INTO
EVERYWHERE

INTO EVERYWHERE

PAUL McAULEY

GOLLANCZ

LONDON

First published in Great Britain in 2016
by Gollancz
An imprint of the Orion Publishing Group
Carmelite House, 50 Victoria Embankment,
London EC4Y 0DZ
An Hachette UK Company

A CIP catalogue record for this book
is available from the British Library

ISBN 978 1 473 20398 3

1 3 5 7 9 10 8 6 4 2

Typeset by Born Group
Printed in Great Britain by
CPI Group (UK) Ltd, Croydon, CR0 4YY

www.unlikelyworlds.blogspot.com
www.gollancz.co.uk
www.orionbooks.co.uk

This one is for Pat Cadigan,
and (of course) for Georgina.

1. Ghost In The Head

There were some days now when she didn't think about the ghost in her head. Or there might be a moment when she'd wonder if it was asleep or awake, if it was looking out through her eyes, and then the moment would pass and she'd get on with whatever it was she happened to be doing. It hadn't shown itself for eight years. It had receded into the background hum of her life. But then there was the day when it returned in all its terror and glory. Black lightning snapping in the cave of her skull. A thunderous swell obliterating all thought.

Lisa's dog was nuzzling her neck when she came back to herself. She flapped a hand, trying to push him away or gather him close, she wasn't sure. Pete sat back on his haunches and wordlessly barked, once, twice. She was sprawled in the yard, halfway between the house and the barn, looking up at the cloudless dark blue sky. Someone had hammered a nail into her skull, right between her eyes.

She pushed onto her elbows, managed to sit all the way up. A greasy swell of nausea washed through her and she rested her head between her knees for a minute or so. Her mouth tingled with a metallic taste like a battery's kiss. The sharp pain in her head began to diffuse into a general skull-cramp; she noticed that her pipe wrench lay next to her. She'd been fixing something, a leak in the water supply to the hurklin pens. She'd gone to fetch the wrench from the toolbox in her pickup truck . . .

Pete told her that she had fallen over.

'I'm okay now,' Lisa said, although she was very fucking far from okay. She was frightened and confused and angry. After all

1

this time it had happened again. After all this time her ghost had woken in thunder and lightning and had knocked her on her ass.

Later, she told her friend Bria that she didn't know what had triggered it.

'I haven't been handling any especially weird shit. Just the usual tesserae, sympathy stones, so forth. And anyway, I haven't had a client for two weeks now. More like three. I haven't eaten anything I haven't eaten a hundred times before, I'm clean and sober . . . I can't figure out what I did to set it off.'

'You sound like you're trying to find some way of blaming yourself,' Bria said.

They were sitting in Lisa's kitchen, drinking coffee. Lisa dressed in her usual blue jeans and denim shirt, Bria in a pale green pants suit, caramel-coloured hair done up in a high curly ponytail. She'd been in a business meeting when Lisa had called, had insisted on driving over.

The two of them went way back. They had both come up and out to First Foot on the same shuttle trip, had both started out working as coders in the Crazy 88 Collective. Lisa's freelance career had run onto the rocks, leaving her with a reputation as a brilliant eccentric whose best years were long behind her; Bria, ten years younger, with a relentless work ethic and good people skills, had founded one of the first code farms in Port of Plenty, was happily married with two kids. A rambling red-tiled house in the burbs, school runs, dinner parties, a subscription to the city's theatre, weekends at the country club where she was attempting to reduce her golfing handicap with the focused zeal that characterised her work. The whole aspirational middle-class-professional bit. Lisa had once asked her friend if this was how she had imagined things turning out when she had won her emigration ticket; Bria had said that back in the day the so-called Wild West had opera houses and gas lighting, and wasn't she dealing with weird alien shit every day, down on the code farm?

'It's been eight years since the last time. Eight years, three months, nine days. What I'm wondering,' Lisa said, 'is did Willie's ghost give him a kick in the head too? I gave him a call, but it went straight to voicemail. So then I phoned around the hospitals and clinics. You know, just in case. No sign of him anywhere, but that doesn't mean he wasn't zapped. Maybe he shrugged it off. Or he's lying hurt somewhere . . .'

'Have the two of you ever been affected at the same time?'

'Sure. During the Bad Trip.'

'Apart from that.'

'Not that I know of. But Willie and I aren't exactly close any more.'

Bria raised an eyebrow.

'So he stops by now and then,' Lisa said. 'But he doesn't tell me everything. I can't help thinking he had some kind of accident. That maybe something happened to him and woke up his ghost, and that's what woke up mine.'

'He's probably scratching around in the City of the Dead, out of phone range,' Bria said. 'Or he's in the drunk tank after one of his parties.'

She didn't have much sympathy for Lisa's ex.

'If Willie had been arrested I would probably know,' Lisa said. 'Because he would have asked me to bail him out.'

Willie had once bought a serious muscle car after making a good find, and a week later had totalled it during a street race in Felony Flats. He'd walked away with a broken collarbone, but the cops had busted him for dangerous driving and he'd served two months, six suspended. Willie was smart and funny and sweet, but he had poor impulse control and was about as dependable as the long-range weather forecast.

'He's like one of those cartoon characters,' Bria said. 'You smack him down with a hammer, he springs right back up. Forget about him, honey, and for once think about yourself. You had a shock. You need to rest. And you need to get yourself checked out. Seriously.'

'I'm fine.'

'If you're worried about paying for it, don't be. I'll cover it.'

'No need. I already had Doc Hendricks look me over.'

'The old guy with the chicken farm?'

'It's also a clinic. And Doc Hendricks knows his stuff. He told me that it wasn't a stroke or an epileptic fit. Nothing organic. As if I didn't already know that. My ghost gave me a little kick, that's all. The way it used to, the first few months after the Bad Trip. I don't need to go to hospital. I don't need any tests. I'm fine.'

Bria gave her a steady, serious look. 'You're very far from fine, honey. Otherwise you wouldn't have called me.'

They pushed it back and forth. After Lisa refused to make an appointment with the consultant who'd tested her after the Bad Trip, no way was she going back to being a lab rat or to being zombified with anti-epileptic drugs, Bria changed tack, said that she was worried about Lisa being out here on her own.

'I have Pete.'

'I mean if it should happen again.'

'This is the first time in more than eight years,' Lisa said. 'I really don't think it's going to happen again any time soon.'

But the flat fact was that she had no idea why the ghost in her head had woken up after so long. She didn't know what it wanted; she didn't even know exactly what it was. Despite the batteries of tests that she and Willie had put themselves through after the Bad Trip, hoping for a fix that had never materialised, no one could tell them whether they had been infected with an eidolon that had full agency, or some fragmented algorithm which threw random glitches. All she knew was that it was old and alien, like all the revenants and ruins on this old, haunted world, that it manifested as unusual activity in the temporal lobe of her brain, and that after eight years of inactivity, after she had begun to allow herself to hope that it might have faded away, it was back. It was awake again, fully present. It was as if something she couldn't see was standing at her back. A visual stutter. A blind spot that jumped past something unimaginable.

Lisa didn't tell Bria about that. She hadn't talked about that aspect of her haunting with anyone except Willie. Maybe that was why she had felt the urge to get in touch with him: he was the only person who understood how it was to have something old and alien living inside your head, amongst your thoughts.

But Willie still wasn't answering her texts and messages.

She told herself that her feeling that something awful had happened was just a hangover from the seizure, and tried to get back into her routine. Watering and feeding the hurklins. Mulching her vegetable beds and planting out eggplant and winter squash. Picking and canning tomatoes. For the first time in a couple of months she went to an AA meeting and testified and drank bad coffee and put some money in the hat. Keeping busy helped to cover up the hole in the world the seizure had made.

But then the geek police came, and everything changed again.

2. Wizards Of The Slime Planet

When the perimeter alert slammed down the pipe Tony Okoye was lying on his command couch and one of the hands was braiding his hair. He raised a finger to still the clever fingers of the man-shaped machine and said, 'I hope this isn't another cosmic-ray impact.'

'Not this time,' the ship's bridle said.

'Because if it is, I swear I will modify your detection filters with an axe.'

'Then I'm almost glad I'm looking at an actual intruder,' the bridle said, and opened an arc of windows in the dim warm air.

Tony sat up, bare-chested in lime-green 'second skin' shorts, pushing a fall of loose hair from his face as he studied multi-spectrum images, vectors, estimates of the intruder's capability. She was real. She was big. A G-class frigate ten times the size of his C-class clipper, bristling with weapon pods and patches. She had come through the mirror less than two minutes ago, she was already driving straight for the slime planet, and she was displaying a police flag. CPF *Dauntless*.

'What are the police doing here? Have they said what they want?'

'They haven't said anything. And they aren't the police,' the bridle said. 'The *Dauntless* is a G-class frigate, but that G-class frigate is not the *Dauntless*. The configuration of her assets is wrong, and her flag's certificate is a clever fake. Clever enough to fool the average freebooter, but not quite clever enough to fool me.'

'Are you certain?'

'I can show you my workings.'

Tony flicked through images of the intruder. It looked a little like a weaponised jellyfish got up from shards of charred plastic: a convex shield or hood three hundred metres across, trailing three stout tentacles ornamented with random clusters of spines. No one knew what the original function of G-class Ghajar ships had been, but plating their shields with foamed fullerene and attaching weapon pods and patches around their rims turned them into formidable combat vessels.

'If they aren't police,' he said, 'they must be pirates. Claim jumpers.'

'The possibility is not insignificant,' the bridle said.

'A ship that size, running under a fake flag? It is the only possibility. The Red Brigade has frigates, doesn't it?'

'So do a number of other fringe-world outfits. We should challenge it,' the bridle said. 'You can use your notorious charm to get its crew to reveal who they really are and what they want.'

Her personality package, presenting as a bright eager capable young woman, was the front end of the AI that interfaced with the mind and nervous system of the actual ship, which like the frigate, like all ships everywhere, had been built by the Ghajar thousands of years ago. Tony's C-class clipper was called *Abalunam's Pride*, but no one knew its real name. The name its maker had given it long before it had been extracted from a sargasso orbit, refurbished and modified, and purchased by his grandmother. The secret name it might still call itself.

Tony said, 'I already have a pretty good idea about what they want. And it is possible that they do not know we are here. So we will maintain radio silence and continue to monitor them. And if they contact us, we will tell them that we are just a freebooter with an exploration licence and nothing to hide.'

'Which we are.'

'Which we are. But my family has a history with the Red Brigade. And if that really is one of their frigates . . .'

Tony grazed the cicatrices on his cheek with his thumb as he thought things through. He was scared, yes, shocked and sort of numb, but he also felt alert and focused. Babysitting Fred Firat and his crew of wizards while they probed the ancient secrets of the slime planet had proven to be astoundingly tedious. There were no beasties to hunt, and the scattered Elder Culture ruins weren't anything special. Junot Johnson was supervising the wizards' work; Lancelot Askia was keeping them in line; after completing the survey of stromatolite sites and setting his little surprises, Tony had mostly stayed aboard the ship. Now, for the first time in four weeks, he was fully awake. At last he had something to do. And if that frigate really was one of the Red Brigade's ships he would have a chance to test his skill and cunning against his family's old nemesis.

He said, 'How long before it gets here?'

'Nineteen point three eight hours, if it maintains its current delta vee,' the bridle said.

'We will have a lot less than that if it fires off scouting drones. What about our assets at the mirror? Has our unwelcome guest pinged them, tried to spoof them, knocked any of them out?'

'Not yet.'

'It could have left behind assets of its own when it came through. Have one of the drones scan the mirror and the volume around it out to five thousand kilometres, but keep the rest dark. And shoot a message to Junot, brief him on the situation and tell him that the wizards should start packing up their stuff straight away.'

'Then we're going to make a run for it,' the bridle said.

'I am not going to sit on the ground and wait to see what that frigate does next,' Tony said. 'Check the mirror, message Junot, and raise the ship and aim it at the wizards' camp.'

'Shall I have the hand finish braiding your hair, too?'

The bridle had a nice line in sarcasm, but Tony took the offer at face value.

'Why not?' he said, settling back on the couch. 'If those claim jumpers do want to talk to me face to face, I should look my best.'

Five minutes later, *Abalunam's Pride* was sliding sideways and low above eroded sheets of ancient basaltic lava. The lifeless black plain stretched away in every direction, studded with puddles and ponds gleaming orange in the level light of the soft sun, which at this high latitude was fixed just above the southern horizon. The slime planet, in close orbit around a cool, quiescent red dwarf star, was tidally locked, one face permanently turned to its star, the other to the outer dark. It had no name, only a number assigned by a rip-and-run survey team before the rise and fall of the two empires, and it was old, about twice the age of Earth. The tectonic plates of its lithosphere had set in place after its outer core had cooled and solidified; any mountains it might once have possessed had long ago weathered to dust; after its magnetosphere had decayed most of its original atmosphere had been blown away by the solar wind of its star. It had been cold and virtually airless when the so-called Old Old Ones, said by some to have been the first of the Jackaroo's clients, said by others to have been the Jackaroo's precursors, had arrived, thickening its atmosphere and rebooting its hydrological cycle by bombarding the vast ice cap on the dark side with comets diverted from the red dwarf's threadbare Oort cloud. Now the slime planet was cloaked in a reducing atmosphere of nitrogen, methane and ammonia, and a shallow sea turbid with ferrous iron spread across its sub-stellar hemisphere, broken by a single sodden land mass near the terminator between light and darkness. Enormous rafts of sticky foam generated by blooms of photosynthetic bacteria floated everywhere on the sea, and colonies of stromatolites grew in a few muddy bays on the sunward edge of the lone continent.

Those colonies were what had brought Tony Okoye and the crew of wizards here, in a three-way partnership with the broker on Dry Salvages who had purchased the old survey team's report. Unprepossessing mounds like melted candle stumps, built from layers of sediments and bacterial filaments and slime, the stromatolites contained nodes of archival genetic material and communicated with each other via a wide-bandwidth transmission system constructed from arrays of microscopic magnetic crystals. The chief wizard, Fred Firat, believed that they were the remnants of a planetary intelligence, a noosphere woven from algorithms that were the common ancestors of the various species found in active artefacts left by the Elder Cultures. A root kit or Rosetta stone that would unlock all kinds of secrets, including the causes

9

of sleepy sickness, Smythe's Syndrome, counting disorder, and other meme plagues.

Fred Firat had the grandstanding rhetoric and unblinking gaze of someone who carried the fire of true crazed genius, and like all the best salesmen, prophets and charlatans he was his first and best convert to his cause. He was convinced that the scant data buried in the records of that old expedition pointed towards something of fundamental importance, had sold the idea to Ayo and Aunty Jael during a virtuoso performance via q-phone. Which was how Tony had found himself embarked on what might be the biggest score of his freebooter career.

But extracting data from the stromatolites' archival genetic material had been more difficult than anticipated. Tony had to park his ship fifty kilometres inland because *Abalunam's Pride* leaked a variety of electromagnetic emissions that interfered with the stromatolites' transmission system, the wizards had to isolate experiments on individual specimens inside Faraday cages to prevent feedback, and they and Aunty Jael had spent more than two weeks developing new tools and probes before getting down to the real work. But although they had sequenced the archival genetics, they had yet to discover how to read the data those sequences contained, or how to hack into the transmission system. And now a fully loaded G-class frigate had driven through the mirror, come to hijack their work or worse. There was no doubt about it. It was time to pack up. Time to boot.

The first glint of the sea had just appeared at the horizon when the ship's q-phone lit up. It was Tony's uncle, Opeyemi, saying with his usual brusqueness, 'I hear you're in trouble.'

'I can handle it,' Tony said, doing his best to hide his dismay. 'And while I would love to talk, uncle, I *am* rather busy. What with having to get the wizards stowed away and so forth.'

He had always known that Lancelot Askai was his uncle's man, seconded to the mission to the slime planet from his usual work of suppressing anti-family sentiment, but had not realised until now that the rat was equipped with a q-phone. Opeyemi had been monitoring everything, Tony thought with a throb of anger. Waiting to pounce on any mistake.

'Am I right in thinking,' his uncle said, 'that you believe this so-called intruder is a Red Brigade ship?'

'It is heavily armed, it is displaying a false flag, and it has been aimed at this remote and insignificant planet when we are in the middle of our work. Its crew must have found out about the stromatolites, and want to steal what is rightfully ours. And of all the pirate gangs, the Red Brigade is the only one that has tangled with our family before, and everyone knows that it covets ancient knowledge above all else.'

'But you have no actual proof that these are no more than ordinary criminals,' Opeyemi said. 'Your desire for revenge is understandable, nephew. But do not let it cloud your judgement.'

'Tell me, uncle,' Tony said, trying to keep his tone light, 'does Ayo know about this call?'

'It is four in the morning here. The alert came straight to me, and I see no need to disturb your sister.'

Tony pictured Opeyemi in his bare room up in the west tower of the Great House, some four thousand light years away. A slender unsmiling man with a shaven skull and deep-set eyes and a steady gaze. He would be sitting at the edge of his military cot, or perhaps he was standing at a narrow window, looking out at the tumbled roofs of the town stretching away in darkness to the cold dark iceberg-flecked sea. After the great betrayal and the deaths of Tony's parents, Opeyemi, a lieutenant colonel in the Commons police, had resigned his commission and taken charge of his brother's orphaned children, serving as acting head of the family until Ayo had reached the age of majority. Tony had often rebelled against his uncle's exacting discipline, still resented the influence he wielded, and flinched now from the admonitory sting in his voice. It was exactly like all those times when he had been called to account for some minor transgression. The hot flush of shame and impotence. Trembling anticipation of his uncle's minatory gaze.

He tried to assert himself, saying, 'Perhaps you should disturb her anyway, uncle. After all, she signed off this deal. She deserves to know that it has gone bad.'

'You did not think to trouble her yourself.'

'I was planning to tell her as soon as I had the situation in hand.'

'You like to think you are an independent operator,' Opeyemi said. 'You are not.'

'You have made that abundantly clear.'

'And you will not risk the ship, a valuable family asset, by making a stand against these claim jumpers. If that is what they are.'

'The idea never crossed my mind,' Tony said.

He had played endless games of Police v. Red Brigade when he was a kid, setting up ambushes in the courtyards and corridors of the Great House, staging skirmishes in the fields and plantations, but the frigate effortlessly outgunned *Abalunam's Pride*, and he wasn't as crazy foolish as some of his family believed. Reckless freebooters did not last long.

'We will get our revenge when we're good and ready,' his uncle said. 'You are neither the arm nor the instrument. Round up the wizards and make a straight run for the mirror. If these claim jumpers see that you are abandoning the prize, they will not waste their time trying to stop you.'

'Absolutely.'

Tony had his own idea about how to evade the claim jumpers but he was not about to run that past his uncle. The crusty old fucker would probably forbid it.

'Bring the ship home,' Opeyemi said. 'The wizards too.'

'I thought I should head back to Dry Salvages first.' Hopefully without the G-class frigate on his tail, but he would deal with that if and when. 'I want to have a hard conversation with Raqle Thornhilde about how this claim jumper found me.'

'You will do no such thing,' Opeyemi said. 'You have no proof that the broker is to blame. And if she is, she will be expecting you to come after her, and you would be meeting her on her territory, on her terms. No, it is too dangerous, and I will not allow you to endanger the family's reputation out of some reckless notion about revenge. What you will do instead is bring the wizards to Skadi, where they will complete their work with the help of Aunty Jael, as already agreed.'

'An agreement that Raqle Thornhilde will have invalidated if she told someone else about the stromatolites.'

'We will make enquiries about that. Meanwhile, we will keep to our side of the bargain.'

'This is something I must discuss with Ayo,' Tony said.

'She will tell you the same thing. Good luck and Godspeed. We will talk again very soon,' Opeyemi said, and cut the connection before Tony could think of a riposte.

That was only the beginning of his humiliation.

The broken latticework spire of the Ghajar landing tower appeared off to the west; Tony saw a huddle of blue tents and the glinting pyramid of the Faraday cage at the edge of the shallow bay as the ship swung around and dropped lower, hovering on a warp in the planet's gravity above a calm sweep of ochre water and the pavements and clumps of the stromatolites. Fred Firat and his six acolytes, dressed in uniform blue pressure suits, gathered in a mutinous clot as Tony rode a gyro platform from the ship's cargo hatch to a slant of black rock at the water's edge. As soon as he landed, the wizards' leader stepped smartly forward, Junot Johnson and Lancelot Askai falling in on either side. Their pressure suits were white, like Tony's, with the red and black triangle of the family's flag on their shoulders.

'You have compromised the local transmission system with this stupid manoeuvre,' Fred Firat said. 'You may have damaged the entire noosphere.'

Tony ignored him, looked at Junot. 'Why aren't these people packing up, as I ordered?'

He was fizzing with anger. Anger at his uncle's intervention; anger at his failure to assert himself; anger at the wizards' insubordination.

'We need more time,' Fred Firat said, before Junot could answer. 'We've made a good start, but a start is all it is. And now you've set us back by bringing the ship here. I realise you are upset by these so-called claim jumpers, Mister Okoye, but you should have known better. You should have thought things through.'

Tony met Fred Firat's bright bold gaze. 'You have isolated some specimens in the Faraday cages, haven't you?'

'Of course, but that isn't the point.'

'Didn't you tell me once that their memory is holographic? Which means, I think, that a small portion will contain everything in the whole.'

'We hadn't done enough work to prove that it was. And anyway, that's not really how holograms work,' Fred Firat said. He was an old man, eighty or ninety, with the squat build of someone born and raised on a heavy planet. He stood foursquare in front of Tony, arms crossed over the chestplate of his pressure suit, the faceted oval of his ancillary eye, socketed in the middle of his forehead, glinting behind his visor like a gunsight.

'Nevertheless, you are done here,' Tony said. 'Load those specimens and whatever else you have as quickly as possible. The window for escape is closing fast.'

'You aren't listening,' Fred Firat said. 'I have a plan.'

'It's you who are not listening,' Tony said, thrusting his face so close to the wizard's that their helmets almost kissed. 'Another ship is coming here. A big ship, well armed, ready to take us prisoner and steal what is rightly ours. We have to boot as quickly as possible. You and your people should be packing up your equipment and your specimens, not quibbling about my orders.'

'I have a better idea,' Fred Firat said. 'You can take the specimens and most of my crew. I'll stay behind with a couple of volunteers. We can hide in the Ghajar ruins – we have mapped a network of voids beneath them. We'll wait out the claim jumpers, and after they leave we'll start work again, and you can bring back the rest of my crew.'

Tony couldn't believe it. No, he could. Wizards were clever but naive, put their faith in friction-free models of messy reality, and lacked any kind of common sense.

He said, 'That isn't going to happen.'

'If you force me aboard at gunpoint, I'll sue you and your family for breach of contract,' Fred Firat said. 'But if you leave me here to finish my work, I promise that I'll make all of us rich.'

'It isn't going to happen because there won't be any stromatolites left for you or the claim jumpers to exploit,' Tony said, and ordered the ship's bridle to implement Plan B.

A hatch opened amongst the jags and points of the ship's base and a black cylinder tumbled out, splashing into the shallow water.

'That is a pop-up high-impulse thermobaric bomb packed with powdered aluminium and nanoparticles of isopropyl nitrate and RDX,' Tony said. 'Powerful enough to sterilise this bay and the surrounding area.'

Fred Firat and the other wizards cried out in shock and fury; a tall skinny young man broke away from the group and ran head down and howling at Tony, who stood his ground and took a half-step sideways at the last moment, blocking his attacker with his hip and using the man's momentum to pivot him off his feet and smash him onto his back. The man stared up through the curve of his faceplate, wide-eyed with shock, as Lancelot Askia stepped forward and aimed his pistol at him.

'Don't,' Tony said, and felt a wash of relief when the enforcer shrugged and lowered his weapon and turned back to the other wizards.

'There are other colonies,' Fred Firat said. 'We will work on them.'

'No, you won't,' Tony said. 'Because I have planted bombs in every colony along this shore. They will be triggered when we boot. The only stromatolites left will be those we take with us.'

'I don't believe you.'

'Too bad. Get your crew moving. We boot in two hours. Anything that isn't on the ship by then will be left behind.'

'And if I refuse? What will you do? Kill me?'

'Why not?' Lancelot Askia said and raised his pistol and shot Fred Firat through his helmet visor.

The wizard collapsed. Blood splashed the inner surface of the crazed visor: the round had nailed him through his ancillary eye.

In the moment of shocked silence, Tony told Lancelot Askia, 'I needed that man. You had no *right.*'

'Orders,' the enforcer said calmly. 'I was told that anyone who suggested staying behind could be the one who betrayed us.'

'And now we will never know if he did.'

'Of course he did. That's why I shot him,' Lancelot Askia said, and turned away and ordered the wizards to shape up and get moving. 'You can pack your shit and get on board the ship or you can join your dead boss. Your choice.'

3. The Geek Police

After the Bad Trip, after she'd been discharged from hospital, after she'd broken up with Willie because he wanted to go right back out there and find the thing that had fucked up their heads, Lisa tried to forget everything by self-medicating with booze and shine. She lost her apartment and let her business slide away, was living in a rented room in Felony Flats, doing zero-hours piece-work for corporate code farms, when an intervention by Bria and several other friends made her realise that she needed to make some changes in her life. So she sobered up and scraped together enough money to buy a trailer home and a pioneer licence for a patch of scrub in the tableland north of Port of Plenty, where she hired a local guy with a bulldozer to cut a track to the nearest paved road, sank a well and capped it with a wind pump and a filter to remove the gypsum from the groundwater, and fenced off a hectare of caliche and grew catch crops of tweaked clover and soybean and ploughed them in with kelp hauled from the coast until the soil was rich enough to support a vegetable garden.

Looking back, Lisa couldn't believe her energy, her single-minded focus. A cold determination to prove that, by taming this little patch of First Foot's strangeness, she could reclaim her life from the accident that had derailed it.

She built a little house with the help of friends and her new neighbours. Rammed-earth and tyre walls faced with lime render, solar paint on the corrugated-iron roof. Bria gave her a tweaked Labrador puppy as a housewarming present, and Lisa soon learned to understand Pete's rough speech. Amazing what you could convey with just a couple of hundred words. Supposedly

17

a guard dog, he was better company than protection, although he was pretty good at running down the rabbits that were multiplying everywhere in the tableland after some misguided settler had released half a dozen into the wild.

Lisa tried to raise goats at first, but when her little herd was cut down by a wildfire pulmonary infection she turned to hurklin ranching instead. She and Pete survived sandstorms, lightning storms, biblical hailstorms, a plague of hoppers that stripped crops, scrub and the insulation from power cables, two years of drought, and a hundred smaller difficulties and hardships. And after five years, by the terms of her pioneer licence, she owned the place free and clear.

By then, she had made a slight return to the Elder Culture biz. Rebuilding her client list, testing and evaluating their finds, advising an academic who was trying to map the taxonomic relationships between different kinds of Elder Culture code. She and Willie were still married, technically. He stopped by now and then, and sometimes they'd sort of accidentally fall into bed. There'd been a few casual relationships too, and one semi-serious – a biologist surveying the flora and fauna of the high desert who turned out to have a wife and three kids in the city – but she mostly lived on her own now, a cantankerous forty-something desert broad scraping by like her neighbours, watching the city creep over the hills and edge into the tableland. Strip malls and motels and big box stores along Highway One; tracts on the western edge of the tableland pegged out for future suburban subdivisions; settlements and developers entangled in lawsuits over water rights. Every thirty-three days the shuttle returned from Earth and disgorged five thousand new settlers; many more were arriving on Ghajar ships reclaimed from orbital sargassos. Human civilisation spreading out in a grand and futile project to 'normalise' First Foot and the other worlds gifted by the Jackaroo more than thirty years ago.

Willie liked to quote a kōan he claimed to have learned from a Buddhist monk he'd met just before he'd come up and out: a man climbing a remote mountain finds a pocket of smooth unmarked summer snow in a shaded hollow, and jumps into it with his big boots. Later, Lisa discovered that the bit about the Buddhist monk was more of Willie's bullshit, and his so-called kōan had actually been written by this canny old Scottish guy years before the Jackaroo came with their gifts and their offer to help. And although it was a neat image of humanity's irrepressible urge to despoil pristine nature, it didn't quite fit the brave new age of expansion. The fifteen gift worlds and the worlds of the new frontier weren't like unmarked snow, or blank pages waiting to be inscribed with human history. Everywhere people went, they found the footprints of previous clients of the Jackaroo. Elder Culture ruins, scraps of Elder Culture technology, Elder Culture eidolons, fetches and ghosts. Remnants of unknown, unknowable alien histories bleeding into human culture and human history.

Lisa knew all about that. She and Willie had been indelibly marked by the Bad Trip. It had changed them, changed their lives, and they still didn't know exactly what it was, what had happened to them.

About a year afterwards, Willie found a recent excavation site out in the Badlands, claimed it was the spot where they'd been zapped, and elaborated a bunch of paranoid riffs about what had been dug up, who had taken it, and where it was now. Even though she'd been on the long slide to her nadir, Lisa knew that it was just another of Willie's fantasies. No one could keep that kind of thing secret. The hole in the ground was just a hole in the ground, and the thing that had zapped them had probably been some kind of one-shot affair – an ancient machine, maybe, that had hoarded its energies for tens of thousands of years and discharged everything it had in one last spasm when they'd come into range. Eventually, they stopped arguing about it, and Lisa did her best to put the whole wretched affair behind her. But then the ghost in her head woke up, reminding her that she'd never be free of it. And then the geek police came knocking.

Lisa was changing the oil in the wind-pump gearbox when Pete barked a warning. She looked up, saw a little cloud of dust out in the tawny scrubland. Two, three vehicles negotiating the swales and dips of the track, headlights on, dust boiling up behind them.

19

By the time Lisa had clipped the chain to Pete's collar and walked with him to the gate, the vehicles were cutting around the shelter belt of cottonwoods. The county sheriff's patrol car leading two powder-blue Range Rovers, new models with slit-like windscreens that gave them a mean squint, badges on their doors and hoods. The UN Technology Control Unit. The geek police. Lisa had been visited by them half a dozen times since she'd moved out here: routine, random inspections of her workshop and equipment as per the terms of her licence. But they'd never before turned up mob-handed with the sheriff.

'Don't do anything dumb,' she told Pete as the vehicles slowed and stopped.

Sure thing, he said, but his ears were pricked and his body was tense, the way he got when he saw a rabbit, and he barked twice when the door of the patrol car popped open. Lisa told him to hush, watched the sheriff ease out of his car, set his white straw Stetson on his head and walk up to the gate.

'It would make things easier if you chained up your dog some-where, ma'am,' he said.

'It would make things a whole lot easier if your friends turned around and headed back to the city,' Lisa said.

'I don't disagree, but they have a job to do and so do I. It would be best for everyone if you allowed us to get on without any fuss.'

The sheriff, Scott Bird, was a rangy man about Lisa's age, the brim of his Stetson angled low over his creased face. He'd been a deputy in Denton County, Texas before he'd come up and out; now he was sheriff of the Carolina Land District. A little old-fashioned, but a decent fair-minded man. Lisa liked him, had twice voted for him to stay in office.

She said, 'I'm sorry to see they asked you to do their dirty work.'

Sheriff Bird held out a folded sheet of paper. 'Sometimes I have to do things I don't agree with. Comes with the badge and the territory. Which includes, I regret to say, serving this warrant on you.'

'Are you arresting me?'

'No, ma'am. This is a notice to search your property.'

Lisa felt Pete stir beside her as she reached out and took the warrant. She could feel the ghost at her back too, briefly wondered what it made of this little human charade.

She said, 'You happen to know what they are looking for? Because I don't have the faintest idea.'

Sheriff Bird hesitated, then said, 'I also have some bad news. Maybe we could step over to your house.'

'And let your friends trawl through my stuff while you distract me? Anything you want to tell me, you tell me here,' Lisa said, and saw the serious look on the sheriff's face and felt as if she'd hit an air pocket.

'It's your husband,' Sheriff Bird said. 'I'm sorry to tell you there's been an accident.'

Lisa thought at once of the seizure.

She said, 'Is he hurt? How bad?'

Sheriff Bird took off his hat. 'He was working with a crew on a big dig out in the Badlands. There was some kind of accident, and everyone involved looks to have been killed.'

'You're kidding,' she said, but she knew that he was not.

'Why don't we go sit down somewhere, ma'am, so I can tell you what I know?'

Lisa saw two figures step out of one of the Range Rovers. One a tall grey-haired man in a cream suit, the other dressed in a black tracksuit, moving with the sinuous gait of a dancer, golden highlights gleaming on a smooth skull. A Jackaroo avatar.

She knew then that she was in serious trouble. She lifted her chin and said to Sheriff Bird, 'Tell me everything. Right here, right now. You can start by explaining what that thing wants.'

4 · Rogue Moon

Junot Johnson swore that he had no idea that Lancelot Askia had been liaising so closely with Tony's uncle. 'That Askia man and me, we hardly talked. He spent most of his time in his tent, or running out across the rock. He has those plastic muscle extenders – he can sprint like a ziphound. And even when he was out and about with the wizards he didn't say much more than yes or no, and shut you down with a sharp look if you tried to be friendly. What with that and trying to keep track of the work, I didn't have the chance to get alongside him.'

'He had a q-phone,' Tony said. He knew that he was angry with the old sidesman because he was angry with himself, and because he had been so thoroughly and publicly humiliated, but he couldn't help himself. 'How could you have not known about that? It was your *job*.'

'I know I failed, young master. And I'm more sorry for it than I can say,' Junot said.

A sturdy broad-shouldered man with a mass of curly grey hair squashed inside his pressure suit's helmet, dutifully loyal and patient, he was from one of the families which had been with the Okoyes long before they had been given Skadi as a reward for their part in the overthrow of the Second Empire, and had served aboard *Abalunam's Pride* for two years and counting.

'What about Fred Firat?' Tony said. 'Was there any sign that he was communicating with someone off planet?'

'That I think I would have seen,' Junot said. 'I was as close to him as his shadow for the most part. And if he had a q-phone, he hid it cleverly. It wasn't in his personal stuff.'

Tony had sent Junot to check the dead wizard's possessions before they were packed up with the rest of the camp. They were standing in the shadow of the ship now, watching the wizards stack equipment and folded tents onto a pair of sleds. Two of the ship's hands moved smartly to and fro amongst them, carrying unfeasibly large loads, their white carapaces luminous in the level light of the eternal sunset. Lancelot Askia stalked up and down, now and then stopping to check a crate or package. They were taking everything, even the garbage. Everything except the body of Fred Firat. That lay on a flat rock nearby, wrapped in a winding sheet of pyrotechnic explosive printed by the ship.

'He was a very clever man,' Tony said, softening a little.

'Do you really think he was a traitor, young master?'

'It would be awfully convenient if he was, wouldn't it? It would justify his execution, and show me up for a fool. In any case, his death will put a serious crimp in the work, which will please my uncle no end. He has been against it from the start.'

'One thing I know to be true,' Junot said. 'There really is a labyrinth under those Ghajar ruins. Some of the wizards essayed a little expedition into them. They were looking for eidolons that might have absorbed something of the stromatolites' code. But they didn't find anything, and neither did I when I checked the place a few days after they finished. Just endless tunnels lined with dirty white plastic.'

'Could Firat have kept himself hidden from the claim jumpers down there?'

Junot shrugged. 'It would depend on how hard they searched for him, and how hard he worked at staying hidden. But those tunnels do go a long way back, and a long way down, too.'

They watched the wizards work for a while.

Junot said, 'Can we get home safe, you reckon?'

'Oh, I have a good escape plan,' Tony said. 'Which also involves a tunnel, oddly enough.'

At last, after everything had been loaded onto the ship, Lancelot Askia marshalled the wizards in front of their leader's body. They stood quiet and still in orange sunlight and long shadows while Tony said that if anyone had any last thoughts for their former chief they should think them now. He gave them a minute's grace before he triggered the pyrotechnic shroud. It burned with a brief fierce intensity, sending up a plume of greasy smoke that the wind bent out to sea. Ash fell all around, on the black rocks, on the water of the bay, on the wizards and Lancelot Askia and Junot Johnson and Tony. Ten minutes after the fire had guttered out, leaving only a smear of sludgy soot on the rock, everyone was aboard the ship. The wizards and the tanks containing half a dozen live stromatolites were locked down in the cargo bay. Junot Johnson and Lancelot Askia were locked down in their cabins. And Tony was back in command.

The ship's bridle reported that the claim jumpers' frigate hadn't changed its heading, said that as far as she could tell it hadn't deployed any assets around the mirror or sent drones to scout the slime planet ahead of its arrival. 'But I'm afraid that my surveillance ability is very limited, and the frigate may possess superior security and stealth tech.'

'There is only one way to find out,' Tony said, and dropped the go command.

The bridle counted down from ten in the traditional way, booted at zero. As the ship jolted away in a long rising arc above the dark sea and its archipelagos of bruise-yellow foam, Tony detonated the thermobaric bombs he had planted in every stromatolite colony, glimpsing the chain of flashes just before the coastline dropped below the horizon. When the claim jumpers arrived, they would find only a couple of dozen flooded craters floored with baked mud and rubble.

The ship punched out of the atmosphere, fired off a package of tiny cube satellites, and continued to rise. The horizon rounded and the dull spark of the slime world's solitary moon rose above it, a skull-shaped chunk of rock fifty kilometres across, with an erratic retrograde orbit. Fred Firat had believed that it was an asteroid that had been moved into orbit by some Elder Culture for some unclear purpose; deep radar scans had revealed that it was riddled with tunnels, including a shaft that pierced it through its rotation axis.

After *Abalunam's Pride* matched the little moon's orbital velocity, Tony took control for the final manoeuvre. Blipping the ship's drive, setting her on a trajectory that would intersect with the moon's surface. This was the fun part. The target area was relatively small, and there was only a narrow window before the frigate appeared over the horizon of the slime planet.

The moon swiftly grew, its lumpy cratered landscape raked with fault-line scarps. *Abalunam's Pride* swung around it, dawdling towards the flat top of a debris cone: the north polar entrance to the shaft that pierced the moon, created by unimaginable energies that had vaporised fifty kilometres of rock. Much of that vapour had boiled away, escaping the grip of the moon's feeble gravity; a small fraction, cooling, had fallen back to the surface and formed symmetrical cones at the poles.

Tony mirrored the visual feed to his passengers so that they could watch some real piloting skill, killed the last of the ship's forward momentum as the cone's flat top slid past, and dropped into the black circle of the shaft's entrance. He fired off a package that would anchor itself to the shaft's lip and allow him to keep in touch with the cube sats, and then *Abalunam's Pride* was falling between smooth melt-rock walls, slowing, slowing, until it was floating freely at the midpoint of the shaft, balanced at the null point of the asteroid's feeble gravity.

'We will wait here until the frigate puts down,' he explained over the common channel. 'And when it does, we'll make a run for the mirror.'

He had to wait almost twelve hours, half a day in old money, while the G-class frigate swung around the slime planet in a near-polar orbit that would enable it to scan almost every part of the surface. No doubt they had checked out the little moon, too, but Tony was pretty sure that his hiding place was safe. Radar scans could render the moon transparent, but their resolution was limited. The claim jumpers would not see his ship until he wanted to be seen.

At last, the frigate fell out of orbit in a smooth trajectory aimed at the lone continent. Tony told his passengers to brace themselves, and exactly a hundred seconds later booted the ship. Maximum acceleration. The walls flashed past; a star of sunlight flared ahead and widened into a perfect circle; *Abalunam's Pride*

25

shot out of the shaft like a cannonball, still accelerating. The moon dwindled astern, and the slime planet dwindled too, rounding into a half-globe that shrank into the big dark like a pebble dropped down a well.

The frigate sent an interrogatory message. Tony ignored it. He was back in control, back on track. All he had to do now was reach the mirror.

It orbited the L5 point where the slime planet's gravity balanced that of its star. Tony flew a flat geodesic trajectory, accelerating all the way. This was the part he loved. He was cradled in his command couch, ramped up on combat drugs and plugged into the ship's bridle and her radar, EM and optical feeds. Flying free into the unknown. Master of his own fate.

He was more than halfway there when the feeds from the cube sats he'd left in orbit around the planet went dark. No problem. He had been half-expecting it after the claim jumpers' frigate had pinged him. But as he closed in on the mirror the assets that had been keeping watch on it went dark too.

It was the usual rock sculpted into a long cone, with the wormhole throat embedded in its flat base: a round dark mirror two kilometres across, framed by the chunky braid of strange matter that kept it open. The only mirror in orbit around this star. The only way in, the only way out. When he had come through, Tony had dropped off a package of drones that had established wide triangular orbits around it. They had not detected anything sown by the frigate, but it had set traps all the same.

Abalunam's Pride was briefly painted by radar and launchers planted around the mirror's rim flung a cloud of disrupter needles: electronic countermeasures packaged in little blades of cubic carbon allotropes denser than diamond, designed to lodge in the hulls of Ghajar ships and paralyse their nervous systems. There was no time for any kind of evasive manoeuvre. Tony shot a drone carrying a totally illegal pinch-fusion bomb with a yield of point six kilotonnes from *Abalunam's Pride*'s launch cannon. Ayo had given it to him just before he'd set out two years ago, telling him that it had been held back when the family's armoury had been stripped by the Commons police, and was to be used only as a final measure in extreme circumstances. Well, if this didn't count as an extreme circumstance he didn't know what did. The bomb detonated scant seconds after launch, obliterating the needles in a furious fireball, and Tony screamed in triumph and blind terror as the ship slammed through the expanding shell of superhot plasma, plunged into the mirror of the wormhole throat, and emerged eight thousand light years away.

5. Breakout

The next day, Lisa met up with Bria in Port of Plenty and down-loaded everything she knew. Everything that Sheriff Bird and the boss of the geek police team, Adam Nevers, had told her. It wasn't much. It was heartbreaking.

It seemed that Willie had found something out in the Badlands, something too big to dig out on his own. He'd partnered up with a crew and they'd uncovered a powerfully malignant artefact that had got inside their heads and turned them against each other. Five people were dead; three, including Willie, were missing, believed to be buried under tons of rubble at the bottom of the excavation shaft after someone had blown it in, possibly in a futile attempt to contain the breakout.

'Do you remember the thing in Bitter Springs, two years ago?' Lisa said to Bria. 'The police said it was like that.'

A prospector had brought an artefact into the little desert settlement of Bitter Springs, the local assayer had woken the eidolon inside it, and there'd been a breakout and a massacre. People attacking each other with teeth and nails and fists and feet. Neighbours and strangers. Husbands and wives. Mothers and children. Lisa had seen the artefact in the Port of Plenty museum after it had been purged of every trace of its algorithms. A smooth slim black needle about the size of a spearhead, gleaming and sterile in its glass case. A reminder of the awful unknowns yet to be unearthed.

'Now I know what caused that seizure,' Lisa said. 'It was the same day the breakout happened. No way is that a coincidence. No. Fucking. Way.'

Bria reached across the little table and gripped her hands. 'Oh, Lisa.'

They were sitting outside the big Starbucks that anchored the western end of Pioneer Square. Lisa was drinking iced tea sweetened with half a dozen packets of sugar, Bria a flat white. Pete sprawled under the table with a dish of water. All around, people sat at café tables in the late-afternoon sunlight, perched on broad steps that dropped to the well where a gout of water pulsed and plashed. Smart little yellow trams ran along one side of the square, which was bordered by office buildings and the plate-glass windows of high-end shops. A sliver of Earth jammed into this alien world, where a dozen or more Elder Cultures had lived and died out or ascended to some unfathomable stage of consciousness, leaving behind ruins and artefacts, scraps of technology, algorithms and eidolons. A perfectly ordinary scene that, distorted by Lisa's blind spot and the intimate presence of her ghost, seemed weirdly unfamiliar, like a hyper-real simulation where everything was a banal, idealised version of itself and nothing fit together properly.

'Willie finally went and did it,' Lisa said, squeezing Bria's hands. 'After all this time, he finally found the thing that zapped us. It zapped him again, zapped the people he was working with. And it reached out to me. It woke the ghost in my head.'

'What did he find?' Bria said.

'The geek police wouldn't tell me. They think I already know. They think I'm involved.'

'But you aren't.'

'Of course not!'

Pete lifted his head, looking up at Lisa. She let go of Bria's hands and pushed her hair out of her face, the frizz of grey corkscrew curls she'd stopped dyeing a couple of years ago. She was bone-tired, had spent most of the night looking at the ceiling of her bedroom, her head like a beehive.

'I haven't seen him for three months,' she said. 'I had no idea what he was into.'

'And you told the police that.'

'It didn't make any difference.'

29

Lisa told Bria about the man who'd led the raid on her property. Investigator Adam Nevers of the UN Technology Control Unit: a tall Englishman with a neatly trimmed salt-and-pepper beard, dressed in a cream linen suit, light blue shirt and dark blue tie, polished brown brogues powdered with the red dust of her yard. He'd been very polite, very proper, but there had been a coldness in his manner, an Olympian condescension, as he explained that the search-and-seizure warrant had been issued because it was possible that Willie might have sent Lisa something potentially dangerous, or left behind something she believed to be harmless but actually wasn't.

'I think I'd know if he had,' Lisa said. 'It's kind of how I earn my living.'

'When you last saw him, did he tell you that he had found something in the Badlands?' Nevers said.

'Not a word.'

'Did he tell you he was going out there with a crew to dig something up?'

'I'd definitely remember that because Willie always worked alone.'

'Did you notice anything strange in his manner or behaviour?'

'No. He was just himself.'

'"He was just himself."' Nevers frosted the words with disdain. 'Exactly what do you mean by that?'

'Exactly what I said. He turned up one day, we caught up on what each other had been doing, and after a couple of hours he left.'

'So it was purely a social visit.'

'As far as I was concerned.'

It was hard to think of Willie, hard not to. Lisa saw his smile, his gold tooth flashing. The deep lines around his eyes. His black hair brushed back and held by a bandana folded just so. The warmth of him, his sour-sweet smell. They hadn't slept together the last time he'd stopped by because Lisa had been irritated by his presumption and they'd fallen into the groove of one of their old arguments. His selfishness; her stubbornness. She hoped that she wasn't going to have cause to regret the way they'd parted, that last time. She hoped that Willie had managed to escape unharmed, that maybe he hadn't been there when the trouble had kicked off. And then she thought of her seizure, and knew, with numb certainty, that he must have been caught up in it.

Nevers led her through the banal details of their last conversation, then threw her a curve ball, saying, 'Could your husband have visited your property without your knowledge?'

'I guess. I mean, I'm not here all the time.'

'So he could have left something here. Hidden it.'

'What kind of something?' Lisa was beginning to feel uneasy, because it was exactly the kind of stupid stunt that Willie liked to pull. Had liked. Jesus.

'That's what we want to find out,' Nevers said.

The other agents, two men and a woman, were walking in and out of the lean-to workshop tacked onto the end of Lisa's house, carrying away equipment and stacking it inside the two Range Rovers. Her ultrasound probe, her binocular microscope, the compact oven of her printer, her Reynolds trap . . .

The gold-skinned Jackaroo avatar stood between the vehicles, still as a statue. It had helped Adam Nevers perform a preliminary survey of the house and barn while Lisa sat with Sheriff Bird in his patrol car, trying to stay calm because she knew that if she lost her cool they'd definitely arrest her. She was still trying to stay calm, but it was getting harder while she watched her livelihood being ransacked and Nevers treated her like someone who was either incredibly naive or incredibly dumb. When she saw one of the men wheel out the tall black box of her massively parallel computer on a hand truck, she started towards him, saying indignantly, 'You can't take that!'

Nevers caught her arm, gripping so hard she could feel his fingers pressing on the bone. He said, 'You'll be given an inventory of everything we take. And if there isn't a problem it will be returned to you as soon as possible.'

Lisa watched, heartsick, as the man wrestled the computer into one of the Range Rovers. Everything its hard drive contained was deeply encrypted, she wasn't about to hand over the keys unless compelled by a court order, and she had a backup that the police hadn't yet found, but she'd built the machine herself and she couldn't afford to replace it.

Nevers said, 'I understand that you were a hotshot coder back in the day. You worked out how to crack Ghostkeeper algorithms, and gave away the method.'

'It was a kernel defining an environment where people can run the algorithms. And I put it out under a Creative Commons licence. Not quite the same thing as giving it away.'

'But you didn't make any money off it, while other people did,' Nevers said.

No point trying to explain to the man that she'd been part of a collective, that she'd just happened to have had the crucial insight that helped move forward a communal effort, that everything back then had been different, more hopeful, not yet thoroughly tainted by commercial interest and the social Darwinism of neoliberal capitalism. Nevers clearly had marked her down as some kind of eccentric hippie who'd not only been fucked up by an alien ghost, but had also squandered her intellectual property out of misplaced idealism.

She said, 'You can let go of my arm. I'm not going to try to stop your people doing their work. Even if it is legalised theft.'

'We're dealing with a serious breakout, Ms Dawes,' Nevers said blandly, releasing her. 'We'll return your equipment after we've examined it. As long as it isn't contaminated, that is.'

Lisa resisted the urge to rub her arm. It felt like the man had left a bruise the size of Nebraska. 'My containment protocols are as good as anyone else's.'

'Then there shouldn't be a problem,' Nevers said, and handed her a business card. 'If you remember anything that might help us find out what happened to your husband and his friends, don't hesitate to get in touch.'

'So are business cards still a thing, back on Earth?'

'I'm no newbie, Ms Dawes. If that's what you're trying to imply. I've been working on cases like this for a very long time. Longer than you've been working on Elder Culture code, I dare say.'

'Well you don't appear to have learned very much,' Lisa said.

That bounced right off Nevers. He said, 'I saw the funny tortoise-things you have in the barn. Is that how you make your living now?'

'The hurklins? Yeah, I ranch them.'

'For meat?'

'You can't eat them. They have funny amino acids, use vanadium in their blood . . . What it is, they shed the outer layer of their shells as they grow. It's like very fine-grained leather, naturally tinted.'

She thought of Willie again, his ancient leather jacket, his cowboy boots with their silver tips and conchos. Oh, Willie.

Nevers was saying something about having had a tortoise as a pet when he was a kid. 'An age ago, in London. I painted the shell once, my idea of dazzle camouflage. But I wouldn't have thought to try to wear it.'

It was hard to imagine him as anything other than what he was, tall and straight-backed in his cream suit, radiating the stern rectitude of an old-time preacher. His flinty probing gaze, his shuttered expression. One of the agents came over with a tablet that displayed an inventory of the things they'd taken. Lisa studied it carefully before she signed it.

'We'll email you a copy,' Nevers said. 'Oh, one more thing. Your phone.'

'My phone?'

'Please,' Nevers said, holding out his hand.

Lisa thought of arguing, but knew that if she refused the agent would grab hold of her and Nevers would pat her down. She took out it out and said, 'Make sure you add it to your inventory.'

'Thank you for your cooperation, Ms Dawes,' Nevers said. 'If we have any more questions, we'll be in touch.'

She barely heard him. She was watching the Jackaroo avatar approach. Its elegant dancer's walk, as if gravity were optional. Its immaculate black tracksuit. Its gold-tinted face, eyes masked by sunglasses – exact copies of Ray-Ban Wayfarers. Jackaroo avatars presented as male, composites of fashion models and movie stars, but their gender was as superficial as a mannequin's, and more than thirty years after First Contact they were still unfathomable enigmas.

Humanity had been hard-pressed back then. Countries fighting over dwindling natural resources; riots, revolutions and counter-revolutions, and the constant low-level attrition of netwars; a billion refugees made homeless by famine, flood or extreme weather events. All of this craziness culminating in the Spasm, when more than a dozen capital cities from London to Karachi had been damaged or destroyed by low-yield tactical atomic bombs and a limited nuclear missile exchange.

The Jackaroo had arrived a year later. They brought with them fifteen wormhole mouths and fifteen colossal shuttles, infiltrated the world's communication networks, and declared that they were here to help. The wormhole mouths led to habitable worlds orbiting red dwarf stars – smaller and cooler than Earth's sun, the most common type of star in the galaxy – scattered across the Milky Way; winners of the UN emigration lottery travelled up and out on the shuttles, hoping to begin new lives in these new worlds, which turned out not to be so new after all. Previous clients of the Jackaroo, the so-called Elder Cultures, had col-onised the worlds and altered them in various ways before either dying out or moving elsewhere, leaving behind ancient ruins and artefacts.

No one knew what the Jackaroo actually looked like, where they had come from, or why. They presented only as avatars, no one had ever visited their ships, and they wouldn't ever discuss their motives, what had happened to the Elder Cultures, what might happen to the human race. *We're here to help* was all they said. *Every client's path is different.* Lisa, who'd been in high school back then, remembered the wave of optimism that had swept across the world after First Contact. Humanity was no longer alone in the universe. The Jackaroo were benevolent ambas-sadors of an advanced culture whose gifts promised the kind of utopian future, packed with miracles and marvels, that had long seemed for ever out of reach. Mining Elder Culture ruins had yielded room-temperature superconductors, construction coral, self-healing plastics and new meta-materials, entangled pairs of electrons that allowed instantaneous transmission of information across interstellar gulfs, and much else. And then there was the discovery of ships abandoned in orbital sargassos by the Ghajar, and the wormhole network of the New Frontier . . .

Lisa had bought into that dream when she'd won a lottery ticket and come up and out, but she knew all about its dark side now. The Bad Trip, possession by an ancient alien ghost, addiction to a drug distilled from an alien plant . . . And she'd had a close encounter with a Jackaroo avatar once before, in hospital soon after the Bad Trip, when she'd told her story and had been left feeling that she'd been judged by some higher being and found wanting.

So she clenched up as the avatar, maybe the one that had interviewed her back then, maybe a colleague, impossible to tell, walked towards her. It held out a hand, palm up. A small sharp-edged stone lay there, black against translucent golden skin. After a blank moment, Lisa realised that it was her only tangible souvenir of the Bad Trip.

'Remember the stone you helped me test for activity all those years back?' she told Bria. 'That one. I must have picked it up before Willie and I were zapped, and found it in the pocket of my jeans a month later.'

Lisa had hoped that it might contain some clue about what had happened to her and Willie out in the Badlands, but it had turned out to be just a rock. A little chunk of chromite, commonly found where erosion exposed the igneous rocks that underlaid the sandstone of the Badlands; an unknown Elder Culture had mined seams of chromite ore in the far south, leaving huge terraced sinkholes.

She said, 'I kept it in a bowl in the living room, with a bunch of pebbles and spent tesserae. Souvenirs of the places Willie and I excavated. I guess the tesserae pinged the avatar's radar – you know how they can track down stuff like that. And when it found them it also found the little black stone, and wanted to know what I knew about it.'

'What did you say?'

'That it came from someplace I couldn't recall out in the Badlands,' Lisa said, remembering the avatar's blank scrutiny and pleasant smile as it asked her if the stone had ever manifested any kind of activity. Although it was a shell of gold-tinted translucent polymer, remotely controlled by God-knew-what, God-knew-where, its face was mobile, disturbingly alive, disturbingly almost-but-not-quite human.

'Of course not. It's just a stone,' Lisa told it.

'Nevertheless, I must keep this for now,' the avatar said, and closed its fingers around the stone and walked away, while Nevers reminded her to call him if she had any questions or remembered anything germane.

'First time I've ever heard someone use the word in cold blood,' Lisa told Bria. '"Germane."'

Bria said, 'He didn't charge you, threaten to charge you?'

'He didn't need to. He confiscated my shit, and sooner or later he'll offer to give it back if I tell him what I know about Willie's jackpot. And the thing is, while I don't know anything but what Sheriff Bell told me, I'm definitely tangled up in it.'

'Because of your seizure.'

'Exactly. Listen, I was sort of wondering if you could maybe do me a favour or three.'

'You only have to ask, honey.'

'First, I have a feeling I might need a lawyer.'

'Of course. I have a good man on retainer.'

'The second thing, I thought I'd ask around in the Alien Market, tap into any gossip about Willie's jackpot. And while I'm doing that, maybe you could find out if he did the right thing for once in his life, and registered a claim.'

'Is that all? It doesn't seem like much.'

'Also, I need you to help me redeem my truck from the parking garage. I bought this piece-of-shit phone to replace the one Nevers took, and I can't figure out how to get it to interface with the payment system.'

6. Serious Throw-Weight

A hundred and fifty years ago, not very long after the Jackaroo made themselves known, human explorers found the entry point to a vast, multi-stranded wormhole network that spanned the outer arms of the Milky Way. Despite the discovery of a dozen or more Ghajar navigational datasets, despite the efforts of scholars, wizards and amateur obsessives who had broken their minds trying to find patterns in the clustering of mirrors and links between mirror pairs that might span a dozen or ten or fifty thousand light years, the network was still mostly unmapped. It had been called the New Frontier at first, but then an empire jacked itself up from its first settlements, ruled by a warlord, Truman Johnson I, whose fleets controlled choke points in the network of mirrors, taxed every ship that passed through them, and attacked worlds which refused to acknowledge his primacy. Only Earth and the fifteen gift worlds were spared, protected by the UN's navy and separated from the nearest wormhole mouth in the New Frontier by a gulf that made it impossible to mount a sneak attack.

Eventually Truman Johnson was assassinated by his eldest son, Able Truman Johnson, whose brief reign, the so-called Second Empire, was even more brutal than his father's. When he executed a general who refused to carry out his order to use nuclear weapons against the only city on the desert world Karnak V, officers loyal to the dead woman became the focal point of a rebellion that spread through the empire's navy, spanning four years and much of the wormhole network, and ending with the disappearance of Able Truman Johnson. A rumour that he had been murdered by two of his younger brothers was never substantiated; neither was the

37

story that he had discovered a ship with a version of the fabled faster-than-light Alcubierre drive, and had set out to discover the location of the Jackaroo's homeworld.

After his disappearance, Able Truman Johnson's empire fragmented into squabbling apanages that were swiftly subjugated by elements of the rebel navy. The victors formed a loose commonwealth that acknowledged the power of a security council and its police to referee disputes and patrol the volume of the wormhole network, but after eighty years its stability was as fragile as ever, threatened by territorial disputes, civilian rebellions and breakaway groups that attempted to set up independent principalities on fringe worlds or turned pirate, preying on merchant traffic and staging quick raids on the worlds and resources of the Commons.

Tony Okoye believed that he had been claim-jumped by one such rogue group, maybe his family's old nemesis the Red Brigade, maybe someone else. And although he had escaped their trap, his ship was half-blinded by its own countermeasures and he was still a long way from home.

As soon as *Abalunam's Pride* passed through the mirror, the bridle threw up images and scans, saying, 'The claim jumpers must have spoofed our assets and fed us fake telemetry – there was some serious throw-weight emplaced around the mirror. One-shot X-ray lasers, shrapnel missiles, ship-killing warheads . . . But they didn't use them. They tried to cripple us, but they did not try to destroy us.'

'Because they discovered that all the other stromatolites are gone, and they want what we are carrying,' Tony said. 'That's good. It means that they will not do anything that could endanger our cargo. And that means that they will not do anything that could endanger *us*.'

But if Raqle Thornhilde had told the claim jumpers about the expedition to the slime planet, they would know who owned *Abalunam's Pride*. They would know where his family lived. He would have to deal with that as and when. Right now, he still needed to make good his escape.

As the mirror of the wormhole throat dwindled into the starry scape he dropped a couple of drones that would keep watch for the claim jumpers' frigate, and reprogrammed and deployed a drone that clamped itself to the ship's prow. It was a poor replacement for the arrays which had been burned away when he had taken out the disrupter needles, but at least he could see where he was headed.

The mirror orbited a brown dwarf, a small sub-stellar object whose dim disc rapidly expanded ahead as *Abalunam's Pride* swung past on a gravity-assist manoeuvre. Ragged shadows of silicate vapour clouds stretched across the faint violet glow of the brown dwarf's inner layers like dirt streaked across a failing neon globe, suddenly filling the sky and then whipping past and falling away as the ship flew on. Its velocity had increased by the small amount of orbital energy it had stolen; it was now aimed at the brown dwarf's sun, a K0 main-sequence star over six billion kilometres away, with a swarm of more than five hundred mirrors orbiting at the inner edge of its habitable zone.

Powered by zero-point energy, warping the gravitational constant to create a local propulsive gradient, *Abalunam's Pride* drove towards the mirror-swarm and safety at an acceleration equivalent to 2.3 g, the maximum acceleration permitted by her bias drive, the maximum acceleration of the bias drive of every Ghajar ship, from A-class jaunt ships to U-class haulers. After more than a hundred years no one knew if this was an inherent property dictated by fundamental physics, or a limit built into the drive for some inscrutable reason – some argued that it was the maximum acceleration force the Ghajar, which appeared to have been fragile gasbag colonies of specialised individuals, had been able to survive. But it meant that, after using the wormhole to traverse thousands of light years in a blink of an eye, *Abalunam's Pride* would take eleven days to cross the void between the brown dwarf and the mirrors orbiting the K0 star.

Tony moved around as little as possible in the heavy pull of constant acceleration, spent most of his time on his bed's silicon-gel mattress. One of the ship's hands gave him full-body massages and spread soothing salves on his aching back and limbs. He sent a text message via the q-phone. *All well. Homeward bound as instructed.* He wanted to talk to Ayo about the close encounter with the claim jumpers, Opeyemi's interference and the execution of Fred Firat, but because his uncle had taken control of the q-phone link it would have to wait. He made regular checks on the drones stationed at the mirror orbiting the brown dwarf, and Junot Johnson kept him informed about the wizards. After arguing about whether they should continue to work after the execution of their boss, they'd turned to intense discussions about the data they'd obtained during their stay on the slime planet. It seemed like a hopeful sign to Tony. He was also monitoring Lancelot Askia. The man spent most of his time sleeping or grimly exercising, and as far as Tony could tell had not used his clandestine q-phone to talk to Opeyemi.

The claim jumpers' frigate came through the mirror two days after *Abalunam's Pride*. An hour later, the bridle told Tony that someone had hacked the carrier signal from the watch drones and was attempting to infiltrate the ship's comms.

'Shut them down,' Tony said.

'The drones or the comms?'

'Both.'

Four days later, he turned *Abalunam's Pride* through one hundred and eighty degrees and began to decelerate, the first stage in preparing to rendezvous with the mirror-swarm. If the claim jumpers intended to destroy his ship, they would continue to accelerate, overtaking *Abalunam's Pride* and knocking her out with shrapnel or smart gravel. But the frigate made its own turnover manoeuvre two days later, and was still lagging behind when Tony aimed his ship at one of the mirrors and passed through into orbit around a young yellow star surrounded by a belt of churning rocks and ice and gas a billion kilometres across. A giant structure orbited the far edge of this protoplanetary disc, a flat, fractal snowflake several thousand kilometres in diameter and of unknown provenance and purpose, as yet undisturbed by the monkey curiosity of humans.

The mirror from which *Abalunam's Pride* exited was one of eight in close orbit about each other. Tony aimed his ship at the nearest, emerging in orbit around a ringed gas giant that orbited a blue-white B0 star. And felt a little better: the claim jumpers would have seen which mirror he had used in the wilderness, but they couldn't know which of the seven possible exits he'd just now used.

Tony lingered only for the handful of hours it took to traverse to the next mirror, and then he was somewhere else, out in another wilderness of mirrors fifteen thousand light years away, this one at the L5 point in the orbit of an Earth-sized planet tidally locked to its red dwarf star, with a narrow habitable ring between the ice cap of the dark side and the howling desert of dust seas and volcanoes of the sub-stellar hemisphere. There were hundreds of worlds like it, most of them littered with the usual Elder Culture ruins, the usual secrets waiting to be unlocked. This one had been colonised by an atechnic cult sixty years ago. Maybe they were living the life of pastoral utopianism they'd planned; maybe they had descended into savagery and were roasting and eating prisoners of war captured in tribal wars fought with stone-tipped spears. No one knew nor cared.

Abalunam's Pride transited three more times, and after twenty-eight hours emerged into the familiar light of a M0 red dwarf star and aimed herself at a rocky world with an equatorial belt of ocean pinched between ice caps that covered most of its northern and southern hemispheres. Skadi. After two years of banging around the galaxy as a freebooter, Tony had come home.

7. The Alien Market

When Lisa arrived on First Foot, the Alien Market had been on the very edge of Port of Plenty: a maze of converted shipping containers, Quonset huts and flat-roofed mud-brick buildings crammed into a narrow triangle between Elysian Creek and the meatpacking district. Tomb raiders and prospectors who came in from the back country to do business had camped out on the far side of the creek, and every Sunday there had been an unofficial flea fair along the main drag where dealers, collectors and scouts haggled over unlicensed artefacts and other finds.

Now the city's low-rise sprawl spread far beyond the creek. A Holiday Inn stood where the tomb raiders had once camped, the slaughterhouses and cold stores of the meatpacking district had moved out to Felony Flats, the flea fair was no more, and most of the assayers, analysts, traders, chandlers, coders and pawn shops had been displaced by bars, coffee shops, bubble-tea houses and restaurants, shops that sold gimcrack souvenirs and replicas of famous finds, stuffed animals and the shells of biochines, and expensive field kit and utility clothing that no prospector would ever use. It was a popular weekend destination. You could eat brunch, buy a pair of hurklin-hide shoes, a snow globe containing a replica of the spires of Mammoth Lakes, jewellery made from spent tesserae, or a phial of blue sand from the so-called Arena of Kings, and round off your day in one of the quaint themed bars.

But some of the old businesses still clung on, and Lisa could map moments from her past as she led Pete through the passages, alleyways and courtyards. Here were the shallow steps down to the cellar bar where she and Willie had spent way too much time back when; here was her favourite sushi counter; here was the ground-floor room in the three-storey stack of shipping containers where she'd first set up business on her own, although the containers had recently been painted in bright primary colours, and what had been her workshop was now a store front advertising 'genuine gemstones and geodes'.

And here was the place where she'd once tried to make contact with her ghost. She'd been desperate back then, in the first year of her possession. She'd broken up with Willie, had begun to numb herself with booze because she was scared of the thing in her head, of what it might do, of what it might already have done. There had been anxiety attacks, lurid nightmares, the whole nine yards. She pestered her friends, asking them if they thought she'd changed, looking for confirmation of her fears in their gaze, in casual conversations. Her obsession had driven many of them away, confirming her belief that she was turning into something else. That she was carrying in her head a monstrous entity whose loathsome aura horrified and repulsed other people.

Back then, a dozen mediums and psychics had been operating in the Alien Market, claiming to be able to channel the spirits of ancient intelligences from Elder Cultures, tap into deep wells of weird wisdom, exorcise unwelcome eidolons and talk to the human and alien dead. Coders and assayers made fun of their mystic woo, but there was an undercurrent of self-recognition in the jokes: both psychics and coders were attempting to quantify the unquantifiable, and their jargon and methodologies echoed each other. Eidolons v. ghosts. Avatars v. spirits. Reynolds traps v. crystal balls. Code stripping v. cold reading.

Lisa hadn't given psychics much thought before the Bad Trip, but after her neurology consultant had told her that it was impossible to remove the eidolon without causing serious brain damage, she began, like a cancer patient who'd been given a terminal diagnosis, to search for cures outside mainstream medicine. Meditation and mindfulness. A sleep machine that was supposed to modify her alpha waves. And then she finally nerved herself to walk into the psychic parlour she passed every day on the way to work.

She waited until the place was about to close. Feeling, as she slipped inside, like a kid trespassing on a grouchy neighbour's lawn. There was none of the paraphernalia – velvet drapes, antique furniture, wax-encrusted candelabra, batteries of crystals – she'd expected. Just two plastic stacking chairs either side of a small glass-topped table, recessed lights in the ceiling, a doorway screened with a waterfall of plain glass beads that clicked as a young man pushed through them.

He wore a white shirt, black pants and wire-framed glasses, looking more like an architect or a college lecturer than someone who communed with alien spirits. Holding up a hand when Lisa began to explain why she was there, giving her a lingering look, saying that he could see that she was troubled, that she wanted help. It was her aura, he said. It was an unhealthy colour and had a swollen, lopsided look.

'You have a guest with deep roots. How did it find you?'

She found herself explaining about the Bad Trip. The young man listened attentively. He did not seem to judge her. When she finished talking there was a short silence; then he told her that understanding what possessed her was the first step on the road to self-knowledge.

'That's why I'm here.'

Lisa paid a hundred and forty dollars for an initial consultation. They sat either side of the table and the psychic took out a small parcel of silvery mylar cloth and unfolded it to reveal a pale, thumbnail-sized tessera. He centred it between them, told Lisa that he was going to evoke his familiar and that she should not be frightened.

'I've seen eidolons before,' she said.

'The Butcher can be intimidating to some people.'

'The Butcher?'

'It is what I call him,' the psychic said. 'His actual name has no real human equivalent, of course.'

'Of course,' Lisa said, beginning to feel that she'd made a mistake.

The psychic told the lights to dim, touched the tessera. And his eidolon was suddenly there, filling the room like a faint fog of cigarette smoke. The psychic closed his eyes. His hands rested palms up on the table, thumb and forefinger pinched together. Lisa expected him to speak in a sonorous voice, channelling his spirit guide, offering nuggets of wisdom, asking leading questions. Instead, the fog began to thicken and coalesce behind him, and she had the brief impression of something larger than the room leaning in, looking down at her. Then the smoky fog blew away, vanishing beyond the walls of the dim little room, and the young man stood with an abrupt motion that knocked over his chair.

'Go,' he said. He looked as if he had been punched hard in the stomach.

'What about my reading? What did you see?'

There was a stinging metallic taste in Lisa's mouth, a headache pulsing behind her eyes.

'Just leave. Please. I can't help you. I can't . . .'

For a moment the young man stared at her, a look that was half longing, half revulsion, then turned on his heel and shouldered through the glass-bead curtain.

Lisa started to take a longer route to work so that she could avoid the psychic's parlour. One morning, three or four weeks later, she found a small parcel of mylar cloth on the doorstep of her office. She didn't unwrap it: she knew what it contained. And when she finally nerved herself up to visit the psychic's parlour she discovered that it was boarded up; according to one of his neighbours the owner had fallen ill and given up the lease.

Lisa didn't ever scan the tessera he'd left. She knew that it would be empty, wiped clean by her ghost. Call it an exorcism in reverse. Shortly after that, she was starting her mornings with a shot or two to numb herself, and then she got into shine and lost her business and quit the Alien Market.

Now she was searching for clues about the identity and nature of her ghost again. She was certain that the geek police weren't going to tell her anything; a brief phone conference with Bria's lawyer had confirmed that as far as that went she was pretty much screwed.

'At this point I recommend patience,' he'd said. 'If your equipment has not been returned in, let's say, four weeks, it might be possible to lodge an appeal based on the distress caused to your business.'

'What about the distress caused by their harassment?' Lisa had said, but the lawyer had told her that it would be hard to argue that the police had been doing anything other than implementing the usual procedures in their investigation.

She planned to make the rounds of friends and business acquaintances, asking about Willie's find and who he'd crewed up with, asking if he'd brought in anything for analysis, and she lucked out on her first stop. Her old boss Valerie Tortorella, who'd heard about the breakout on the tomb-raider gossip board.

Valerie was in her late sixties, a shrewd, laid-back Canadian who'd come up to First Foot on the seventh shuttle cycle, back when Port of Plenty had been no more than a tent town pitched on the shore of an alien sea. Lisa had worked for her before she'd met Bria and joined the Crazy 88 Collective, and Valerie had been part of the intervention that had rescued her from her low point after the Bad Trip.

They sat in Valerie's workshop, sipping mint tea. Pete sprawled beside Lisa; her ghost leaned at her shoulder. Perhaps it was interested in the fossil that sat on the workbench, under an articulated magnifier lamp: a hand-sized sandstone slab printed with a glistening spiral, the burrow made by some worm-like animal or biochine in the mud of a lake that had dried up half a million years ago, lined with an organic polymer salted with copper and iron. Valerie had shown Lisa how a pair of gold-tipped needle probes attached to an oscillator elicited high pure tones from different parts of the fossil. 'Maybe the worm-things sang to each other with magnetic pulses. Or maybe it's an accidental feature of some deeper property. Who knows?'

Lisa told her old boss about the raid on her homestead by the geek police and admitted that she still didn't know how she felt about Willie, said it hadn't really sunk in yet. Valerie said, 'I heard the police haven't found his body. Is there still a chance . . . ?'

'If anyone could turn up after a catastrophic breakout, it would be Willie. But the guy in charge of the case said that it was really bad, it looked like everyone had turned on everyone else . . .' Lisa paused, then said, 'You know that corny old thing about twins feeling each other's pain? How if one twin dies the other knows about it, even if they're half a world apart?'

Valerie looked at her over the top of her bifocals. Her grey hair was pulled in a tight bun skewered with a steel needle. She was dressed in a work apron over jeans and a thin cotton sweater. 'It was like that with you and Willie?'

'I think it was like that with our ghosts,' Lisa said, and told Valerie about her seizure, said that she thought that Willie had been digging up something related to the Bad Trip.

'So I suppose you want to know about that weird tessera he brought in for analysis a few weeks back,' Valerie said.

Lisa rode out the moment of freezing shock and said, 'This was from the place he was digging up?'

'He didn't say. You know Willie. One day he would be bragging about some jackpot that turned out to exist only his imagination, the next he was Mr Mystery.'

'That's why he was such a terrible poker player. He'd clown around until he got some good cards, and then he was deadly serious. He'd say, "Are we playing or are we playing?" and everyone knew to throw in their high cards and low pairs.'

'The same when he was trying to get a price on something, for sure,' Valerie said.

She told Lisa that Willie had asked her for a second opinion on the tessera. 'It was active, but didn't express the usual eidolon. Instead, it contained some kind of Ghajar code. Not my kind of thing, so I sent him over to Carol Schleifer. She has handled a couple of fragments of ship code from that crash site in the City of the Dead.'

'This was definitely a tessera.'

'And not a piece of ship wreckage that looked like a tessera? That's what I wondered,' Valerie said. 'So I zapped it with my chemcam. I also did a CT scan. Chemical composition and fine-grain structure were identical with late-period Ghostkeeper tesserae. Composition, isotopic ratios and tracks left by cosmic rays dated it at between forty and fifty thousand years old. Again, consistent with late-period tesserae.'

'So how did Ghajar code get inside it?'

'You'd have to ask Carol. It's outside my area of expertise. Do you think it could have something to do with what happened to you?'

'I'm not sure. Maybe. Did Willie happen to tell you where he found it?'

Valerie shook her head. 'He was holding that card close to his chest.'

'He partnered up with a crew,' Lisa said. 'I was wondering if you heard anything about that, know anyone who went with him.'

Valerie studied her for a moment. 'Are you sure you're all right? Because if you don't mind me saying so, you look like you're running on empty.'

Pete agreed, saying that Lisa was bad tired.

'Say again?' Valerie said.

'He said I've had a couple of rough days,' Lisa said. 'I should go talk to Carol. If you hear anything about this breakout, what the geek police are doing, maybe you could pass it on.'

Carol Schleifer's office was in Prometheus Row, a narrow street of mud-brick buildings that stepped down towards Elysian Creek. It was cluttered with little restaurants and shops selling trinkets and printed replicas, but some of the original businesses lingered at the far end, down by the old cast-iron bridge where day trippers posed for selfies and love-sick teenagers fastened padlocks scratched with their initials to the railings. Carol Schleifer shared a storefront with a business that advertised energy-dispersive X-ray spectroscopy. She made a fuss of Pete, as if he was a pet instead of a working dog, and told Lisa she was sorry to hear about Willie. 'Sometimes you hit the jackpot and sometimes the jackpot hits you, I guess.'

Lisa ignored that, asked about Willie's tessera. Carol told her that it had contained Ghajar code all right, but it wasn't ship code.

'It was narrative code, so-called. Rare stuff, usually found in scraps of grapheme laminate recovered from Ghajar ships. I asked him if he'd been poking around the City of the Dead. You know, the site of that crashed spaceship. He just winked. He was acting *muy misteriosamente*,' Carol said. 'Said he'd found something big but wouldn't tell me what.'

She didn't think it odd to find Ghajar code in a Ghostkeeper tessera.

'Ship code got into hive rats that dug a colony in the site of that crashed ship. And it got inside a couple of coders working on it, too. It's labile. So I wouldn't be surprised if narrative code is labile too. Do you think it got inside Willie's head? It would find it pretty crowded in there, I should think,' Carol said, reminding Lisa exactly why she'd never really liked the woman.

'Did Willie say anything at all about where he'd found it?'

'He said he'd made a lucky strike, wouldn't say where. Did anything ever come of it? Why I ask, he still owes me,' Carol said. She was a brisk, brittle New Yorker, her sharp blue eyes lasering Lisa over the top of spex with thin gold frames. 'I told him that I could get him a good price for that tessera. Enough to pay off his debt, and then some. I know most of the collectors, and there's someone at Peking University trying to decode the language. If it is a language. But Willie blew me off, said he had other plans.'

'He went back out with a crew. I'm trying to find out who they were.'

'I wouldn't know anything about that. You could ask his girlfriend, I guess.' Carol smiled. 'You did know he has a new girlfriend?'

'I'd be surprised if he didn't,' Lisa said.

According to Carol, this one was a pretty newbie who'd come up a few months ago. 'Say, how about this? You pay what he owes me, I'll knock twenty per cent off, you get the girlfriend to pay you the full amount and keep the difference. That way we both make a little something.'

'I don't think so.'

'I help people, this is what I get,' Carol said. 'You guys were still married, weren't you?'

'Only technically,' Lisa said. 'Don't think that it makes me liable for his debts. But listen, maybe his girlfriend is holding on to something that might raise a little cash. Do you happen to know if he was still living in that motel over in Felony Flats?'

8. Risk Management

Tony Okoye was in the middle of offloading his passengers and their strange cargo when three police cruisers came scurrying across the landing field. He was required to attend an extraordinary council meeting; no use protesting that he had far better things to do. He told Junot to oversee the transfer of the crew of wizards to Aunty Jael's laboratories, climbed into the lead cruiser, and in a whirl of lights and blare of sirens was driven at speed along the coast highway and through the crooked and winding streets of Victory Landing to the Great House.

Tony had been away for more than two years, but nothing seemed to have changed. His rooms were as clean and anonymous as a hotel suite. Hands had set up artful arrangements of pine boughs and the blood-red feathers of some kind of native foliage here and there, laid out a selection of fresh clothes, and drawn a sudsy bath. As soon as he was alone, he called Ayo on her hard line. He was certain that Opeyemi was behind the security theatre and the meeting, wanted to find out if his sister was on his side, wanted to discuss how they could neutralise this charade, but her secretary told him that Madam Ayo was at present unavailable.

'Tell her it's her young brother, back from a grand adventure with a great prize.'

'She knows all about your arrival, sir. And she asked me to tell you that she is looking forward to hearing your report.'

'I have to talk to her before the meeting.'

'The meeting is already under way, sir. You will be sent for shortly.'

Tony was pacing in a tight circle to work off his frustration. 'Sent for? What am I, a package?'

'I believe that you will appear as a witness, sir,' the secretary said drily.

Perfumed from the bath, dressed in a red brocade jacket with gold frogs, matching trousers with a gold stripe, and a felt cap denoting his status, Tony was escorted by a coronet and two troopers to his sister's offices. Lancelot Askia was in the anteroom, dressed in a plain black suit and talking to a pair of senior executive officers. He glanced at Tony across the big room, smiled, and looked away. According to the handsome young aide who greeted Tony, the man had just given evidence to the council.

'My version of events should be all they need,' Tony said, feeling that he had walked into an ambush.

'They must consider all the facts, sir,' the aide said. 'This way, please.'

As he followed the aide to the council chamber, Tony opened a window, called up the ship's external feeds, and checked its perimeter. The wizards and the shielded aquarium containing the stromatolites were gone; there was no unusual activity on the whitetop of the landing field; the bridle confirmed that everything was quiet.

'Are the wizards safe?'

'They have arrived at Aunty Jael's laboratory. I regret that I have no access to her security.'

'Stay alert. We may need to leave in some haste.'

In the chamber, Ayo and her secretary were waiting with four members of the executive council. Aunt Felicia, the Lady of the Market; Uncle Socrates, who ran the family bank; the justice minister, Avon Abbas Acholonu; and Opeyemi, who returned Tony's greeting with a stiff unsmiling nod.

Ayo kissed Tony's cheeks and welcomed him home. It was always a surprise that she was so much taller than him. 'It has been far too long,' she said. 'We have missed you.'

'And I have missed you, Ayo. But is this any way to greet your prodigal brother? I was hoping for a parade. Or at least one of

51

our walks in the woods. You could tell me how lumber production has gone up and milk yields have fallen, and I could try to amuse you with outrageous lies about my adventures.'

'For once, the truth is outrageous enough,' Ayo said.

She was dressed in a white business suit, looked tired and careworn. Tony had been away for two years, but his sister seemed to have aged at least ten, with new lines in her forehead and streaks of grey in her crown of twisted locks.

'That it is,' he told her, trying to keep it light, trying to show that he would not be intimidated. 'Full of thrills and close encounters, and the promise of a wonderfully happy ending.'

He took his seat, facing the others across the table, and explained what the wizards had found on the slime planet, described his escape from the claim jumpers, and restated his belief that the G-class frigate had been owned by the Red Brigade. Felicia and Socrates kept interrupting him for clarification of some point or fact in the fussy way they had, but otherwise he thought that he carried it off pretty well. But as soon as he'd finished, Avon Abbas Acholonu started in, telling him that he had no evidence that the frigate was one of the Red Brigade's ships.

'Ordinary claim jumpers do not run to frigates,' Tony said. 'It was flying a false police flag—'

'It could belong to one of the other honourable families,' Avon said. 'On a clandestine mission like yours, searching for the same fool's gold.'

'No honourable family or corporation would pretend to be the police.'

Tony was smiling, still keeping his tone light, but he was somewhat unnerved. Avon was Ayo's man; he was the only commoner on the council, and she had promoted him after his meteoric rise through the ranks of the civil service. His direct challenge suggested that Tony couldn't count on his sister's support, let alone anyone else's. The council chamber, with battle flags hung from the ceiling and cases of heirlooms and battle trophies along the walls, an antique gold-visored spacesuit standing beside the double door, all the weight of the family's storied history, suddenly seemed like a trap.

Avon said, 'Someone who wanted us to believe they were Red Brigade might fly under a false flag. And the police's black-ops crews have been known to emulate the pirates they are trying to catch. Lacking any hard evidence as to the claim jumpers' actual identity and intentions, any story we tell is as valid as any other.'

'Surely the simplest explanation is the best,' Tony said. 'Which is that the claim jumpers had been sent by the Red Brigade to steal the ancient knowledge we had uncovered. I know that Opeyemi agrees with me. It's why he told me that it was too dangerous to return to Dry Salvages and confront the broker.'

'Not exactly,' Opeyemi said. 'I told you that *if* Raqle Thornhilde had a connection with the claim jumpers, you should do nothing to endanger yourself. But it is now obvious that she was not to blame. It was the leader of that crew of wizards, Fred Firat.'

Socrates said, 'It doesn't really matter who the claim jumpers were, nephew. The point is that this sorry incident underscores the unnecessary risks you have been taking.'

'There's a feeling,' Ayo said quietly, 'that your ship and your talents might be better used elsewhere.'

Tony appealed to her directly. 'We agreed that there was no better mission than finding a cure for sleepy sickness. That's why you gave your assent to the deal.'

'It was not properly scrutinised by the council,' Felicia said.

'And it was hardly a commercial venture,' Socrates said. 'More of a reckless adventure that nearly ended in disaster.'

They were twins, Felicia and Socrates, seventy years old, with the same round face and broad nose, the same brown eyes. Socrates wore his grey hair in beaded braids; Felicia's was piled high and wrapped in a brightly patterned scarf.

'And you don't have a cure,' Avon said. 'You were pursuing what might at best be described as a wild hypothesis.'

'I have brought back ancient code stored in living libraries,' Tony said, 'and a crew of wizards who even as we speak are preparing to unravel its secrets. And I saved those secrets from capture by people who clearly believe they are important. The mission has been a howling success, yet I've been forced to account for myself before this so-called emergency meeting. What is it that I'm missing? What do you think I've done wrong?'

He had been speaking to Ayo, but it was Opeyemi who answered. As always, his uncle, rail-thin and straight-backed, was dressed in severe black, saying, 'We accept that the stromatolite code is ancient. And we accept that it may have some small commercial value. But there is no evidence that it has anything to do with finding a cure for sleepy sickness, and the idea that it does was advanced by a man who turned out to be a traitor.'

'It wasn't entirely his idea,' Tony said. 'It's widely held that the various kinds of Elder Culture code have a common root.'

'Quite,' Opeyemi said. 'The idea he sold you was not even his. And then he sold you out.'

'We can't be certain of that,' Tony said, 'because you had him killed before I could put him to the question.'

'Mr Askia determined that it was necessary to eliminate the traitor before he could do more damage,' Opeyemi said. 'I agree with that decision, as does the rest of the council. And we have also agreed that his death has put an end to the matter.'

'You decided all that before consulting me,' Tony said, with chilly dismay.

'There has been much discussion about the mission and its unfortunate termination,' Ayo said. 'The council has concluded that it represents a considerable risk, and has come to a decision as to how that risk should be managed. The point of this meeting is not to assign blame to you or to anyone else, but to explain that decision to you.'

'A hundred days,' Avon said.

'A hundred days?' Tony said.

'It has been decided that if examination of the stromatolites yields nothing useful in a hundred days, our support for it will be terminated,' Avon said.

'Then you may as well terminate it now,' Tony said. 'Because unravelling the code will not be easy. We knew that from the beginning. That is why our contract promised to give the wizards open-ended support. A hundred days will not be anywhere near long enough.'

'There was a strong argument that we should have nothing more to do with it,' Ayo said, 'but we reached a compromise.'

'If your wizards fail to discover anything useful after a hundred days, they will be returned to Dry Salvages, where they can continue their work in any way they see fit,' Avon said. 'I have drawn up an addendum to the contract. It is actually quite generous. We still expect to share in the profits from any commercial application, but that share will be reduced pro rata, reflecting the reduction in our support.'

'We are certain that Raqle Thornhilde will agree,' Felicia said. 'After all, it is an opportunity for her to increase her share of any profits by increasing her support.'

'This is the person who may have betrayed us,' Tony said.

'We know who betrayed us,' Opeyemi said. 'And it was not the broker.'

'It's a question of balancing the investment we have already made with the increased risk of exposure,' Socrates said.

'This meddling in things unknown and potentially dangerous is exactly the kind of behaviour that could attract the attention of the police,' Felicia said. 'Especially as your so-called claim jumpers know about it.'

'A hundred days is recklessly generous,' Opeyemi said. 'It's my opinion that we should destroy those stromatolites now. You're lucky that some on the council hope to salvage a little profit from this farrago.'

Avon said, 'We have a contract with the wizards and the broker. This is the best compromise.'

'Yes, yes,' Opeyemi said, irritated by the reminder of an argument he had lost, giving Tony a stern look across the polished tabletop. 'You can make amends for your foolishness, nephew, by making sure that those wizards of yours do not cause any more trouble. If they let loose something that overturns everything we have done to rebuild our standing in the Commons I can assure you that you will learn the true meaning of trouble.'

'I see,' Tony said.

He knew now that Opeyemi had taken advantage of the adventure on the slime planet to undermine Ayo's authority, and that the rest of the council had turned on her when it became clear that the enterprise had exposed them to unacceptable risk.

'I hope you'll excuse me,' he said. 'I must convey this bad news to the wizards at once. They deserve no less.'

Opeyemi opened a window in the air, prodded at something inside it. 'There is something else,' he said. 'It has been decided that the family would benefit if *Abalunam's Pride* was redeployed. Returned, that is, to its former duties.'

'Running cargo? But we already have ships doing that,' Tony said.

'It is good steady work,' Socrates said.

'Necessary work,' Felicia said.

'It is in your best interests,' Ayo said.

'It is in the best interests of the family,' Opeyemi said. 'You have had a narrow escape, nephew. A *lucky* escape. One that highlights the risks this freebooting nonsense has exposed us to. We could have lost a valuable asset.'

'Thank you for your concern, uncle.'

'I meant the ship,' Opeyemi said, and skimmed the window across the table to Ayo.

'I'm sorry,' she said to Tony.

'Wait,' he said. 'What's in that window?'

'An executive override,' Opeyemi said. 'Ayo, if you please.'

Ayo set her palm against the window's glow, and there was a sudden empty silence in Tony's head. The ship's feed had been cut off.

9. Love And Marriage

Felony Flats was a low-rise clutter of light industry, bungalows, apartment buildings and public housing spread across reclaimed marshland east of the city. Boxbuilder ruins and patches of local vegetation on scattered low hills that had once been islands. Wind-turbine farms. Smallholdings and compounds fenced with corrugated iron. A threadbare grid of paved streets and dusty tracks where Lisa had lived during her nadir, amongst the poor and the dispossessed.

She overtook an ancient bus crowded with people inside and out. She drove past a young boy leading a beautiful chestnut horse along the edge of the road. She drove past a cement factory, past a muddy channel where clinker-built fishing boats lay on their sides, waiting for the afternoon tide.

The motel where Willie had pitched camp for the past three years was in a flyblown commercial strip near the shore: a two-storey string of rooms, an empty swimming pool painted sky-blue, and a sign advertising air conditioning, clean rooms and free adult movies. The manager, a skinny young Sikh with pockmarked cheeks and a prominent Adam's apple, remembered Lisa from the time she'd covered Willie's back rent after he'd got in a hole over a gambling debt. He folded away the fifty-dollar bill she slipped him, told her that Brittany Odenkirk worked in a bar a couple of blocks down the street, and asked if this was about the trouble yesterday.

'That depends on the trouble.'

'Police trouble.'

'The police police, or the geek police?' Lisa said.

'Excuse me?'

'The UN Technology Control Unit. A guy name of Adam Nevers.'

'Yes, that was the man in charge,' the manager said. 'He sealed Mr Willie's room with tape and told me I couldn't rent it out again until his investigation was finished. What investigation this was he would not tell me.'

'He's chasing ghosts,' Lisa said, and held up another fifty and asked if she could check out Willie's room.

'If the police find you there,' the manager said, 'I don't know anything about it.'

The room was pretty much as Lisa remembered it, apart from the women's clothing in the chipboard chifferobe and the make-up and box of tampons in the bathroom. Hard to tell if it had been tossed by the police or not, but she bet that if Willie had left any souvenirs behind, Nevers and his Jackaroo pal probably had them now.

Feeling like a detective, she drove the two blocks to the bar, a low flat-roofed shack islanded in a big dirt lot. A neon sign over the door flickered weakly in the sunlight. Chillies Spot. Behind it, spiny jags of elbow bush caught about with litter sloped down to the steel-grey water of a broad inlet. A warm breeze carried the bitter tang of the sea, subtly different to the scent of the seas of Earth.

Lisa told Pete to sit tight in the back of the pickup truck and keep a look out for men in black, adding, when Pete said he didn't understand, 'Like the people who visited us yesterday.'

Pete wagged his tail and said no problem.

Chillies Spot was a dim cave reeking of cigarette smoke, stale beer and disinfectant. Bottles racked in front of mirrors behind the well bar, vinyl booths, a scuffed pool table. It was as if Lisa had time-travelled back to one of the dives where she'd hid from the world in the bad old days. It was alarmingly like coming home.

She spotted Brittany Odenkirk at once – a pale blonde girl, pretty in that brittle way that went quickly downhill after the brief glow of youth faded, talking to a couple of old geezers at the far end of the bar counter – and took a seat and waited. After a couple of minutes the girl drifted over, asked her what she was having.

'I'd like to ask a couple of questions about your boyfriend.'

Brittany Odenkirk gave Lisa a weary look. Her eyes were bruised. She'd been crying, Lisa realised, and felt a touch of shame. She hadn't yet shed one tear for Willie, had come here for entirely selfish reasons.

The girl said, 'If you're from the police, I already told everything I know.'

'As a matter of fact,' Lisa said, 'I'm Willie's fucking wife. Let me buy you a drink, and we can talk about our mutual loss.'

They sat in one of the booths, with a tall glass of a green concoction called Jackaroo Blood for Brittany and a what-the-fuck bottle of imported Dos Equis for Lisa. Still tasting damn fine after crossing twenty thousand light years. She told herself that she'd be careful and only have the one.

After Lisa told Brittany about the raid on her homestead, the girl said that she'd found out about Willie's accident when the police came to search their motel room yesterday, at four in the fucking morning.

'A guy and, can you believe it, a goldskin.'

'An avatar?'

'In a tracksuit and box-fresh kicks like some gnarly old MC.'

The girl had a Californian lilt and was, as Carol Schleifer had said, very young. Twenty, twenty-two, traces of acne in the corners of her mouth. Lisa felt sort of protective, wondering about the brief sad trajectory that had brought her to Felony Flats, and Willie.

'They came to my place, too,' Lisa said, and described Adam Nevers.

Brittany nodded. 'Like an older, not quite as handsome version of that actor who played Batman in those movies? He was English too, right?'

'Did they take anything?'

'What's it to you, if you don't mind me asking.'

'Did Willie ever tell you about the Bad Trip?'

'You mean the ghost in his head? Yeah, he liked to tell that story. Said it helped him see things differently. Gave him what he called a Martian perspective, whatever that was.'

'Did he tell you I was there with him?'

'Well, not exactly . . .'

'I have a ghost in my head, too,' Lisa said. 'Courtesy of the Bad Trip. It gave me a kick when the breakout killed Willie and his friends. So I'm pretty sure that whatever happened out there has something to do with me, and that's why I need to find out what Willie was into.'

Brittany looked off at something that wasn't in the dim room. When she looked back, she said, 'Can your ghost . . . Does it know if he's really dead?'

'All I know so far is what the police told me.'

'He was so up before he went away,' Brittany said. 'Bouncing around because he'd made a find. He said there was a big payday coming. Promised me we'd be rich.'

'Did he tell you what he'd found? Where he'd found it?'

'He had like one of those little stones you can find in the City of the Dead?'

'A tessera?'

Lisa felt like Spider-Girl just before the baddie tries to whomp her.

'Yeah. A little black squarish thing. He said it was special. Said he was going back out to dig up a lot more of them.'

'Did he tell you where he found it?'

'All I know is it wasn't from the City of the Dead, but someplace out in the Badlands. And yeah, I wish I'd asked about it, but it wouldn't have meant anything to me. I only ever went out with him the one time. Dust and sand and really old ruins that really didn't look anything much like tombs or whatever. More like heaps of rubble, holes in the ground. Willie dug up a bunch of these what-do-you-call-them, tesserae, but nothing special. He got a couple of hundred bucks for some of them from this guy in this little desert town, let me keep the rest.'

'The town – was that Joe's Corner?'

Brittany shrugged.

'Can you remember the name of the guy who bought those tesserae?'

Another shrug.

'Calvin Quinlan, does that ring any bells?'

Calvin Quinlan was an assayer Willie had done business with, back in the day.

'I don't know. Maybe.'

'When Willie went back out,' Lisa said, 'did he leave any documentation behind? Maps, samples, maybe a data stick with photos on it?'

'The police guy asked me that. I said go ahead and look. All they found were the little stones Willie gave me.'

'Were any of them haunted?'

'Willie said they were just stones. Said he'd buy some silver wire and make me a necklace, but he never got around to it . . .'

Brittany sniffed loudly, tipped back her head. To keep her tears from running and ruining her mascara, Lisa realised, and handed her a napkin.

'Thanks,' Brittany said, and dabbed at her eyes, blew her nose. 'When he told me he'd found something big? Frankly, I didn't really believe him. He was always talking about making a big score. Finding something out there that would make him rich. He'd make a joke about it, you know? But I think it was the one thing he was serious about.'

'Willie didn't lack ambition,' Lisa said.

'Yeah, and look where it got him.'

Brittany took a big sip of her green cocktail; Lisa drank down the last of her beer. Lord but it tasted good. She had to step hard on the impulse to order another.

'The police told me there were other people involved in that breakout,' she said. 'Do you know who they were? Tomb-raider pals of Willie's, what?'

'He got in with this company?'

Lisa's spider-sense was tingling again. 'Do you happen to know its name, or where I can find it?'

'I don't know where their offices are. Somewhere in the city, I guess. They're called Outland Archaeological Services? Willie came in here to get the contract checked out. One of our regulars, he used to be a lawyer.'

'Outland Archaeological Services. Okay. That's good.'

'You know who they are?'

'Not yet.'

'It was Willie's life, looking for that alien shit out in the desert,' Brittany said. 'I should have been more interested in it, but to tell the truth? That one time was enough. The sand getting everywhere, and the heat, and the weird creepy-crawlies? Thanks, but no thanks. Also, I have this job now. Ten hours a day behind the counter with a smile painted on and my legs turning to wood, and even with tips it barely covers the rent. And I can't take time off, I'd get canned. Even after that raid yesterday, finding out what happened to Willie . . . The next day, here I am. The trip we made, that was before I got started here. When we first met.'

She'd hooked up with Willie three months ago, soon after she'd arrived on First Foot. A guy she was sort of seeing had taken her to a house party, and she'd left with Willie.

'I've always gone for older types. And he's fun to be with, you know?'

'At first, yeah.'

Brittany looked sideways at Lisa. 'Are you really married to him?'

'I really am.'

'It's just that he never mentioned it. And I didn't think he was the marrying type.'

'He wasn't,' Lisa said. 'And you don't have anything to apologise for. We split up years ago. Just never got around to getting a divorce.'

'That sounds like Willie.'

They shared a smile.

Lisa said, 'Willie had a sort of glamour about him. A free-spirit thing, and also a kind of helplessness that made you want to look after him. But someone like you? Frankly, and not wishing to speak ill of the dead and all that, I think you can do better.'

'I did love him,' Brittany said, with a sharp stubborn look.

'How did you come up here? Shuttle or scow?'

'Shuttle. I won a lottery ticket.'

'There you go. You're a winner. Don't piss it away. Don't be like Willie.'

'Were you a lottery winner too?'

'Yeah, I was. And yeah, I know, I ended up marrying Willie. Don't make my mistake is what I guess I'm trying to say.'

'So how did you guys hook up?'

'I was kind of bored with the way my life was going,' Lisa said, 'and Willie happened along.'

After the high point of designing the virtual space where Ghostkeeper code could be run safely, she'd quit the Crazy 88 Collective and sort of lost direction. Her next big idea, an attempt to construct a logic engine to map common features in algorithms from a variety of Elder Cultures, had run into serious difficulties. It seemed that her best work was behind her, that like many mathematicians she'd burned out early. She'd been working in the Alien Market back then, testing finds for prospectors and tomb raiders, analysing algorithms and code for commercial potential. It paid the rent and groceries, but it was mostly dull routine, and she was beginning to believe that it was what she'd be doing for the rest of her life when one day Willie Coleman turned up with a tessellation panel for analysis.

When he'd won a ticket in the emigration lottery, Willie had been a thirty-year-old farm-equipment salesman in Duluth. He left behind an ex-wife and two daughters, a rented apartment and an ancient Subaru Outback held together by rust and duct tape, and completely reinvented himself on arrival in Port of Plenty, becoming a swashbuckling prospector who roamed the vast necropolis of the City of the Dead in a sand-blasted Holden Colorado truck, scraping a living selling tesserae and other small artefacts, always hoping for the life-changing jackpot of discovering a fragment of novel technology that he could sell or licence to one of the big companies. He wasn't exactly handsome, but he had a charmingly boyish enthusiasm and a quick wit, and carried off his rock-and-roll gypsy look – fingers knuckly with silver rings, long hair tied back with a red bandana, loose white shirts carelessly unbuttoned under an ancient leather jacket – with total unselfconsciousness. Lisa knew about his string of girlfriends and his self-mythologising, but she'd allowed him to flirt with her, he'd stayed the night, and returned a week later to ask if she wanted to go on a trip. And she'd said why not?

'You got together with him while you were depressed,' Bria once said, as if Lisa's black dog had prevented her from making any good decisions. But at the time Willie had been right for her. He'd helped her to escape herself.

Three months after their first trip to the City of the Dead, they married on impulse in a *Star Trek*-themed chapel in Mammoth Lakes. They'd gone there to test Lisa's method for beating the house at blackjack. She'd mentioned Edward Thorp's card-counting technique after Willie had almost lost his truck in a poker game, and he'd said that he bet she could come up with something better. Lisa accepted the challenge and spent some serious time on the project, but after winning nine hundred and forty dollars at one of the ten-dollar-minimum blackjack tables in the Galaxy Rio Casino she was spotted and thrown out. It didn't help that she pointed out to the shift manager who accused her of card-counting that her method actually used an equilibrium distribution strategy based on a variant of Markov chain analysis. In the end, she wasn't charged because she hadn't been wearing a computer or been caught using a code to signal to confederates. She'd been allowed to keep her winnings, but she'd been banned, permanently, from the Galaxy Rio and the other casinos on the Strip.

'It isn't about the money,' she told Willie, when he'd asked her how much she'd won. 'It's about proving that the system worked. Which it did.'

'Apart from the getting-caught part.'

'A hazard of field experimentation that doesn't invalidate my conclusion.'

'It kind of invalidates the potential profits, though. Maybe you could sell it to someone else,' Willie said. 'Let them try their luck.'

'It's been busted,' Lisa said. 'All the casinos will know about it now. Mei told me that they share information on attempts to game the system.'

'Mei?'

'The shift manager.'

'You and her got pretty cosy, it sounds like.'

'The problem is that the pattern of wins and loses isn't random. That's how I was caught. An AI plugged into the surveillance cameras spotted the periodicity. Anyone else trying to use it will be caught too.'

'Why I hate the modern world,' Willie said, 'is working people can't catch a break. But hey, at least you got your mojo back. Didn't I tell you it would be fun?'

They celebrated in a bar, and after half a dozen cocktails came to the mutual decision that it would be a blast to get married. So Lisa bought a couple of rings in a pawnshop and they did the deed in the hotel chapel, reading their vows in Klingon off an iPhone in front of a guy in golden robes and Spock ears.

Waking up in the motel room the next morning with her new husband snoring beside her, Lisa didn't regret it, not one little bit. Willie was self-centred and narcissistic, and wasn't half as bright as he thought he was, but he was also kind and thoughtful, in his way, the sex was amazing, and he was a fun guy, fun to be with. Lisa worked on other people's finds in the Alien Market and took trips with Willie into the back country searching for finds of their own, and for a couple of years she was happy. They even began to talk about settling down one day, having kids. Lisa still sometimes thought of the children she hadn't had, the chances she'd missed, because the Bad Trip had fucked up their heads and everything else, and Willie had gone his way and she had gone hers, and that was that.

Brittany said, 'If you don't mind me asking? You split up like years ago, you think he's a loser . . . So why do you still care for him?'

'My reasons for wanting to find out what happened, they're mostly selfish,' Lisa confessed, feeling that she should be honest with this girl, who'd clearly fallen hard for Willie. 'I'm hoping that it might help me evict the ghost in my head. But beyond that, I guess Willie and I still had a kind of connection. Whatever it was he found out there, it shouldn't be up to Adam Nevers and the geek police to decide what to do with it.'

'So what are you going to do now?'

'Check out that company. Outland Archaeological Services.'

'And if they can't help you? Like if they all went out there?'

'A friend of mine is looking at the register of Elder Culture sites, in case Willie or maybe this company made a claim. And if that doesn't work I'll just head out there and see what I can find. I still know some people in Joe's Corner. Maybe they'll know something.'

Brittany took a big sip of her drink, looking at Lisa over the top of the glass. 'There is something else that might help you,' she said.

'Yeah?'

'That stone Willie found? The one that started off this whole thing? I still have it.'

10 · The Singer Not The Song

'That's him,' Òrélolu told Tony.

'The one with the cornrows?'

'Danilo Evangalista. A real heartbreaker. He can sing, too. Wait until you hear him sing, cousin. If I wasn't married . . .'

'Oh, he's luscious, no doubt,' Tony said. He was a little drunk. Brandy at the Great House when he had met up with Òrélolu, and now gin flavoured with pine resin. 'Is this why you brought me here? To see a little songbird who has turned your head?'

They were in a basement café in the Old Town quarter. Rough stone walls, wooden benches and tables, a toilet where you put used tissues in a bin instead of flushing them. Tony and Òrélolu sat in a booth whose original occupants had been evicted by the café's owner; the man couldn't stop telling them what an honour it was to have two such distinguished guests. The booth was to one side of the low stage, where a poet was machine gunning staccato verses under a blue spotlight. The young singer sat with two men on the other side, tall and slender in a simple white shirt and black trousers.

'I'll introduce you,' Òrélolu said. 'We can have a drink together after his set.'

'Whose idea was this, Òrélolu?'

Tony's cousin shrugged. 'You wanted to talk. Here is as good a place as any.'

'Oh, Òrélolu, you were always such a bad liar,' Tony said. 'You know why? Because when you tell an untruth you always break eye contact. Also, pandering really isn't your thing. So who put you up to it? Actually, I know. It was Ayo. Ah, and there we have

67

it. Because now you are trying so very hard not to look away that you are staring at me without blinking. Ayo will not talk to me, but she feels sorry for me, and here we are. Well, you can tell her that I'm not looking for a boyfriend.'

Òrélolu smiled. 'He really is a good singer.'

'I would rather talk about Opeyemi.'

'To what point? The decision has been made. Nothing can undo it.'

Tony ignored that. 'He has been waiting for an excuse to shut me down. And when he finally finds one, he uses it to wreck what could have been a great chance for our family to turn its fortune around.'

'The thing is, T, it isn't all about you,' Òrélolu said.

'It isn't? Then why am I the one who has lost his fucking ship?'

'I don't know how to put this delicately,' Òrélolu said. 'So I will speak plainly, and you will have to forgive my bluntness. There is a majority in the family who believe that Ayo has been taking us in the wrong direction. That she has been taking too many risks. That she has been gambling with our fortune and reputation. You know how badly she was affected by the death of Ngoze. Some say that she has not been thinking straight ever since.'

'I know that she threw herself into her work. And that she resolved that it was time the family took back its rightful place in Commons affairs.'

'You've been away a long time, cousin. She has become some-what erratic. Careless, even. She has made some bad decisions. People are rightly worried.'

'Are you one of these people?'

'You know very well that I keep out of that kind of thing,' Òrélolu said. 'I care about patients, not politics.'

He was almost exactly Tony's age, a calm plump man dressed in the local fashion – homespun wool trousers dyed purple by a lichen extract, an embroidered cotton shirt, a goatskin waistcoat with horn buttons. They had grown up together, and after two years away Tony was surprised and grateful that they were still good friends, despite the different paths their lives had taken. Òrélolu had married three years ago, he and his husband had a son, conceived using the sperm-fusion technique and carried to term by a surrogate mother, and he had devoted himself to his

68

work at the clinic where scions of honourable families and the rich suffering from sleepy sickness lived out the last of their days. The place where Ayo's eldest son, Ngoze, had died.

Tony said, 'For someone who claims to have nothing to do with our business, you seem to know an awful lot about it.'

'Even if you have no influence over the weather, you cannot ignore it,' Òrélolu said. 'Ayo has lost crucial support in the past two years. Your adventure brought things to a head. Even those who still support her felt it was a step too far. Running contraband and cutting deals in the shade is one thing. Meddling in dangerous Elder Culture stuff is quite another.'

'I heard all that from the doubters, and I am sorry to hear it from you,' Tony said. His glass was unaccountably empty; he clicked his fingers to summon a waiter.

'I am merely reporting how things are,' Òrélolu said blandly. 'I am sorry you will not accept it.'

'How things are, I have been given a hundred days to prove that this "meddling" could increase our fortune and standing,' Tony said. 'And I will. Don't doubt that I will. Despite the murder of their leader, my wizards are pressing on with their work. And Aunty Jael is doing all she can to help.'

But digging out the information from the stromatolites had turned out to be extraordinarily complicated. According to the wizards and Aunty Jael, sequences packed into the archival genetics were organised in overlapping frames, which meant that they could be read in hundreds of different ways, producing hundreds of different code strings. And they were also badly corrupted. The stromatolites were millions of years old, and although the microorganisms that had built them were highly modified and possessed a variety of proof-reading and post-replication mechanisms to ensure accurate copying of the data stored in their archival genetics, as well as the data transmission system that cross-checked and corrected copy families in different colonies, serious errors had accumulated. Information had been erased, or had been imperfectly copied, or had been compromised by insertion of multiple copies of nonsense sequences. Two weeks after they had started work, the wizards were still separating signal from noise. Only then, Aunty Jael said, could they begin to attempt a full translation of the archival genetics, and try to understand what it contained.

'At least she sees the importance of what we found,' Tony told Òrélolu. 'She knows what is at stake. But no one listens to her. They treat her as if she is just another hand.'

'I know that she is so much more than that,' Òrélolu said. 'I owe her my career. She encouraged my interest in biomedicine. She gave me a space for my studies. Without her I would not be where I am now.'

'Oh, I did not mean you, Òrélolu. You are one of the good guys.' Tony drank half his new drink and said, 'So how are things with you? With your work? There was a D-class barge on the field when I touched down. Lowloaders were trundling hibernaculae out of the hold, and there were a dozen coffins stacked on the whitetop. New patients for the clinic arriving, I suppose, and the dead returning to their families. How many are you treating now? How many could be saved, if the doubters would allow my wizards to work as they should?'

'I admire your ambition, cousin,' Òrélolu said. 'But it is not as simple as you seem to think. Even if there is a clue to the origin of sleepy sickness in those stromatolites of yours, it will take years to develop a cure.'

'Yes, and thanks to Opeyemi we have only a hundred days. And he didn't order the so-called execution of Fred Firat because he believed the man was a traitor. He did it to sabotage the work. He wanted us to fail.'

'Do you know how many wizards claim that they are close to finding a cure?' Òrélolu said, with a spark of exasperation.

'Too many, I suppose. But the information that the stromatolites contain is old. Old enough to be the common link to all other Elder Culture code. That has to count for something.'

'Your sudden faith in science is touching,' Òrélolu said. 'And I wish I had the power to help you. I really do. But I chose to take a different path.'

'Yes, you chose to help others rather than our family.'

The words tasted bitter, and Tony regretted them at once.

'I always hope that by helping others I am also helping our family regain its honour,' Òrélolu said mildly. 'Now, hush. Let's not argue. He's about to sing.'

The young man, Danilo Evangalista, had taken his place behind a small upright harmonium. Glass beads woven into the cornrows that criss-crossed his shapely skull sparkled in blue light as he bent over the keyboard and picked out a brief melody before he began to sing: an old choro standard about songs so good and true they outshone the faults of their singers.

'So simple, and so lovely,' Òrélolu said, when the young man had finished.

'I told you. And you can tell Ayo. Thanks but no thanks.'

'You feel wounded. It's only natural. But try not to see everyone as your enemy.'

'It is hard not to see those who would take away my ship and my work as friends. Opeyemi has no imagination, Òrélolu. He does not understand what Ayo and I are trying to do.'

'Is that ship really more important than your home and your family?' Òrélolu said. And then: 'Wait. What's wrong?'

Tony was pushing to his feet. He had recognised the introduction to the young man's next song. 'The Sky Has Closed Over Us.' A bright breezy tune with lyrics lamenting the cruel separation of two lovers after Skadi had been cut off from interworld trade because of the so-called treachery of his family. After his father had been killed during negotiations with the Red Brigade. After his mother's so-called suicide.

The singer fell silent when Tony stepped onto the stage. Someone in the audience laughed nervously. Tony mashed the harmonium's keyboard with his fist. The squealing discord echoed in the silence at his back.

'You have no right,' he said. 'You have no right to sing that song.'

'What would you have me sing instead?'

The young man's gaze was level and calm. There were flecks of gold in his warm brown eyes.

'Sing something happy, goddamn you,' Tony said. His sight swam with stupid tears. 'Stop trying to break my heart.'

11. The Bad Trip

'It looks like an ordinary tessera,' Lisa told Bria. 'But I'm pretty certain that it'll yield Ghajar narrative code when I tickle it. Brittany kept it in the safe of the bar where she works – she'd had some jewellery stolen from her motel room. When Nevers and his Jackaroo pal came knocking, they didn't think to look there.'

'And then she sold it to you,' Bria said.

'She loaned it to me. And in return, when this is over, I'll sell it for her on a zero-commission basis. We co-signed an agreement. One of her customers, he used to be a lawyer, drew it up. I'm not certain it'll hold up in court, but I intend to stick to it.'

'Drew it up on what, a napkin?'

'Her tablet. Brittany printed out two copies, had a couple of customers witness them, gave me one. She's smarter than she lets on.'

Lisa was at a roadside food truck near the shuttle terminal, talking to Bria on her new phone and sipping strong earthy Ethiopian coffee from a paper cup. Pete was sitting in the loadbed of the pickup truck, watching traffic scooting along the dusty two-lane blacktop. A flat-roofed factory building sprawled on the other side; beyond it, the level plain of the shuttle field stretched towards foothills shimmering in the deep orange light of the setting sun. A single ship hung above the field – a bulbous, spiny S-class scow forty storeys tall. Ghajar ships, revived and repurposed, weren't an uncommon sight these days. Governments and private companies used them to transport people and goods between Earth and the Jackaroo gift worlds, and the worlds of the New Frontier. Anyone with a couple of thousand dollars could afford a ticket. But this one nagged at Lisa's attention – perhaps her ghost was interested in it for some reason. The damn thing had woken up again, a spooky presence at her back, always just out of sight.

Bria was saying, 'The girlfriend sounds like a bill of goods.'

'I liked her. And she loved Willie, in her way. That was one thing he was good at. Getting inside your heart.'

There was a pause, and then Bria said, 'Have you been drinking?'

'Not really,' Lisa said, and knew it sounded evasive. 'Just this one beer. To be sociable while I had my heart to heart with Brittany. Right now I'm sipping some damn fine coffee made by an Ethiopian woman who was in Ethiopia just three months ago.'

'Because you sound a trifle manic.'

'Maybe that's because I'm absolutely, one hundred per cent certain that Willie found the place where we were struck down. Not that stupid hole in the ground, but the real deal. Wherever it is, whatever it is, he couldn't afford to excavate it on his own, so he partnered up with this outfit his girlfriend told me about. Outland Archaeological Services. I just now paid a visit to their offices. Police tape across the door, no one home. This guy in the insurance brokers next door told me they'd been closed for several days, and the police had been around first thing yesterday. He said they carried out everything in the place. And he also said, get this, that there was a Jackaroo avatar poking around. Adam Nevers's sidekick. First they raid Outland's offices. Then, when they couldn't find anything, they go after Brittany and me.'

'I don't think I've ever heard of them,' Bria said.

'I googled them,' Lisa said. 'Turns out they're funded by this nonprofit outfit, the Omega Point Foundation.'

'The one owned by Ada Morange?'

'She doesn't exactly own it. But her company, Karyotech Pharma, is its major benefactor.'

Ada Morange was famous in the way that Albert Einstein and Abe Lincoln were famous. The kind of fame that was in the air, in the water. She had been involved in the discovery of the first Ghajar ships, the ones that a kid infected with some kind of eidolon had called down to a ruined spaceport on Mangala

– people called it a spaceport, although no one could say exactly what it was. A place those two ships knew, at any rate. And a couple of years later Ada Morange's company had located the first orbital sargasso. She was one of the richest people in human history, and most of her wealth was channelled into the Omega Point Foundation, which subsidised big astronomy projects, exploration of the new worlds of the New Frontier and research into Elder Culture technology, artificial intelligence and life extension, and promoted the idea that humanity could bootstrap its way to transcendence without the help of the Jackaroo.

Lisa told Bria that Outland had bought out the site in the City of the Dead where a Ghajar shipwreck had infected a hive-rat colony. 'And they were involved in digs looking for other traces of the wreck.'

'So is that what Willie found?' Bria said. 'Something to do with the wreck?'

'It's possible. According to Carol Schleifer, this tessera contains Ghajar narrative code. Which until now has only been found in Ghajar ships. I need your help, Bria. I need to take a look at this code.'

'Right now what you need to do is go home and get some rest.'

'And meanwhile the cops are digging up whatever it was that Willie found out there,' Lisa said. She was walking up and down at the shoulder of the road. She couldn't keep still. 'I need to look at this code, and I need you to go check recent excavation licences again. Willie didn't register his find, either because he couldn't afford the fee or because he knew it was something big, was worried that it would attract the wrong kind of attention. So he took a risk and kept it secret. But maybe Outland took out a licence after he hooked up with them.'

'We'll have to do that tomorrow,' Bria said. 'The licence office will be closed now.'

'Okay. But first thing. First thing tomorrow. The licence and the code.'

'Are you sure,' Bria said, 'that this isn't something to do with the ghost? That it isn't driving you towards this place? The place it came from, where Willie and everyone else was killed.'

Lisa realised that she was staring at the big ship hanging out there across acres of concrete. Had the Ghajar built those ships before their version of first contact with the Jackaroo, or had they found them afterwards, cast off by some previous client race? She deliberately turned her back on it and said, 'This isn't about helping it. It's about understanding it. Finding out what it is so I can get rid of it.'

'You just had a seizure,' Bria said. 'And then there was the bad news about Willie. Either one of those would have definitely put me in a spin.'

'I'm chasing it *because* I had a seizure,' Lisa said. 'Because Willie found something that woke the ghost in my head.'

'But first, maybe you should to take a step back and think this through. Think about what you really want. Think about the consequences of going up against the geek police. Not to mention the Jackaroo.'

'I don't want to get into a fight with anyone,' Lisa said. 'I just want to find out what it was Willie found. Find out exactly what it was that fucked us up.'

After all these years she still didn't have a coherent picture of what had happened to her and Willie during the Bad Trip. They had set out from Port of Plenty on one of their expeditions into the back country, and next thing she knew she woke up in the clinic in Joe's Corner, battered and bruised and sick, no memory of how she got there. Apparently she and Willie had ditched their truck in the City of the Dead and had been found by a tomb raider, badly dehydrated and suffering from heatstroke and retrograde amnesia. She'd lost almost three weeks of her life. Wiped clean. Gone. Later, she was visited by little flashes of disconnected memory fragments – a sense of deep panic, as if she was struggling for her last breath deep underwater, dust whirling up around her, fighting with Willie over control of the truck as they fled helter-skelter from some vast black flapping doom – but neither she nor Willie could ever recall where they'd been, how they'd got there, what they had found.

A couple of local tomb raiders had tried to follow their trail back into the Badlands, but the Badlands were big and empty, and the sandstorm season had arrived early and put an end to the search. A year later, Willie found that small excavation pit in what he claimed to be the right place, but although he dug all around it he hadn't turned up anything.

But something had happened. Something that had stimulated a flight reaction, forcing them to run mindlessly until they could run no more. Something that had wiped out their memories and left atypical neurological activity in the temporal lobes of their brains. An infection with some kind of algorithm. An eidolon. A ghost.

Although actively malign artefacts were rare, all Elder Culture algorithms possessed some degree of toxicity. Despite using virtual sandboxes, Reynolds traps and other precautions, most coders and analysts suffered from headaches and transient visual or auditory hallucinations, while prospectors and tomb raiders, exposed to unshielded artefacts, risked all kinds of neurological damage, from hysterical blindness to pseudo-Parkinson's and the zombie delusion. There was always some old-timer in the corner of a tomb raiders' bar with the staggers and the jags, or an imaginary friend, or a demon on their back, or missing fingers or ears they'd cut off to prove that they were actually one of the walking dead. Lisa and Willie were haunted, but according to their neurology consultant their ghosts were mostly benign. They had been lucky to escape without suffering more serious damage.

Apart from the deep brainburn of knowing that they might never understand what had happened to them.

Apart from their marriage falling apart.

Apart from the bone-deep need to find out what Willie and his friends from Outland Archaeological Services had discovered out there in the Badlands. Maybe Bria was right. Maybe what Lisa thought she wanted was something the ghost wanted. Some deep alien urge to return to where it had come from, or something weirder and deeper. But at that moment she didn't care.

Bria said, 'One thing is certain: it's deeply and dangerously bad. And then there's the agent in charge of the investigation. Adam Nevers. I told you I had a contact in TCU? She says that he's one of their most senior field agents. Smart and tough, very experienced. And he has history with Ada Morange. He was on Mangala when she brought down the first Ghajar ships.'

'You're kidding.'

'He's hardcore, Lisa. Not someone you want as an enemy. A few years after the Mangala thing, he shut down one of Ada Morange's companies in France. Something to do with importing biochines without the proper licences. After that he was part of a big investigation into her affairs, just before she moved most of her business out to the New Frontier. And now he's here, and it looks like he's still on her case.'

'Which means that this is something important. That it's not just some trivial breakout.'

'Which means,' Bria said, with the exaggerated patience she used on her sons when they were acting up, 'that you don't want to get caught up in the middle of a feud between them. My advice? Forget it. It's Chinatown.'

'Bria, the whole fucking planet is Chinatown. We come up and out and build shopping malls and golf courses and pretend we've civilised the place. But there's a couple of million years' worth of weird alien shit lying around everywhere. Do you really think we can just ignore that? Do you really think it ignores us?'

Bria finally agreed to a meeting at the code factory the next morning. Lisa drove home through the stop-and-go traffic of the city's sprawl, through the hills on Highway One amongst the windy roar of big rigs and road trains, with the dazzle of oncoming high-beams on the other side of the highway nagging at her and a headache beginning to build behind her eyes. She was short of supplies and had planned to stop at the community store on the way home. Instead, she pulled into the lot of the Shop'n'Save on the commercial strip at the junction with the high desert road, one part of her mind knowing exactly what she was thinking of doing and hating herself for it, another part knowing that she needed anonymity.

She told Pete to guard the pickup truck and went inside and uncoupled a shopping cart and patrolled the towering aisles. She bought bags of dog chow and rice, cans of beans, a couple of kilos of frozen hamburger meat. Bathroom tissue. Fresh-squeezed orange juice. And here was the liquor aisle and the shelves where half a hundred brands of vodka were displayed, from generic gallon jugs to high-end Russian and Polish brands. Clear glass gleaming like a queen's ransom.

12. Wizard Work

'Wizards work because they want to work,' Aunty Jael told Tony. 'There's no need to bully them into doing it. No need for threats. It's what they do. It's their vocation.'

'The problem is not their work ethic,' Tony said. 'It's that they don't seem to realise they must find something that can be used to win them more time.'

They were standing, Tony and the hand that Aunty Jael was currently using, in a glassed-in gallery overlooking the hangar-sized work space. Accommodation pods were stacked at one end; the big bubble of the aquarium stood in the centre, half-obscured by monitoring equipment. Inside, the stumps of the live stromatolites squatted in two metres of murky water; around it, the six wizards, dressed in traditional white coats emblazoned with heraldic stains, scorch marks and hand-lettered slogans in archaic fonts, scurried to and fro as they set up their latest experiment.

'Things might go more quickly if we had access to more processing space,' Aunty Jael said.

Today she was present in a skinny ball-jointed hand with glossy white plastic skin and a small head crowned by a circlet of stalked eyes. A number, 7, was stencilled in black ink on its chestplate. The 7 had, in the antique style that Aunty Jael favoured, a dash across its stem.

Tony's grandfather had purchased her fifty years ago, but she was much older than that – although she claimed to have forgotten her original identity and the circumstances of her death and lamination, she said that she had been born on Earth and could remember what it was like before the Jackaroo had arrived in the aftermath of the Spasm, with their offer to help. And while she was an imperfect simulation running in the laminated architecture of her original brain, got up from bundles of reflexes, habits and memories, Tony never doubted that there was an actual person behind the hands and windows she used to interact with the world: astute, absent-minded, and somewhat remote, wryly amused by what she called the eternal theatre of human folly, and unswervingly loyal. She tutored the family's children, was involved with Òrélolu's work on sleepy sickness, supervised research on introducing salmon into Skadi's icy ocean, increasing the efficiency of the kraken-oil refinery and improving the cultivation of pine trees and the quality of their timber. She had advised Tony about the deals he had made during his two years of freebooting, analysed artefacts he had sent back to Skadi, and expressed enthusiasm for the slime-planet adventure, whose success now hung on the fraying hope that the wizards would find something in the stromatolites' archival genetics that could be linked to sleepy sickness.

This was not the first time she had asked Tony to provide more processing space; like all laminated minds she tended to repeat herself, was locked in the deep grooves of old obsessions. He patiently explained that he had twice asked the council to grant the wizards access to the city net, and had twice been refused for the same reason. 'They want the work quarantined. They are worried that an eidolon will leak out. Or some kind of meme plague even worse than sleepy sickness.'

'Did you tell them about the firewall I devised?'

'They were not convinced. We must manage with what we have.'

'Unless we access the city net anyway.'

'We cannot do that without permission from the council.'

'I need only permission from a member of the family, Master Tony.'

Tony glanced across the work space to the kitchen area, where Lancelot Askia sprawled in a chair, watching something in a window. Hopefully one of his pornographic war fantasies, not a feed from a drone that Aunty Jael had failed to find and subvert.

He said, 'Have you talked to anyone else about this?'

'Of course not. They would not agree to it.'

'Neither can I. It would be sedition.'

'I agree that it would be a drastic measure,' Aunty Jael said. One of the stalked eyes that crowned the hand's stubby trunk was watching the wizards working below; the rest were aimed at Tony. 'But shutting down this research would be a bad mistake. The archival genetics are rich in unrealised potential. Since you cannot extend the time granted for this research, I feel that it is my duty to suggest ways of making the most of what you have.'

Tony thought for a moment, then said, 'Could you link me with my ship?'

He missed her more than he could say, was always aware of the silence in his head, of being trapped alone in his skull.

'I'm afraid not,' Aunty Jael said. 'I do not have access to that system.'

'Then think of something else. Think of a way of making our wizards do what they're actually supposed to be doing.'

The wizards had been working in Aunty Jael's laboratory for twenty-nine days now. Tony and Aunty Jael were supervising them; Junot Johnson sourced the materials and items of equipment they required; Lancelot Askia was a permanent reminder of Opeyemi's disapproval, skulking around, examining the wizards' notes and worksheets, asking awkward questions. Their new leader, Cho Wing-James, claimed that the work had already yielded some very interesting results. He and the other wizards had dissected the complex molecular machinery that replicated the archival genetic material, were developing a working model of the stromatolites' data-transmission system, and had disproved several theories about the mathematical systems of the Old Old Ones. The problem was that Cho Wing-James's ideas about what was interesting had very little overlap with Tony's, and none at all with the family's.

Cho Wing-James was the beanpole who had charged at Tony after the thermobaric bomb had been planted, an animated, untidy scarecrow with a ragged mop of hair, given to mumbling cryptic snatches of internal dialogue and smacking his forehead with the heel of his hand as if trying to dislodge a jammed gear train in the mechanism of some internal argument. He claimed that he was from Earth. From London, England. He'd come all the way out here, he said, because this was where the shit was at. The real shit, not Boxbuilder ruins or Ghostkeeper tombs, or even archival genetics containing secrets millions of years old. He believed that there were Elder Culture artefacts so wild and strange that people had not yet recognised them for what they were.

'The Jackaroo gave us wormholes and shuttles,' he said, 'and we understand those because, hey, shuttles are basically big old spaceships, and we already had crude spaceships when the Jackaroo made contact. And although we didn't know how to open wormholes, we had theories about them, so the idea that they allow near-instantaneous travel to every part of the Milky Way wasn't new or startling. It's the same with most Elder Culture tech. It's the kind of stuff we might have come up with, in time. But there are a few artefacts that are so weird we barely recognise them as artefacts, and can't begin to understand their function, and it's not much of a leap to believe that there's stuff we don't even recognise as technology. Stuff so advanced that it makes us look like insects walking through the interface of a qube. At best we might glimpse a bare flicker of light, but we'd have no way of knowing what it means.'

He could happily elaborate his ideas about hyper-evolved Elder Cultures for hours, said that it was quite possible that there were aliens far more advanced than the Jackaroo – civilisations that could harness the entire energy output of stars, construct megastructures like Dyson spheres and stellar engines, manipulate space-time, and organise information flow across the galaxy or even the entire universe. These beings, Cho said, would be like gods. Incomprehensible, unknowable, unseeable.

'I don't mean that they look and behave so differently we think they're animals, or biochines, or like the trees you have here,' he said. 'If they are trees.'

'We call them trees,' Tony said. 'Because that's what they are.'

'Well, they look more like giant kelp to me, or big mops stuck in the ground and spray-painted unnatural shades of yellow and orange. This world, it's like it's always autumn. You know? The chill in the air, the colours of the vegetation. Or what passes for vegetation. But the angle of light, the verticality of it, is tropical. It's a weird combination. Anyway, the kelp-mop-tree-things, they could be an Elder Culture species, communing through what passes for their root systems, through chemicals they release into the air. Thinking really slow thoughts that take decades to complete. But mistaking them for trees when really they're sentient beings is only a category error. Trying to detect and understand a truly advanced civilisation would be a completely different order of difficulty. And that's what makes it so exciting,' Cho said.

He was not interested in the uses of knowledge; he was interested only in how it confirmed or changed his theories of how the world worked. A common failing in wizards, who dosed themselves with drugs that accentuated obsessive-compulsive traits, and infected themselves with memes and partial eidolons to help them intuit the workings of Elder Culture algorithms. Unlike Fred Firat, who'd struck Tony as a sturdily practical sort, Cho Wing-James treated the stromatolites' archival genetics as an intricate and fascinating puzzle rather than a library of ancient and potentially valuable secrets. He and his crew had squandered days studying some kind of Ghajar algorithm lodged in the magnetite arrays of the stromatolites; Cho had claimed that it might have been some kind of translation tool left over from an attempt by the Elder Culture to crack the archival genetics, but nothing had come of it.

At last, frustrated by his inability to persuade Cho to focus on finding something, anything, that could persuade the family council to extend its deadline, Tony took the wizard up to the clinic to show him what was at stake. It was Danilo Evangelista's idea, actually. After listening to Tony vent one day, the young singer had asked if Cho had ever seen the effects of sleepy sickness. It turned out that the wizard hadn't. It wasn't something that had ever interested him, he said.

Tony was astonished. 'Even though I hauled you and your friends out to the slime planet because Fred Firat claimed that the stromatolites would help us understand meme plagues?'

'Oh, I know that Fred believed that,' Cho said airily. 'But I was only ever interested in the actual science.'

'Sleepy sickness is an actual thing, too,' Tony said. 'It's time you realised that.'

Tony, Danilo and Cho Wing-James travelled out to the clinic the next day, flying north in a spinner helmed by Lancelot Askia – a condition imposed by Opeyemi in return for permission to take the wizard on the little trip. Danilo pressed close to the transparent aluminium of the spinner's bubble, pointing out sights to Cho as the spinner rose above the close-packed roofs of the city and flew out over patchwork farms and pine plantations, and the orange and yellow native forest climbing the slopes of the foothills. Snowy mountain peaks were chalkily sketched against the blue horizon, the boundary between the northern edge of Skadi's habitable strip of land and the vast ice cap that stretched away towards the north pole.

Tony was charmed by Danilo's innocent delight in these vistas. The singer wore the white fur jacket that Tony had given him for this trip, his long legs encased in tight red jeans. When he looked around and asked if that was the clinic ahead, his smile turned Tony's heart.

'Yes,' he said. 'Yes, it is.'

'It's bigger than I thought it would be,' Danilo said.

The spinner was flying above a lake towards rugged cliffs divided by the white ribbon of a waterfall. The heaped geodesic domes of the clinic straddled the swift river that fed the waterfall, glinting in cold sunlight and caught between steep slopes of yellow forest.

'When I had a work placement here, eight years ago,' Tony said, catching Cho's gaze, 'there were just over three hundred patients. That was bad enough. Now there are more than two thousand. All of them children, sent here from every world in the Commons. And all of them will die here, for want of a cure.'

Òrélolu greeted them at the landing stage and took them up to his office, where he and several staff members explained that the clinic had been founded by Ayo after the death of her eldest son, and gave a short description of its work and research programme. Cho sat through this quietly, but said at the end that he was pleased to see that they were using randomised trials. 'A lot of what you people call science is indistinguishable from magic. Claims of secret knowledge and special talents, all kinds of weird rites and ceremonies, and so forth. It's so rare and refreshing to find this kind of old-school methodology out here. Hopeful, even.'

'Aunty Jael must take most of the credit for that,' Òrélolu said. 'She devised the experimental programmes. But despite all our work, we still have no idea what causes sleepy sickness, or how it is transmitted. And although we have prolonged the lives of some of our patients, we have yet to cure a single one.'

'That is why your work is so important,' Tony told Cho. 'We hope that it will give Òrélolu and his crew a new direction.'

As they set out across a covered walkway that swooped above the river, linking the stark cube of the administration block with the accommodation domes, Òrélolu took Tony's arm and said, 'I hear that you have moved out of the Great House and moved in with Danilo. Is it love, or just a silly stunt to piss off Opeyemi?'

'I can assure you that there is nothing silly about it.'

'You shouldn't use the boy to score petty points, Tony.'

'You set us up, cousin. And I am glad, now, that you did. And grateful. But frankly? Our relationship is none of your business.'

'Then why did you bring him here to rub my nose in it?'

'This visit was Danilo's idea, actually. And it was also his idea to come along. I told him that he would see things that might break his heart; he said that if he shed a tear or two it would help my pet wizard to understand the reality of this. He is tougher than he looks.'

'Even so, he is just an ordinary kid,' Òrélolu said. 'Suppose Opeyemi decides to get at you by hurting him?'

'I will make sure he won't,' Tony said. 'Oh, and by the way? The sex is amazing.'

They entered an observation cubicle raised high in the side of one of the domes. Below, fifty or so children shambled about the black-sand floor. Some dressed in pyjamas or cotton gowns, some naked. Some moving in little groups, some following solitary paths, some standing still, staring off at something beyond the walls of the dome.

All were pre-adolescents between ten and fourteen, and all were in the second stage of sleepy sickness. To begin with, sufferers began to sleep for longer and longer, eventually passing into a state of unconsciousness that lasted for as long as forty days. Most woke and showed no other symptoms, but one in a hundred developed aberrant behaviour similar to sleepwalking, becoming increasingly withdrawn until at last lapsing into a catatonic state and shortly afterwards dying.

Òrélolu told Cho Wing-James that the patients in this dome were local children whose parents had volunteered them for tests and experimental drugs and other treatments. Therapies developed here, he said, were used to treat children of parents who could afford to send them to Skadi.

'So basically, the rich kids benefit from their suffering,' Cho said, seeming more amused than angry.

'And the local children benefit from care they could not otherwise afford,' Òrélolu said.

'I guess I have a hard time understanding it because we don't have your kind of social hierarchy on Earth,' Cho said. 'The honourable families thing, and so on. But you'd have a much bigger sample group, and a better chance of finding an effective treatment, if all of your patients were treated in the same way.'

'We hope that your work will give us a much better chance of finding a treatment that would benefit everyone,' Tony said.

'Including your family,' Cho said. 'A cure for sleepy sickness would be worth a tidy sum.'

'Perhaps we would give it away, increasing our reputation instead of our wealth,' Tony said, and half-believed it. The clinic was a reliable source of off-world income, but a selfless act would do more to repair the damage to the family's standing amongst the other honourable families than any amount of money.

Òrélolu picked up the thread of his lecture, telling Cho Wing-Jones that sleepwalkers kept in isolation soon died. They were obligately gregarious, he said, forming gangs or tribes with unclear affiliations, marking their territories with piss and daubs of excrement, stronger gangs attacking weaker ones, weaker ones attacking singletons. The aggression was mostly low-level but sometimes flared into serious fights. Sleepwalkers could be badly injured if hands controlled by the clinic's staff failed to intervene quickly enough.

'But at least the sleepwalkers' behaviour has counterparts in ordinary human society,' Òrélolu said. 'The final stage is worse because that is where the real madness lurks. Let me show you.'

Another dome, this one cupping a bell of dim red light, its floor a maze of crooked tunnels pieced from scraps of plastic and foam sheeting. The patients who inhabited this maze were in the terminal stage of their illness. They spent their time entirely inside their tunnels, rebuilding them from within and daubing them with patterns made from their own excrement.

'We have been able to extend the sleepwalking phase of the illness by several months, but every patient eventually enters the final catatonic stage, and its course is remorselessly swift,' Òrélolu said, and called up images of naked and emaciated children, blank faces under tangles of filthy hair. Eventually, they fell into a permanent stupor, he said. They stopped eating and drinking; even if they were force-fed and attached to drips they quickly died.

Tony felt the same queasy mix of pity and disgust that had gripped him during the long weeks he'd spent as an intern at the clinic, part of his education in the family business. The sleepwalkers were children, but they were no longer human. They were running an alien algorithm in their brains. They were trying to express alien thoughts, alien behaviour. Whatever they had once been had been fragmented, overwritten. You never got used to that.

Danilo put his arm around Tony's shoulders, asked him if he was all right.

'I'm remembering how it was when I worked here. Nothing seems to have changed.'

Lancelot Askia was staring at them, his fists jammed in the slant pockets of his leather jacket, his pistol holstered at his hip. Tony stared back until the man looked away.

'Let me try the thing we discussed,' Danilo said, and stepped away and turned his back, standing quiet and still while Òrélolu told Cho Wing-James about the characteristic long slow waves in the brains of sleepwalkers about to enter the catatonic phase. With his back still turned, Danilo began to sing a slow, aching song about a mother who gave up her sick son to the clinic and came to visit him every day, until at last she realised that she no longer remembered what her son had been like before he had fallen ill, and wished that she had never come at all. He sang with his fists clenched and quivering under his chin, his clear voice resonant in the small space. Tony and the others – even Lancelot Askia, his arms folded sternly across his chest – listened in silence. When the song ended and Danilo turned and sketched a small bow, Cho Wing-James gave Tony a long, thoughtful look before returning to the discussion about the sleepwalkers' neural activity.

The next day, in Aunty Jael's laboratory, the wizard told Tony that his crew wanted to make another attempt to crack the Ghajar algorithm they had isolated from the magnetite arrays. 'We will run copies in the ablated shells of a wide variety of eidolons, and compare their behaviour with controls containing native algorithms. The differences between Ghajar hybrids and controls will help us understand how to control the algorithm. And then, hopefully, we will be able to use it to explore the archival genetics.'

'You are still assuming the algorithm is a translation tool,' Tony said, with the sinking feeling that this was another frivolous diversion from the main task.

'If it turns out to be something else, we will go back to trying to build our own translation tool,' Cho said. 'But this could be the kind of quick and dirty fix you have been urging us to try.'

The experiment was as strange and solemn as an ancient religious ritual. The lights in the work space were dimmed. The bubble aquarium tank that housed the stromatolites glowed like a cauldron. Flickering columns of glyphs cascaded through windows as the wizards, robed in their white coats, chanted obscure instructions and readouts, and in the centre of their rough circle the smoky shadows of ablated eidolons flickered as the Ghajar algorithm was downloaded into them. Up in the walkway with Aunty Jael's hand, Tony held his breath, felt his blood tingle and his hair stir. But the eidolons remained stubbornly inactive: either the interface protocols were incorrect, or the algorithm the wizards had inserted into them was so badly corrupted that it was no longer functional.

Cho Wing-James dismissed the failure. 'We have learned what not to do,' he said. 'Next time we will do better.'

'Soon there won't be time for a next time,' Tony told him.

'Unfortunately, we are not in the miracle business.'

'That's a shame. Because if you want to stay in business, a miracle is exactly what you need.'

13. Code Farm

Lisa meant only to knock back a few stiff ones to calm herself and numb the feeling of the ghost at her back, but of course that wasn't how it ended up. She woke on her couch sometime the next morning. The empty bottle on the tile top of the coffee table; the parched-mouth pinch-skulled hangover; the black fog of remorse and self-loathing. She managed to feed Pete and check the hurklins, then collapsed on her bed and dozed into the afternoon, waking with a stab of unfocused panic that crystallised into the realisation that she'd missed her appointment with Bria at the code factory. She used her piece-of-shit phone, cursing its nannying autocorrect, to send a text — she'd come down with some twenty-four-hour bug, could she come in tomorrow, same time? — and then hauled her sorry carcass into the shower. Bria replied while she was in there, confirming that tomorrow was fine, asking how she was. *Convalescing*, Lisa texted, not wanting to get into a conversation, made a pot of coffee and choked down a couple of slices of toast, and used her phone again, found there was an open meeting that evening in a church basement in Three Rocks.

On the drive over she steeled herself to confess her lapse, but lost her nerve and blurted out a lame apology when the chairperson took her aside at the beginning of the meeting and asked if she wanted to speak. She sat at the back and listened to the testaments of two volunteer sinners, left as soon as she decently could, and cursed her stupidity and cowardice all the way back home. Her lapse had badly frightened her. Reminded her that she was always just one drink away from reverting to her bad old ways, hiding inside a bottle, using booze to numb the inescapable presence of the thing in her head. She would atone by rededicating herself to finding out everything she could about the cause of the breakout that had killed Willie and the others. She would avenge his death by defeating her own ghost. Every day was day one. Every day you started over.

So the next morning she rose at dawn and spent three hours mucking out the hurklin pens and topping up the dry-feed hoppers and checking the water dispensers. They looked more like ambulatory oysters than tortoises, hurklins, perched on random arrangements of unpaired peg-like legs that made soft clickings as they shifted about. Now and then feathery sense organs flickered from under the margins of their shells, tasting the air like snakes' tongues; strings of crude, crystalline eyes were set in the leading edges of their shells, but they mostly found their way by taste and touch. There were almost a hundred of them in the pens, some standard stock, some part of a breeding experiment, crossing a big old male she'd bought from her one of neighbours with selected fresh-caught females from a guy over in Stone Creek. The first-generation crosses included three females with deep green shells marked with pleasingly random swirls of black. Lisa was planning to inbreed them with one of their brothers to see if their patterns stayed true.

After she had cleaned herself up, she drove into the city for the second time in three days, pretty much a record. Pete rode on the passenger seat, happily sticking his head into the slipstream. She'd asked him one time why dogs did that, and he'd told her it was fun, she should try it.

The code farm was in a business park halfway across town from the Alien Market. Inside its anonymous box a clutch of egg-shaped work pods were set out in an eight-by-four grid; the servers and a chill-out area were tucked under the platform that supported the conference room and Bria's glass-walled office. No basketball hoops, table football, air hockey or antique arcade machines, none of the testosterone-fuelled competitive atmosphere and raucous bonding rituals of most code farms, which exploited a transient population of young, mostly male coders by working them remorselessly for two or three years and replacing them with new recruits after they burned out or were flamed by exposure to raw algorithms. Bria employed more women than men, gave them long-term contracts with benefits, shared out bonuses from exploitable finds, encouraged her coders to decorate their pods according to individual taste. One had been made over into a replica of a spaceship cockpit; another was lined with a thin shell of polystyrene carved and painted like antique stone; the one that Bria and Lisa commandeered (from a young woman who told Lisa that she had been inspired to become a coder when she'd studied sandbox code at college, which made Lisa feel like a relic from deep time) was tiled with picture postcards from Earth – anodyne views of beaches, mountains, monuments, city streets and parks – and little vitrines containing robots dressed in a variety of national costumes. It was at once knowingly kitsch and deeply nostalgic.

Lisa and Bria closed up the pod, activated its Reynolds trap and deployed the security protocols, worked their way through checklists and alerts. The soft green glow inside the shuttered pod and the ozone whiff of the humming trap were calmingly familiar, somewhat abating Lisa's uneasy mix of guilt and shame. Bria hadn't mentioned yesterday's missed appointment beyond asking Lisa how she was feeling, but Lisa suspected that her friend knew that she'd taken a tumble off the waggon. It was an echo of her paranoia from the bad old days, when she'd worked zero-hour contracts in corporate code farms and sneaked carefully calibrated doses of shine during her shifts, and put a certain distance between the two of them.

At last, Bria activated the multi-spectrum scanner and told Lisa that she should do the honours. Lisa snapped open the little acrylic box and used silicon tweezers to pluck the tessera from its nest of cotton wool and set it in the foamed-plastic cradle.

It didn't look like anything special. A small flat chip of tile, roughly rectangular, surfaced with a dark grey sheen that had flaked off along one edge to reveal a tangle of fine black threads and a fugitive glitter of micronodules in a ceramic matrix. No different to the thousands of tesserae scattered across the walls of tombs in the City of the Dead in patterns that no one had been able to prove were anything other than random.

Lisa angled the Reynolds trap over the cradled tessera and with delicate concentration advanced the ball of the ultrasound probe until it kissed the smooth grey surface. Checked the frequency and timer settings, touched the on/off icon.

Most tesserae were inert. Some, triggered by the proximity of animals, biochines or humans, tickled optic nerves and generated hazy glimpses that might have been fantasies or fragments of the lives of the Ghostkeepers, the Elder Culture that had built the City of the Dead. And a few contained active intelligences. Ghosts, eidolons. But no eidolon appeared when the probe sang its mosquito song. Instead, the tessera was immediately enveloped in a flowing silvery-grey fog. Lisa believed that she could see movement in there, but it was hard to make out what it was. For a long moment, the rest of the world folded into the blind spot where her ghost lived . . .

The timer shut off the ultrasound probe; the flow vanished. Lisa tried to blink away silvery after-images. Her eyes prickled hotly and she felt the stab of an incipient headache.

Bria said, 'Are you okay?'

'I saw something. Like fog, or water . . .'

Lisa wondered if Willie had seen it, too. She watched eels of phantom light swim through the dim air of the pod while Bria ran through checks on the sandbox, finally announcing that the mirroring had been successful and bringing up the looped playback on the big 3D screen.

The code's graphic display was simpler than most, appearing as the same kind of silvery currents that had briefly enveloped the tessera, but with far greater resolution. Lisa could see rippling moiré patterns in the flow now, like the play of sunlight on white sand at the bottom of a shallow sea. A Cartesian grid distorted by continuous coordinate transformation. And she was beginning to see repeating elements emerge in the fractal complexity, although the overall pattern seemed to be endlessly variable. She remembered a quote about architecture and frozen music. But this was moving, liquid, alive.

Bria brought up a wire-frame model of the grid, said that the initial results from decompiling, pattern matching and reverse lookup had already located several points of glancing similarity with Ghajar narrative code. 'I guess Carol Schleifer was telling the truth. But no one has ever found this stuff in a tessera before.'

'Run it again,' Lisa said.

There was something compelling about the rippling patterns rolling through the screen. A weird hypnotic beauty. After a little while Lisa glimpsed a flash of movement, as if something had momentarily come into focus, there and gone. She leaned in, trying to spot it again, and there it was, a brief distortion in the flow, dividing it as a fish divides a river current, blinking out as suddenly as it had appeared.

'There!' she said. 'Did you see that?'

Bria hadn't. Lisa asked her to rerun the last thirty seconds of the playback, pointed to the anomaly when it reappeared.

'I'm not sure what I'm supposed to see,' Bria said. She was leaning side by side with Lisa, bright lines gliding across her face.

'There's a kind of displacement in the flow,' Lisa said. 'Let me loop it.'

She saw, as the loop ran over and again, chains of flashes flickering in the anomaly's wake. Bright vortices emerging, spinning away in the silvery stream. She froze the playback, pointed them out to Bria.

'I think I see something,' Bria said. 'But maybe only because I want to see it.'

They seemed very obvious to Lisa. Cream-into-coffee swirls that flowed across the Cartesian grid without distorting it. Fingerprints on a blank page. Gas clouds birthing stars. Ghostly jellyfish caught in a rip tide . . .

After a timeless interval, Bria said, 'I think that's enough.'

'Just a little longer,' Lisa said. 'There's so much detail in here.'

'You've been staring at that loop for almost an hour now.'

It had seemed like a handful of minutes, but when Bria switched off the display and cracked open the pod Lisa realised that her eyes were dry and painful. Her mouth was dry, too, and there was a bone-deep ache in her lower back.

Pete, lying in a splash of sunlight by Bria's free-form desk, looked up and wagged his tail when they came into the office, asked if the hunting had been good.

'We definitely caught something,' Lisa said. 'All we have to do now is figure out what it is.'

She paced back and forth, drinking from a bottle of spring water. She was gripped by an electric excitement. She was thinking, in no particular order or pattern, about manipulation of three-dimensional superimpositions, interference transitions, Steiner structures, Floquet-Bloch states and high-lying Rydberg states, K-theory topology, harmonic oscillators, optical manipulation of topological quantum matter, selection components in a system-density matrix . . . If asked, she couldn't have explained why these particular concepts and conjectures seemed relevant. She knew only that they might have some kind of correspondence with the vortices spawned by the displacement in the flow of narrative code, might help her fix the alien and unfamiliar within the topologies of conventional maths and Elder Culture algorithms.

She said, 'It isn't a simple data matrix. There's definitely something active in there. But is it an intrinsic property of the stored information, or is it something else? An emergent property, some kind of observer effect . . . What? What's so funny?'

'You have the look,' Bria said.

'What look?'

'The look when you've hit upon what you call an interesting problem.'

'I think Willie must have seen it, too.'

'Because of his ghost?'

'I think so. Yes. Because our ghosts interact with the code in some way.'

'Of course, we still don't know that the tessera came from the breakout site,' Bria said. She was playing devil's advocate, as she so often had back in the day, trying to prevent Lisa's wilder flights of speculation from soaring off into the wild blue yonder. 'We don't even know where the site is, or if it has anything to do with what happened to you during the Bad Trip.'

Bria had checked the records; Outland Archaeological Services hadn't registered Willie's jackpot. They'd gone wildcatting.

'It's a *clue*, is what it is,' Lisa said. 'A clue about what Willie found out there, what he was hoping to find . . .'

Perhaps she didn't need to find out where the tessera came from. Perhaps it contained everything she needed to know, if she could only figure out how to decipher it.

She said, 'I need to read up on Ghajar narrative code. Carol Schleifer said that someone at Peking University is trying to crack it, read the text, whatever. Maybe I should talk to them. Could you do me another favour, let me use your q-phone? It would be a lot quicker to talk directly than exchange emails. And what about decompiling and reverse look-up? How long will it take to check this code against the catalogues?'

Bria held up her hands as if trying to fend off an unstoppable force. 'Before we do anything else, perhaps we should think about taking this to the police.'

'And have Nevers take it away from me, like he took everything else? No way.'

'But if it's linked to the breakout that killed the Outland crew, that killed Willie—'

'Willie left the tessera behind for a reason. Maybe he wanted me to find it. Maybe he wanted me to see whatever it was I saw in the code. And he knew I'd be able to see it, because of my ghost. This could help me understand what the Bad Trip did to me, Bria. It could help me find a way of fixing the damage it did. But if I give it up to Nevers he'll destroy it, or deep-six it in some vault. Because that's what people like him do with stuff like this. And then I'll never know what it is, or what it can do. But if you want out,' Lisa said, because she knew how much she was asking of her friend, 'I understand. I can take it elsewhere.'

'And have some cowboy outfit rip you off? No, I'll do the decompiling and all the rest,' Bria said. 'But there's a lot of data to process, I'll have to steal time on the cluster when my girls and boys aren't using it . . . It will take at least a day. Maybe two. And while you're waiting you should definitely take a stress pill.'

It was their old code for time-out when one of them had spent too many sleepless hours trying to crack a problem and needed the other to tell them to take a break, to eat, shower, sleep.

Lisa smiled. 'Absolutely.'

'And there's something else you should think about. You said that Willie found it. But suppose instead it found him?'

14. Traitors

The Red Brigade was an alliance of a dozen gypsy tribes that had evolved from a rogue element of the survey arm of the Second Empire's navy, haunting the lawless territories beyond the reach of the Commons and linked by q-phones, darknets and stochastic democracy, a perverted blend of chaos theory and behavioural psychology used by the Brigade's leaders to shape their plans and control and discipline their followers. Like other pirate groups, they claim-jumped finds, infiltrated trade routes and hijacked ships, ransacking their cargoes and ransoming their crews, but they had also turned science into a religion. They were bound by elaborate occult rites and deliberately infected themselves with algorithms, partial eidolons and ghosts ripped from Elder Culture artefacts. They were searching for the home worlds of the Elder Cultures and the origin of the Jackaroo and the !Cha. They were searching for ancient secrets that would enable individuals to transcend universal laws and every kind of ethical code. That would make them gods.

Twenty years ago, the Commons police had raided one of the asteroid reefs colonised by the Red Brigade, assassinated several of its prominent wizards and leaders, and destroyed more than a dozen of its capital ships. The Red Brigade's newly elected philosopher queen, Mina Saba, had sued for peace, and the Commons had agreed to a parlay at HD 115043, a planetless yellow dwarf star orbited by a scattered wilderness of mirrors. But the parlay had been a trick, an act of revenge for the police action. A Red Brigade attack wing had ambushed the Commons delegation and destroyed their ship and most of their escorts. Nonso Okoye,

Tony's father, was one of the murdered delegates. Two days later, Tony's mother was found dead in her hotel suite in the fleet city of Great Elizabeth on Ràn, the water world that was the seat of the Commons' political and military power. An apparent suicide that her family suspected was an assassination, part of the putsch that had given hardliners control of the government. The Okoye family and other liberal elements that had played a role in the so-called appeasement of the Red Brigade had been purged and disgraced; its world had been subjected to a ten-year trade embargo.

Like everyone else in the family, Tony was marked in blood and bone by the shame of its dishonour. That, and the humiliation of the council meeting, was why he thought Danilo Evangalista had been mocking him with a song about the human consequences of the embargo. But after his drunken outburst and a reconciliation engineered by Òrólolu, Tony and Danilo had talked long into the night, and Tony had wound up in Danilo's bed and two days later moved out of his rooms in the Great House and moved in with the singer.

Danilo lived in an efficiency apartment in a crumbling stone building in Old Town, where they still called the city Yapurá, the name it had been given by the original pioneers half a century before the Okoye family had been given control of Skadi and had renamed its only city Victory Landing. The apartment overlooked Rua Santa Clara, a long street that bustled with a produce market during the day and at night glowed with the neon signs of two dozen restaurants, bars, cellar clubs and cafés. Handwoven rugs covered the apartment's varnished floorboards; Danilo's musical instruments and clothes hung from pegs on the yellow plaster walls; there was the carved pine bed, a sagging armchair, a low table with a hammered brass top, a microwave and a small icebox. Bunches of dried flowers in glass vases, scarves muting the glow of little floor lamps, the scent of cedar and lemon. Tony loved it. The simplicity of it. The romance of it. He loved the cries of stallholders drifting up from the street in the day, and the music from the cafés and bars in the evening. He loved the old men who drank tiny cups of coffee and played chess in the apartment building's foyer. And he was in love with the idea of being in love with the singer, Danilo Evangalista.

They spent their nights in cafés and bars. Danilo played a set or two, gossiped with musicians and poets and hangers-on about everything and nothing. He and Tony would eat late, sometimes with the cooks and waiters of a restaurant after it had closed to paying customers, sometimes at a street stall, sometimes in the house or room of one of Danilo's acquaintances, where there would be more music, more talk, and towards dawn they would walk back to the apartment, past stalls setting up in the produce market, and tumble into bed and make love. Danilo had the ability to seem more naked than anyone Tony had slept with before. The singer would massage him, using his elbows, using his hands, his strong knowing fingers, the whole of his long supple body. Gliding caresses would slowly turn to sex. Afterwards, they would sleep until noon, Tony would drive out to Aunty Jael's laboratory to discuss the wizards' work, and in the evening he would find Danilo in one of his haunts and the night's round would begin.

Once, Tony flew the singer out of the city to picnic in a glade in the native forest by a waterfall of glacial meltwater that tumbled into a broad pool; another time they flew to a long beach of black sand where they walked hand in hand in the freezing whip of the wind. Gavots floated on long narrow wings above surf exploding on the beach's steep slope, the broken temples of icebergs twinkled out to sea, and the two of them were consumed with happiness. And one day he took Danilo out to the space field to show him the ship.

Danilo marvelled at *Abalunam's Pride*'s size and strangeness. The way she hung vast and still above the shadow she cast on the ceramic whitetop. Tony told Danilo that he wished that he could take him to other worlds and amaze people with his music. He told him about some of the things he had seen and some of the stories he had heard out there, asked if Danilo could use some of them in one of his songs. The singer laughed and said that such strange marvels were beyond him, that he wrote small songs about the small change of ordinary lives, and Tony wondered if Danilo would ever sing about him, his high-born lover. Some regretful lament that encapsulated their brief moments of happiness.

He knew that Òrélolu was right: knew that their affair was in part a rebellion against his family's attempt to control him. He knew that it could not last. Sometimes, in a brief flash of self-awareness, he told himself that he would have to be careful not to hurt Danilo. That sooner or later this interlude would end. But he also told himself that the singer was tough and streetwise, and several of Danilo's friends had hinted that there was an older man somewhere in the mix, a lover or mentor wisely keeping out of the way. And sometimes he tried to absolve his conscience by telling himself that Danilo probably hoped to cash in on the relationship, like most commoners who become involved with someone in the family. That he would break Tony's heart by asking for a favour, the use of his influence in some way, before Tony could break his . . .

At the beginning, Danilo had explained frankly that Òrélolu had asked him to be nice to Tony. 'It was just a favour to a friend. But I liked your passion. That grand gesture when you leapt up and told me to sing something that would make you happy, not sad.'

Tony said he'd already apologised for that.

'Oh, don't apologise! It made me want to find out who you really were.'

'Who am I, then? Really?'

Danilo studied him with a serious expression. 'Someone who is hurt. Someone who runs away from that hurt but always comes back. Someone who's looking for something he can't define. Maybe you're trying to find out who you really are, not what your family thinks you are.'

'I don't want to be what they want me to be.'

'Then don't be.'

'It is not as easy as that.'

'Because of who you are.'

'Yes. Because of who I am.'

'So be someone else.'

'I am, with you . . .'

Maybe it was not love, but there was real passion. A kind of hunger only partly satiated by sex. Tony wanted to be Danilo; he wanted to understand how it was to be him, what it was like to inhabit his skin, his life.

The singer had lived by himself ever since his father had died. The father had been crippled by an accident in one of the maker forges and Danilo had nursed him for a year as he lingeringly deteriorated, blind and racked by fits. His mother had died in childbirth long before that; the baby, Danilo's sister, had died too. After his father's death, Danilo had used what he called his small talent to support himself. His mother had been a singer, from a family of musicians, and several of Danilo's cousins were in the same business. They played in cafés, at private parties, at weddings and christenings, at rent parties thrown when one of their number was short of funds. Old songs brought with them from the old country; new songs in the old tradition.

And so the days passed. The wizards were no closer to being able to read the archival genetics in the stromatolites. Opeyemi's men watched Danilo's apartment from the street, and people Tony had hired from the local police watched Opeyemi's men and followed Danilo wherever he went, ready to protect him from harm. Sooner or later, Tony knew, Ayo or Opeyemi would step in and try to put an end to his little show of defiance. He was not sure, yet, how he would handle that.

After the church service one Sunday Tony was waiting by the great double doors, hoping to intercept Ayo, a mission he'd failed to accomplish the past five Sundays, when Opeyemi suddenly appeared beside him and clutched his elbow in a bony grip and leaned close. 'Walk with me if you would, nephew.'

Tony could not help looking towards Ayo. But his sister, her hair wrapped in a purple gele, was talking with the minister at the centre of a circle of people that included guards and Tony's cousin Julia, who was in charge of the Great House's security. Julia and two guards had intercepted Tony the last time he had tried to get close to Ayo. Julia told him that he had no right to harass Ayo in church; when Tony had asked loudly and angrily why he did not have the right to talk to his sister, Julia had said that perhaps he would be able to talk to her when he was calmer, and the guards had, humiliatingly, escorted him out.

Opeyemi saw his glance and said, 'Given the circumstances, it would be better for you if you did not trouble her today.'

'It is hard not to hear that as a threat.'

'It is useful advice. As is what I want to tell you. Come. It will not take long.'

Tony followed Opeyemi to the edge of the promenade that fronted the church. Beyond a slope of orange twitch moss, the roofs of the city tumbled towards the harbour. A bank of mist hazed the sea; the sun was a pale coin in the white sky. Tony shivered in a cold wind that carried the fresh salt scent of the sea and the burned plastic odour of the refinery. He was ready to hear the worst about Danilo. He was certain his uncle was going to make an end of it. Perhaps he already had: a shoot-out outside the apartment building, a kidnapping, Danilo ransomed for a promise of obedience . . .

Opeyemi leaned on the low slate-topped wall and looked out towards the sea, as if measuring the advance of the mist's tendrils as they groped towards the harbour's sturdy breakwater. He said, 'You visited the space field a little while ago.'

'I cannot check on my ship remotely any more.'

'There is no need for you to check.'

'She is still my ship.'

'But not for much longer.'

Opeyemi had the look that Tony remembered from childhood games of chess: the look that meant he was about to make a killer move Tony had failed to spot. Despite the difference in their ages, Opeyemi had never given any quarter. 'Talent counts as much as experience,' he would say. And: 'If I let you win, the game will be spoiled for you for ever. Don't expect anything in this life to come easily, just because of who you are.' Tony had never managed to beat him, but he had never given up trying, either, and Opeyemi's rare words of praise had been better than any victory. Tony had so much wanted to be like his uncle then: cunning, clever, and calculating. It was only when he had grown up a little that he realised that Opeyemi was a lonely man trapped in a role he had put on like armour, only to discover that he could never again take it off.

'How is the work with your wizards?' Opeyemi said.

'Even if we do not find a cure, I'm sure that we will find something else. Something useful. Something valuable. But we need time to do that, and you refuse to give us time because you have already decided that we will fail.'

'Talking of failure, your last experiment didn't go too well, did it?'

There had been more attempts to animate eidolons with the Ghajar algorithm isolated from the stromatolites. The last, just two days ago, had ended in confusion when the eidolon turned into a cauldron of virtual fire that filled the workspace with roaring blue light. Everyone had fled, half-blinded, and because there had been no way to extinguish the display it had raged for several hours until finally dying back of its own accord.

Tony said, 'It proved that the algorithm we have discovered is active, with coherence and internal consistency. Another step towards cracking the archival genetics.'

That was what Cho Wing-James had told him. He and Aunty Jael had seemed pleased by the virtual conflagration, and were designing a superconducting pipe containing frozen photons of crystal light that would, according to them, resonate with the Ghajar algorithm and mirror its quantum properties. It still seemed a long way from finding out how to read the ancient information stored in the stromatolites, but Tony wasn't about to admit that to his uncle, or tell him how, two nights in a row, he had woken beside Danilo from nightmares to the creepy feeling that someone else was in the room.

'Actually, I'm beginning to believe that there may be something of value,' Opeyemi said. 'Because someone else does.'

'Yes. The Red Brigade. From whom I escaped by the skin of my teeth.'

'Whoever the claim jumpers were, the traitor Fred Firat called them down on your head,' Opeyemi said. 'And now it seems that there is another traitor. Someone in that mad little crew you are supposed to be supervising has been sending reports of their work to someone on Dry Salvages.'

The mist was creeping through the streets. The buildings nearest the harbour were almost entirely drowned; only their red-tile roofs and the upper storey of a stone tower showed above a white sea.

Tony said, 'That is a serious accusation, uncle. I hope you have serious proof.'

'Deadly serious,' Opeyemi said. 'My people have discovered encrypted packets steganographically inserted into communications traffic in the common exchange.'

Commoners did not have access to q-phones, which transmitted messages instantaneously across any distance. Instead, their off-world communications were sent via an exchange linked to a q-phone network. Messages could hop through a dozen or more exchanges and q-phone pairs, zigzagging across the Milky Way until they reached their destination.

'It was cleverly done,' Opeyemi said, 'using a variation of the classic chaffing-and-winnowing technique. Fortunately, our security protocols detected and pieced together two messages, including headers that addressed them to Dry Salvages. As to their content and who they were sent to, we have not yet broken the encryption. But it is only a matter of time before we do.'

'If you have not read the messages, uncle, how do you know that they came from one of the wizards?'

'Because they began to be sent after you returned home. And they were traced back to Aunty Jael's laboratory.'

'I need to see them.'

Tony was afraid and angry. He half-hoped that this was some trick of his uncle's. A bluff with nothing behind it, an attempt to shut down the work on the stromatolites before the deadline expired.

Opeyemi said, 'My word should be enough, but I'll arrange it.'

'Who knows about this?'

'Don't worry, nephew. I came to you first. If you follow my advice and act quickly, you will be able to come out of this with some kind of honour. First, you should shut down the research. Suppose your wizards actually found something? The traitor could send the information to their friends. Second, you should put the wizards to the question. I will be happy to help you with that. My people have considerable expertise.'

105

Two years ago Tony would have surrendered to the canon law of Opeyemi's counsel. But he'd been tempered by hard lessons in the freebooting business since then, and knew a thing or two about countering threats and intimidation. He met his uncle's blinkless stare and said, 'I'll find this traitor, but I will do it my way. For now, everything will continue as normal. I will do nothing that could alert the traitor and give them the chance to destroy all evidence of their actions before they are brought to justice.'

'And exactly how do you propose to do that?'

Tony flatly lied. 'Oh, don't worry, uncle. I have a few ideas.'

'Then you had better get to work,' Opeyemi said. 'If you don't identify the traitor soon, I will be forced to act for the good of the family, and you will lose what little reputation you have left.'

'Oh, I rather think this enhances my reputation,' Tony said. 'After all, other people believe that the research is important. And sending the wizards to Dry Salvages is no longer an option, because the recipient of those messages might well be Raqle Thornhilde. Once I have got to the bottom of this, I will ask the council to reconsider its deadline.'

15. Crashing And Burning

On her way out of the city, Lisa stopped at Skate Planet, the only skateboard store in Port of Plenty, on the whole damn world, and bought a twelve-pack of Club-Mate. The soda, juiced with caffeine-laden yerba mate, had powered the Crazy 88's exploits back in the day: Lisa had a lot to do and sleep didn't figure in her plans.

When she got home, she dug up a plastic box buried in the pounded earth floor of the pen of the big male hurklin. Inside, wrapped in layers of polyester soft-shell material, was the exabyte drive that contained a mirror of the files in her confiscated massively parallel computer. She placed Willie's tessera in the box and reburied it and stamped the earth flat, cracked open the first bottle of golden rocket fuel, and fired up Sorabji's *Opus clavicembalisticum* on the sound system (Pete gave her a soulful look and padded out of the room). She liked to work to music, mostly solo piano pieces, some ambient stuff, Pink Floyd's *Wish You Were Here*, her father's favourite album. Silence was a big empty room in which every distraction echoed; music was a train that took her somewhere useful, sharpened her focus, inspired connections and little leaps of logic, shut down extraneous thoughts. And for deciphering this mad strange code, what better inspiration than Sorabji's enormous, wild, incantatory masterpiece? As its opening bars rang out, she plugged the mirror drive into the powerful tablet she'd borrowed from Bria, and got down to it.

She was certain that the narrative code was connected with the mystery artefact that had zapped her on the Bad Trip: that was why she could see the distortion in the silvery flow, the sparks

107

in its wake. Something that had reached out to her. She needed to find out what it was. What it did and how it did it.

She brought up a sandbox, froze the playback when the distortion appeared, and used the zoom tool. She was hoping to glimpse some kind of fractal activity, but the edges of the distortion were smooth all the way down to the limits of resolution. She ran the looped playback over and again, watched the distortion appear and disappear until she couldn't really see it any more, closed the sandbox with an angry gesture and shut off the sound system. She felt threadbare, shaky, sick with frustration. Silvery eels swimming everywhere she looked. The ghost leaning at her back.

She needed to run the real thing again. She needed the data from Bria's decompiling, pattern matching and reverse lookup. She needed to sleep, but knew that she couldn't. She needed a fucking drink and swore that she wouldn't. Instead, she opened another bottle of Club-Mate and began to read up on Ghajar algorithms.

The Ghajar had been a gypsy species that had left almost no trace of its civilisation or culture apart from its ships and a few so-called landing towers. Most of their ships had been abandoned in orbital sargassos, but several crash sites had been identified on First Foot and other Jackaroo gift worlds. Some archaeologists believed that the Ghajar had beached their ships much as whales and smaller cetaceans, because of disease or panic or suicidal ennui, had stranded themselves on beaches on Earth. Others said that the crashed ships were casualties in a war between factions of the Ghajar, and suggested that so-called mad ships recently discovered in a remote sargasso, which killed or drove crazy anyone who approached too closely, were weapons which had been used in that war.

One thing was certain: all Ghajar ships were infested with algorithms, quantum stuff embedded in the spin properties of fundamental particles in the molecular matrices of their hulls, riddled with errors and necrotic patches that had accumulated during millennia of disuse. Coders analysed and catalogued the algorithms, stitched viable fragments together, and spent hours and days trying to get them to run in sandboxed virtual spaces.

Ghajar ship code had played a pivotal role in the development of various kinds of quantum technology and had helped to solve four of the so-called hard mathematical problems; one of Ada Morange's companies had used it to develop the AIs that acted as interfaces between the ships and their human pilots. But Ghajar narrative code was another country. Unmapped, untranslated, incomprehensible. Lisa googled some scholarly articles, most of them by a professor at Peking University, no doubt the researcher Carol Schleifer had mentioned. Lisa had trouble following his deep theoretical analyses, but the conclusions were plain: no one knew what narrative code did, what it contained, or how to read it. And no one ever seemed to have observed the distortion she'd seen, either.

It was four in the morning. She was wired but bone-tired, and was still seeing little flashes in the air. She crashed for a couple of hours, woke around dawn and fed Pete, brewed a pot of coffee and whizzed two chopped bananas with almond milk in a blender and drank her breakfast while watching the looped playback just one more time. Okay, another.

It was too early to phone Bria. Lisa called anyway. It went straight to voicemail.

She was in the barn, checking on the hurklins, when a car horn sounded out in the yard. Sheriff Bird was standing at the gate, and a black SUV and a powder-blue Range Rover were parked behind his tan patrol car. The geek police were back.

16. Conceptual Breakthrough

Tony went straight from church to the laboratory. Junot Johnson intercepted him outside the workshop, saying that there had been a development.

'The wizards have been working all through the night,' he said. 'They believe they have made what they call a conceptual breakthrough.'

'Is this something real, or some kind of theoretical business no one else would ever be interested in?'

'Maybe one, maybe the other,' Junot said. He had a grainy, blood-shot look: he must have been up all night too. 'They're working on that Ghajar stuff again—'

'After I told them to give it up? Has time started running backwards here?'

'I know, Mr Tony. They're a stubborn lot. But this time they may be on to something. That last experiment? The blue light you told me about? They think it was some kind of eidolon. They think it's done something to their heads, lets them see stuff they couldn't see before. They think that it could help them to read the stromatolite data.'

'What kind of eidolon? Is it harmful?'

'I don't know. They're more interested in what it does than what it is.'

'I could be infected, too. So could you.'

'It's possible, Mr Tony. Although if you remember, I was in the city at the time, buying elements for their maker.'

'You should have told me what they were doing from the very first,' Tony said. He was angry and scared. First Opeyemi, and now this. It was as if everything was spinning away from him. 'I

110

have just had a very difficult conversation with Opeyemi – I am certain Lancelot Askia told him all about this. But you waited until now . . . It's unacceptable, Junot. Completely unacceptable.'

'I realise that, Mr Tony. And I'm sorry,' Junot said, with a hangdog look of contrition.

'"Sorry" will not fix this mess. But there is something you can do. Opeyemi told me that someone is sending clandestine messages off-world. He believes it is one of the wizards. If he is right, we must deal with the traitor straight away. Are they working on this so-called breakthrough right now?'

'They're all in the work space, yes.'

'Good. I want you to search their accommodations. Look for anything that could be used to connect to the city net. It might be a phone, it might be some sort of homebrew device. Turn everything upside down and inside out. If you don't find anything, I want to be certain that it is because there is nothing there, not because you fucked up again.'

'I will do my best. Although the man Askia searches their stuff regularly, and he hasn't found anything I know of.'

'Yes, because he could have planted something. Because this traitor may not exist outside of Opeyemi's scheming.'

'I don't follow, Mr Tony.'

'My uncle knows about this breakthrough, and will have guessed that I would want to use it to argue for an extension of the council's deadline. So he may have had his man plant damning evidence that one of the wizards is a traitor, and when I fail to find it he will accuse me of incompetence. You see it now?'

'Clear as ice, Mr Tony.'

'Then get to work. Search every square centimetre of the wizards' accommodations. Meanwhile, I will get up to speed on this discovery of theirs.'

The wizards were clustered around a big window in the work space. One of Aunty Jael's hands stood behind them – this one tall and very thin, clad in polished black plastic that reflected a stream of silvery light waterfalling through the window. Lancelot Askia sat in his usual place in the kitchen area, watching everything with sleepy insolence.

The hand did not turn as Tony approached. Instead, an image of the face that Aunty Jael chose to present to the world floated around the screen that ringed the flat-topped cylinder of its head, saying, 'Something wonderfully interesting has happened.'

'So I heard,' Tony said, and asked Cho Wing-James if he had cracked the archival genetics.

'Not exactly,' the wizard said, running his fingers through his disordered mass of hair. 'But I think that we have cracked something that can.'

His explanation came in an eager rush of technical terms. Tony held up a hand to silence him, asked Aunty Jael for a summary. It seemed that the storm of virtual light had contained densely packed sequences of information that had interacted with the wizards' visual cortices and printed copies of an eidolon in their brains.

'The eidolon is a kind of translation tool,' Aunty Jael said. 'The Ghajar appear to have used it to hack into the archival genetics via the stromatolites' transmission system, extract data, and render it into so-called narrative code.'

'That is what we are studying now,' Cho Wing-James said.

'And can you translate this narrative code into something I can understand?' Tony said.

'That's a very interesting question,' Cho said, and opened a small window that displayed a kind of starburst with lines of unequal length radiating from a central point. The wizard set it rotating, asked Tony if he had ever drawn something like it, or if it had featured in any of his dreams.

Tony felt a clammy twinge of unease and said, 'You had better tell me exactly what this eidolon has done to you.'

'To begin with, it helps you see patterns in the narrative code,' Cho said. 'Eli and Rael saw them first.'

'We were running the code in different configurations, and it suddenly popped out at us,' Eli Tanjung said. She was the youngest of the wizards, a solid, solemn young woman with glossy black hair and a trace of a moustache on her upper lip. A plastic circlet spiky with plug-in circuitry was clamped around her head.

Rael Manzano also wore a circlet. 'We could not believe what we saw,' he said. 'We stared at it for an hour at least. Such unexpected beauty!'

'I believe a demonstration is in order,' Cho Wing-James told Tony. 'We'll run it from the beginning, let you see for yourself.'

The silvery flow in the big window blinked out, resumed. At first, Tony saw only a uniform stream of mercury light, but then he felt a weird moment of doubling, as if he was watching himself watch the window, and began to make out knots and vortices like unstable whirlpools, or the teardrop shapes that water currents made in rivers when they divided around obstacles. The patterns were everywhere he looked, and there were patterns within the patterns. An eternal silver braid flowing past, beautiful and compelling . . .

'That's enough, I think,' someone said, and the window blanked and he came to himself with a start.

'You see?' Cho said. 'You see?'

'I saw something,' Tony said. 'But I don't know what it was.'

'Similar patterns were discovered more than a century ago,' Cho said. 'Only those infected with a specific and very rare kind of eidolon can see them. Apparently, that is what infected us.'

'And it has spoken to us,' Eli Tanjung said. 'It has shown us the way.'

'Some of us have felt a compulsion to draw diagrams similar to the one I showed you,' Cho said. 'We believe that it is something encoded within those patterns. Its meaning isn't clear, not yet, so we are hoping to stimulate our eidolons into providing us with more examples.'

That was what the wizards had been doing when Tony had arrived. Taking turns to wear circlets that with pulsed magnetic fields poked and pried at the eidolons in their heads, trying to stimulate them, trying to make them reach into the narrative code and pull out something comprehensible. If the stromatolites contained data relevant to sleepy sickness and other meme plagues, Cho said, tugging at stray strands of his hair, this was their best chance of finding it.

Tony told Aunty Jael again that he wanted a word in private. When he climbed up to the balcony, pushing through the dull hum of its privacy screen, another hand was waiting there – one

113

of the skinny white-skinned hands, this one with a stencilled 3 on its chestplate.

'Just how dangerous is this eidolon?' he said.

Thinking about it made the inside of his skull itch.

'It is hard to say. However, it appears to interact only with Ghajar narrative code.'

'I suppose that I'm also infected. As is Lancelot Askia.'

The idea that his uncle's man harboured a copy of the eidolon gave Tony a thin satisfaction.

'I have tested the neural activity of the wizards,' Aunty Jael said. 'All of them possess the characteristic signature of the eidolon. If you like, I could also test you. As for Mr Askia, I doubt that your uncle would give me permission.'

'What about you? Are you infected?'

'Alas, no. My mind is fixed. Also, the eidolon appears to have infected only those in the immediate vicinity of the light storm. Several of my hands were caught up in it, but my mind was, of course, elsewhere.'

Tony remembered when he had first seen Aunty Jael's true self. He had been eight, about to become her pupil. Ayo had taken him down to the basement of the laboratory, to a small room lit by a warm blood-red glow, with a ladder of shelves holding what looked like the spines of printed books. His big sister had put on white cotton gloves and pulled out one of those books, showed Tony that it was a slice of brain just a few nanometres thick in a rectangular leaf of grainy plastic.

'The plastic contains circuitry that infiltrates the laminated cytoarchitecture,' Ayo had said, holding the plastic leaf in gloved hands. 'And the circuitry of each leaf is connected to all the others. The brain provides the template for the mind that is generated by all of this, and the circuitry animates it. All this, everything on these shelves, is needed to support an imperfect simulation of a single human mind. Remember that, little brother. Aunty Jael may appear cleverer than us, but that is only because she is able to think faster. It is a shallow kind of thinking, and her viewpoint is fixed. Unlike us, she is unable to change. And that, in the end, is what counts.'

Tony said now, 'So far all it has given us is that funny diagram. And we do not know what it means.'

'Not yet,' Aunty Jael said.

'And even if they can use this eidolon to translate the stromatolite data, they may not find anything that can be used to understand and treat sleepy sickness.'

'I am cautiously optimistic,' Aunty Jael said.

'But it isn't anything I can take to the family council,' Tony said. 'And there's another problem. The thing I came here to tell you.'

He quickly explained Opeyemi's story about one of the wizards sending messages, his belief that it was a ploy to undermine the little authority he had. But when he threw the link that his uncle had given him to Aunty Jael, expecting her to find something that would prove that the clandestine messages were fake, she said that they not only appeared to be genuine, but packet analysis showed that they had originated in her laboratory.

'Do you know who sent them?'

'I'm afraid not.'

'How it was done? How anyone could hack the common exchange from here? I thought you had locked down comms.'

'There are no direct lines, but there are a number of devices and utilities that communicate their status with central services. Someone appears to have used one of those connections to tap into the city net, and then reach out to the common exchange. Fortunately, a unique numerical string is inserted into every communication with central services, identifying the device that sent it. These messages were all sent from the same place: the power transformers.'

'Are you certain?'

'While we have been discussing this, I have used one of my hands to locate an unauthorised device attached to the downlink with central services. It is accessed by a simple transceiver, similar to those used to control various probes in the stromatolite aquarium.'

'Show me.'

Aunty Jael's opened two small windows, one showing a small bead inside a cable junction box, the other the X-ray image of the scrap of circuitry it contained.

'I looked for fingerprints but found none,' she said. 'Likewise with DNA. Traces of talc suggest that the person who built and installed it wore gloves.'

'So we know how these messages were sent, but we still do not know who sent them.'

'Correct.'

'I don't suppose you can break the encryption.'

'Oh, I'm certain that I can. But it will take time.'

'How much time?'

'Less than that left before the heat death of the universe,' Aunty Jael said.

'Is that supposed to be a joke?'

'I thought it very like one.'

'If I were you, I'd stick to wizard work,' Tony said.

'Your culture does not recognise me as a human being, and I was long ago stripped of all the rights that human beings enjoy,' Aunty Jael said. 'I became a chattel, and was purchased by your grandfather for my skills and expertise, not for who I am or who I once was. Since then I have always carried out my instructions without complaint, have always tried to do my best for your family. I have especially enjoyed working with you, Master Tony. Your adventures have been thoroughly stimulating, reminding me of my younger self and giving me a sense of freedom I thought I had long ago lost. And I hope that my endeavours on your behalf have given you some small respect for my judgement, and that you will listen carefully to my advice now. Because I have a very good idea about how I can help you catch this traitor.'

Later, Tony realised that Aunty Jael had been warning him about her own plans. That her little speech was both a confession and a boast. But at the time, he thought that it was a plea to be taken seriously. And the thing was, her idea did seem like a good one. Simple, direct, and something they could try at once.

17. Under Caution

Lisa was fingerprinted and photographed in a clinical room somewhere in the basement of the UN building, the inside of her cheek was scraped for a DNA sample, and she was taken up in a freight elevator to an open-plan office and left in a small side room painted Disney Princess pink. Sitting in a plastic chair bolted to the floor, handcuffed to a battered table like an actual criminal. Headachy light from a buzzing fluorescent circlet bounced off the pink walls. Someone had scratched their tag, Bullpup, in wonky Gothic lettering in the plastic tabletop. The door was slightly ajar. She could glimpse people coming and going in the office, hear clipped exchanges on a police radio.

She tried a couple of breathing exercises to calm herself.

She tried not to stare at the black eye of the camera up in one corner of the ceiling.

After about twenty minutes, the agent who had escorted her through booking and processing returned and asked if she wanted anything to drink.

'I think this is where I say I'd like to speak to a lawyer.'

'There'll be time for that later, ma'am.'

The agent was a trim young African-American woman with an accent from somewhere in the Deep South. She'd taken off her jacket to reveal her shoulder harness and the automatic pistol holstered under her left arm. According to the photo ID she wore on a lanyard her name was Aimee Cutler.

Lisa said, 'Exactly what have I been charged with, again?'

'That is what we are here to determine, ma'am. The coffee's not so bad. Or if you like I can fetch a soda.'

After Agent Cutler delivered a cardboard beaker of thin burned coffee, Lisa was left alone again. A tactic to weaken her, she supposed. To let her worry about the deep shit she was supposedly in.

More than an hour passed before the agent returned, toting a tablet and a document case, followed by Adam Nevers. Lisa did her best to hide her relief that this time he wasn't accompanied by the Jackaroo avatar. She didn't know if she could stand being cooped up with the fucking thing in this cramped cell.

'Agent Aimee Cutler and Chief Investigator Adam Nevers questioning Lisa Dawes,' Nevers said, after he had settled on the other side of the table. He gave the time and date, told Lisa that the interview was being recorded and that she should remember she was under caution.

Lisa looked him in the eye and said, 'I'd like to talk to my lawyer.'

Nevers smoothed the point of his neat little beard between finger and thumb, a gesture that reminded Lisa of a second-rate stage magician she'd once seen. 'We can do that,' he said, 'but it would put things on a formal footing. Are you sure you want that?'

He was dressed in a grey silk suit today, a burgundy tie with a yellow stripe on the bias, his usual crisp white shirt.

'I'm handcuffed to this table,' Lisa said. 'How much more formal can it get?'

Nevers glanced at Agent Cutler; the woman stood up and unlocked the handcuffs. Lisa massaged her wrists while Nevers told her that she wasn't under arrest because at the moment he didn't see the need.

'So am I free to leave?'

'You're under caution. If you refuse to cooperate or demand legal representation, I'll have to charge you. Under the terms of the Technology Security Act we can hold you for forty-eight hours without access to legal support, and you'll be asked the same questions I'm going to ask you anyway. So I hope you see that it's to your advantage to keep things informal.'

'Charge me with what?'

Nevers ignored that. 'You are here to help us with our inquiries. As is your friend, Ms Mendoza-Trujillo. I've just had a very interesting conversation with her. I hope you'll be equally cooperative.'

He paused, letting Lisa think about that. A classic prisoner's dilemma tactic. Threaten two suspects separately, offer each of them the chance to betray the other. But Lisa was certain that Bria would have told Nevers everything he wanted to know. She was an upstanding citizen who believed that she didn't have anything to fear from the police, and she would be concerned about her business, her employees, her livelihood. Yes, absolutely, she would have talked, and Lisa didn't blame her one little bit.

'Let's start with the stone,' Nevers said. Agent Cutler unzipped her document case and took out a plastic bag and laid it on the table. It contained the tessera.

Lisa was certain it had been truffled out by the avatar which had accompanied Nevers and his agents when they had pitched up at her place for the second time. So much for her hiding place.

Nevers said, 'For the record, I am showing Ms Dawes evidence article number BK89 slash zero three eight. Do you recognise it, Ms Dawes?'

'It looks like a tessera,' Lisa said.

'Is it the tessera formerly owned by your husband, William H. Coleman?'

'I'd have to take a look at what it contains before I can answer that.'

'We dug it up from its hiding place inside your barn,' Nevers said. 'Would you like to reconsider your answer?'

'It isn't illegal to possess tesserae,' Lisa said. 'I deal with them all the time.'

'And where did you get this particular tessera, Ms Dawes?'

'I think you know where.'

'I'll remind you again that you're under caution. Refusal to answer my questions could have serious consequences.'

'If you're going to arrest me then arrest me.'

'If I arrest you, you'll stay in jail overnight, come back here tomorrow. And you'll still have to answer the question. And if, as you believe, we already know the answer, what will you have proved?'

Lisa decided to call the man's bluff, partly out of stubborn pride, partly because she did not like him. 'I can't tell you because I signed a contract with my client.'

'So you are claiming, what? Client confidentiality?'

'Exactly.'

'Show Ms Dawes evidence article number BK89 slash zero two six,' Nevers told Agent Cutler.

The woman extracted a sheet of paper in a plastic sleeve from her document case, laid it on the table in front of Lisa.

'That was found on your kitchen table,' Nevers said. 'Could you tell me what it is?'

Lisa saw that he was definitely enjoying this. She wondered, with a flush of shame, if they had also checked her waste bin, found the empty vodka bottle.

'You know damn well what it is.'

'For the record. Please.'

'It's a contract.'

'Is that your signature?'

'Yes.'

'And the contract is between you and a party named Brittany Odenkirk,' Nevers said. It was not a question.

Lisa nodded.

'For the record, Ms Dawes confirmed that this is a contract between herself and Brittany Odenkirk,' Nevers said. 'It concerns the tessera, doesn't it?'

'If you know about it, why ask me?'

'We're trying to establish what you know, and your level of cooperation. Which is, to be frank, disappointing,' Nevers said, fixing Lisa with his gimlet stare. 'Am I correct in thinking that Ms Odenkirk was your husband's girlfriend?'

'We were only technically married.'

'Your husband gave her the tessera. And she gave it to you.'

'She lent it to me,' Lisa said, with a pang of guilt.

'Did your husband give her anything else?'

'You'd have to ask her.'

'If you could answer the question,' Nevers said.

'I did. I don't know.'

'You work as a freelance analyst.'

'On and off. Mostly off, these days.'

'Amongst other things, you extract and analyse algorithms stored inside tesserae.'

'Stored inside some of them.'

'I believe that you analysed this particular tessera yesterday. Would you like to tell me what you found?'

'It contains Ghajar narrative code,' Lisa said. Nevers would have got most of the story from Bria, and his techs would have ripped out the files in the borrowed laptop besides. 'No one knows what it does, what information it contains, but it's basically harmless.'

Nevers was giving her that look again. She wondered if the Jackaroo avatar was watching on CCTV, had a wild thought that Nevers could be a puppet, fed orders by some kind of implant. There were stories, urban legends, that the Jackaroo had cultivated human avatars – a secret race bred from people kidnapped thousands of years ago, raised in Jackaroo ships or on some alien planet, and sent back to Earth to observe and report to their masters, or to interfere directly with history. If anyone was a Jackaroo spy, it would be Adam Nevers, with his semi-detached manner and barely hidden contempt for other people.

He said, 'You examined the tessera with the help of Ms Mendoza-Trujillo, didn't you?'

'She had the equipment I needed to extract the code safely and securely,' Lisa said. 'I don't, any more, because you took my stuff. You still have it, as a matter of fact.'

Nevers ignored that. 'And you were also studying it at your home. Wasn't that rather dangerous, seeing as you didn't have the right equipment?'

'I didn't need a trap because I was working with a mirrored image of the code, in a virtual sandbox. Bria helped me extract and mirror it. It was entirely routine.'

'Entirely routine, except for the fire in the code farm owned by your friend Bria Mendoza-Trujillo.'

'A fire? What kind of fire?'

'The serious kind,' Nevers said. He was watching her with clinical interest, like a lab technician noting the reaction of a rat after it had been given an electric jolt.

'Is Bria all right? Her people?'

'No one was hurt, as far as we know. The fire marshals are working up the scene right now. According to them, the place is a total write-off.'

121

'When did it happen?'

'It was called in at a little past midnight. Are you saying that you didn't know about it until now?'

'If you're trying to imply that the code did this, I don't buy it,' Lisa said. 'We used standard quarantine protocols when we worked on that tessera. And as I've already said, there was nothing about the code that suggested it was in any way malign.'

She was remembering the fire in the code farm that had discovered the Ghajar navigational data some years back – work that had led to the opening of the New Frontier. There had been talk back then that the Jackaroo had been responsible, either as punishment for the code monkeys' presumption, or as a preventative measure, destroying as yet unanalysed algorithms and datasets that contained deeper secrets. The location of Elder Culture home worlds, say, or images of the actual Jackaroo, the unseen creatures that controlled the avatars. Lisa had always discounted that kind of truther conspiracy bullshit until now.

Agent Cutler woke her tablet, showed Lisa the image it displayed. It took her a moment to figure out what she was looking at. Everything was charred and ruined, wet ashes and blistered wood and the melted remains of a desk chair.

'Do you recognise it?' Nevers said.

'It looks like a workstation,' Lisa said, with freezing caution.

'Is it the workstation where you and Ms Mendoza-Trujillo extracted the code from the tessera?'

'I can't say for sure.'

Agent Cutler tapped the tablet; it yielded a new image. A sooty surface shingled with blistered rectangles.

'Ms Mendoza-Trujillo says that the workstation was decorated with postcards,' Agent Cutler said. 'Postcards like these.'

'Then I suppose this could be where we were working,' Lisa said reluctantly.

'Ms Mendoza-Trujillo says that it was,' Nevers said. 'And the fire marshals believe that it was the seat of the fire. Where it started. So tell me, Ms Dawes, do you still believe that this so-called narrative code is "basically harmless"?'

18. The Slint

Aunty Jael's plan was elegantly simple: break into the transceiver, force it to send a fault signal, and wait for the traitor to come to check it out. She told Tony that they should wait for three or four days before baiting the trap because the traitor might become suspicious if the transceiver failed immediately after the discovery of the Ghajar eidolon, but he told her that he wanted it done straight away. If they waited too long, Opeyemi might tell the family council about the traitor, and that would be the end of everything. And it was also a matter of pride. Opeyemi's discovery of the clandestine messages was a humiliating black mark that could be countered only by an audacious act of cunning and bravery.

That was why, after the transceiver had been hacked, Tony chose to wait inside the transformer shed with Junot Johnson and one of Aunty Jael's hands. He wanted to arrest the traitor himself, saw himself standing in front of the council, explaining how security had been compromised, how he had intervened, and why it meant that the work was vitally important. He would win more time for the wizards; they would find something astonishing; he would get back his ship. It was all good.

He sat on the floor with Junot Johnson in the humming, ozone-scented darkness, sharing a small window that displayed feeds from drones stationed outside the shed, trying not to think about the eidolon in his head. Aunty Jael had scanned his brain activity and confirmed its presence, told him that it had imprinted itself within a small tangle of neurons in his temporal lobe and was at present mostly inactive.

'My work with the wizards suggests that it is stimulated only by the narrative code,' she had said. 'If it is no more than a simple translation device, it is nothing to worry about.'

Which did not mean that he was not worried. Far from it. Like every freebooter, he had heard all kinds of cautionary tales about wild algorithms infecting the unwary and driving them crazy, and now something very like those storied horrors was curled up like a tapeworm in his brain. He wanted to believe Aunty Jael's reassuring diagnosis, could not help wondering how he would know if he began to think thoughts that were not his own . . .

Hour bled into uneventful hour. Tony fell into a doze, woke from a muddled dream about chasing Cho Wing-James through a host of inhuman statues carved from stromatolites. Junot said quietly, 'Someone is coming.'

'Give me the window.'

Tony recognised the stolid silhouette at once: Eli Tanjung. He and Junot stood, pulling up the snorkel hoods of their camo cloaks. They were armed with fat-barrelled guns that fired sticky foam pellets, ready to immobilise the traitor as soon as she touched the transceiver. Aunty Jael's hand, crouching up in a corner of the ceiling, was backup, and was recording everything. Tony planned to show the video of the arrest to the family council.

The door concertinaed back; Eli Tanjung stepped inside; the lights, usually motion-sensitive but presently controlled by Aunty Jael, came up at half-strength. But the woman didn't cross to the junction box where the transceiver was located. Instead she hung by the door, nervous and uncertain, saying, 'Where are you?'

Tony sweated inside his cloak, gripping his gun, willing the woman to step towards the junction box. She called out again, her uneasy gaze sliding past Tony, coming back. He saw her expression change, knew that she'd seen the contours of his cloak. As he brought his gun up, motion exploded from shadows above him and the spidery hand collided with Eli Tanjung. She spun around and fell backwards, and the hand pinned her to the floor with its wiry limbs.

Tony pulled down his hood and stepped forward, aiming the gun at the young woman. 'Tell me why you are here,' he said.

Eli Tanjung stared up at him, started to say something, seemed to choke on the words. Then she was arching under the hand, balanced on her heels and the back of her head, pink foam spattering her lips, bubbling at her nostrils. Junot rushed forward, cradled her head with one hand and with the other gripped her jaw and forced it open and stuck his fingers inside, trying to clear her airway. But her face darkened and her eyes rolled back and she shuddered and fell limp.

Junot was straddling her, pumping his laced hands on her chest, when Lancelot Askia walked in.

Eli Tanjung had killed herself with a tailored neurotoxin favoured by the Red Brigade. It suggested that Tony's guess about the identity of the claim jumpers had been correct, but that counted for nothing when he stood before an extraordinary session of the family council. He was commended for his actions in locating and neutralising the traitor, but his plea that the wizards should be given more time to complete their work and his offer to travel to Dry Salvages and confront Raqle Thornhilde were brushed aside. A majority vote supported Opeyemi's proposal that the wizards should be transferred to the care of the Commons police as soon as possible

'My uncle broke his word,' Tony told Danilo. 'I did as we agreed. He should have supported me. Instead, he whispered in people's ears before the meeting, telling them that Eli Tanjung's duplicity meant that we could not trust any of the wizards, and spreading lies about the dangers of the research. And now everything will be lost. The police will shut down the work and exile the wizards to some remote facility on an otherwise deserted planet. That is what they do with any discovery that threatens the status quo. They lock it away, or they destroy it. And the funny part is this: I helped them. I blew up the stromatolites left behind on the slime planet, to keep them out of the hands of the claim jumpers. Now the police will get rid the rest.'

Tony had drunk too much gin, knew that he was letting all his anger and self-pity show, and didn't care. He had not told Danilo about the eidolon in his head, had not told Ayo or anyone else, either. He felt wretched and soiled.

When Danilo said that the news feeds were claiming that Tony was a hero, Tony told him that it was the family's spin. 'I failed. I failed to take the traitor alive. And I failed the wizards. I had a contract with them, and I have reneged on it. My ship will be taken from me, and sooner or later I'll be shunted into an off-world marriage . . . And then I will lose you, because I will have to go and live with my husband. That is how my family gets rid of embarrassments like me.'

'Well, but at least you won't starve,' Danilo said. 'Even if the worst comes to the worst you'll still have everything most people can only dream of.'

'I won't have you.'

Danilo smiled. 'You're sentimental because you're drunk.'

Tony took the singer's hands in his. 'I mean it.'

'You'll forget me soon enough.'

'Never. There's a freighter coming in two weeks. I could have a word with its captain, arrange to stow away on it. Run off to another world.'

'That isn't something people like me do.'

'Of course it is. How do you think your ancestors got here?'

'And anyway, your family would find us. And what would happen to me then?'

'I'll make sure nothing ever happens to you, Danilo. I swear.'

He would buy his lover a café, or a bar. Make sure he was set up for life. It was not much by way of making amends, but it was the least he could do before his family found a way of exiling him. But when he told Danilo about his plans, as they held each other in the dark, the singer said that he didn't need his help, that he knew how to look after himself. And anyway, why was Tony talking of leaving?

'I am talking about losing you.'

'Silly man. I'm right here,' Danilo said, and put his hand on him, and tenderly squeezed.

'Yes. Yes, you are.'

But Tony knew they had only a little time left.

Two days later, Ayo invited him to go hunting in the hills with her and her eldest son, Chidike. They hiked up through plantations of pine and larch into the forest of native trees (although they weren't really native to Skadi, had been introduced ten or a hundred thousand years ago by an Elder Culture known as the Constant Gardeners), where spires clad in leathery black plates soared skywards, sprouting clumps of feathery yellow sporangia at their midpoints, topped with mops of filmy orange and red banners. Chidike walked ahead of his mother and Tony, a crossbow slung over his right shoulder. Ayo was likewise armed, even though this was more of a ramble than a serious hunting trek. Two forest rangers and a pair of house servants followed at a discreet distance.

Tony told his sister about his latest plan: he could join the Commons police, sign up and ship out, and enhance the family's honour by serving on the line.

Ayo smiled. 'We already have two hostages. We don't need another.'

'Abass and Henry are hardly hostages.'

Abass was a police flight commander; Henry an executive officer in the civil service.

'They entered public service to prove our loyalty to the Commons,' Ayo said. 'But they have suffered because of our history. Henry should be a director general by now. And Abass should be a commodore, working on one of the fleet worlds. Instead, he is commanding a little no-place watch station, and knows he will never be given any more responsibility than that.'

'I wouldn't care,' Tony said. 'Anywhere up and out would be better than being stuck at the bottom of a hole.'

'As holes go this is rather lovely, don't you think?'

It was a cold crisp day. Clouds had swallowed the mountain peaks and snow was predicted, but here in the foothills sunlight lanced between the trees and splashed on granite boulders and patches of creepmoss, and high above translucent red banners snapped in the crisp breeze.

Tony barely noticed the beauty of the native forest. He was still trying to come to terms with Opeyemi's betrayal, the possibility of exile, and the stark realisation that he would never fly with his ship again. The silence in his head reminded him of losing a tooth when he'd been a child. How his tongue would keep going back to probe the tender gap.

He said, 'You could give me back the ship, Ayo. All you have to do is say the word. I will do good out there. I will make you proud.'

'I am not the queen of the world, Tony. I am merely the chief executive of our family's business. We tried to do something different, you and I. And I think we made a good go of it. But our family has decided that it has reached an end point, and we must abide by the majority decision.'

'Even though the majority are frightened of their shadows. Even though, as a reward for my service, I suppose I'm to be sent away and married off. That's not my life, Ayo, and you know it.'

'Right now the kind of life you want is not possible. But I have been thinking about how you can best be employed, and I believe that I may have a solution.'

'So we have come around to the point of this little walk.'

'I wanted to talk to you about it before I put it before the council,' Ayo said, and told him that he could make good use of his experience of trading by becoming the Lord of the Market. 'It is past time Felicia retired. She has made several deals lately that were not to our best advantage. Trade has become harder. Worlds are turning inwards. But you might have some good ideas about shaking things up, brother. You would work with Felicia at first, as her assistant. And after a few years you would take her place. And in a few years more, who knows, you might need to go up and out to make some deals.'

'But not on my ship.'

'*Abalunam's Pride* was always the family's ship. Think carefully about this. Do not dismiss it out of hand. It is important work, I think you'll be good at it, and you can stay here, with those you know and love.'

Tony wondered if that was a reference to Danilo. He knew that Ayo wanted to help him and he tried to show a little gratitude, saying, 'You will have to get it past Opeyemi and his little gang. I hear that he wants to put me in charge of one of the tank farms.'

'Let me deal with the council. Now, let's make the best of this lovely day. Let's find Chidike. He has got ahead of us.'

They walked on through the trees, and saw the boy leaning behind a flat-topped rock, resting his crossbow on it. As they approached, he turned and put a finger to his lips, then pointed. Tony saw the banners of a tree in the middle distance threshing in the windless air, then saw the slint reared up at the tree's base, clasping the scaly trunk with its middle set of limbs, rubbing and scraping it with its armoured forelimbs. He touched Ayo's arm and she nodded. She had seen it too.

Tony and Ayo sidled up to Chidike's lookout spot. Behind them, the servants set down their packs and the rangers unslung their rifles and moved forward on either side.

The boy, grinning with excitement, said, 'It's a big one. A mother.'

Slints had three sexes. Males and females were small swift carnivores that hunted in bonded pairs; mothers were big, slow plant eaters that incubated eggs injected into their body cavities by females and fertilised by males. Males and females died immediately after impregnating mothers, and after they had been impregnated by a dozen or more male-female pairs, mothers dug burrows in which they hibernated, never to wake again. In the spring, the young hatched in the bodies of their torpid mothers and ate them from the inside out. This one was big, more than six metres from the flat stub of its tail to the tip of its needle snout, and was still patched with the oranges and yellows of its summer coat.

'It is marking the tree with scent glands on its forelimbs,' Chidike said. 'Leaving a trail so males and females can find it.'

He was a sturdy boy with a spray of freckles across his flat nose and a prominent gap between his front teeth that showed when he smiled, dressed like a sheep herder in felt trousers and a woollen jerkin. He loved hiking and hunting, and was being given tutorials by Aunty Jael in the patchwork ecologies of the world. Now he asked his mother if he could shoot the slint. Speaking in a low whisper, not taking his eyes from his prize.

'It's very big,' Ayo said doubtfully.

'Exactly,' Chidike said. 'Think how fine it would look on display.'

'Suppose you only wound it?' Tony said. 'It might charge at us. How fast do those things run?'

'Pretty fast. Twenty kilometres an hour on flat ground. And it's no use climbing trees to get away from them, because they can

129

climb too,' Chidike said. 'But don't worry, uncle. My crossbow bolts are hollow-tipped, and contain a fierce neurotoxin.'

'One bolt might not be enough for such a big beast,' Ayo said.

'Then I will shoot it twice.'

'And what will it be doing while you rewind the crossbow?' Ayo said.

'It won't be able to do much, because of the toxin,' Chidike said. 'But if it somehow manages to look menacing, Vic and Charity will shoot it dead.'

Vic and Charity were the two rangers.

'They are here to protect us, not to help you kill animals,' Ayo said. 'No, I think we will let this one live.'

'Listen to your mother, lad,' Tony said. 'If you want to take a slint as a trophy, you need to prepare in advance. Let this one make more baby slints, and you will have a chance at them next year.'

Ayo was looking at him.

He smiled and said, 'I still have a little common sense, sister. Contrary to Opeyemi's slander.'

Off in the distance, the slint mother stopped pawing at the tree and turned its tiny head towards them. Perhaps it had heard their whispered conversation, or had caught their scent. In the corner of his eye, Tony saw one of the rangers raise her rifle. But the slint dropped to the ground and with a fast, scuttling gait headed further up into the forest. When it was at last lost amongst the trees, Ayo said that it was time to go home.

On the way back to the spinner that would fly them back to the city, Tony thought of that slint. Did it know of its destiny – that it would be eaten by children not its own? Would it do anything differently if it did?

19. Control

Lisa was released at eight in the evening. She refused Nevers's offer of a ride home, called Bria as soon as she walked out of the UN building. She wanted to apologise for the trouble she'd caused, compare notes, work out what to do next, but the call went straight to voicemail, and when she phoned Bria's husband he told her curtly that his wife was still being interviewed by the police and hung up before Lisa could ask any questions. Well, fuck.

She found a coffee shop and sipped a flat white and thought about her options. Finally she called Valerie Tortorella and asked for a lift home.

As they set off towards Highway One in Valerie's beat-up Honda, Lisa said, 'I hope this won't get you into trouble.'

'For giving a buddy a ride?'

'I didn't tell them you'd handled the tessera,' Lisa said. 'They didn't ask, I didn't volunteer it. But they knew all about my visit with Willie's girlfriend. They could know I visited you, too.'

'If the geek police come snooping around I'll tell them the truth,' Valerie said. The tight bun of grey hair at the back of her head was skewered with two chopsticks today. She wore an ancient Pearl Jam T-shirt, blue jeans speckled with acid burns. 'I can't see what harm it could do. And it won't be the first time those cock-knockers have asked me about a customer.'

'Nevers isn't your ordinary geek police. He has a beef with Ada Morange that goes way back, and now I'm caught up in it. He told me, just before he let me go, to be extra vigilant. Told me that although Outland Archaeological Services was eliminated by the breakout, there might be other followers or sympathisers of

131

Ada Morange active in Port of Plenty. Said that I could have put myself at risk from them because of what he called my meddling.'

'Did he offer you any kind of protection?'

'No, and I didn't ask for it. I think he was trying to put a scare in me so I wouldn't go any further with this thing. But here's the thing,' Lisa said. 'That tessera definitely has something to do with Willie's jackpot. I think that he found it before he partnered up with the Outland crew, and left it with his girlfriend because he wanted to sell it on the side. But it can't have anything to do with the breakout. If it did, Nevers wouldn't have sat across a table with me, and he wouldn't have let me go, either. He would have slammed me straight into quarantine. And it didn't have anything to do with the fire at Bria's place, either. Remember how people said the Jackaroo were responsible for the fire in the code farm where the Ghajar navigational data was discovered?'

'I remember some thought it was an inside job,' Valerie said. 'An insurance thing. And others thought a rival crew did it.'

'I reckon Nevers and his gold-skin friends burned down Bria's place to cover up something. It's all about control. They confiscated my copy of the records, took Willie's tessera . . .'

'They wouldn't have needed to break into the code farm,' Valerie said. 'They could have knocked on the front door with a warrant.'

'Then maybe they burned it down as a warning to others. You know – stay away from this shit or this could happen to you. But there's no way a mirrored copy of the code could have generated some kind of salamander eidolon from inside a sandbox. And I had the original, in the tessera. It didn't burn down my barn. And it didn't burn down the bar where Brittany Odenkirk had stashed it, either.'

'You're trying to make sense of what just happened. Trying to justify it. In a few days you'll get some perspective.'

'The only way I can get any perspective on this will be to go out there and find it.'

'Why is it I get the feeling you aren't going to let this go?'

'Willie's jackpot killed him,' Lisa said, heart-stung by a fresh pang of grief. According to Nevers, the geek police were still digging out the collapsed shaft. Willie and several other victims of the breakout were still down there in the dark. 'It put me in this shit. Bria too. And it has something to do with the Bad Trip. It's not exactly the kind of thing I can let go.'

There was a silence. Valerie negotiated the junction at Highway One and drove north at exactly the speed limit, overtaking road trains strung with constellations of lights. Lisa's mind buzzed with half-realised ideas and patterns. Wave functions she couldn't yet collapse to a single eigenstate because she lacked crucial data.

The homestead was quiet and dark when they arrived. The gate was open; so was the door to the barn. And there was no sign of Pete, no response when Lisa hollered and whistled. She remembered how he'd chased the Range Rover as she was driven away. Maybe he'd given Nevers's people the slip when they'd tried to round him up. He'd come back when his blood had cooled down.

Then she found the receipt on her kitchen table.

It was a yellow form filled out in a neat angular script, listing everything that had been confiscated. Bria's laptop, the contract, the tessera . . . And paper-clipped to the form was a scribbled note advising her that her livestock and her guard dog had been taken away and put down because of the danger of cross-infection with an unknown algorithm.

She read the thing again. Her heart a cold stone.

When Valerie asked what was wrong Lisa thrust the form at her. 'Nevers took my fucking hurklins. And he murdered Pete.'

20. Sky Fall

Snow fell overnight and continued to fall through the day. Fat flakes thickly whirling out of a pale sky, falling on the forest and farms, falling on the city's roofs and streets, slanting past the towers of the Great House. By nightfall the blizzard had blown out to sea and the sky was clear and the black air bitterly cold. People bulked up in fur coats and down jackets jostled through the Rua Santa Clara street market, past stalls that sold spiced wine, toffee apples, pastéis, doughnuts, fries with melted cheese, nutmeg coffee and little cups of thick hot chocolate.

Trailed by two different security detachments, his own and Opeyemi's, Tony walked through the crowds towards the club where he had arranged to meet Danilo. His heart jumped when he saw a tall slim man in a white fur coat, hair braided in cornrows, at a stall selling bolinhos de peixe, but then the man turned and Tony saw he was not his lover.

He was numb with shock. The desolation of bereavement. The hammer finally had come down. He had come straight from the Great House and a brief meeting with Ayo, who had told him that a police ship would arrive in six days to collect the wizards and the stromatolites, and that the family council had decided to sell *Abalunam's Pride*. Once a suitable buyer had been found Tony would climb aboard his ship for the last time and null the keys that linked him to the bridle. Meanwhile, he would begin shadowing Felicia's work, and in the fullness of time would take her place.

Ayo had delivered the news with brisk sympathy. She had told him that it was best to get it over with now so that he could move on. He had tried to marshal a defence, protesting that he had been given no warning that the family wanted to get rid of the ship, that it would traduce half a century of tradition, that by giving in to Opeyemi and his allies Ayo was fatally weakening her position. No use. Ayo had told him that like everyone else he must put the interests of the family first, and had ended the meeting before he could say anything more.

Now he would have to find a way of breaking the news to Danilo. Tell him that he had lost his ship and would have to return to the Great House. He could see his future unrolling along a narrow path hedged by duty and tradition. Working as an assistant to his aunt before taking over her office. His formerly unbounded life shrinking to the curtilage of the Great House and the petty politics of the family; an arranged marriage and the occasional sop of an off-world business trip. He supposed that he would be allowed to keep Danilo as a lover, but knew how that would go. An apartment in the good part of the city. Visits that he would always have to arrange in advance; the high days and holidays Danilo would spend alone; coded gossip in the news that he owed his career to his association with Tony. No, it was impossible. It would be best for both of them if Tony set him free. And it would be best to do it as soon as he could. But not quite yet. He would not be as brutal as Ayo. He would find a way of disengaging that would cause Danilo the least pain. And tonight he would mourn the loss of his ship and forget all his tomorrows by getting gloriously, roaringly drunk.

He had just glimpsed the sign of the club above the heads of the crowd when Junot Johnson called.

'Something's come up,' the sidesman said.

'What have they done now?'

'Not the wizards,' Junot said, with a bluntness that meant he was seriously worried. 'The police stationed here got a heads-up from their commander. A problem raised by traffic control. It looks like an intrusion. I had one of them give me a copy. Here.'

Tony opened a window: an image of white streaks across black sky, radiating from a single point. It reminded him of the diagram several of the wizards had begun to draw after they'd been infected with the eidolon. He had caught himself sketching it in the condensation on the glass mirror of the shared bathroom yesterday. He had tried to persuade himself that it was autosuggestion, but it had left him feeling unsettled for the rest of the day.

He said, 'What am I looking at?'

'Contrails,' Junot said.

Tony stopped dead, scarcely noticing the passer-by who bumped into him.

He said, 'Incoming ships? How many? When?'

'Sixteen of them, about twenty-five minutes ago,' Junot said. 'They're small. About the size of escape pods. Traffic control is looking for the ship that dropped them. The thinking is it snuck through the mirror after the freighter that touched down yesterday.'

'Have they been tracked all the way down?'

'Not quite. There's a ninety-five per cent probability they landed here,' Junot said, and sent a map.

The ellipse occupied a sizeable portion of the foothills. Its nearest edge was some eighty kilometres west of the city.

Tony said, 'That's if they didn't adjust their course as they came in.'

'Escape pods can't do that. They fall, they don't fly.'

'If they are escape pods. What are the police doing?'

'They're locking down the lab.'

'I mean about the pods,' Tony said.

'I think they're sending people to investigate.'

'Find out. And round up the wizards, find a place of safety. You could use one of the cold stores. Switch off the refrigeration and lock them in.'

'At once, Master Tony. Would you be thinking these are friends of the G-class that gave us trouble?'

'That's what I'm going to find out,' Tony said, and saw a commotion in the crowd and told Junot he would call back directly.

People were pressing back from a face-off between his security people and Opeyemi's men. Both sides had drawn their weapons and were shouting at each other; then his people collapsed, all at once. Tony saw glints flickering in the black air above the crowd – drones – and turned and plunged through the crowds towards the club.

Danilo was sitting in a booth at the back with several of his friends. He jumped up when he saw Tony, a hand rising to his mouth. Tony was breathless and trembling. He pulled his lover close and said in his ear, 'We have to leave. At once.'

'What's wrong?'

'The sky just fell in,' Tony said, and the trio on the stage suddenly stopped playing and someone screamed.

He turned to face Opeyemi's men as they barged through the tables. Their leader told him that he had to come with them now.

'I'm bringing my friend,' Tony said.

He was holding Danilo's hand; Danilo was holding his.

The man, a sturdy ruffian with the badge of the family's security service pinned to the collar of his black leather coat, did not so much as glance at the singer. 'My orders are to bring you, sir. No one else.'

'Either both of us go, or I stay here.'

Something floated down. A fist-sized drone floating under triple rotors, its sighting laser glittering blood-red in Tony's eyes.

The man said, 'You can walk out or we can carry you out.'

'You will regret this,' Tony said.

'Yes, sir. But right now I have to take you to the Great House.'

'I want you to assign one of your people to look after my friend. Do that, and I will forget about this unpleasantness.'

'All right,' the man said. 'Alice, you take care of the kid.'

'Thank you,' Tony said, and turned to Danilo, told him he had to go. 'I won't be long.'

Danilo looked at the security man. 'If you are arresting Mr Okoye, you can arrest me too.'

'It isn't like that,' Tony said. 'It's family business. I want you to go to the apartment. I want you to wait there, with Alice. I will come find you as soon as I can.'

'Are you in trouble?'

'No more trouble than anyone else. Will you do as I ask?'

'Family business?'

'I'm afraid so.'

'Damn them. And you.'

'Absolutely. But I want you to do that one thing for me.'

'The apartment. Wait there until you find me.'

'Don't leave until I do. Alice will look after you.'

'I can look after myself.'

'This is just in case.'

'Tell me that you aren't about to do something stupid,' Danilo said.

'I will come back as soon as I can,' Tony said, and kissed him.

Police drones hung above the crowded street, blue lights strobing across the canvas roofs of stalls. A stentorian voice was telling people to disperse. A spinner dropped out of the black air and the security people hustled Tony aboard. Pinned between two of them, he called Junot and got no reply. Aunty Jael: no reply. Cho Wing-James: no reply.

The spinner was descending towards the Great House. The towers and snow-covered gardens inside the triangle of the great granite walls, the church at its prow gleaming white as snow in banks of spotlights. Then the spotlights went out; lights went out across the city. In the sudden darkness, Tony saw a distant flicker of flame. The refinery was on fire.

21. Ashes

The next day, Bria still wasn't picking up her calls.

Lisa tidied the house, even did the damn washing-up, and went out on a supply run to the Shop'n'Save. She felt kind of queasy about the supermarket after her stupid fucking lapse, but she didn't want the people at the country store asking her where Pete was. She bought tomatoes and potatoes, oranges and grapes, gallon jugs of spring water, cereal bars and pitta bread and Graham crackers. Canned beans, canned ravioli and canned beef stew, jars of peanut butter and strawberry jelly . . . And three new smartphones. She was damn sure Nevers had bugged the one that had been returned to her when she'd been let go, and dumped it in the recycling bin.

Back at the homestead she dug out her camping stuff from the barn and carried it into the yard and beat the dust from it. The frame of her pup tent had lost its memory of the shape it was supposed to assume, and her spider-silk sleeping bag was filthy, but otherwise everything was pretty much okay. She washed the sleeping bag by hand and was pegging it out in the sunshine when Sheriff Bird's cruiser pulled up at the gate.

They sat in the kitchen, drinking coffee. The cardboard tube containing Pete's ashes stood on the table between them, next to the sheriff's Stetson. It was squat and green, the tube, sealed with yellow tape printed with *Property of the UN Technology Control Unit.*

Lisa said, 'Did you find out why they killed him?'

'I understand that he had the language tweak,' Sheriff Bird said.

'He had about a hundred words. Mostly he preferred to bark, the dumb mutt.'

'It seems that the tweak makes animals susceptible to memes and such,' Sheriff Bird said. 'Which is why, well, what happened happened.'

'Did they bother to test Pete first?'

'Excuse me?'

'Did they test my dog before they killed him, or was it a summary execution?'

'They told me that it was standard procedure.'

'And killing my hurklins, that was standard procedure too?'

'I don't like what they did. But Mr Nevers had a warrant and I had to let him execute it.' Sheriff Bird's hair was slicked back; there was a dent in his forehead where the brim of his hat had rested. He said, 'If you want to make an official complaint, I'll be more than happy to explain the procedure.'

'Is there any point? Nevers wanted to intimidate me, show me he can do what he likes. And it was "standard procedure".'

'He neglected to inform you. That could be grounds for complaint.'

'He neglected to inform you, too. Was it because he has trust issues with his law-enforcement colleagues, or because he didn't care that it would cause you trouble?'

'I don't know that I'd call him a colleague.' Sheriff Bird took a sip of coffee, then said, 'That other thing you asked me about. I'm afraid I don't have much to tell. I'm sure you know that Nevers was involved with the discovery of those two spaceships on Mangala.'

'That's when he first went head to head with Ada Morange,' Lisa said. 'When her company found and flew the first Ghajar ships.'

'He was serving in the London police force at the time,' Sheriff Bird said. 'He had to take early retirement, afterwards. But he was recruited by the UN straight away, and was fast-tracked. I guess they thought his experience counted for something. He worked in the UK and Europe, was sent out to Yanos and worked there for a while. And then he came here. That was four years ago. He's been involved in some high-profile cases, but as far as I can tell he hasn't stepped out of line the way he did on Mangala. Or if he has, the UN and our government have kept it quiet. The only other thing I can tell you, he definitely has something going with the Jackaroo. He liaises on cases they're interested in.'

'Like this one.'

'It seems so.'

'I suppose you can't tell me why the Jackaroo are interested in me.'

'I doubt even Nevers knows. Those avatars like to observe, like on a ride-along. But they don't give away much.' Sheriff Bird took out his phone and set it on the table and turned it towards Lisa. 'There isn't anything else I can tell you. Officially. But you might want to think of doing a bit more digging into that space-ship thing on Mangala. May I use your bathroom?'

As soon as he was gone, Lisa leaned forward to check the phone's screen. A phone number and a name she recognised from her research into Nevers's background. Chloe Millar. One of the people who had been involved in 'that spaceship thing'. She had been helping the kid infected with the Ghajar eidolon, and Nevers had followed them to Mangala, where the whole thing had gone down. From the phone number's code, it seemed that she was still there.

When Sheriff Bird returned, Lisa thanked him, said that she hoped this wouldn't get him into trouble.

Sheriff Bird said that it wasn't something he was going to lose sleep over. 'The thing is? When I volunteered to bring you your dog's ashes, wasn't a person I talked to at the TCU thought it was necessary.'

22. 'I just need your head.'

Tony found Ayo in the operations room under the Black Tower. It hadn't been used since the food riots during the blockade, the air smelled faintly of mould and furniture was stacked along one wall and covered with drop cloths, but it was bustling with edgy purpose now. Aides, clerks and security flacks coming and going, studying windows, talking to each other or to the air. Tony saw images of flames roaring amongst the refinery's pipework towers and a rolling gout of flame and black smoke as a tank ruptured, aerial views of city streets, infrared views of random patches of countryside, live maps, streams of data. Opeyemi and Julia were in conference with the house's master at arms; Ayo was talking with her secretary and the city's chief of police.

Tony darted in when the chief of police left, flung out his arms and said, 'Ayo. Sister. This is all my fault.'

'Not now, Tony,' Ayo said, and started to turn away.

Tony got in her face. 'The claim jumpers want the stromatolites. Or the wizards. Or both. They failed to seize them at the slime planet, and now they're here.'

Ayo looked at him. 'If you know anything that could be useful, tell me now. All of it.'

'The claim jumpers came after the stromatolites on the slime planet, but I escaped with a few specimens and destroyed the rest. Then one of the wizards was feeding them information about our research, but we shut that down. And now the Commons police are about to take the wizards into custody, and the claim jumpers have come to snatch them.'

Ayo said, 'If they came for the wizards, they missed their target by almost a hundred kilometres.'

'Traffic control couldn't track those pods all the way down. Some may have landed in the foothills to draw us away, but the rest landed closeby. They took out the refinery, and I think that they also raided Aunty Jael's laboratory. If you don't believe me, try calling Aunty Jael. She isn't answering. Neither is my man, nor the wizards' leader. If you don't have any assets there, you should send some right now.'

'The police are guarding it,' Ayo said, but told her secretary to call Aunty Jael.

After a moment, the man said, 'She is not picking up, ma'am. There seems to be a problem with the local network.'

'Find out if the police know anything,' Ayo said.

The secretary nodded and turned away.

Tony said, 'Now would be a good time to give me back my ship. It has survey drones. They can reach the facility in a couple of minutes.'

'We already have plenty of drones.'

'They won't be much use when the claim jumpers head up and out. But I can give chase—'

'Not another word about your ship,' Ayo said. 'This isn't the time.'

Her secretary said that the police guards at the laboratory had reported that nothing was amiss.

'You see?' Ayo told Tony. 'Everything is fine.'

'The last I knew, there were only two guards.'

Ayo looked at her secretary. 'Have the police sent any additional support?'

'I have been told that all available personnel are either searching for the fallen escape pods or guarding the clinic, ma'am. The police believe that this may be an attempt to kidnap some of the patients. Many of them are children of important and powerful people.'

'If the police are protecting them,' Tony said, 'no one is protecting the wizards or Aunty Jael.'

'Send some people over there, just in case,' Ayo told her secretary. 'A single squad will suffice.'

'I want to go with them,' Tony said.

'Everything is under control,' Ayo said.

'The wizards are my responsibility,' Tony said. 'If you won't let me use my ship, I should ride with that squad. And if I cannot ride with them, I will find my own way there.'

Ayo studied him for a moment. 'Tell me this isn't about getting your ship back.'

'Absolutely not,' Tony said, hoping she would not catch the lie.

'All right,' she said. 'Go. But as an observer. You will do everything the squad commander tells you to do. If she tells you to stay in the flitter, you will stay in the flitter.'

'Thank you, sister. I won't let you down.'

'Get upstairs. I will order them to pick you up from the plaza.'

Tony heard the flitter coming in to land as he hurried out of the Black Tower's entrance. Its skids kissed the marble slabs of the plaza and he ran through the prop wash and climbed the steep ramp into its belly, fell into one of the bucket seats as the craft leapt into the air with a roar of turboprops, almost fell out of the seat as it made a steep turn.

Someone came towards him, stepping easily despite the tilt in the deck and the jolting ride. Sade Oyecan: a tough wiry woman whose family had been in service of Tony's for ever. She had trained him in use of weapons and personal security fifteen years ago. He remembered her sharp voice echoing under the high roof of the gymnasium during krav maga sessions, the whiplash of her scorn, the relentless exercises, the happiness he had felt whenever she doled out rare praise.

She dumped an exosuit in his lap, told him to put it on. 'You won't be armed. It might make you reckless, and I remember your attempts at marksmanship. You're liable to hit one of us if there's any excitement.'

'I want to help in any way I can.'

'You can do that by staying out of trouble. Keep to the rear, move only when I tell you to move. Understood?'

'Absolutely.'

Sade helped him buckle into the exosuit. Its musculature woke with a shiver, tightened at his ankles and knees and hips, his shoulders and elbows. Sade handed him gloves and a visored helmet. 'Remember how this works?'

Tony scanned the symbols and readouts of the visor's head-up display, nodded. His mouth was dry. He felt as if he had swallowed a knot of thorns.

Sade rapped the top of his helmet. 'Stay back. If there's any trouble throw yourself flat and wait for me to tell you when to move. The place is dark. I'm hoping that's the police's idea of defence. My people will set up a perimeter and sweep the area, and then we'll walk in. You tell the wizards to evacuate; we'll escort them out. Okay?'

'Okay.'

The flitter made a sudden sharp turn, then dropped faster than the Black Tower's express elevator. Tony grabbed a strap and hung on, bit his tongue when the little craft banged down. He swallowed a spit of blood, followed Sade and the half-dozen guards down the ramp into a cutting wind that blew flat out of the freezing dark. Snow up to his knees. He remembered how to toggle the visor's starlight view and slogged after the others to a fence half-buried in a smooth white wind-sculpted wave.

The long, low laboratory building stood beyond snow-covered fields. No lights showing anywhere. On the command band, one of the guards was telling Sade that drones were not picking up any movement.

'Try another sweep,' Sade said. 'And give me a line to the police in there.'

She talked to someone, a brief exchange of mostly yeses and noes, told Tony that the lab had been locked down and everyone was safe.

'Tell whoever you are talking to that I want a word with Junot Johnson,' Tony said.

'All's quiet here, Mr Tony. The hostiles are way to the north-west, up in the foothills.'

'Don't be so sure. Tell them to put my man on the line.'

Sade leaned close, said quietly, 'If you have cold feet, you can go back to the flitter. Wait until we've secured the place.'

'If you were so certain nothing was wrong, why didn't you land outside the entrance? Ask them to put Junot on.'

Sade asked. She told Tony, 'They say he isn't around right now.'
'Something isn't right.'

'Maybe your man is looking after the wizards.'

'I told him to lock them in one of the cold stores. And the greenhouses should be lit up. Aunty Jael is running experiments in them. Tell the police I want to talk to her.'

After a moment, Sade said, 'Apparently she's busy. I think you're right, Mr Tony. Something's wrong.'

'Ask one of the police to come out. Tell them to bring Junot with them. Tell them it is on my order.'

Sade passed on the message. Silence. Stars twinkled brightly everywhere overhead. Seeing them from a planet's surface was very different from being aloft. They seemed so very cold and remote.

'They've cut the channel,' Sade said, and a moment later a constellation of little sparks crackled and died in the dark air above the laboratory.

'The drones are down!' a man shouted, and the flitter's rotors spun up with a roar, blowing a huge gust of snow over them. As the machine lurched into the air, something screamed across the fields. Tony saw the flitter's shadow against the starry sky, saw it tilt hard right, and then it burst in a flower of bright flame and someone banged into him and knocked him face down in the snow.

'Okay,' Sade said after a few moments, and helped Tony to his knees. A cauldron of flames was tilted in a stand of pine trees, throwing huge flickering shadows across a stretch of snow pockmarked with fallen debris and little fires. And in the other direction thin dark figures were running across the snowy fields, moving with curious high gaits . . . Tony's visor popped brackets around them and zoomed in. They were four of Aunty Jael's hands, packs strapped to their chests.

'Suicide bombers,' Sade sang out. 'Put them down.'

There was a brief soprano squall of gunfire. Three of the figures collapsed. The survivor came on, zigzagging through spurts of snow, and Sade jacked her carbine to her shoulder and squeezed off three shots. The hand collapsed, headless, a hundred metres off. A moment later, a plume of dirt and snow erupted where it had fallen and the clap of the explosion echoed out across the dark flat countryside.

In the freezing silence Sade stood up and told the guards they were going in. She was calm and matter-of-fact, saying they would cross the open ground as quickly as they could, selecting one group to take the main entrance, another to take the loading bay. The guards rose up and ran; Tony chased after Sade. His exosuit took over, pounding through knee-deep swales of snow. His head-up display was cluttered with signs and portents as the suit analysed and dismissed likely targets; he ached for a gun. His breath was a harsh engine. Muscle memory from the combat games he had played as a kid, an echo of childish glee, and a sick apprehension growing because this was not a game where you died in half a dozen ways before going home to supper.

Three guards cut away towards the main entrance; the others, led by Sade, ploughed straight on. Tony stumbled and fell flat on his face in a deep snowdrift, pushed to his feet and sprinted to the corner of one of the greenhouses where Sade and the guards crouched. Silence. Nothing moving in the dark shadow of the laboratory.

Sade put a hand on his shoulder, pointed to the lab's loading bay. Tony nodded to show he understood.

'Now!' she said, and they were up and running again. Over a fence, across a yard, halting in the shelter of a big tractor. The loading bay was a dozen metres away when a sudden thunderclap of red flame rolled up beyond the laboratory's flat roof. 'Booby-trapped,' someone reported breathlessly on the command band. Then: 'Hands coming at us,' and there was the sound of small-arms fire.

Sade said to Tony, 'How many of those things does Aunty Jael have?'

'Ten or twelve, I think. She can control some of the equipment, too. Low-loaders and so on.'

'Is there a kill switch?'

'I don't know.' Tony was not sure that the hands were being run by Aunty Jael, either. He had a bad feeling about her and Junot and the wizards.

'Then we'll take them down one by one,' Sade said.

One of the guards scrambled onto the loading bay's platform, plugged something into the keypad by the door, flattened against the wall as the door rolled up, took a quick peek inside, gave the all-clear thumbs-up. Sade and the other guard dashed forward; all three vanished inside. Tony took a few seconds to nerve himself up and follow them. He had almost reached the loading platform when bright flame blasted out of the door and a hard jolt of noise and air slammed into him.

He was on his back. Dazed. A high ringing in his ears. The front of his exosuit was smouldering; pockets of blue flame guttered in the snow around him. He could not move. His exosuit was locked.

Someone leaned in above him. A young man with a pale face and a stiff brush of blond hair, a black band painted across eyes that gleamed silver. Tiny crosses for pupils. Tony tried and failed to scrabble backwards. He was trapped in a rigid lobster shell, helpless as the man reached down and unlatched his helmet, saying, 'I just need your head.'

Tony saw the glint of a knife blade, his bowels liquefied, and then the man grunted and flew sideways. Tony lay there, sweating inside the shell of his suit. He had pissed himself, could feel it soaking into the liner, warm then cold.

Sade knelt beside him, asking if he was okay, her voice distanced and flattened by the ringing in his ears. She had lost her helmet and the right side of her suit was scorched and her arm was strapped to her torso with a grappling cord.

'I can't move,' Tony said. The words were barbs in his throat.

'I can fix that,' she said, and stuck something into the port under his chestplate.

The hard shell of the exosuit relaxed. Tony rolled over, got to his knees, stood up. The pale man lay in the snow, a raw red crater in his chest, one arm flung above his head and a saw-bladed knife lying nearby.

'We were hit by a booby trap,' Sade said. 'A hand ran up and exploded. Killed Tokun. Are you okay?'

'Sade, I owe you my life.'

'We're not done yet. Can you walk?'

He could walk. They headed towards the main entrance. The floor of the lobby was shattered and scorched; overhead, shredded tiles dangled from twisted struts. One of the guards met them, said that aside from the booby trap there had been minimal resistance. 'We knocked out about a dozen hands. Two hostiles took off in a spinner. It looked like they were loading equipment when we came in.'

Tony said, 'What about the people who were working here?'

'They didn't make it, sir,' the guard said. 'I'm sorry.'

The dead were in the work space, lying in stinking black water that had spilled from the smashed ruin of the stromatolite aquarium. A man and a woman in Commons police green, Junot Johnson, three wizards in their white coats. The wizards had been decapitated. Tony recognised the heraldic formulae scrawled on Cho Wing-James's lab coat and looked away.

'I think they took the heads of the wizards because they are infected with a Ghajar eidolon,' he told Sade. That was why the man she had killed had wanted to cut off his head, he realised. He was infected, too.

According to one of the guards, all of the dead had been electrocuted.

'Like with a taser but a lot more voltage,' she said. 'The filaments are still stuck in their skin.'

Sade, surveying the dismal scene, pointed to several small hands lying in the flood. One, the plastic shell of its torso badly cracked, was still twitching. 'It looks like they were attacked by the hands, and made a last stand here,' she said. 'But who was controlling the hands?'

Tony was certain that Junot Johnson, loyal to the last, had smashed the aquarium to prevent the stromatolites falling into the hands of the raiders. He asked the guards if they had swept the building.

'This floor is clear,' one said.

'Two of the wizards are missing. We need to check the basements,' Tony said.

There was no one in the cold store, and the door to Aunty Jael's room was open. Her laminated brain and the apparatus that supported it were gone.

'I think Junot and the others were attacked and killed before the raiders arrived,' Tony said. 'Someone mobilised the hands against them, and sabotaged the comms so they couldn't call for help. And I think I know who did it.'

'You mean the two missing wizards?' Sade said.

'Not the wizards,' Tony said. 'It was someone who knew everything—'

Sade raised a hand and half-turned away and began a brief conversation with someone on the command band.

Tony realised that the intruders could not have known that he would come to find them at the laboratory. And because they wanted the eidolon in his head they would have gone to look for him . . . A panicky convulsion passed through him. 'I need to get back to the city,' he told Sade. 'I need to get there right now.'

She turned to him. Her expression behind the overlay of symbols and little windows in her visor was serious and sad. 'I'm sorry, Mr Tony,' she said.

'If you can't take me there I will find some other way.'

'It isn't that,' Sade said. 'You're under arrest.'

23. Chloe Millar

Lisa scattered Pete's ashes on a flat ridge that overlooked the dry wash where they'd often walked in the evening. Pete always running ahead, investigating rocks and undergrowth, chasing after critters he'd raised up. He had never lost that artless enthusiasm, the dumb old dog. Sometimes he would disappear for a couple of hours, tracking the spoor of something intensely interesting, returning with a sidling guilt he'd shake off as soon as Lisa forgave him. As she always did. She'd lived with Pete for six years, and in all that time the world had been ever fresh for him, born anew every day. She'd loved him for that, and he'd given her his unconditional love in return. Flopping beside her while she worked, putting up with her moods, sleeping at the foot of her bed at night. He'd loved Willie too, greeting him in a frenzy of delight whenever he turned up.

Lisa remembered the times when she and Willie had perched up here of an evening. A little fire flickering in a circle of stones. Stars coming out above the darkening shrub-steppe tableland as they talked about their lives and people they knew, talked about anything and everything except the Bad Trip and how it had split them in two. Willie had done most of the talking, now Lisa thought about it. His wild tales. They'd come out here on his fortieth birthday with his road dogs, the little gang of bikers he'd fallen in with after he'd bought a second-hand Harley Davidson Roadster. A year later he'd had to sell that bike to settle a gambling debt, but they'd had a fine old time that night. Building a big fire, firing roman candles at the stars, dancing to old songs and howling at the little lopsided moon as it jumped up from the

151

western horizon. Lisa remembered how Willie had ridden his bike through the fire, scattering galaxies of sparks into the night.

Oh Willie. Oh Pete.

She climbed into her pickup truck and in the last light picked her way across country until she struck a county road, and then drove to the Trading Post, a store with a pit barbecue out back. She needed to eat before she set out, and it was a popular joint. If Nevers was somehow keeping watch on her, it would be good cover for what she needed to do.

She sat at one of the picnic tables under coloured bulbs strung criss-cross on poles, a couple of dozen people eating and chattering around her, and placed a call to a service that patched ordinary phones to a q-phone exchange. She gave the number Sheriff Bird had passed to her and while she waited for the call-back worked through a pulled-pork sandwich and a side order of slaw, demolished a portion of pecan pie. She was on her second coffee refill when her new smartphone rang and the exchange operator told her that the call was connected. A few moments later, a cool English voice was asking what she wanted.

'My name is Lisa Dawes. You don't know me, but we have an acquaintance in common. Adam Nevers.'

It was the usual miracle – talking in real time to someone on another planet halfway across the galaxy. No delay, the signal so clear she might have been gossiping with her next-door neighbour.

A pause. Then Chloe Millar said, 'How did you get my number?'

'My place was raided by Adam Nevers. He works for the geek police here on First Foot. The TCU. They killed my dog, and someone passed on your number because he felt bad about that.'

'Adam Nevers killed your dog?'

'Euthanised him because, allegedly, he might have been infected with an eidolon. I just now scattered his ashes. What it is, I'm in kind of a tight spot thanks to Mr Nevers. I'd be really grateful if you could spare a couple of minutes and tell me anything that might help me deal with him.'

'Before this goes any further,' Chloe Millar said, 'I have to tell you that you aren't the first person to call me about Adam Nevers.

And I have to ask you, as I asked the others, not to go into any details about the kind of trouble you're in.'

'Okay.'

'I looked you up when the exchange got in touch about this call. I know you deal in artefacts. I know you were involved in some kind of incident with one some years ago. And that's all I want to know. I'm trying to have what passes for a normal life, even though I'm living on an alien planet full of alien ruins. I have a husband, two kids. I don't want to become involved in anything that could attract attention. I don't want my family involved.'

'I understand,' Lisa said. 'But since you kindly agreed to talk, maybe you could tell me about your encounter with Adam Nevers. Your history with him.'

'I haven't seen him for a long time. Eight years. He came back to Mangala once, made a point of seeing me. He felt that it was important to let me know he was still working. It was a matter of pride as far as he was concerned.'

'I think I know what you mean.'

'Is he still suited and booted?'

'Excuse me?'

'What does he wear, these days?'

'Suits, silk ties, cufflinks . . . Sort of like one of those old movie stars. Pretty fancy for a cop.'

'I noticed his clothes the first time I met him. Which isn't something you can always say about a man. Especially a policeman. That was back in London, when he and I were on different sides of the search for these two kids who'd fallen under the influence of a Ghajar eidolon.'

'And you found them, and they led you to the Ghajar ships.'

'We found the place the ships returned to after spending who knows how many thousands of years in mothballs. And Nevers persuaded his bosses to allow him to chase us all the way to Mangala, and tried and failed to arrest us. The one thing you should know about him,' Chloe Millar said, 'is that he really does believe that he's doing the right thing. And he doesn't give up, and he has friends in high places.'

'If you mean the Jackaroo, he brought an avatar along the first time he visited my place,' Lisa said. She was about to explain about the raid and the follow-up, then remembered that Chloe had asked her not to give any details.

'Was it Bob Smith?' Chloe said.

'Excuse me?'

'That's what the avatar Nevers was working with back then called itself.'

'We weren't introduced,' Lisa said. 'It was mostly tagging along as an observer.'

'Nevers was carrying a kind of wire that generated a copy of that avatar,' Chloe said. 'It got into a fight with the Ghajar eidolon that called down the ships, and it lost. One of the !Cha once told me that the Jackaroo make a thing of preventing us finding and using certain kinds of Elder Culture technology because they know it will make it seem all the more desirable to us. Forbidden fruit, the apple in the Garden of Eden and so on. I don't think Nevers understands that. That he may be helping the Jackaroo to manipulate us.'

'You make him sound like some kind of fanatic,' Lisa said.

'He's deadly serious about the dangers of Elder Culture technology. And he more or less lacks a sense of humour. Goes with his vanity, the way he presents himself. My advice is to take him as seriously as he takes himself. Because if he believes that you are dangerous, or if he thinks that you have found something that could be dangerous, he won't let it go.'

'That's kind of why I called you.'

'Because you aren't going to let it go, either. Whatever it is that we aren't going to talk about.'

'I won't go into any detail, like you asked,' Lisa said. 'But Ada Morange has an interest in this thing I'm caught up in. And I've reached a point where I may have to decide whether to throw in with her.'

A silence on the line. At the table next to Lisa's a woman said loudly, 'He told me he was so over it. But he so wasn't.'

Chloe Millar said, 'I can't advise you about that. I haven't met her or heard from her in years.'

'But you chose to work with her, once upon a time.'

'I was working for her from the beginning. For a little company, Disruption Theory, she'd bought a controlling share in. And then I got involved with the two kids infected with that Ghajar eidolon, and she gave us a great deal of help. She can be a good friend when your interests coincide with hers, but like all successful business people she can also be pretty ruthless. Using people to get what she wants.'

'Nevers warned me about her followers. He made it sound like she's running some kind of cult.'

'I wouldn't know about that,' Chloe said. 'She wanted me to stay on, afterwards. I said no thanks, and we parted I guess you could say amicably. But Fahad Chauhan, one of the kids infected with that Ghajar eidolon? He stayed on. And at first it worked out pretty well. He helped her company work out how other people could control Ghajar ships; she paid him a good salary, protected him and his little sister from a shitload of legal trouble. But she also encouraged him to take off on solo voyages, go anywhere he wanted to, because she believed that his eidolon might lead him to something super-interesting. The Ghajar home world, some place with a living remnant of an Elder Culture species . . . He was one of the first pilots to explore the New Frontier, and one day, about five years ago, he went out into that wormhole network and he didn't come back. You could say that it wasn't Ada's fault. That he would have gone out there anyway. But she encouraged him. She enabled him. She used him for her own ends.'

'So if I throw in with her, I should watch my back.'

'Like with any business deal.' Chloe paused, then said, 'If you do throw in with her, you'll probably meet a !Cha who calls himself Unlikely Worlds. He's following her story, the way the !Cha do, and she lets him. Partly out of vanity – that's one of the things she and Adam Nevers have in common. Partly because she thinks he can be useful to her. If you do meet him, be careful.'

'Is this the one who told you about the Jackaroo?'

'I think that the !Cha manipulate people too,' Chloe said. Most people didn't bother with it, but she had the pronunciation of the click consonant, halfway between a sneeze and the sound of a cork pulled from a bottle, down to a T. 'The Jackaroo do it because they want to help, whatever that means. The !Cha do it to jazz up the stories they're following. At the end of the thing with the Ghajar eidolon, Unlikely Worlds gave me something I thought I wanted. As a reward, you know, for making Ada Morange's story more tasty. I'd been looking for it for the longest time. I guess you could say it was my heart's desire. It turned out that it wasn't what I wanted at all, but that wasn't his fault . . .'

Another pause. Then Chloe said, 'My mother died in the Spasm. The suitcase nuke that took out Trafalgar Square, in London? She was there.'

'I'm sorry,' Lisa said.

'I tried to find out how she died,' Chloe said. 'What she was doing, whether it was slow or mercifully quick. It was sort of how I got involved with Disruption Theory, so I suppose you could say it was how I got caught up in the Ghajar eidolon thing, too . . . Anyway, Unlikely Worlds showed me her last moments, and it was quick. Thank God. She died quickly. But that isn't the point. The point is that he knew. I don't mean that the Jackaroo and the !Cha had anything to do with the Spasm, or any of that truther nonsense, but they definitely knew about it. They knew what was going to happen. Where it was going to happen. And they let it. They let it happen, and then they came to help.'

'They'd been watching us for a long time before First Contact,' Lisa said.

'Yes. And they know more about us than we can imagine. They know us better than we know ourselves. So watch out, if you meet Unlikely Worlds. Because he might try to fuck around with you. To spice up the story he's following, or because it's his idea of fun.'

'Okay.'

'I'm afraid I haven't been much help.'

'I think I have a better idea about what I'm up against.'

'As far as I'm concerned? I still don't know the half of it, and I probably never will. But whatever you choose to do, I hope it works out. I really do,' Chloe said, and terminated the call.

A couple of moments later, a robot voice told Lisa how much it had cost. It was a healthy bite from her bank account, but she thought that it had been worth it.

She went into the rest room, pulled out the smartphone's SIM card and snapped it in half and flushed it. An hour later she was out on Highway One, heading for the desert and the City of the Dead.

24. On The Farm

Tony was exiled to a tank farm some forty kilometres north-west of the city. He was supposed to be learning how to run the place – starting afresh from the bottom and working his way back up, as Ayo put it – but it was really just one step away from house arrest. He had been stowed there because the family had chosen to reserve their decision about how best to punish him until after the Commons police had completed their investigation of the assault on Skadi. Out of sight, out of mind.

He had not been allowed to attend the funeral of Junot Johnson, the quiet, wry man who had served with him for two years of freebooting. Running errands, giving him unobtrusive advice during negotiations, checking out markets and rivals and potential clients . . . A dutiful, loyal sidesman, and also, Tony realised, too late, a good friend.

His phone privileges had been revoked. He could not access the family or the public nets, could not communicate with anyone outside the boundary of the farm. And Ayo refused his request to arrange a meeting with Danilo. That little fling was over, she said.

'I know that isn't your idea,' Tony said. 'It reeks of Opeyemi's petty spite.'

'It was going to end sooner or later, brother. That kind of affair always does.'

'Danilo was an innocent party in all this,' Tony said. 'Promise me that he will not be hurt. Give me that, at least.'

'He has been interrogated and released. And he will be of no further interest to us as long as you keep away from him.'

'What do you mean, interrogated? Was he put to the question?'

'He gave a statement about your little affair,' Ayo said. 'Nothing more than that. We are not monsters, Tony.'

She looked exhausted. Worn down and overburdened. She had agreed to the freebooting venture that had culminated in the work on the stromatolites, and now she had to deal with the fallout of the raid, and with Opeyemi's self-righteous crusade to defend the family's honour. Her authority had been weakened. She could no longer protect Tony because she could no longer protect herself.

While the city's emergency services had been dealing with the attack on the refinery, raiders had infiltrated the city and headed for Danilo's apartment building. Security forces had spotted them entering; there had been a firefight; the raiders had triggered explosives they had been carrying. Three city blocks had been obliterated and more than five hundred people had been killed or badly injured. Danilo had survived only because his bodyguard had ignored Tony's orders and had taken him to one of the deep shelters instead of his apartment.

It was the only bright spot in what was otherwise a comprehensive fiasco. Tony had been interrogated by Opeyemi, and then interrogated all over again by the family council. There was general agreement that the raiders had wanted to snatch the stromatolites and the results of the wizards' research, but no one apart from Tony believed that they were part of the Red Brigade – the dead they had left behind had lacked any kind of identification – and Opeyemi had more or less accused him of collaboration. Although they had been carried out in private and Tony had sworn her to secrecy, Opeyemi knew all about Aunty Jael's tests. He said that the eidolon which had infected Tony had affected his behaviour and judgement, said that Tony's failure to inform the family council about it was an irresponsible and wholly selfish decision that proved he was unfit to serve in any capacity.

Tony's offer to chase after the raiders had been refused; Ayo had told him to admit his guilt and take his punishment. If he kept a low profile and showed suitable contrition, she said, it was quite possible that he would be forgiven.

'Opeyemi has other ideas,' Tony said. 'He wants me to stand before a police tribunal and be prosecuted for sedition. He wants to sacrifice me to save the family's reputation. You would think, sister, that I had stolen the fucking freighter.'

It was clear now that the K-class freighter which had landed the day before the attack had been hijacked by the raiders. They had launched the escape pods as the freighter had approached Skadi, and the pods had followed long spiral orbits that had intersected with the planet's atmosphere eighteen hours later. The police were still trying to find out why traffic control had failed to spot this manoeuvre. And at the end of the raid, several hands acting as suicide bombers had damaged the only police ship and killed eight and wounded twenty more in the barracks and the control tower, and the raiders had sneaked back aboard the freighter and booted.

Tony's suggestion that Aunty Jael had infiltrated traffic control and prevented it spotting the incoming pods, that she had used the hands to kill Junot and the police guards and attack the space field, and had told the raiders that he was living in Danilo's apartment, was comprehensively ridiculed. She was a laminated person, unable to show any kind of initiative. She had not escaped; she had been stolen. The family's official story, given to the police and distributed across news feeds, was that Eli Tanjung and the two missing wizards had been traitors, communicating with the raiders and feeding them inside information, and that Tony was entirely responsible for this catastrophic failure in security.

So he was exiled to the farm, accompanied by Lancelot Askia. In case, Tony supposed, he tried to poison the fish or lace the banana crop with hallucinogens. It was a relief to get away from the Great House and his family, the looks and pointed silences, the whispers at his back, but he had little to do but brood in the office he had appropriated from the farm's supervisor, or wander the catwalks above the tanks and hydroponic platforms, where tomato vines, yams and banana plants, queen's pineapple, efo tete and ugo grew in the sharp light of grow-lamps. The secret flicker of carp in the green depths of the tanks; a hundred hungry mouths kissing the skin of the water when they were fed. The taste of a freshly picked apple banana. The calm odour of growing plants in the damp warmth. Moments of pleasure in the desolation of his misery.

He went for long walks in the snowy plantation. Rows of tall pines stretching away in cathedral quiet. The sun pale and heatless in the white sky. Tracks of animals and biochines printed here and there in the snow. The crackle of ice crystals breaking under his boots. The smoke of his breath.

Lancelot Askia followed a dozen or so metres behind, a rifle slung on his shoulder and a pistol at his hip. Tony was unarmed. He was not even allowed to carry a knife.

Sometimes he fantasised that Opeyemi had given the order for his execution. A merciful bullet in the back of his head as he plodded through the snow. The crack of the shot echoing off through the trees, vanishing into the rapt chill silence.

Sometimes he fantasised about overpowering the man and escaping. But where would he escape to?

Sometimes it felt as if there was a third person walking with them. The feeling was so strong that Tony could not help looking around, seeing only his guard and the sentinel ranks of pine trees.

Once he came across a patch of trees that had been colonised by a congregation of kites. Clusters of the black diamond-shaped creatures clung to the treetops, overlapping each other like badly laid flagstones. Tony stepped towards the nearest tree and walked all the way around it, studying the kites. They were mostly motionless, but now and then an edge of a wing would ruffle, or a whip-like clasper would coil a little tighter, or an eye or three would extrude, blink, and withdraw.

The colour of them was like burned vinegar in the cold still air.

He clapped his hands. Softly and tentatively at first; then, after nothing happened, as hard as he could. Cupping his palms and smashing them together, the impact stinging under his gloves. Above him, several kites shuffled and stirred. One raised a ventral clasper to reveal its secondary sensory cluster: white stones randomly set in creased black leather.

Tony laughed, clapped some more. He was seized by a careless exhilaration. Maybe the kites would attack him, maybe they wouldn't, but in the moment it felt as if he had regained control of his fate. He was so keyed up that he actually jumped when

Lancelot Askia's hand fell on his shoulder. It was the first time the man had touched him.

'We must leave,' Lancelot Askia said. 'They could kill us if they startle.'

'They don't care,' Tony said, and raised his voice. 'They. Don't. Care.'

'Please,' the man said firmly, and tried to pull Tony away.

Tony lashed out and smacked him in the face, a hard blow that sent him reeling back. He wiped a bright bubble of blood from his nose and stared at Tony with a hard loathing. His eyes were small and dark, set close together under a heavy brow.

'I didn't ask to look after you,' he said. 'You're the one who infected me with a fucking alien ghost. I should kill you for that. But unlike you, I respect the chain of command. I have been given my orders, and I will carry them out as best as I can.'

Tony realised that the man had not been sent here to spy on him or kill him. No, Opeyemi wanted to make sure he did not try to commit suicide before the police tribunal arrived.

He said, 'Why are you even alive? Why weren't you in the laboratory? Why weren't you killed like the others?'

Lancelot Askia glanced up as a couple of kites stirred high overhead, looked back at Tony. 'If I have to knock you out and carry you, I will.'

'If you lay a hand on me again, I will have you skinned for your insolence.'

Lancelot Askia stepped forward. Their faces were a handspan apart, the clouds of their breath mingling. 'No, you won't,' he said. 'Because you don't have any power any more. Now let's take this pity party home.'

25. The City Of The Dead

Lisa perched on the hood of her pickup truck, peeling an orange with her clasp knife, watching the first sliver of the sun simmer at the horizon, silhouetting the mounds and arthritic coral trees of the City of the Dead. She was bone-tired and stiffly aching after the long drive and a few hours of snatched sleep on stony ground, was trying to ignore the feeling that something was in the cab, sitting behind the steering wheel, staring at her through the windshield. Light sparked off a distant string of Boxbuilder ruins that crested a low ridge. A flock of harmless little eidolons that had crept out to watch her in the night suddenly swirled into the air and fled into a nearby crevice like flakes of burned paper sucked down a flue. Something whoop-whoop-whooped close by; in the middle distance something else cleared its throat with a brisk pneumatic rattle.

The alien desert waking around her, ancient and vast and full of mystery.

First Foot huddled so close to its cool red dwarf star that it should have been tidally locked like Earth's Moon, its orbital period matching its rotation so that one face was always turned towards the star. Sunrise was a daily miracle courtesy of the unknown Elder Culture which had spun up the planet's rotational speed around the time a long drought had been driving the ancestors of hominins into the plains of Africa.

Lisa remembered trips with Willie in the first flush of their marriage. Banging across stony flats in the old Holden Colorado, soundtracked by the Rolling Stones, Neil Young, Joni Mitchell, and the Grateful Dead. Willie grokked the music from three or four

163

generations ago. He said that he had an old soul, claimed to be the reincarnation of the singer Gram Parsons. He'd had a chart drawn up by a Tibetan monk, or so he said, that tracked his soul back to when it had previously entered the bardo: 19 September 1973, when Parsons had died in the Hi-Desert Memorial Hospital in Joshua Tree National Monument, California. Parsons's friends had hijacked his body and attempted to cremate it out in the desert, and that was what he wanted when the time came, Willie said. Forget some sterile crematorium oven. He wanted a pyre out in the desert. Wanted to mingle his molecules with earth and sky.

He liked to speculate about whether the souls of people who died on First Foot stayed there, or if they transmigrated back to Earth. He wondered if human beings shared souls with Elder Culture species. 'We could have been Ghostkeepers in former lives, Lize. Maybe that's why we're drawn to the City of the Dead.'

Lisa remembered their stoned, intense conversations under the huge desert night sky. Their lovemaking on a blanket by the camp fire. The prickle of Willie's beard. The taste of his sweet breath. She remembered falling asleep with him under alien stars. And she remembered the long quiet days fossicking amongst the tombs.

There were millions of them in the City of the Dead, scattered across fifty thousand square kilometres. Built from small round-edged clay bricks that some believed had been excreted by the creatures that had created them, the so-called Ghostkeepers. No one knew if they really were tombs. Although they appeared to memorialise fragments of the lives of their builders, they might be temporary shelters, like Boxbuilder ruins, or works of art or religion, or the equivalent of the cells created by wasps or bees, a vast nest that had spread across the desert for five thousand years, until the Ghostkeepers had suffered the equivalent of colony collapse and vanished.

Willie had taught her tomb taxonomy. Their different sizes and shapes. How some clustered close while others were spaced in radial patterns with teasing asymmetries. Lisa had learned about the plants and animals of the desert, too: a patchwork of clades from the various worlds of the various Elder Cultures which, one after the other, had inhabited First Foot. She had studied the morphology of the desert. Alluvial fans. Bajadas. Hoodoos. Blowouts. Ventifacts. Rimrock. The difference between calcrete layers and caliche. Mesas and buttes. A mesa is wider than it is high. A butte is higher than it is wide.

Most of the tombs were small, and most had collapsed or been buried by wind-blown sand that over thousands of years had cemented into friable rock. In certain places, tombs had been built on older tombs, creating tells ten or twenty strata deep. Most were empty, but fragments of Elder Culture technology, usually sympathy stones or the mica chips that contained the entangled pairs of electrons that underpinned q-phone technology, could be found in some, and tesserae were embedded in the walls of others. No one knew if the tesserae had been created by the Ghostkeepers, or if the Ghostkeepers had excavated them from ruins left by other Elder Cultures and used them as decoration or markers for reproductive fitness. Almost all of them were inert and of only archaeological interest; those that still generated active eidolons were highly prized.

Like all tomb raiders, Lisa and Willie had eked out a living from sales of mundane finds while dreaming of discovering the kind of jackpot that would kickstart a new industry or technology and make them so rich that they would never have to work again. They sifted through the middens of abandoned hive-rat nests – the fierce little creatures dug deep and sometimes brought up artefacts. They found their way into intact chambers where eidolons might kindle from shadows and lamplight. When everything else failed, they sank shafts into the mounds of collapsed tombs. Willie disliked digging. Not just because it was hard work, although that was a consideration, but because it disturbed what he called 'the flow'.

The City of the Dead was a sargasso of history, according to him, with strange tides and currents, backwaters and eddies. Everything flowing into everything else.

If they found no intact tombs or abandoned nests, Willie preferred to dowse rather than dig. He would wander over the parched landscape with two lengths of copper wire bent into a pair of L-rods, delicately pinching the short arms between thumbs and forefingers and narrowly watching the quiver and dip of the long arms. Circling a spot when the rods began to twitch, insisting that Lisa start digging if they violently see-sawed.

Willie's dowsing had a surprisingly good hit rate – slightly better than chance, according to Lisa's Chi-squared tests – but he preferred spelunking, and so did Lisa. Finding their way into spaces untouched for thousands of years, where the psychic traces of the creatures that had built them yet remained. She remembered spiral tombs augered into the earth. She remembered labyrinths of broken stone. She remembered one huge, cool, bottle-shaped chamber lit by a shaft of sunlight from a high crevice. As Willie had climbed down the swaying rope ladder, orange fronds clumped in the splash of sunlight on the floor had suddenly broken up and scurried off in every direction, seeking the safety of shadows. A kind of colonial beetle-thing, it turned out, with symbiotic plants growing on its shells. Lisa remembered another chamber, this one long and low, where eidolons had exploded around them like bats: after they'd sold the tesserae that generated them, she and Willie had lived high on the hog for two months.

She remembered the time the truck's LEAF battery had run out of charge at the western edge of the City of the Dead, a long way from the nearest settlement, with the eroded range of mountains that marked the edge of the Badlands shimmering at the horizon. Willie had pulled his trail bike from the load bed and roared off with the battery strapped behind him. He'd said that he'd be directly back, but a day passed, and another, and there was no sign of him and Lisa couldn't pick up a phone signal. She discovered that she didn't mind being stranded. She had plenty of food, enough water to last a couple of weeks. She slept in the back of the truck's crew cab during the day and watched the starry sky at night. Dissolved into the antique silence of the desert. Looking back, she'd never been happier.

On the fourth day a hot wind out the south blew white sand from the crests of sand dunes. The sky grew milky and the sun faded to a dull smear and the horizon closed in. The truck's door seals couldn't keep out the dust and Lisa had to tie a handkerchief over her nose and mouth. Everything was covered with a fine white bloom. Her eyes itched madly.

Willie drove out of the tail end of the storm towards sunset. He'd been caught up in a business deal, he said, but it hadn't panned out. Lisa didn't bother to ask. It might have been a lead on Elder Culture ruins or a poker game, a girl or a spell in jail. In the morning they mounted the recharged LEAF battery and drove to Joe's Corner and bought water and food and went on.

Those were the days of their lives until they finally hit their jackpot. Until the Bad Trip.

Now here she was again, searching for the origin of the ghost which had driven her away from that life. Grainy and strung out from driving most of the night, watching her rear-view mirror. As soon as she'd hit the eastern edge of the City of the Dead, she'd gone off-road. Navigating by starlight along trackways constructed from ceramic plates laid by an Elder Culture that had left no other trace but these spidery networks.

The trackways had grown rougher as she moved deeper into the City of the Dead, driving deeper and deeper into the past. Her and Willie's past, and the long-gone past of the planet's previous tenants. The past that Willie had uncovered, out in the Badlands. At last, about twenty kilometres north of Joe's Corner, she'd pulled up at the edge of a salt pan, under the shelter of the knitted branches of a cluster of coral trees (they weren't really trees, but a kind of leathery blood-red giant lichen), and dozed in the pickup's cab for a few hours.

As the desert lightened around her, she scanned it for signs of vehicles and checked the sky for drones. She couldn't believe that she had managed to escape, yet here she was, and a strange calm had settled over her. She'd burned her old life and everything was new and strange again.

She ate the last orange segment and pulled out one of her smartphones, checked that she had a signal, and called Bria again. Straight to voicemail. Well, she had tried. She climbed into the pickup truck, started the engine – and the phone rang. Bria, according to the display, but Lisa let it ring for almost a minute, thinking hard, before she answered.

'Where are you?' Bria said.

'Out and about. How are you?'

'Worried. Hoping I can talk you out of doing something foolish.'

Lisa felt a prickle of apprehension. She said, 'Let me guess. Nevers has been telling tales out of school.'

'He said that you'd run off,' Bria said. 'And that you could get into serious trouble if you didn't come back right away.'

'Are you in trouble too?'

'Only the trouble I'm already in. Regarding that, he said it would help me if I could persuade you to see sense.'

'I apologise for what went down. The fire. But it wasn't anything to do with the code.'

'It was everything to do with you,' Bria said.

'It was everything to do with Adam Nevers and his Jackaroo pal,' Lisa said, and knew that she was being unreasonable. 'But yeah, I asked you for a favour and it got your business burned down. And I'm sorry for it, I really am.'

'I have insurance,' Bria said. 'And because the police are saying that the fire was caused by a rogue algorithm, the insurers will probably pay up without too much trouble. Meanwhile, fifteen people have lost their jobs. They're good coders, so they'll probably find work elsewhere, but I'll have to start over from scratch. That's okay. I can do it. But I also have to deal with Nevers. He's threatening to revoke my licence. My lawyers say that he doesn't have a case that'll stand up, but he can drag me through the courts and cause me all kinds of trouble. So if you really are sorry for everything you've done, if you really want to help, you should come back and face the music.'

'Nevers let me go,' Lisa said. 'Without a charge. After murdering Pete, by the way. If we're going to talk about losses. Not to mention confiscating and killing my hurklins. So what does he want with me now?'

'All I know is he wants you to come back to Port of Plenty,' Bria said. 'And frankly? I really think you should, before you get into more trouble.'

Lisa remembered that flat unforgiving tone of voice from the time Bria and her other friends had confronted her and, after a fierce three-hour struggle, she'd agreed to go to an AA meeting, her first. And here they were again, Bria telling her what she should do for her own good, but this time Lisa knew that she couldn't take her friend's advice.

She said, trying to explain, trying to be reasonable, 'All it is, I want to find out what happened to Willie. Whether or not it has anything to do with the Bad Trip. Is that so wrong?'

'It's grief,' Bria said. 'You aren't thinking straight.'

'If I can find what caused the Bad Trip, I can fix the ghost in my head.'

'How do you know that what you think you want isn't really what the eidolon wants?'

'I don't. But I'm going anyway.'

'You're throwing everything away.'

'If he doesn't put me in jail, Nevers will probably do his damnedest to make sure I can't work in the Elder Culture biz ever again. So I don't have a whole lot left to lose. I really hope we can sit down and sort things out when this is done. I really do. But if I don't see you again, I just want to say that I'm sorry for everything,' Lisa said, with a rising flush of shame and guilt, and rang off.

She extracted the smartphone's SIM card and broke it and tossed it out the window. It was purely a gesture. She was certain that Nevers had been listening in, that his people had a fix on her location. But fuck it, it was pretty obvious where she would be going next.

169

26· Colonel X

One day, Tony found a tightly rolled strip of plastic at the bottom of his morning cup of coffee. When he flattened it out, words began to run from right to left, black on translucent white in a neat handwritten script: *We shall meet in the forest at midnight. A servant will show you the way.* As the last word followed its predecessors over the left-hand end, the strip faintly fumed and disintegrated into fine ash.

There could be only two possibilities. Either it had been sent by someone who had news or wanted to help him, or it was the work of an enemy who wanted to lure him into an ambush. Not Opeyemi, who would like him to take the blame for everything, but someone else, someone unknown. Tony discovered that he did not much care about the risk. He was excited by the promise of action and the possibility of change. And the form of the message was intriguing. He wondered it had been sneaked into his cup by the farm's supervisor or one of the workers, or perhaps by Lancelot Askia, working as a double agent. He studied the man during that day's constitutional around the perimeter of the farm's snowy fields (he had been forbidden to walk anywhere else after the incident with the kites), but as usual his face was as tightly closed as a fist.

Sleep was impossible, of course. Tony was sitting in the dark in his room, fully dressed, thinking about ways of sneaking past Lancelot Askia and the farm's security, when, at exactly forty-five minutes before midnight, the door opened. One of the farm's hands stood outside, a tripedal servitor like a skinny black bar stool, its flat sensor plate level at waist height. The little machine

170

did not respond to any of Tony's questions as it led him to the mud room. It waited while he pulled on cold-weather gear, then it opened the outer door and led him into the night, across the fields into the pine plantation, heading due north.

The hand skated lightly over the snow, barely leaving any tracks; Tony plodded behind, picking his way by starlight. His face tingled in the cold and his blood tingled too. They crossed the far edge of the pines into the native forest, where spires clad in frosted banners reared into the black sky like rockets of the Space Age, before the Jackaroo had come with their gift of easy travel to other planets. At last, at the edge of a clearing around a frozen pond, the hand halted and a shape detached itself from the shadows between a pair of trees that stood close together.

A tall pale-skinned man drifted forward, dressed in a black jacket and black trousers, dainty black slippers that didn't quite touch the snow. An avatar, a projection.

'I'm glad you came, Mr Okoye,' he said.

'Who exactly are you?'

'Call me Colonel X. These days I work for the Special Services section of the Commons police. I'm sorry that we can't talk face to face, as they used to say. Unfortunately I have to be elsewhere. I'm entertaining an old friend. Someone I haven't seen in an age.'

Colonel X's voice was soft and clear in the stillness of the night; his English strangely accented. His eyes were dark stars in the pale mask of his face. Tony felt as if he'd fallen into an old story about a traveller losing his way in a dark forest and meeting a spirit that offered him his heart's desire in exchange for his soul.

He said, 'You could have called me. It would have avoided a cold walk.'

'Cold for you, not for me. And given the present political climate within your family, any official conversation would have been severely compromised. As would any conversation in your present residence. But we can speak candidly to each other out here, in the presence of God and no one else.'

'Why exactly are you interested in me?'

'Do I need to spell it out?'

'In the spirit of candour.'

171

'Very well. The archival genetics in the stromatolites. The interest of the Red Brigade in that archive, beginning with your encounter at what you call the Slime Planet. The kidnapping of two wizards and the slaughter of the rest, and the escape of the laminated brain you know as Aunty Jael.'

'You think she escaped?'

'I know that you do. It's a pity your family refused to believe you. It would have made things easier. But here we are anyway.'

Tony realised that Colonel X, whoever he was, must have access to the records of the family council. Perhaps one of his relatives was an agent who could not risk being compromised by openly helping him . . . In any event, it meant that it wouldn't cost him anything to talk frankly. Colonel X must know everything he had to say. He said, 'So what do you want from me?'

'You are in something of a pickle,' Colonel X said. 'I'm here, as the Jackaroo like to say, to help.'

'It was definitely the Red Brigade who claim-jumped the slime planet and was behind the raid.'

'Definitely.'

'And Aunty Jael is not all she seems.'

'She's an acquaintance of mine – a sparring partner from days gone by. Someone even older than me, and that's saying something.'

'And the wizard, Eli Tanjung, was not the traitor. She did not contact the Red Brigade. It was Aunty Jael.'

'Indeed.'

'And Aunty Jael poisoned her before she could protest her innocence.'

'Using the neurotoxin favoured by the Reds was a nice touch, wasn't it?'

'What I can't figure out is how Aunty Jael lured Eli to the generator shed.'

'Oh, that's easy,' Colonel X said. 'In addition to the neurotoxin, there were traces of a novel binary drug in Eli Tanjung's blood. Like most wizards, she had been tinkering with her consciousness. And she was also the youngest of the crew, with the lowest status. I believe that your Aunty Jael hooked her on an especially tailored neurological booster, no doubt promising that it would give little Eli an advantage over her colleagues. The usual appeal to vanity – I'm sure that a freebooter like you is familiar with the technique. Aunty Jael supplied the drug clandestinely, dose by dose, lured Eli to the generator shed with the promise of more of the good stuff, and killed her before she could protest her innocence. The neurotoxin bolstered your idea that the Red Brigade was involved, so you were happy to believe that the silly young wizard was a traitor who committed suicide to avoid interrogation.'

'At first I was, yes.'

'But then you realised that the Red Brigade must have had inside help. You realised that Aunty Jael could have used her hands to kill the police guards and your servant, and attack your family's troops. And you realised that she had made a deal with the Red Brigade, offering the stromatolites and the Ghajar eidolon in exchange for helping her escape from her bondage with your family.'

'If you know so much, why do you need me?'

'As I said, I'm otherwise occupied at present. But I would very much like to talk to Aunty Jael, and I believe that you will be able to track her down.'

'And what do I get, if I agree to help you?'

'Apart from your freedom, your honour, and your ship?'

'You can do that?'

'Your family have been too busy cleaning up the damage after the raid to get around to putting her on the market. Here.'

It was like a window opening inside his head. The familiar connection streaming in like sunlight through a window. The sense of the shape of the ship and the status of her systems. Tony and the bridle of *Abalunam's Pride* asking each other if they were all right.

'What have they done to you?' Tony said.

He was on his knees in the snow. He didn't remember falling to his knees.

'They cut off my comms. They would not tell me why,' the bridle said.

'My family were scared of what we found,' Tony said. 'They are still scared. And I am in a little trouble.'

173

'Of course you are,' the bridle said. 'How bad is it?'

'Nothing that can't be fixed.'

Tony was running a swift and superficial systems check. The ship appeared to be free of any extra layers of security or surveillance. He would need to go deeper to discover if anything had been implanted by his family, and wondered if he would be able to tell if Colonel X had inserted something . . .

And then it all went away again. He was back in the snowy forest, facing the avatar of Colonel X.

'I can give you everything you want,' Colonel X said, 'as long as you agree to help me. And since we both want to find out the same thing, the obligation is hardly onerous.'

'If you really are working for the Commons police, with all its resources, why me?'

'This particular investigation is off the books. Like you, I haven't been able to convince those who call themselves my superiors of the importance of this. So I must work with what comes to hand. If it's any comfort, you are by no means my only irregular.'

'I suppose your superiors refuse to believe that the stromatolites' archival genetics may contain a cure for sleepy sickness.'

'Oh, it was never about that,' Colonel X said airily. 'That was a story got up by your Aunty Jael. Have you been drawing lately? Scribbling?'

'You mean the pattern.'

'I mean the map. The Ghajar found something, long ago. I believe that it has something to do with the so-called mad ships and a certain wormhole route,' Colonel X said. 'As to where that leads, and what's at the end of it, I don't yet know. Something old, something powerful, something that might have destroyed the Ghajar, and may destroy us if it falls into the wrong hands. You should start with the person who pointed you towards the slime planet. The broker, Raqle Thornhilde. She may have collaborated with Aunty Jael.'

'I need some time to consider this,' Tony said.

He wanted to escape his punishment and his shaming, wanted to prove that he was right. And after the brief moments of contact with the bridle, he ached for his ship more than ever. But he also felt a prickling caution: this really did seem like one of the old stories where someone made a pact with a devil, only to find out that the bargain was deeper and more dangerous than it first appeared.

The ghostly avatar of Colonel X said, 'I'm afraid that you'll have to make your decision now. Ten minutes ago someone discovered my tampering with the security system of the farm. And four minutes after that they found that you are not in your room. They are searching the farm for you; it won't be long before they will realise that you escaped, and find the tracks you left in the snow.'

Tony knew that Colonel X could be lying to force his hand, but he also knew that he did not want to return to the farm. He said, 'All I have to do is find Aunty Jael.'

'Yes. What happens after that is up to you.'

'I want full control of my ship.'

'Of course.'

The ship's bridle was back inside his head again, and he was back inside her. She started to apologise for having been cut off; he told her to get ready to boot.

'You bet.'

Tony tore his attention away from her and looked at Colonel X. 'You won't ever touch my ship again.'

'Now she's back with her rightful owner? Of course not.'

'I am doing this for my family, not for myself.'

'Of course you are.' It was impossible to tell if the avatar was mocking him. 'Take command of your ship, Mr Okoye. Go to Dry Salvages, or wherever else you think your search should begin. We'll talk again soon.'

As the avatar began to fade out of the dark air, Tony said, 'Wait! You said that Aunty Jael was an old acquaintance of yours. Who is she really? What is her name?'

The avatar's face brightened briefly, it said two words, then popped out of existence. A moment later something shot up from where it had stood, a tiny bright spark rising past the tops of the trees and accelerating as it rose higher, vanishing amongst the fixed stars. A drone, no doubt equipped with a q-phone and a caster. The hand was moving too, marching past Tony, following the tracks he had made in the snow. It ignored him when he ordered it to stop. He wondered, watching it disappear into the dark between the trees, if it would have killed him if he had turned down Colonel X's offer.

He asked the bridle if she knew his location.

'Of course.'

'Come and get me. Right now.'

'I am already on my way, and will rendezvous with you in two hundred and thirty-two seconds. Traffic control is unhappy.'

'Ignore traffic control. Are you connected to the net?'

'Yes. That came back after the block on communicating with you was removed.'

Tony thought of sending a message to Danilo Evangalista, explaining that he was setting out to right a great wrong and would carry Danilo in his heart until he returned. But he told himself, thinking of the oubliettes beneath the Great Tower, the interrogation suite stark as an operating theatre, that there was every chance that Opeyemi would intercept any message, that it would be stupid and selfish to put his lover in harm's way. No, he thought, with a cold, lonely but not ignoble feeling, this was no time for explanations or sentiment. He must slip away into the night, and hope that finding Aunty Jael and bringing her to justice would exonerate him.

So instead of calling up his phone, he gave the bridle the password to the family's archives, saying, 'I want you to compile a file on someone called Ada Morange. Find everything you can before we boot.'

27. Joe's Corner

Apart from her recent slip and a couple of early lapses, Lisa had been clean and sober for almost six years. But the old cravings were never far away, ambushing her at odd moments, sneakily sliding in the idea, when she passed a bar or a billboard advertising liquor or saw the bottles glinting behind the sliding doors of the country store's chiller cabinet, that a cold one would hit the spot right about now. As she drove south in early morning light, striking the two-lane blacktop and blowing down it, she felt something like those cravings rise up inside her – the need to find the site of the breakout, to find what was there, what it had done to Willie and the others. Bria had asked if she'd come out here because she really wanted to, or because she was being driven by her ghost. Well, the thing was fully present now, like a shard of sun-dazzle at the corner of her sight, and Lisa was certain that it wanted to find the site as much as she did. Maybe it wanted to go home. Maybe it would slip away from her and return to the artefact which had generated it, the way that little pack of eidolons had fled from the sunrise into the tomb and their tesserae.

She slowed, passing the sign for Joe's Corner, Pop: 523, and discovered that the little crossroads town had been overrun. RVs, SUVs with big all-terrain tyres, pickup trucks and Humvees were nose to tail along its main drag, crowding the parking lots of the three motels and the flying-saucer-shaped coffee shop. She saw a polished aluminium Slipstream caravan, saw customised camper vans with elaborate paint jobs depicting galaxies, desert landscapes, a Jackaroo avatar riding a T. rex rodeo-style. An old school bus converted into a travelling restaurant; a food van serving tacos. A gaggle of Harleys cruised throatily past, ridden by women with shaven heads and leather armour, reminding Lisa of the road dogs Willie had run with back in the day.

As usual after someone hit a jackpot, tomb raiders had come a-running. It didn't matter that the find had killed the people who had dug it up. Tomb raiders believed they made their own luck, were exemplars of confirmation bias, retrospective determination and the gambler's fallacy who thought that they were invulnerable because nothing, so far, had proven that they weren't. Some believed that they possessed special talents, gifts and knowledge that those killed in breakouts or driven into irretrievable psychosis so obviously lacked; others deployed trademark rituals and methods for invoking luck and appeasing the alien dead, wore amulets, bones, and rings to ward off ancient curses, or were tattooed with signs meant to baffle spooks and defuse bad algorithms. Lisa remembered one woman who used the *I Ching* to decide where to search. Remembered another who'd always burned fake paper promissory notes, big red bills, before entering a tomb. And here they all were, hoping to cash in on someone else's bad luck, planning to head into the Badlands as soon as the geek police lifted their quarantine. No doubt some of them were already out there, trying to sneak past the patrols and drone pickets.

Lisa found a parking spot at the far end of town, walked back. Ten-thirty in the morning, and there was a pool party at the Westward Ho! Beer coolers and a barbecue and a sound system pumping out A-pop. She didn't recognise anyone. She'd been away a good long while.

She was planning to have a serious conversation with Willie's old friend, the assayer Calvin Quinlan. There had always been a sour atmosphere between her and Calvin. It ran deeper than professional rivalry, although he always made it plain that he resented Lisa taking on the business of analysing Willie's finds. Maybe it was because Calvin was a boozehound who kept a bottle in his desk drawer and had recognised the same weakness in Lisa long before it had surfaced. Despite this old enmity, she figured that he wouldn't find it easy to blow her off if she turned up unannounced, but discovered that his storefront was shuttered and dark and there was yellow police tape across the door. She walked straight past, scared that someone could be watching the place, and turned down a sandy alley and turned again, following a track behind the commercial strip as she tried to work out what to do next.

There was a stretch of elbow bush at the edge of the parking lot behind the flat-roofed single-storey Sheriff's Office building. And in the lot, under the microwave mast, were three white Toyota Land Cruisers with Outland Archaeological Services in blue lettering on their doors, and a burned-out pickup truck squatting on wheel rims. A Holden Colorado, paint scorched from its cab, all glass gone, the door on the passenger side hanging loose, displaying the charred interior. Lisa stopped and stared. It was Willie's truck, had to be, but there was something missing, something she wasn't seeing . . .

A door opened in the back of the building, someone stepped out, and Lisa started walking. A dry clicking followed her down the length of the elbow-bush hedge as its long spines rotated towards her. She followed an alley that led back to the main strip, thinking about the truck, and right across the street was Don's Joint, the bar where she and Willie used to hang out back in the day, dancing to old tunes on the jukebox, talking till three in the morning with other tomb raiders, the scores they'd made, the scores they were going to make . . .

It was dark and cool inside, mostly empty. Lisa stepped hard on the impulse that had brought her there, ordered a Diet Coke, and fell in with Jayla and Shelley Griffith-Fontcuberta, a couple of good old girls she'd known slightly back in the day. Jayla was as intense and impatient as ever, jiggling in her chair, jabbing a finger when she wanted to make a point; Shelley was about fifty pounds heavier than when Lisa had last seen her, her gorgeous waves of hair dyed blood red. They had heard about Willie, of course, and commiserated with Lisa on her loss.

'The cops brought in the vehicles from the site two days ago,' Jayla said.

179

'Willie's truck had been set on fire,' Shelley said. 'It broke my heart to see it.'

Lisa nodded. She didn't trust herself to speak.

'It's beyond fucked up is what it is,' Jayla said.

'There has been a serious disturbance,' Shelley said.

'She felt it coming,' Jayla said, daring Lisa to contradict her.

'Even those without the Gift could feel it coming,' Shelley said.

She was a self-proclaimed Sensitive who believed that a web of quantum entanglement linked the City of the Dead and all the other Elder Cultures sites on First Foot, and that she could sense changes in its traffic of information. Why not? As far as Elder Culture tech was concerned, no one had yet found the limits of the possible.

Shelley said that eidolons were spooked everywhere in the City of the Dead. She said that someone had seen a vast cloud of them pouring out of a vent, rising high into the sky and heading south. She said there had been heat lightning and ripples of light like auroras, tombs collapsing, sightings of strange creatures that dissolved into thin air when approached, cries and wild music on radio bands, packs of animals and biochines fleeing as if from a forest fire. People prospecting around the spaceship crash site north of Joe's Corner had been visited by ghosts at night: tall and slender and pale, stooping amongst vehicles and tents. Others had thrown fits or had seen visions of a celestial city rising into the sky.

'So,' Lisa said, 'are you planning to go out there, find out what's causing this shit?'

'We might have one or two ideas about that,' Jayla said. 'The geek police have thrown up a big-ass quarantine zone. We've located a bunch of hotspots in there.'

'I dowsed the map,' Shelley said.

Lisa told them that she was looking for someone who might know how to find a way inside the quarantine zone; they said that they'd be happy to partner up with her, a straight three-way split on anything they found. Hoping, no doubt, that either Lisa knew exactly where she wanted to go, or that she would act as a human dowsing rod and lead them directly to the good stuff.

'We can get in right now, no problem,' Jayla said. 'The zone's too big to police properly. And there are plenty of blind spots. Draws, dry washes, places that fuck up radio transmissions . . . You want in, we can find a way.'

'But you'd better make up your mind quick,' Jayla said. 'We aren't going to hang around town much longer.'

'It's getting pretty heavy here,' Shelley said. 'The cops are cracking down.'

'They came in here last night,' Jayla said. 'Arrested this guy who'd been mouthing off that he knew where the breakout site is.'

Lisa said, 'Did he?'

Jayla said, 'Did he know? No, it was just drunk talk.'

'They arrested a good number of people,' Shelley said. 'There's talk they're planning to arrest more.'

Lisa asked about Calvin Quinlan: did they know why his store was closed?

Jayla shrugged. 'I expect he was caught handling hot shit. Wouldn't be the first time that's come back to bite old Calvin.'

Lisa hardly heard her. Someone had come through the door, a big guy in biker gear. Someone she recognised. And, with a click, she realised what had been missing from Willie's burned-out truck.

28. Rumours And Ghosts

The trip from Skadi to Dry Salvages took twenty-three days and six transits. Three involved passing through systems with inhabited planets, but although he was flying what was technically a stolen ship, Tony was not challenged by police or traffic control. There was no watch notice posted, no sign of pursuit. He doubted that his family, especially Opeyemi, had decided to let him go, suspected that Colonel X had finessed his free passage. Another debt to someone he knew nothing about, except that the man (if he was a man) had the power to reach across the galaxy and get deep inside the Okoye family's security. And he had a serious interest in Aunty Jael, who was, he claimed, the laminated remains of his old 'sparring partner' Ada Morange.

The ship's bridle had been able to ransack every corner of the family's database during the two hundred and thirty-two seconds it had taken her to travel between the space field and the forest, but the information she had gleaned about the dead woman was disappointingly thin. Ada Morange, born sometime in the twentieth century, had been a biotech wizard who had pioneered the exploitation and re-engineering of Elder Culture artefacts, discovering how to manipulate the growth of construction coral, mapping eidolon activity in human brains, and acquiring and learning how to control the first Ghajar ships. She'd moved to the New Frontier after that, where she had been prominent in the first attempts to explore the wormhole network and the worlds it linked, and had developed a considerable interest in the so-called mad ships.

This last fact had not come from the family's database, but from the Commons police station on Skadi. When Tony asked her how she had managed to hack police security, the bridle said that she did not know.

'It came to me that I could do it, so I did. Did I do something wrong? Are you unhappy with my initiative?'

'I'm startled.'

Tony was wondering if Colonel X had given the bridle some kind of access protocol, and was also wondering what else the man might have done, such as introducing spyware or overrides.

'It surprised me, too,' the bridle said.

She had also discovered that Ada Morange had been active until the rise of the First Empire, when she would have been around a hundred and thirty years old, but after that she had disappeared from view. Either she had died, or had managed to purge every trace of her life from public records, or those records had been destroyed or corrupted. There was certainly no mention of her name in the bill of purchase for the laminated brain that Tony's family had owned for the past fifty years.

'The people who sold her to your family called her Jael,' the bridle told Tony. 'Your grandmother added the honorific. Much of the work she did for her previous owners involved manipulating eidolons and tweaking crop species and bioforms, an odd combination consistent with Ada Morange's interests, but I was unable to find any other link. Colonel X must know something I do not.'

'Or he wants me to check out a hunch,' Tony said.

'A hunch?'

'An evidence-free guess. If he has been searching for this Ada Morange for a long time, he will have exhausted all of the best leads. By now he will be chasing rumours and ghosts.'

'Will we be in trouble if it turns out that Aunty Jael is not Ada Morange?'

'Even if she was once Ada Morange, she is not Ada Morange now. She is a laminated brain with only a residual resemblance to her original. Besides, we were not asked to find out who she was, but where she is. And I have my own reasons for tracking her down.'

Colonel X wanted to find Aunty Jael because he believed that she had once been the long-dead biotech wizard with whom he had unfinished business. But Tony wanted to find her because she had tricked him, because her escape had caused his downfall and disgrace, and because he believed that she had found something in the Ghajar algorithm that the wizards had overlooked. She had sold that knowledge to her friends in the Red Brigade, and she had also given them the two missing wizards. Not because of what the wizards knew, but because of what the Ghajar eidolon had done to their heads.

Because of what it had done to his head.

He wanted her to pay for what she had done. Her betrayal; his disgrace. But before he turned her over to Colonel X and the Commons police, he planned to find out what she had discovered. He would offer it to his family, and if they spurned it and refused to forgive him, it would provide the foundation for his own fortune, his own dynasty of freebooters.

Tony shared this and other fantasies with the bridle. She indulged him because that was how she had been made. She listened to him talk about Danilo, too, and the brutal end of their relationship. It had been a point of pride, a discipline, to conceal his emotions from Opeyemi and the rest of his family, but he could grieve openly now. Wallow in self-pity, and curse himself all over again for having failed his lover.

One day, on the way to the last mirror pair, the bridle told him that there was a problem.

Tony thought she meant the upcoming transit, but no: *Abalunam's Pride* was decelerating exactly as planned through the outer edge of a small wilderness, and would make her final transit in a little under four hours. Everything was nominal.

'What is it?' he said.

'There is someone else aboard,' the bridle said.

Tony immediately thought of the eidolon. It had been quiet all this time – he had not been troubled by strange dreams, had not once absent-mindedly sketched that diagram – but he supposed that it might know that they were closing in on their destination.

He said, 'Has it been talking to you? Asking questions? Demanding information?'

'It has been talking to the ship.'

184

'The actual ship? Its mind? What have they been talking about?'

'The great highways. Deep time. Other things I do not understand.'

Tony said, 'Can you talk to them? To this intruder, to the ship?'

'I have always been able to talk to the ship's mind,' the bridle said. 'But this is different.'

'What do you mean?'

'Another part of the ship is awake. One I did not know about until now.'

She could not explain how this newly wakened part of the ship was different to the part with which she was linked, and was unable to give Tony any specific details about the snatches of conversation she had overheard. He thought of the travellers' tales about ships which had rebelled against the smart apes who'd press-ganged them into service for trivial ape business. Ships which murdered their crews and passengers and lit out for parts unknown, or enslaved their human pilots, using them as puppets for their own fell purposes. He told the bridle to find a way to open up a line of communication and ran his own checks on the ship's systems, but failed to find any irregularities.

By now, the mouth to the last mirror pair was dead ahead. Tony slipped into the ship's navigational systems and gave the transit his complete attention.

It was entirely uneventful. *Abalunam's Pride* emerged into the light of a M0 red dwarf star and drove on towards the desert world at the inner edge of its habitable zone. The ship might be haunted by the eidolon, but right now Tony was still in control. Riding the rails of his determination towards Dry Salvages and Raqle Thornhilde.

29. Road Dogs

'You're a long way from home, Bear.'

'We ride where we want to ride, Lize. You know that.'

'Where are the rest of the dogs? Or are you riding alone?'

'Come to that, you're a long way from home too.'

'I think you know why I'm here, Bear.'

They were talking by the dumpsters in back of the bar. Bear – his birth name was Joshua Davis, but after he'd come up and out no one but the police had ever called him that – was a big guy dressed in a denim vest, filthy jeans, motorcycle boots. Hair greased back and matted with road dust; glasses with black plastic frames; a necklace of hive-rat soldier teeth hung on his bare chest; arms wrapped in full-sleeve tats.

He said, with an unconvincing shrug, 'There are a bunch of tomb raiders out here chasing this jackpot. Thought I'd check it out.'

He'd never been a good liar.

Lisa said, 'You found Willie, didn't you?'

Bear's mild blue eyes widened behind the thick lenses of his glasses. 'Where did you get that idea?'

'I saw his truck,' Lisa said. 'In the parking lot of the sheriff's office, where it was towed. His trail bike wasn't in the load bed. How I see it, he escaped the breakout somehow, and took off on that bike. And then he called on his friends for help. So where is he?'

Bear met her gaze, looked away.

Lisa said, 'It's okay, Bear. It's me. His old lady.'

'Not exactly his old lady any more.'

'Not exactly not, either. We split up, yeah, but we never divorced. Remember the last time we were all together, out at my place? Willie's fortieth? Did it look like I didn't care for him?'

Bear shrugged again.

'I want to help him, Bear. Any way I can.' She really did. She could feel the weight of it settling on her. She said, 'At least tell me that's he's alive.'

After a moment, Bear nodded.

Lisa could have hugged the sweet dumb old road dog. 'Is he okay? Is he hurt?'

Bear's Adam's apple bobbed. 'It's fucked, Lize.'

A chill gripped Lisa's heart. 'Oh, Bear. How bad is it?'

'Why I came into town, it was for supplies from the pharmacy. But honestly? I don't think they'll do much good.'

'You have to let me see him.'

She watched Bear think about that. At last he said, 'I gotta make a phone call first.'

They headed into the City of the Dead on Bear's hog. Lisa rode pillion, feet on the pegs, the small of her back against the chrome rest. The familiar throaty burble and rush of hot wind, the tang of burned gasoline – the road dogs brewed their own in anaerobic stills, from wood chips and tweaked algae. It was like the old times when Willie and his dogs would stop by the homestead and hang out for a day or two.

After the Bad Trip, Willie had spent a couple of years riding the roads with them. To get his head straight, he'd said, but it had seemed to Lisa that his exploits with the road dogs had been howls against the void. They were lost boys, riding out into the alien wilderness and the ruins of millennia of alien colonisation in search of something they probably couldn't even begin to define. Outriders of a Mad Max future in which civilisation had been destroyed by imperfectly assimilated alien wonders, and deracinated tribes haunted by powerful eidolons wandered the Earth and the fifteen gift worlds. She'd been pleased when Willie had sold his Harley to settle that gambling debt, and had gone back to full-time tomb raiding. She had thought that it was a kind of progress. But he had never quite cut his connection with the road dogs, and she was grateful for that now, riding behind Bear as his low-slung hog jolted down sandy tracks that twisted through a maze of mounds and half-buried tombs.

They rode a long way. Heading west and north through the City of the Dead, as far as Lisa could estimate, towards the range of hills that was the gateway to the Badlands. She entertained all kinds of scenarios about the breakout, and how Willie had escaped. She wanted to believe that he was basically okay, wanted to believe that she could do something to save him, but she kept coming back to the way Bear had looked when he'd told her that no one could help Willie now. The soft sadness of his gaze. The knowledge of finality that it contained.

Bare rounded hills slashed by arroyos and draws resolved out of the heat haze. Their slopes glowed in the afternoon light and the shadows between them were dark and deep. A trackless maze where Ghostkeepers had cut tombs into sandstone laid down by an ancient sea, built them into the overhangs of eroded ledges.

At last Bear swung the Harley into a slot canyon pinched between cliffs banded by pink and yellow layers of sandstone and mudstone. The beat of the exhaust echoed off the high close walls and then they leaned into a sharp turn and the canyon suddenly opened out into a narrow valley. Grey scrub and a scattering of mounds, a row of Boxbuilder ruins on a high shoulder of stone, glittering against the cloudless sky, and off to the right a thin thread of smoke rising against a red cliff.

Lisa suddenly had a funny itch in her head, like a scratch in the cornea of her eye or an aching tooth that the tongue keeps returning to.

The camp fire was burning just outside an overhang at the base of the cliff. As she and Bear puttered in, threading between big boulders, Lisa saw bikes parked in the overhang's shade and her heart overturned when she spotted Willie's stud-tyred trail bike amongst the Harleys. And now men were standing up, big and muscled in leather and denim. Shaved heads, beards, tats. Wolfman Dave. Little Mike. Mouse. And Sonny Singer, unfolding from the shelf of stone where he'd been sitting, strutting over as Lisa swung off Bear's bike.

Sonny addressed Bear first, punching him hard on the shoulder, asking him if he remembered what he'd been told.

'Come on,' Bear said uneasily. 'When I phoned you said I should bring her in.'

'I also said you shouldn't have let yourself get compromised.'

'This is Willie's old lady, dude. I don't see how she compromises anything.'

Sonny ignored that. A black and white doo-rag was knotted around his shaven skull; his eyes were masked by mirrorshades. 'I trusted you to do the right thing, Bear. Before you left, what did I tell you?'

'You said don't talk to no one. Get the painkillers and shit and come straight back. But this —'

Sonny punched him again. 'Goddamn, Bear. You had just the one job.'

Lisa stepped up. 'I came to see my husband, Sonny. Where are you keeping him?'

Sonny Singer had always intimidated her. He'd been a dentist before he'd come up and out, was the most intelligent and least predictable of the road dogs, his laid-back Southern charm masking an indelible meanness. He never forgot a slight, talked down to everyone, especially people he suspected might be brighter than he was, and knew exactly when and how to twist the knife of his scorn.

He looked at Lisa and said, 'You know who Willie called when he was in trouble? Here's a clue: it wasn't you.'

'But here I am.' The itch was stronger now, and it had a direction. 'I know you've been trying to do right by him, and I want to help any way I can.'

'Exactly what did you tell her, Bear?' Sonny said.

'She's his old lady,' Bear said again.

'Maybe she was once,' Sonny said.

'We still have something in common. That's why I know he's in there,' Lisa said, pointing to one end of the overhang.

It wasn't exactly as if she'd suddenly acquired X-ray vision, could see through dirt and rock to where Willie lay, but like a compass needle quivering north she knew with absolute conviction his position relative to hers.

'He's hurt bad,' Sonny said. 'And he's sleeping. Maybe you can see him when he wakes. If he wants to see you.'

'He's awake now. And he knows I'm here,' Lisa said, because she could feel that too. Or maybe her ghost could: it was standing at her shoulder, so close that if it had been human she would have felt its breath on the back of her neck. She had to resist the urge to turn around, try to glimpse the unglimpsable.

She said, 'If you men don't believe me, maybe one of you could go check.'

Staring at her, Sonny said, 'Someone take a look,' and Mouse, a white scar Lisa didn't remember dinting his unshaven chin, more chains than ever looped across the front and back of his leather jacket, jangled off.

The men around Lisa relaxed, as if something had been resolved. They started asking questions, how was she, was she still living on the homestead with those critters, so forth. As if this was no more than a social call. She asked them if this was where they'd found Willie.

'More or less,' Sonny said.

'How badly is he hurt? What happened to him?'

'You can't tell?'

Lisa knocked that one right back at Sonny, saying, 'You didn't think to take him to hospital?'

'There isn't anything a hospital can do.'

'Maybe that's something a hospital should decide.'

'We took medical advice,' Sonny said.

'And there's help on the way,' Wolfman Dave said.

'What kind of help?' Lisa said.

'Stick around and you'll see,' Sonny said.

'This is where he wants to be, Lize,' Little Mike said. 'We've made him as comfortable as we can, in the circumstances.'

He took a swig from a half-empty bottle of Jack Daniel's and held it out to her. She refused as nicely as she could. 'How about giving a lady a long drink of cold water? I feel like I've swallowed a couple of pounds of dust riding here.'

Wolfman Dave fetched a bottle of spring water. Lisa was chugging it down when Mouse came jangling back, with the disconcerted, distracted look of a man trying to puzzle out a magic trick.

'Willie knew she was here before I told him,' he told Sonny. 'Says she shouldn't have come, but now she's here he needs to talk to her.'

The road dogs exchanged glances.

'Why don't you take me in to see him?' Lisa said.

The overhang narrowed to a descending slot, the entrance to a chamber lit by a blade of sunlight slanting through a slit in the high ceiling. A scattering of tesserae glimmered on the far wall; Lisa could feel the presence of eidolons, like a flitter of bats in the corner of her eye.

'Over here,' Mouse said, and led her across the sandy floor to an alcove on the far side. A woman rose from a canvas chair as they approached.

'Ms Dawes? I am Isabelle Linder. I am so pleased to meet you,' she said, and held out a hand.

Lisa hardly noticed. She was staring at the thin figure lying on a kind of shelf or fold of rock. It was Willie. It wasn't.

He was bare-chested, a mylar blanket folded to his waist, his head pillowed on a sweat-stained kitbag. His cheeks were hollow, his eyes sunken in bruised sockets. His ribs articulated under his skin with each breath. And there were needles studded in his grey crew cut and his forehead, needles of black glass, different lengths, forming a kind of crown. They rattled when he turned his head to look at Lisa.

'I knew you were coming,' he said. 'I could feel it.'

'Our ghosts,' Lisa said.

'Yeah. Our ghosts.'

She could see, in the same unseeing way she'd been able to tell where he lay, a roil of activity in his body. Nodes under places where the needles stuck him, and a kind of traffic seething through the blood vessels under his skin. His face shone like a foggy mask of milky silver, like the swirl of currents around the anomaly in the Ghajar narrative code.

191

Lisa knelt and took his hand. She could feel the bones inside its loose hot skin.

He said, 'I have some new ghosts now.'

His smile was all teeth.

'Oh, Willie.'

The road dogs and the woman were standing behind her; she briefly wondered at the strange tableau they must make. Like one of those chintzily pious religious paintings. The curve of stone over Willie's makeshift bed was marked with drawings in black Sharpie. Each the same. Lines radiating out from a central point, each marked with different patterns of cross-hatching. She supposed it was some kind of representation of the needles that pierced him. A notebook folded open and tucked between the kitbag and stone showed part of a similar sketch.

Willie said, 'It doesn't hurt. It did at first. But not now.'

'What is it? What happened?'

'I believe that he was infected with a variety of nanotechnology,' Isabelle Linder said. 'As far as I can tell, it is not contagious.'

'It's all through me like bad cancer,' Willie said. 'I tried to cut it out. It hurt like hell and it fucking grew back.'

Lisa turned to look at the others. 'And you thought the best thing for him would be to stick him in this . . . cave?' She couldn't say *tomb*. 'He needs to get to a hospital. Right now.'

'We will do our best to help him,' Isabelle Linder said.

'Are you a doctor?'

'I work for Outland Archaeological Services.'

'I thought you were all dead.'

'My colleagues are dead. Fortunately, I was not there when the breakout happened.'

'Good for you. How do you know what's best for my husband?'

'I have consulted with experts.'

'And why aren't they here?'

'They are on Terminus. But they have been advising me via q-phone. And help is coming.'

Willie squeezed Lisa's hand with surprising strength. He said, 'Ada Morange is sending a ship. All I have to do is hang on until it arrives.'

192

'I can go get help right now.'

'Stay a while,' Willie said. 'Let me tell you how I fucked up.'

He told the story with something of the jaunty self-deprecation of old. Explaining that for the past two years he'd been spending a lot of the time in the hills at the edge of the City of the Dead, where tombs were scattered and hard to find, and there were many dead spots where GPS and phone signals vanished. He'd become obsessed with the place, he said, and at last he'd found somewhere that sang out to him. Ground radar showed the faint trace of a shaft; his instincts told him that there was something useful down there.

'Your instincts, or the ghost?' Lisa said.

'Maybe fifty-fifty. It had become hard to tell where it ended and I began.'

He had spent two weeks excavating rubble. Digging through compacted layers of sand and stone. Dragging out big rocks with a winch. Eventually he uncovered the beginning of a Ghostkeeper shaft, blocked a couple of metres inside by a rockfall.

'But I found something there. A handful of tesserae. They shone like shards of moonlight. Earth's Moon, not our crappy little lopsided flying pebble,' Willie said, and went off at a tangent about different kinds of lunar light and then briefly fell asleep. Mouse bathed his head with a wet cloth and he woke again, slowly focusing on Mouse and Lisa and the others like an astronomer scrying distant worlds. 'What was I talking about?'

'Tesserae that looked like moonlight,' Lisa said. 'They contained Ghajar narrative code, didn't they?'

'You know about that.'

'Your girlfriend gave me the one you asked her to look after.'

'Is she here?'

'Brittany? No.'

'Good. Don't let her know how I ended up, Lize. Tell a few lies. I know some good ones if you come up short.'

'I'll do my best,' Lisa said, speaking around a hard ache in her throat.

Willie explained that his old friend Calvin Quinlan hadn't been able to make head or tail of the tesserae, so he'd had one of

193

them analysed in the Alien Market. And that had attracted the attention of Ada Morange. Her people were on the lookout for Ghajar code; he was pretty sure that Carol Schleifer had told them about his find after he'd paid her to mirror the stuff. The deal had been clinched when they'd seen the drawings he'd been making. Turned out they were identical to a diagram that a Ghajar eidolon had put into the head of the little sister of the guy who had found the first operational spaceships. A map of pulsars that Ada Morange believed might lead to the Ghajar home world or some other equally momentous discovery.

'I made a deal with her people,' Willie said, sounding briefly like his old self. 'A pretty good deal, if I say so myself. They were so excited they didn't care what it cost. It was like taking candy from a baby who happens to own a candy factory. And frankly they got me cheap, considering . . . I should have asked for more, for all the good it would have done me. So anyway, we went out and started digging. We found a chamber tomb, and that's when things sort of went sideways.'

He'd glimpsed some kind of skeleton on the floor, and then eidolons had exploded around him and the Outland crew. The crew had started attacking each other; he'd fled. When he woke, he was in his truck, his nose crusted with blood, bruises on his chest, the windshield cracked. He'd crashed into a stand of iron trees half a dozen kilometres from the site, but had no memory of it. He believed that he'd suffered the same kind of fugue that had seized him and Lisa during the Bad Trip.

He drove back to the excavation site, saw several bodies lying all bloody outside the shaft and realised there'd been a breakout, and freaked out again.

'I thought that the police would think I murdered those people. So I unloaded the trail bike, put together some supplies, and set fire to the truck to cover up my disappearance. Crazy, I know, but I was sort of delirious by then.'

He had ridden until he had stumbled on this tomb, drawn there, he said, by some instinct not his. He slept outside on bare ground under the stars and woke up at first light, feverish and hurting. Needles were beginning to grow through his skin. Trying to cut one out had caused terrible pain. He couldn't go any further, knew he was in a bad way, and had used his satellite phone to ask the road dogs for help.

He believed that the crash site in the City of the Dead, the Bad Trip and his jackpot were all linked. 'The ship was damaged. It fell out of orbit and crashed. One of the crew escaped. Or maybe it was the only crew . . . Anyway, it got away, in some kind of lifeboat. It was hurt. It hid in that Ghostkeeper tomb, and repurposed the tesserae it found there. I think it put some kind of log or diary in them. Some kind of information.'

'What kind of information?'

Willie touched the scribbles on the rock beside him. 'It's out there. I can feel it tugging at me.'

'Where they came from?'

'That would be something, wouldn't it?'

Lisa started to tell Willie about the flow of Ghajar narrative code, the nodes she'd seen that Bria hadn't. He nodded out for a minute or so, woke and focused on her.

Saying, 'We had some good times, didn't we?'

'The best,' Lisa said.

They talked about the old times. Willie said that when he was fixed up he wanted to see some of the other worlds. Said that Ada Morange owed him that.

'You can come with me, Lize. You deserve it.'

'That's a fine idea,' she said, and held his hand until he passed into sleep again.

30. Dry Salvages

Tony touched down outside Dry Salvages's only city, Freedonia, in the middle of the long afternoon of the planet's two-thousand-hour day, and rode a taxi into town. They had ceramic-shell ground vehicles here, propelled by engines that burned alcohol refined from sugar cane, and piloted by actual human beings. This one was red with a chequerboard stripe around its waist, owned by a garrulous middle-aged woman with a lot of curly black hair who drove with casual authority along the buzzing six-lane highway, trying to find out where Tony had been, why he was here and where he was going, offering to introduce him to the kind of good honest trader who was impossible to find in Freedonia without local knowledge. She laughed at Tony's dismay when she swerved around a truck that cut in front of them. 'You space jockeys are all the same. You ride in alien space-cans, zip through wormholes from star to star, but a little light freeway traffic makes you shit your underwear.'

It was actually the prospect of confronting Raqle Thornhilde that was making Tony nervous. Fantasies of revenge were one thing; the reality was something else. He had spent a fair amount of his freebooter career on Dry Salvages, in Freedonia, but everything familiar seemed strange; the gigantic spires reared up ahead like the fangs of some planet-eating beast.

They were between one and a half and two kilometres high, the spires. Crooked and tapering and glossy black, woven from billions of strands of fullerene, a carbon allotrope harder than diamond. Their adamantine foundations went down half a kilometre and the land around them had eroded over the tens of thousands of years since they had been built, leaving them standing on a mesa elevated above the desert plain. Like all such spires, every square centimetre of their surfaces was covered in intricate carvings whose meaning and purpose were as yet unknown. Some believed that they were algorithms encoding the essence of the Elder Culture that had constructed them; others that they were vast libraries containing secret knowledge about the relationship between the Spirebuilders and the Jackaroo, or the entire history of intelligent life in the universe, or instructions that when deciphered would allow humanity to uplift itself into some higher state of being.

The spires that stood in the centre of the vast desert of Dry Salvages's southern continent were the largest known, surrounded by the detritus of Elder Cultures that had come to study, worship or rewrite their texts. This, and the small wilderness of mirrors that orbited Dry Salvages's star and gave access to a mostly unexplored portion of the wormhole network, had attracted freebooters, tomb raiders, scholars, wizards, pirates and hopeful dreamers from every part of the Commons and the fringe worlds. Artefacts and clandestine goods were traded in Freedonia's libertarian economy; brokers bought and sold information about new worlds and unexplored Elder Culture ruins. This was where Raqle Thornhilde had forged a contract with Tony and a crew of wizards, sending them out to track down the rumour of ancient stromatolites left by the Old Old Ones on a remote slime planet. And now he had returned to confront the wily old broker, to ask her who had told her about the slime planet, and to find out what she knew about the Red Brigade, Aunty Jael, and Ada Morange.

The freeway switchbacked through a steep fell field of tumbled rocks to the top of the mesa and the entrance of the great cavern that, carved into one of the spires, housed the city of Freedonia and sheltered it from the extremes of temperature during the long days and nights. The city's low-rise grid spread across the cavern's flat floor. One- and two-storey flat-roofed buildings, open-air shopping malls and food markets, a golf course with swards of artificial grass. Bubble cars and trikes and shoals of cyclists swarming along wide boulevards under illuminated hoardings advertising perfume and clothes, drink and drugs. All this encompassed by black walls, scaffolded at their bases with the platforms where scholars and tourists inspected the spire-builder carvings, that curved up to the dome of the cavern's roof and its fixed constellations of chandelier blimps and fierce stars of piped sunlight. It was like inhabiting the belly of a giant ship.

Tony spent most of his first day in the city recruiting a pair of bodyguards, a taciturn father-and-son team, renting two adjoining rooms in a motel they recommended, and hiring a little runabout. He dearly missed Junot Johnson, and his unflustered ability to sort out mundane matters. The next day he began the rounds of the bars, tearooms and cafés where freebooters and traders hung out. The routine was much the same in every place he visited. With one of the bodyguards stationed outside and the other keeping watch inside he would nurse a glass of tea or cup of coffee and fall into idle conversation with the other customers, working around to the prize that had been hijacked by the Red Brigade. They had murdered a bunch of wizards, he said, not needing to fake his outrage, and stolen valuable stromatolites recovered from a slime planet. Right now he was trying recoup his losses by selling some algorithms, unusual Ghajar stuff, that had been ripped from those stromatolites. Anyone who was interested in that kind of thing should come and see him.

He did not want to approach Raqle Thornhilde directly. It would imply weakness on his part. An admission that, despite the raid on his family's home and the hit to their reputation, it was their fault that they had defaulted on the contract. And besides, although he would have loved to storm her home and put her directly to the question, the broker had powerful connections in the city and was protected by layers of robust security.

The first time Tony had met her, he had been summoned to her house, a rambling sugar-white confection in the exclusive district at the inner end of Freedonia, and had been subjected to intrusive security scans and an actual body search before being escorted by two burly men, alike as identical twins, to a tiled inner courtyard where water pulsed in a little fountain and birds chirped in gilded cages set amongst hanging ferns. He had sat there for more than half an hour before Raqle Thornhilde finally appeared, accompanied by a weircat and two men identical to Tony's escorts: the same burly build, the same scowl, the same beady gaze under a thick monobrow, the same cropped black hair. They were rumoured to be clones of Raqle Thornhilde's dead son. Why not? Many things forbidden elsewhere were legal in Freedonia.

The broker gave no excuse or explanation for the delay, which was clearly meant to underscore the point that this meeting was entirely on her terms. One of her escorts helped her lower herself onto a day bed; the other poured tea into silver-rimmed glasses while she studied Tony with a direct gaze that seemed to X-ray his soul.

'You'll like this,' she told Tony, as she took one of the glasses. 'A single-estate blend I import from Wellington for my own use.'

Her peremptory manner was not so much arrogance as indifference to any opinion that contradicted her tastes and decisions. Her bulk was draped in a scarlet and gold kaftan; her jowly face was powdered white, lips painted red. The weircat sprawled at her feet, long legs folded under its wasp-waisted body, its tiny head aimed at Tony, its red eyes glittering. When its mouth dilated in a kind of yawn, it displayed a rim of crooked black thorns.

After a brief exchange of pleasantries the broker explained that she had a lead on a pre-empire survey report about ancient stromatolites, was looking for someone who could take a crew of wizards to check it out, and believed that he was the person for the job.

'To be frank, I didn't invite you here because I was impressed by your experience, or your ship. It's because your family owns a laminated brain that could be of great help if the wizards actually find some algorithms. Are you still interested?'

Tony, scenting the possibility of a big score, admitted that he might be. Raqle Thornhilde introduced him to Fred Firat, the leader of the crew of wizards she had already recruited; over a dinner of imported oysters and roast beef, the wizard expounded on the expertise of his crew and the potential importance of the find with a fiery passion that was only slightly less impressive when he repeated the performance for the benefit of Ayo and Aunty Jael over a q-phone link. Aunty Jael confirmed that the report was very promising and Ayo shared Tony's enthusiasm, but there was a nerve-racking wait while she sought the approval of the family council. She called Tony early the next morning, told him that she had won the vote at the council meeting and the deal with Raqle Thornhilde and Fred Firat was on. Standing on the balcony of his motel room, still drunk from the night before, the guy he'd picked up in a bar snoring on the bed, Tony had believed that he had passed some kind of audition. That he had finally proven his worth to his family and was about to embark on the first of many fabulous adventures. He had been so stupidly happy.

He knew now that the adventure on the slime planet had been part of Aunty Jael's escape plan, and he wanted to discover if Raqle Thornhilde had been a willing collaborator. If she was, she might know where Aunty Jael, aka Ada Morange, and the Red Brigade had gone, and how to contact them. If she wasn't, she might help him track down the people who had cheated her out of her share of the find.

Innocent or guilty, she would know why he had returned to Freedonia, and suspect that his talk about selling Ghajar algorithms was bait for some kind of trap. But he was certain that she would not be able to resist checking it out. If she was innocent, she'd arrange a meeting and bluster at first, accuse him of cheating her and dodging his contractual obligations, but once they got past that Tony believed that she would be willing to negotiate. But if she had been collaborating with the Red Brigade and Aunty Jael, she would come at him some other way, and he would have to hope that the two bodyguards could protect him. And while she was checking him out and planning her move, he could try to find out if anyone knew why the Red Brigade wanted those stromatolites, and the copies of the Ghajar eidolon.

Mostly, he heard only the same old rumours. The Red Brigade had found the frozen body of Emperor Truman Johnson, and had laminated his brain. Their philosopher queen, Mina Saba, had cloned herself and the clones were riding a hundred ships in a hundred different directions, looking for the Jackaroo's home world. Or she'd already found that world, and ancient secrets she'd uncovered there had enabled her to transcend the limits of the human mind. And there were the usual stories about agents from the Red Brigade spreading sleepy sickness, contaminating water supplies with alien drugs or genetically engineered gut bacteria, launching cube sats that broadcast mind rays . . . The same old same old.

He did hear one interesting tidbit in a small café with people playing backgammon at a couple of tables, under the husks of big silvery bugs hung from a mirrored ceiling. It seemed that a few weeks ago the Red Brigade had raided a police outpost at a small, recently discovered sargasso of Ghajar ships. According to the freebooter who told Tony the story, it contained a number of mad ships, and the police had been making arrangements to transport them to one of the collection sites in the Commons. The sole survivor of the raid claimed to have been interrogated by Mina Saba herself, said that the Red Brigade had made off with a mad ship caged in an automated U-class hauler.

Tony thought of his brother, commanding a similar lonely outpost; thought of Ada Morange's interest in mad ships. He asked if anyone knew what the Red Brigade wanted with their prize.

'Nothing good, you can be sure of that,' the freebooter, a shrewd sensible grey-haired woman, said. 'The Commons police have been rounding up mad ships ever since that terrorist gang, the ones claiming to be the true heirs of the Second Empire, tried to use one to drive an entire city crazy. I was there, one time. On Takama-ga-hara? You can still see the impact crater. Maybe you know the official story: how the mad ship parasitised the multiple-frequency bands the terrorists were using to fly it in by remote control, punched through their firewalls and drove every person and AI on board their ship insane. How it was brought down by a hero pilot who flew her raptor into the hauler carrying it before it could escape. Well, someone in Takama-ga-hara's traffic control told me that pilot flew into the hauler, all right, but she didn't do much damage. What really happened was that the mad ship crashed itself. It reached out to the terrorists and killed them, and then it committed suicide.'

Abass had once told Tony that story. He'd also said that the police team which had located and boarded the terrorists' ship afterwards had discovered a charnel house: its crew had killed each other with their teeth and bare hands.

'You have to wonder, if it really did commit suicide, why it did it,' the freebooter said. 'Maybe mad ships have some kind of ethical code, and it killed itself because it had been misused, and death was a way of making that good. Or maybe it's just that mad ships are crazy. What's your interest, kid?'

'Some wizards I know got themselves involved with the Red Brigade.'

'You probably don't want my advice, being young and immortal and all, but here it is anyway. You should fly on by. Wizards are clever, but they lack caution and common sense. They have moths, where you come from?'

Tony shook his head.

'They're from Earth. Winged bugs, a lot smaller and much prettier than those monsters,' the freebooter said, indicating the silvery husks overhead. 'They mostly fly at night, navigating by the light of the moon. Earth's moon, that is. Nothing else like her in all the known worlds. Nothing so big or so bright. I don't miss most things about Earth, but I miss that big old moon. But we were talking about moths. The point is, any light at night, they're attracted to it. They'll circle a candle until they burn up in the flame. Wizards are like that. And they'll take you with them. If you don't want to get burned, you should fly your own course, not theirs.'

'I hear that,' Tony said, thinking of Cho Wing-James and the others lying dead in the stinking aquarium water. *I only want your head.*

The freebooter said that she'd got the story about the stolen mad ship from a trader who had a contact in the military division that supplied stations that controlled sargassos. So maybe there was a grain of truth in it, just enough to make Tony a little paranoid, to make him wonder why Colonel X hadn't told him about it, and what other information the colonel might have withheld.

The bridle had at first been blithely optimistic about their quest; now she began to echo Tony's unease.

'You should trust your instincts,' she said.

And: 'When you feel it's time to cut and run I'll be ready.'

And: 'Whatever you choose to do, I'll always be there for you.'

Using her newly acquired abilities, she had delved into the records of Dry Salvages's traffic control, but the only G-class frigate to have visited the planet in the past year had been owned by the Commons police, and the three K-class freighters which had recently touched down had all had been registered to governments or legitimate companies, and none were in port right now. So if the Red Brigade had paid a visit to Raqle Thornhilde, they hadn't travelled to Dry Salvages on the frigate which had jumped the claim on the slime planet, and they hadn't used the hijacked freighter to deliver the stromatolites and Aunty Jael to the broker directly after the raid. The bridle had also checked the records of Raqle Thornhilde's previous contracts and trades, but could find no evidence that she had any involvement with the Red Brigade or their known proxies, or any previous interest in stromatolites, the Old Old Ones, Ghajar narrative code, or mad ships.

Tony paid a bribe to a minor official in the city's police who claimed that she would be able to dig up some dirt on Raqle Thornhilde, check for clandestine deals that didn't appear in the records, so forth. But every time he contacted the woman she said that she needed to do a little more work. It looked like the only way he could find out if Raqle Thornhilde was in league with the Red Brigade would be to ask her directly, after she came to him.

She seemed to be in no hurry to do that. Five days passed, six, and there was no sign that she was checking out Tony or probing his ship. He nursed his dwindling funds – his bodyguards' per diem was substantial. He worried that Colonel X hadn't sent him to Freedonia as an independent investigator but to bait some kind of trap. He worried about the eidolon that had infiltrated *Abalunam's Pride*'s systems, the conversation it was having with the actual ship that the bridle still couldn't understand.

He remembered his first trip off Skadi, accompanying his parents on some kind of diplomatic business in Great Elizabeth, on Ràn. Just turned six (the trip was a birthday treat), excited and intimidated by the strangeness of it all, he had asked his nanny to leave the door of his bedroom ajar, to let in a little light from the sitting room. For a long time he had lain awake, listening to the low murmur of his parents' voices, familiar and soothing but indistinct. He told the bridle about this, but she didn't understand the comparison. She wasn't good with analogies because their slippery meanings overflowed the boundaries of logic.

'Keep listening,' Tony told her. 'Keep watching the skies.'

By now she was all up inside traffic control, watching ships in transit between the mirrors in the wilderness, but she saw nothing of interest, and still Raqle Thornhilde hadn't reached out to Tony. And then, one day at breakfast in the courtyard of the motel, the bodyguard sitting nearby (the father, a craggy man with deep-set eyes and a spade-shaped beard) suddenly became alert. Tony looked up and saw someone coming towards him, and knew at once that it was Raqle Thornhilde's emissary.

31. The Invitation

Isabelle Linder told Lisa that a ship had been dispatched from Terminus more than a week ago, after ground-radar images had revealed a chamber at the excavation site. The original plan had been to transport finds from the dig directly to Terminus, bypassing UN controls; now the ship was going to take Willie there for treatment. According to Isabelle it was due to arrive in three days.

Lisa said, 'Then what? Can they cure him?'

'I will be honest,' Isabelle said. 'The experts listened to his story and studied the photographs I took, but it was not enough for them to be able to make a prognosis. When they can examine him properly we will know more.'

'By examine, I guess you mean experiment,' Lisa said.

'He has agreed to it,' Isabelle said.

'I bet. He thinks it's his only chance of surviving this.'

They were walking slowly between boulders and patches of catchclaw. Late-afternoon sunlight glowed on the cliffs that stood above them.

'We really are his best chance,' Isabelle said. 'The Professor has many good people working for her, and I am told she has taken a personal interest. That means everything that can be done for him will be done.'

She was a pretty young woman with a fetching French accent, dressed in a pink T-shirt, hiking shorts with big side pockets, sneakers stained with red dust. She told Lisa that she was Outland's office manager, and had stayed behind in Port of Plenty during the excavation of Willie's jackpot. About a week into the dig one of her colleagues had made a panicky call that had cut off mid-sentence. No one had picked up when she'd rung back, so she had used the company q-phone to call the head office for advice, and had been ordered to go straight to the site.

'I had no idea what to expect, or how I could be of help,' she said. 'So, first I stop at Joe's Corner. We have an understanding with the mayor there, because of our purchase of the crash site of the spaceship. He told me that the police had arrived, that already they have sealed off the excavation and set up a quarantine area. So I was cautious. I hired a tomb raider as a guide, a woman recommended by the mayor. We could not get so close to the site, but we found a spot where we could see it clearly enough. It is at the base of a big rock formation. The kind in cowboy films?'

'A butte,' Lisa said.

'Yes, I think so. A column of rock rising out of the desert floor,' Isabelle said, shaping the air with her hands to demonstrate what she meant. 'Everything bare, like the Sahara. Sand and rocks. And strange plants, some black, some orange. I could see the site very clearly. There were police working there, and also avatars.'

Lisa felt a cold clutch in her heart. 'Jackaroo avatars.'

'Of course.'

'How many?'

'At least three. It was a long way away and they were coming and going around the shaft. And even face to face it is hard to tell them apart. At least three.'

'One visited me,' Lisa said. 'Whatever your people found out there, the Jackaroo don't like it.'

'Yes, that is very clear. We thought we had taken precautions, but alas, they were not sufficient.'

'No kidding. So how did you find Willie? Did he call you?'

'Not exactly. I must tell you that there was a certain amount of distrust between us. He has a certain . . . reputation, shall we say. And although the contract specified that we share all finds, we knew he had held back some items from his initial excavation.'

'Willie always likes to have an edge,' Lisa said, thinking of the tessera he'd given to Brittany Odenkirk.

'Yes. So that is why we placed a tracker in his phone. Simply as a precaution. When I was close enough to check, it showed that he was some distance from the dig site. I followed its signal, and found him here, with his friends. And then you found us, and here we all are.'

'You were lucky to find him. There are plenty of dead spots in these hills.'

'Good luck had nothing to do with it,' Isabelle said.

'I mean for Willie, not you.'

'You might call it predestination,' Isabelle said. 'How paths come together at the right time. Those seeing it from the inside might call it luck. Those who know better would not.'

'You mean the Jackaroo?'

'I mean that the Professor sees much that we do not,' Isabelle said.

There was a kind of shine in the young woman's gaze. Lisa remembered with a twinge of unease that Nevers had warned her about the fanaticism of Ada Morange's inner circle.

It turned out that this wasn't the first of the Jackaroo gift worlds that Isabelle had visited. Two years ago she had been part of a team that had unsuccessfully attempted to raise the remains of a Ghajar ship from silt a hundred metres beneath the surface of the world ocean of Hydrot. She had been there for six months, working out of a tiny office on one of the islands at the south pole, organising resupply and the procurement of new equipment while the underwater excavation work, using remote-controlled robots, was delayed by endless difficulties.

The Ghajar ship had broken apart on impact. The wreckage was scattered across an ellipse more than twenty kilometres long, and each piece had to be dug out of several metres of silt before it could be raised to the surface. The robots were unreliable; the generator of the deep-sea trawler that acted as the expedition's platform kept breaking down; the local workers went on strike after one was killed by a broken cable's whiplash. At last, an approaching hurricane that drove twenty-metre waves ahead of it had brought a premature end to the attempt, but two fragments of memory laminate had been retrieved, Isabelle said, and Ada Morange's scientists were still attempting to crack the narrative code they contained.

Ada Morange believed that the Ghajar had mapped the entirety of the vast wormhole network of the New Frontier, and she was also attempting to piece together their history. There had been a war, that much was clear. Either between opposing factions of Ghajar or against some external enemy – another Elder Culture, perhaps, or even the Jackaroo. Half a dozen crash sites had been discovered on various worlds, and a huge debris field orbited a white dwarf star in the New Frontier: billions of particles and fragments of metal, polymer and deep-frozen organic matter. And then there were the so-called mad ships, which killed or drove insane anyone who attempted to board them. Ada Morange believed that the mad ships were the key to the Ghajar's history, and had invested a significant portion of her fortune in researching ways to neutralise and enter them.

After the expedition on Hydrot, Isabelle had been promoted to a position in the head offices of the Omega Point Foundation, in Paris, France. But her plan to work her way up the management chain had been frustrated by what she called an indiscretion with a senior colleague during a conference on Ghajar technology. The man had made things difficult for her, and eventually she had been dispatched to First Foot.

'I hoped it would be a temporary assignment. Winding up the affairs of the investigation into the crash site in the City of the Dead. But then your husband brought in his find, and now I am caught up in the mainstream of the Professor's interests again,' Isabelle said. 'I am no archaeologist. I am not interested in Elder Culture artefacts, or the "deep time" projects. I have a degree in accountancy. Yet here I am.

'Some say that great people in history make their own luck. I think in the Professor's case that is especially true. She saw the importance of Elder Culture technology before almost everyone else. Without her, the first Ghajar ships would not have been found. She has done much to map the New Frontier. And now this. I am part of that luck, and so are you.'

'It didn't work out so well for Willie, did it?' Lisa said.

Isabelle ignored that, saying, 'You said you were in trouble with the police?'

'One of them, anyway.'

'It is possible we can help you. And you, of course, may be able to help us. Think about it,' Isabelle said, and turned and started to walk back to the little camp under the overhang.

Lisa watched her go, wondering about that unexpected invitation. Wondering what she was going to do about it.

32. The Switch

'I had a time of it, tracking you down,' Brandon Wiley told Tony. 'Anyone would think you don't care about your old friends any more.'

'Right now, I am hoping to sell something,' Tony said.

'Well, maybe I can help you with that,' Brandon said artlessly. 'Are you going to finish those, by the way?'

'The bean cakes? Help yourself,' Tony said.

The motel's maker hadn't done a very convincing job. The fried shells were too dry, the insides half-cooked and gluey.

'I had to skip breakfast. Too much work to do, too many people to see. These aren't bad, whatever they are. Spicy,' Brandon said, biting a bean cake in half. 'You should give me the recipe – I could try them out on a few people I know in the food biz. Maybe they'll catch on. You never know.'

He was dressed in a shabby black jacket and blue jeans, a plump middle-aged man with an untidy halo of curly black hair and the manners of an over-indulged child, half obsequious, half petulant. He had quit his university post in Port of Plenty, First Foot after some vague scandal and had drifted through the fringe worlds before washing up in Freedonia. He worked now as a low-rent trader. Although he lacked the skill and nerve to ever make it big, he was surprisingly good at networking, keeping his contacts sweet by assiduously dispensing gossip, flattery and minor favours. Tony had done a little business with him, once transporting a gaggle of code jockeys who had been stranded after their ride found herself a better deal and booted without bothering to tell them, another time shifting stock confiscated from a bankrupt trader – cheap trainers and cases of a soft drink, Vimto (the last in the universe according to Brandon), that Tony had managed to offload on Wellington for a marginal profit that had been considerably less than the trader had promised.

Brandon took a while to get to the reason for his visit. Tony listened patiently while he complained about the foibles and foolishness of other traders and freebooters, and boasted about his low-ball deals.

'People complain that times are hard,' Brandon said, blotting crumbs of fried beans with a wetted finger and sticking it in his mouth. 'They say trade isn't what it once was because worlds are becoming more self-sufficient, and too many are caught up in this so-called recession. But if you can make your own opportunities there is always a profit to be made somewhere. People like us, we roll with the lows and ride the highs for all they're worth. For instance, here's a nice little deal I'm putting together. An acquaintance of mine has a contract to ship seven hundred gross of prayer flags to Zungqu. You know the kind? They are set out for a year on certain places high on the spires, where they accumulate spiritual energy. Not much money in it, but – this is the sweet thing, Tony – there's a fellow I know on Zungqu who deals in desert rose. A drug distilled from the sap of a native flower. Genuinely native, not some Elder Culture introduction. Found only there. It gives a very fine high, a little like opium. It's legal in Freedonia, of course, but not in the Commons, which means there's a much better profit to be made there.

'So what I plan to do,' Brandon said, leaning in and lowering his voice, as if that would make any difference if anyone wanted to listen in, as if anyone else cared, 'is bring it back in the hollow bases of a consignment of those spectacularly ugly vases they make on Zungqu. You might ask why I would go to such trouble, as all drugs are legal here. The answer is simple. I plan to sell the vases to someone I know who deals in so-called illegal drugs in the Commons. He takes the risk, I make more money than I would if I sold the shit here, on the open market. It's an old trick, but if you know what you're doing, it's a profitable one.'

'It sounds as if you are getting ready to make a big score,' Tony said politely, thinking that it was the sort of deal that inevitably went bad in a hurry.

'I always have the modest hope that my efforts will be properly rewarded,' Brandon said. 'And what about you, Tony? I hear this thing you want to sell, it may be also something big.'

'It could be,' Tony said. 'If I can find the right buyer.'

'I also hear it has something to do with that adventure of yours on the slime planet.'

Tony pretended to be surprised that Brandon knew about it.

'Oh, I heard one bird twittering to another,' Brandon said. 'Something about a cure for sleepy sickness, am I right? If you don't mind me asking, Tony, how did that all work out?'

'We didn't find what we were looking for, but we found something else instead,' Tony said.

'Not in that so-called code of the ancients, I bet. No one has ever cracked it. Probably no one ever will. So what did you really find? Some junk left by some other Elder Culture, or a new kind of slime? Or perhaps something with no practical application whatsoever, except it gives the so-called wizards a hard-on.'

Brandon was trying for an offhand manner, but Tony could see an eager shine creeping into his gaze.

'Something unexpected,' Tony said. 'A Ghajar eidolon.'

'Hmm. Eidolons can be tricky. Harmless or dangerous, most of them. Not much good in either case.'

'This one is a kind of translator,' Tony said. 'I hope you will not take it the wrong way if I don't go into too much detail.'

'Not at all. You don't want to give away too much until you've found someone who has a genuine interest . . . Have you found anyone?'

'Not yet.'

'Just the usual chancers, I suppose.'

'More or less,' Tony said. 'But I am sure that I will find someone who will recognise the value of what I have to sell. Its uniqueness.'

Tony had already rejected the advances of several traders and brokers who, like Brandon, worked at the low end of the market, where it was often difficult to distinguish desperation from greed. So far the real players had kept away, either because they weren't interested, or because they knew about his contract with Raqle Thornhilde. Who, he hoped, had sent Brandon Wiley to sound him out, as pilot fish searched out prey for krakens, hoping to find scraps in the bloodied water after the kill.

'What about the wizards you took all the way out there?' the trader said.

'Oh, there is no need to worry about them,' Tony said. 'They are out of the picture. This is what you might call a personal project of my own.'

Brandon pretended to think about that. He said, 'I know someone who could help. If you like, I can provide an introduction.'

There it was. The first tentative tug on the hook.

'That would be extremely generous of you, Brandon,' Tony said, as casually as he could.

'We are old friends, Tony. And what are friends for, if not to help each other? Let me see what I can do about arranging a meeting. And meanwhile, don't talk about it to anyone else. There are too many people in this city who hope to take advantage of someone who has an unexpected difficulty in moving his merchandise.'

After Brandon had gone, the older of the two bodyguards asked Tony how he could be certain that the trader was fronting for Raqle Thornhilde.

'He asked if the wizards still had an interest in this thing, but he did not once mention Raqle's name, or the contract,' Tony said. 'He will come back with an offer to meet with this person who can help me, and it will turn out to be her.'

And then Tony would find out who had told her about the slime planet and the stromatolites, and all the rest. Trade information for information. He discussed the terms of the meeting with the bodyguards, told them it was possible that Raqle Thornhilde would try to strong-arm him.

'Brandon will suggest a meeting place. At the last moment, we will tell him we have decided to meet somewhere else. Somewhere public where we can talk without either of us worrying that the other will pull some kind of trick.'

The bodyguards said that they knew just the place. Brandon Wiley called the next day, and the negotiations about where to meet his client went down just as Tony had predicted. But after that, everything went to hell.

As the hired runabout trundled towards the rendezvous – a cocktail bar on the top floor of an apartment tower – the youngest of the two bodyguards palmed a black cylinder and screwed it into Tony's neck. A jolt of pain paralysed him; the older body-guard slapped a surgical patch over his eye. He felt something press between his eyeball and its socket, and then his link with the ship's bridle fell over.

'Nothing personal,' the older bodyguard said, ripping off the patch. 'We just got a better offer.'

When the pain had mostly ebbed away and he could think straight again, Tony said, 'I'm going to make sure you never work in this city again.'

'We already have a new job,' the younger bodyguard said.

'A permanent one,' the older bodyguard said. 'No more scuffling for temporary contracts with off-world assholes.'

Tony pulled up his comms menu: most of its icons had turned red. He couldn't even make a simple phone call. The bodyguards would not answer any of his questions – the younger one showed him the black cylinder, told him he would get another taste if he didn't shut the fuck up. Tony hoped that they were working for Raqle Thornhilde. He believed that he could still make a deal with her, but if one of her rivals was trying to muscle in he could be in serious trouble. Freebooters and traders caught in the middle of local disputes had a habit of disappearing.

They headed out of the city on the beetling freeway, turned off onto a service road that cut between huge fields where combines were harvesting catch crops ahead of the long night. Beyond the last of the fields, the service road gave out to a rutted dusty track. The runabout jacked up on its suspension and fattened its wheels and without slackening its speed drove straight on into the desert. They drove for more than an hour, at last rolling to a halt in a broad sinuous valley that might once have been the course of a river, vanished aeons ago.

The bodyguards helped Tony out into dry furnace heat and immense silence. Sculpted saddles of sand dunes; rocks thinly layered like old books. Long shadows lay everywhere. Red rocks and red sand glowed in level sunlight. The spires reared up at the horizon, clawing the sky.

A spark flared overhead: the bubble of a spinner floating down, dust blowing away in every direction as it kissed the ground. One of the bodyguards bound Tony's wrists with a cord that cinched itself tight; the other produced a black hood and pulled it over Tony's head. He was hustled forward, lifted up, dumped on soft padding. A moment later, the world fell away.

33· Death Mask

After sunset, Little Mike built up the campfire against the chill of the desert night and the men sat around it, grilling hot dogs and passing a couple of blunts and a bottle of Jack Daniel's to and fro. Isabelle, sitting in the shadows outside the pulsing light of the fire, politely refused their offers to share; Lisa did her best to ignore the whisky, but took a couple of cautious tokes that levitated her, just a little, above her anxiety and grief.

Little Mike took a couple of hot dogs into the tomb for Mouse, who was keeping watch over Willie, and came back out and said that Willie was still asleep.

'That's a good sign,' Bear said. Firelight glinted on his glasses at he looked around at the others. 'I mean, isn't it?'

'If it helps the man conserve his strength,' Sonny said.

'We did everything we could,' Wolfman Dave said, staring at Isabelle. 'Fuck anyone who says different.'

'Willie and his dogs, man,' Sonny said, and raised the bottle of Jack Daniel's in salute and took a long drink and spat into the fire. Blue flames briefly flared.

Little Mike told Lisa, 'I got a blanket if you need one. Looks like the night air's getting to you.'

This rough kindness pierced Lisa's heart. She excused herself and walked off a ways and wept a little. For Willie. For Pete. For herself, because she believed that she saw in Willie a premonition of her own fate.

She returned to her seat by the fire, nodded off, and was jolted awake by the sound of angry voices. She knew, somehow, that Willie was awake, too. In the leaping firelight, the road dogs were

216

crowding around Isabelle. She looked frightened but defiant, saying, 'My people need to know. If they are to save him, they need to know everything!'

'We should fuck up her ride,' Wolfman Jack said. 'Leave her stranded here.'

'Take her way the hell out into the Badlands, leave her there,' Mouse said.

The men were mostly drunk by now. There was a meanness in the air. They ignored Lisa the first time she asked what was going on, so she stepped between them and Isabelle and asked again.

Mouse was holding up a smartphone, saying that he'd woken to find that Willie was in a bad way, and 'this fucking French bitch' was filming him.

Lisa said, 'What kind of bad way?'

'He may have reached a crisis point,' Isabelle said.

'Like you fucking care,' Sonny said.

'I know how you feel—'

'I don't believe you do,' Sonny said, with a hard stare and a nasty smile. 'But I'll be happy to enlighten you.'

'Give me that phone,' Lisa told Mouse, and he handed it over. She held it up, saying, 'Willie's sick, and you're all out here, arguing about this? What kind of friends are you?'

The men looking at her as she tossed the smartphone, underhand, into the fire. Isabelle had the good sense not to say anything.

Mouse said, 'She's right. We need to go see to him.'

'Don't think we aren't done with you,' Sonny told Isabelle, trying to assert his authority.

'We need her help,' Lisa said, thinking of how strange it was, an actual fucking spaceship coming to save Willie.

Mouse said, 'I think it could be too late for that. I think you'd better come see.'

There was a fluttering agitation in the tomb's dark cool air: eidolons had been loosed from the tesserae scattered across the walls. Lisa felt their attention turn towards her as she hurried towards Willie's makeshift bed. He had pushed his blanket away and his fists were clenched by his sides and his chest heaved with each breath. It was as if he was trying to breathe through a narrowing straw. He turned to look at Lisa when she knelt beside him, and she saw that the blood vessels in his eyes had burst. His pupils were black pools floating on eight-ball haemorrhages.

'The bones in there,' he said. 'If they were bones. Woven, like wicker baskets. Chains of them. That Ghajar. Much bigger than a man, Lize. Much bigger. Wounded I think. In a bad way. Trying to help himself. Used some kind of nanotech. That's what got me. It's trying to fix me only way it knows how . . .'

Lisa took one of his fists in both her hands. It was fever-hot. She told him to hush, said, 'We'll get you fixed up soon. Isabelle's friends are on their way.'

'I won't be dissected, Lize. I won't be cut up. Analysed. Bits of me sold off. Promise me that.'

'Oh, Willie.'

'The things we meddle in. Not knowing what they are. Wonder any of us survive.'

His breath stank like a chemical lab. There was a faint silvery glow under his skin, a flow of unreadable information. She was only dimly aware of the road dogs behind her, and of the faint flutter of eidolons, now near, now far.

'I see it all,' Willie said, 'but I understand hardly any of it. Maybe you'll do better.'

'What do you mean, Willie? Tell me what you see.'

'A planet bigger than its sun. I think it's a planet. A city hidden in a sea of red sand . . .'

Willie started to laugh and it turned into a racking cough. Flecks of blood on his lips. Bubbles of blood in his nostrils. Blood welling from the corners of his eyes, pooling against his nose, slanting down his cheek in a quick red slick. Lisa was gripped by a freezing mix of horror and pity.

He was looking straight at her, saying, 'We don't know anything, Lize. We're like ants. Ants trying to understand algebra. But it's so beautiful, you know?'

Then he was looking past her. Looking past everything.

'Hush now, Willie. Save your strength. Hush.'

He breathed for a minute. Maybe two. It felt like all the time they'd ever had was compressed into that tall dark chamber. The eidolons were gathering close, eager witnesses to this all too human drama.

Willie suddenly started, tried to sit up. For a moment his reddened gaze fixed on Lisa.

'The Jackaroo aren't gods, Lize. That's the funny thing. They aren't even close . . .'

He fell back. The faint silvery flow, the death mask beneath his skin, was fading. His fist relaxed in Lisa's grip and something slammed through her. She felt the eidolons fly back into their tesserae, and then black lightning clawed across the inside of her skull and everything went away.

34. Real Free People

Tony was imprisoned in a shed or shack with a beaten-earth floor and walls of roughly mortared blocks of sandstone. An unglazed slit window above his pipe-frame bed, a low doorway he couldn't quite reach because of the plastic cord that tethered his ankle to the bed. Peering through the window, he could see a cluster of stone shacks and a patchwork of small stone-walled fields. In the distance was the long low barracks where the children were kept.

The sky was on fire with the mad light of the long sunset.

When the wind blew in a certain direction it carried a stench like rot and charred plastic – the smell of decomposing windrows of the self-reproducing photosynthetic monomers that an unknown Elder Culture had introduced into Dry Salvages's shallow seas. So he was somewhere on the coast, but had no idea where he was in relation to Freedonia. Pyotr, the old man who brought Tony's food, would not tell him who had kidnapped him or how long he was going to be kept there, and shrugged off threats of retribution and promises that Tony's family would pay a generous reward for his release.

'We are a long way away from the city and its laws,' Pyotr said. 'We are the real free people. Free to think as we will, free to live our lives. We answer only to God.'

The food was simple but good. Pyotr brought a pail of hot water every morning, and there was an ancient tablet containing a small library – mostly theological texts and tracts, but some fiction, too, all of it predating the arrival of the Jackaroo – and a chess program that even on its simplest setting beat Tony two times out of three. But Tony was not allowed to leave the shack, and whenever Pyotr visited there were always two strong lads stationed outside the door.

The old man was barefoot in a simple shift cinched at the waist by a belt woven from a rainbow of plastic threads, a tough bird with the serene manner of someone who didn't have anything left to prove. There were deep scars on his arms and the side of his neck, inflicted by a weircat ten years ago, when he had been on what he called a walkabout, wandering naked across the desert, living off the land. He had transfixed the biochine with a flint-tipped spear and bashed it to death with a rock.

He belonged to a sect that rejected the hypercapitalism of Freedonia and had chosen instead to live in what they called the real world. They strung kilometres of fine netting to harvest water from the fogs that rose at the beginning of each day, maintained an elaborate system of channels, water lifts and little dams to irrigate their crops of corn, squash, beans, sunflowers and melons, extracted fibrous plastic from seawater evaporated in lagoons and used it to weave mats, baskets and clothing. And they looked after children who had fallen victim to sleepy sickness.

Some were the children of rich citizens who paid for them to be cared for, but most had been rescued after being turned out of Freedonia and abandoned to live as best they could in the coastal margin lands. The real free people provided food and water and shelter, and gave them Christian burials when they died. Pyotr said that all children were God's children, even those whose minds had been overwritten by alien memes.

'What about the Jackaroo and the !Cha?' Tony said.

'Those also.'

'And the Elder Cultures?'

'Of course. The universe and everything in it is Her kingdom.'

'My religion has it that the Jackaroo and the !Cha lack souls, because they were not made in God's image.'

'There are some who believe that the Jackaroo are angels or devils,' Pyotr said. 'Others that they are secular gods, empowered by technology that appears to us to be miraculous, and with a long history we can only guess at. But compared to God, they are no more than we are. Creatures of stardust with finite lifespans and limited powers. It is a matter of perspective. From that of God, all are as children.'

They talked about the differences between the real free people's religion and the religion of Tony's family, whose God was served by lesser deities, orishas, which also controlled the destinies of people and acted as their protectors. Tony confessed that he had fallen out of love with religion, but supposed that his ship – or at least, its bridle – might be a kind of orisha.

'Is the eidolon in your head also an orisha?' Pyotr said.

'Who told you about that?'

Pyotr shrugged.

'My people believe that eidolons are false orishas,' Tony said. 'Because they come from an Elder Culture rather than from God they are as treacherous and evil as any demon.'

'We would say that although eidolons do not come directly from God, they are the creations of God's children. And like God's children, they have the potential for good as well as for evil.' Pyotr paused, then said, 'I was told that there is a possibility that your eidolon harbours secrets that could help us understand sleepy sickness.'

'I was told that too. But so far it has only led me into trouble.'

Tony was not especially afraid. Mostly, he was bored. Pyotr visited twice a day but otherwise he was left to his own devices. The nanotech inserted into his head by the surgical patch prevented him from calling his ship or anyone else, but he was not completely isolated. There was always the sense that something else was with him, in the bare shack. Sometimes he looked around quickly, trying to catch it out, but it always evaded him.

Sometimes he sang. Hymns, snatches of the old, old songs that Danilo had liked to sing. He had always liked to sing in church, loved the exhilaration of raising his voice in communal music, of letting go of himself in a great joyful noise. His voice was at best vigorous, but it didn't sound too bad in the small resonant space. He wondered what the eidolon made of it. And realised, with plangent regret, that he had never once sung with Danilo and his friends in one of their impromptu sessions in an after-hours café or someone's apartment.

He remembered the time he had conjured a window while he and Danilo lay together one night after making love, and he had shown the singer the luminous wheel of the Milky Way, the known stars in the wormhole network marked in red, scattered across its smoky spirals like flowers in a meadow. He had highlighted the stars he had visited, zoomed in through great drifts of stars to the star of Skadi.

'That's where we are,' he said. 'One star amongst four hundred billion. You could spend a lifetime travelling between the known worlds, and not exhaust them.'

Danilo laughed, saying that you could spend all your life in one place and still find something new every day.

'Aren't you curious about the other worlds?' Tony said.

'I'm curious about other people.'

'There are other people on those worlds. Strange and new and wonderful people. People unlike any here.'

'You miss your ship,' Danilo said.

'I miss my freedom,' Tony admitted.

'One day you'll get her back, and then you'll be gone. Out there somewhere, in all those bright stars . . .'

'I could take you with me. I could get permission, and if I didn't I could take you anyway. Show you things you wouldn't believe—'

Danilo placed two fingers on his lips.

'But it isn't about the other worlds, is it?' the singer said. 'It isn't about where you go. It's about the going. The flight. You're like a kite who can't settle on a roost. Always in motion, never at rest. Always between one world and another.'

Tony had tried to turn it into a joke, saying, 'Am I not part of your world?' But he knew now that Danilo had been right. He had only ever been a casual visitor in his lover's life. That was the worst of it. The root of his guilt. He could visit Danilo's world, but Danilo could never visit his. Could never, ever be a part of it.

Two days passed. Three. The conflagration in the sky intensified as the sun laboriously set; the patch of windowlight that fell on the far wall dimmed as it inched towards the ceiling. And then, on the morning of the fourth day of Tony's imprisonment, the door slid back and Raqle Thornhilde ducked under the low lintel. Behind her, stepping daintily over the threshold on three articulated legs, was the aquarium tank of a !Cha.

35. The Pyre

In cold dawn light the road dogs used their Harleys to rope stumpy greasewood trees out of the stony ground and haul them, bumping and jerking, long leathery leaves trailing like the tentacles of dead squid, to the spot where they were building Willie's funeral pyre. They stacked the trees in lengthwise and crosswise layers, taking care not to get the caustic white sap on their skin, and capped the pile with a platform of brushwood and coral-tree branches. And then Willie's body, wrapped in a blanket, was carried out of the Ghostkeeper tomb and tenderly laid on top. Each road dog said his goodbye, gripping Willie's limp hand, telling him *you're in a better place now, bro*, and *ride safe*, and *fuck an angel for me*. Lisa brushed back black spikes and kissed his cold lips. Then Sonny sprinkled a litre of precious gasoline on the blanket and took a burning brand from Mouse and touched it to the congealed puddles of sap at the base of the pyre.

They all stepped back from the heat and flare. White smoke rolled up, stinking like molten road tar. Lisa wondered about contagion. What if the Ghajar nanotech had multiplied in Willie's body, and had been freed by the fire and was rising and spreading on the air?

Something had definitely escaped from him at the moment of his death. She supposed that it was his ghost, or what his ghost had become after the breakout, passing through her as it flew into the tesserae scattered across the walls of the tomb. She hoped that it had taken something of Willie with it. In ten or a hundred thousand years other clients of the Jackaroo might read in those tesserae something of the essence of his life.

Whatever it was, it had left its mark in her. She could see now dim phantoms in the landscape. Faint X-rays of the dead. She could sense the interiors of Ghostkeeper tombs in the cliffs across the valley. Indistinct gestures inhabited the Boxbuilder ruins up on the ridge. Something severe and forbidding stood in the chip of the moon as it fell towards the paling eastern horizon, and she could sense another presence in the sky – an orbiting ship, maybe . . .

There was a sudden jerky movement inside the caul of flame. Willie's body sitting up in the fire, horrible to see.

'It's just muscles contracting,' Mouse told her. 'It don't signify.'

The body fell back into the flames, and a little later the platform on which it lay collapsed into the burning shells of the grease-wood logs. Wild galaxies of sparks swirled up into the vivid blue morning sky. A great banner of smoke streamed down the valley.

The road dogs began to pack, getting ready to move out in case the geek cops spotted the tell-tale smoke and came to investigate. Lisa hugged and thanked them one by one.

'We only did what was right,' Sonny said, his usual belligerence slightly softened. 'You sure you want to go off with that woman?'

'You need protecting from the cops, let us do it,' Little Mike said.

'You don't want any part of the trouble I'm in,' Lisa said.

'Seems to me you're asking for more trouble, going with her,' Sonny said.

'I think she can help,' Lisa said. 'Or at least, I think her boss can.'

When the fire had at last burned down, the road dogs picked through the hot ashes. They found a few shards of bone and buried them near the entrance to the tomb, then swung onto their hogs and saluted Lisa and rode off towards the City of the Dead. After she had prised a couple of tesserae from the wall of the tomb, Lisa walked to where Isabelle Linder was waiting by her Land Cruiser, which had been hidden under a camo drop cloth that imitated the red rocks and grey brush with such fidelity that Lisa hadn't spotted it when she'd walked past it the previous evening.

Two hours later they were parked at the edge of the Badlands, in the shade of a cluster of organ trees, waiting to pick up someone who, Isabelle said, needed a lift. She wouldn't tell Lisa who it was because 'it would spoil the surprise'.

While Isabelle perched on the hood of the Land Cruiser, looking out across a glaring salt pan towards the highway that ran west across the Badlands to the copper mine at Mount Why Not, Lisa sat with her back against an organ tree's scaly column, sipping from a bottle of spring water. Brittle husks were scattered over the gravelly sand, dropped from the chocolate-brown froths of sporangia that sprouted under the notched swords of the tree's fronds. It was fiercely hot, timelessly quiet and still.

There was no sense of the history of Elder Cultures out there. No tombs, no ruins, no ghosts. The desert was empty of any meaning but its own. Lisa found the inhuman silence calming after riding through the far edge of the hills, with distracting glimpses of tombs and their inhabitants and inscrutable fragments of Boxbuilders long dead. She was trying to understand Willie's death. The fact of his death. The manner of his death. She was still kind of numb, the weight of what had happened poised above her head like a landslide. It could bury her if she didn't come to terms with it. If she didn't find some way of understanding it. Or if not understanding, because maybe it was impossible to understand, then at least some way of accepting it. Accepting that she had been changed. Accepting that the ghost tattooed in her brain had been changed too.

She kept touching her face. Half-expecting, half-dreading that she would discover hard points pushing through her skin. She had studied herself in the Land Cruiser's rear-view mirror, and although she had failed to find any trace of the silvery flow of information she'd seen under Willie's skin she supposed that it was only a matter of time before it appeared.

It was the fear of that, of how her ghost might have been changed, of how she herself might have been changed, rather than the possibility of arrest and indefinite quarantine, that had convinced her that she should throw in her lot with Isabelle Linder and Ada Morange. She wanted to talk one-on-one with the Professor, but Isabelle had told her that it was impossible – the Professor had nothing to do with the operations of the Omega Point Foundation or the companies and research initiatives that it funded. Instead, Lisa had used the q-phone Isabelle kept in the glovebox of the Land Cruiser to discuss terms with someone called Malcolm D'Ath, one of the non-executive directors of the foundation. The man had sounded like one of those plummy actors in the British TV soap about old-time aristocrats and their servants that Lisa's mother had liked to watch way back when, but seemed pretty hands-on and straight-talking.

He was in London, England. It was two in the morning there, apparently.

'But not to worry, Ms Dawes. I'm used to keeping strange hours. And I am very pleased that you have decided to get in touch. I think you will be a great help to our programme. And, in turn, we can definitely help you.'

She would be handsomely rewarded if she allowed the Professor's researchers to investigate her eidolon and the tesserae she had taken from the tomb, he said, and assured her that they would do their very best to find a way to cure her.

'But the first thing we need to do is extract you, and get you to a place of safety. Did you know that you are on the TCU's watch list, and that a warrant has been issued for your arrest?'

'I can't say I'm surprised,' Lisa said, thinking of Adam Nevers.

'Our legal people can file an appeal against the warrant straight away. But it would not be wise to remain on First Foot.'

'Where would I be extracted to? London? Paris?'

'That would be a jump from the proverbial frying pan into the proverbial fire. No, our ship will return to its point of origin, Terminus. I am given to understand that the facilities there will be more than adequate to investigate your discovery. And also, of course, to try to rid you of your passenger.'

'Terminus.'

'Yes. A great opportunity, if I may say so.'

'I guess I have no alternative,' Lisa said, with a feeling of weightlessness.

'A simple "yes" will seal the deal.'

'Yes, then. Yes.'

'Very good. Our ship is already on its way, of course. Our agent on the ground will arrange the rendezvous. If I could speak to Mademoiselle Linder?'

'Wait a moment.'

'Yes?'

'Is it raining there?'

'In London? Not at present. Contrary to myth it doesn't always rain here.'

'Are you near a window?'

'Standing in front of one, as a matter of fact.'

'Could you open it?'

'One moment. There.'

'And hold the phone out.'

'Ah. I see. Of course.'

Lisa clamped the shell of the q-phone to her ear. Heard across tens of thousands of light years the faint rustle of a night wind in trees, a siren twisting above the surf of a great city.

Malcolm D'Ath said, 'Was that satisfactory, Ms Dawes?'

'Yes. Yes, thank you.'

'Goodbye, Ms Dawes. And good luck.'

The shadows of the organ trees turned and shortened across the dry stones, began to lengthen again. Ant-sized biochines scuttled from shadow to shadow on wiry multi-jointed legs. At last, Isabelle slid off the hood and called out that their passenger had arrived. Lisa climbed to her feet, dusting off her pants, and saw that a truck had stopped out on the distant highway. After a minute it moved off, the faint whine of its gear train passing over the salt pan as it picked up speed, heading east towards civilisation. A little later, a jiggling shape appeared at the far edge of the salt pan, broken and distorted by layers of hot air. Vanishing, reappearing upside down, vanishing again.

And suddenly it was close: a black, blunt cylinder prinking towards them on three slender legs like a miniature Martian fighting machine. Its flat top was at about the level of Lisa's chest. There were no cameras, no windows, no eyes, but she was acutely aware of the attention of the alien intelligence inside.

'Mademoiselle Linder,' an engaging baritone voice said. 'How good to see you again. And here's Ms Dawes and her guest! How marvellous! What fun we're going to have!'

228

36 · The Children

They made a strange little procession, following a red-dirt path slashed across a meadow of black, close-woven, strap-like plants. Tony and the broker, Raqle Thornhilde, immense in a white kaftan and a wide-brimmed straw hat, the aquarium cylinder of the !Cha raised on its three legs, and three identical bodyguards in white shirts and black kilts. Raqle Thornhilde's weircat ran in swift loops and circles across the meadow, once jumping onto a prow of rock and raising itself on its long legs, silhouetted against the slow apocalypse of sunset.

'She can hear her prey hiding in their burrows,' Raqle said. 'She triangulates the heartbeat, then leaps high into the air and augers down into the dirt. So fierce. So precise.'

Tony didn't know what to say to that. He supposed that it was some kind of warning.

Now the biochine flung itself from the prow rock and sped out across the meadow again.

'I love to see her run,' Raqle said. 'I take her out of the city when I can, but never for long enough. I have too much to do, and many of the people with whom I do business find my sweetheart intimidating.'

'I find *you* intimidating, madam,' Tony said.

'Good. Perhaps you're not as stupid as you seem.'

Raqle had made it clear that his fate was subject to her whim. 'You didn't put up much of a struggle,' she had said, back in the little prison shack. 'I think you wanted to be caught.'

'I wanted to talk to you,' Tony said.

'It was almost clever, luring me to approach you by advertising yourself about town, but it attracted the wrong kind of attention. That's why I had you brought here. It was for your own good.'

'People keep telling me that,' Tony said, thinking of Ayo and Opeyemi.

Raqle said that she had not questioned him until now because she had been waiting for the !Cha to arrive. The alien would be able to detect the slightest deviation from complete truthfulness and sincerity, she told Tony, and warned him that any hint of duplicity would be severely punished.

Tony said that there was no need to threaten him because he would be happy to talk about why he had come back to Dry Salvages. He told the broker and the !Cha about his adventure on the slime planet, and how the wizards had discovered the Ghajar algorithm in the stromatolites and accidentally freed the eidolon. He described the raid on his family's home and its aftermath, explained that he had escaped and set out to find Aunty Jael.

He did not mention Colonel X, hoping that Raqle Thornhilde and her !Cha would not be able to sniff out the lie of omission. The broker was a formidable person, sly and dangerous, and he was at her mercy. But he needed Colonel X as a hole card. He wasn't hoping for rescue, but it was always useful to have something in reserve.

She did not tell him whether she believed his story; nor did she tell him whether or not she had been involved with Aunty Jael's escape. Now, as they walked towards the compound where the children were kept, he was waiting on her judgement.

'Look at her run!' she said. She was still watching the weircat. 'I love her purity. She is a killing machine. Fast and sleek and unforgiving. She feels no remorse when she brings down her prey. And you cannot plead with her, if she targets you. She is what she is. She does not care that she was designed by unknown minds and hands. She is what she is. She does not meddle in things she doesn't understand, or dream that she can become other than she already is. If we were a little more like her and all the other biochines, if we weren't so restless, so stupidly inquisitive, then perhaps we might not be afflicted by meme plagues or possessed by eidolons. We might not have scattered ourselves so widely and

230

thinly, or warred against each other over stupid little differences. We might not be trembling on the edge of extinction.'

'But you would be a great deal less interesting,' the !Cha said.

It was still startling to hear his rich baritone, to remember that his tank was not a drone but a kind of spacesuit for a little colony of smart shrimp.

Tony had never met a !Cha before, although he had once glimpsed one on a city street on a world thirty thousand light years away. Their relationship with the Jackaroo was unclear, but they freely admitted that they were connoisseurs and collectors of human stories, and many believed that they manipulated people and events to make those stories more interesting. This one's name was Unlikely Worlds. Tony supposed that he was following Raqle's story, her life; supposed he would become a small part of that tale. It was not a comforting thought.

'You are biased,' Raqle told the !Cha. 'You like us to burn brightly and briefly because that creates interesting stories, and interesting stories turn on your females.'

'You would create stories anyway,' Unlikely Worlds said. 'It is in your nature to elaborate worlds that do not exist.'

'The point is,' Raqle said, 'we'd live a lot longer if we didn't meddle in things we don't understand. We wouldn't be divided as we are. Our children wouldn't be dying of sleepy sickness.'

'And you would not aspire to glory and godhood,' the !Cha said. 'I do envy you that. And not just because it makes such good stories.'

'No doubt you said that to all the Elder Cultures. And look at them. Like Ozymandias, one and all.'

'I am old, certainly. But not that old.'

'So you'd like me to think. Oh, just look at her!' Raqle said, turning from Unlikely Worlds to look across the meadow again. 'Such speed. Such fierce joy. Now there's something to envy!'

'I'm not so sure,' the !Cha said. 'Weircats are found only on Dry Salvages and two other worlds. And on all three they are scarcely numerous. Each needs a territory of several hundred square kilometres, in the right kind of desert. Made or evolved, they have specialised themselves almost out of existence.'

'Three worlds that we know of,' Raqle said. 'There are thousands we haven't yet touched. And besides, because of us, because we have taken them with us, they live on more than three of the known worlds now. After we die out, the Jackaroo will find new clients, and perhaps they will wonder why certain species are always associated with the ruins of our cities. Perhaps that will be our only legacy.'

'We will remember you,' the !Cha said.

'You collect our stories and turn them into love feasts for your females. What about Mr Okoye? How does his story taste to you?'

'It tastes of truth,' Unlikely Worlds said.

Tony felt a wash of relief, and realised at that moment exactly how anxious he had been.

'That's what I thought,' Raqle said. 'He didn't tell me much that I didn't already know, but it's clear now that I've been played for a fool. And by a laminated brain, of all things.'

'If it's any consolation, she has been playing the game a lot longer than you,' Unlikely Worlds said. 'This is a new chapter in a long and enthralling tale.'

'His story isn't worth much by itself,' Raqle Thornhilde said. 'But I think you'll agree that it definitely adds something to hers.'

'Oh, I think it's safe to say that I haven't been disappointed,' Unlikely Worlds said, and Tony realised with a little thrill of hope that the !Cha was not interested in his story, or Raqle Thornhilde's, but in Ada Morange's. That there was a chance he could turn that interest to his own advantage.

'Then you'll give me your help,' Raqle said.

'We will help each other,' Unlikely Worlds said.

'Yes, we will,' Raqle said, and took out a small golden cylinder and put it to her lips and blew. Tony did not hear anything, but out in the meadow the weircat turned sharply and ran headlong towards them.

They walked on to the place where the children infected with sleepy sickness were kept. A plastic mesh fence strung on concrete posts with three strands of barbed wire stretched along its top; a dusty compound; a long windowless barracks built of the same sandstone blocks as the huts of the real free people.

'It isn't much compared with the clinic run by your family,' Raqle Thornhilde told Tony. 'Pyotr's people do what they can, but there are no trained medical personnel, no hands or drones, no attempts at remedial treatment, no wizards trying to find a cure. But the children have food and water and shelter. They are free to do what they need to do. What their disease needs them to do.'

There were about twenty children beyond the fence. A small group huddled around something Tony couldn't see, but most stood or sat by themselves. Several were staring at the sunset. A tall blonde girl, hands knotted at her chest, sang over and over: 'La! La-la-la. La!'

Raqle Thornhilde stepped closer to the fence, hooking her fingers in its diamond mesh, gazing at the children with fierce tenderness. 'My son died here,' she said. 'He began to show symptoms just after his eleventh birthday. I brought him here, and he died two years later. The kind of medical intervention your family provides can keep them alive for longer, but what's the point? During the first stage of infection, the meme eats their minds while they sleep. When they wake, they are no longer what they once were. They are not even children.'

She spoke flatly, without affect. Tony supposed that it was the only way she could bear to talk about it.

'I cloned my son,' she said, 'but of course it isn't the same. I knew that, even at the nadir of my grief. His siblings may look like him, they share his genome, but I had them tweaked to be stupid and loyal. I wanted him to live, but I couldn't stand the thought of another person wearing his body. Of living the life he had lost. Of living a life different to the life he would have had. He was one of the first, twenty years ago. How it's spread since then! I have not been able to change the quarantine law. I have not been able to stop people turning them out of the city. So I pay the real free people to round up as many as they can, and look after them here.

'That was why I was interested in the stromatolites. I believed the story that there might be a cure hidden in their archival genetics. And you and your family wanted to believe it too.' Raqle Thornhilde turned to look at Tony. She was dry-eyed, quite calm.

233

'I had nothing to do with what happened afterwards. I thought that your Aunty Jael could help to find a cure. I didn't know who she really was.'

'My family and I were fooled too,' Tony said.

'A pleasing symmetry,' Unlikely Worlds said.

Raqle Thornhilde ignored the !Cha, telling Tony, 'You came to me because you thought I'd helped her to escape. I didn't. But I want to find her, as do you. And we're going to help each other. I'm not doing this to get some sort of revenge, or so this fucking school of shrimp can get his rocks off. I want to find out if there's any truth to the idea that there's a cure for sleepy sickness out there. I'm doing it for the children. As far as I'm concerned, it has always been about the children.'

37. 'I can see ghosts.'

Unlikely Worlds was the !Cha Chloe Millar had warned Lisa about, the one who was making a story out of Ada Morange's life. He said that he had come to First Foot because he believed that what he called Lisa's accident was about to become an important part of that story. A story that was, according to him, a great work of time.

'And it is not yet even halfway done. She changed human history with the discovery of the Ghajar ships, and now she may change it again. This time with your help, Ms Dawes, and the help of the eidolon in your head, so recently embiggened.'

Lisa said, 'How do you know it's been . . . What was it you said?'

'Embiggened. A cultural reference. A small joke. Perhaps too obscure? Oh well. We try to please and sometimes we try too hard. As for your eidolon, I can see ghosts. Although perhaps not in quite the same way that you see them. How did it happen, may I ask?'

'Isabelle didn't tell you?'

'I prefer to hear these things first-hand,' Unlikely Worlds said.

His mellifluous baritone sounded like the dead guy who did the voice-overs for the kind of movie trailers that were full of explosions and military hardware and collapsing megastructures, and who was now a kind of ghost himself, an AI that perfectly imitated him. Lisa and Isabelle were sitting on a flat slab of rock in the shade of the organ trees; Unlikely Worlds had folded his three skinny multi-jointed legs to squat in front of them. The flat-topped cylinder of his tank was about a metre tall, matt black and textured with a fine grain, like expensive hand-made paper. He wasn't the first !Cha that Lisa had met. There had been another, Useless Beauty, sniffing around her and Willie after the Bad Trip. Lisa, unsure of the !Cha's authority, had told him what she remembered of the incident; Willie claimed to have strung him along with the promise of some grand tall tales. Hoping for payment that had never come. Useless Beauty had listened to them and had not returned; they had never learned if he had been satisfied with their stories or if he had found them wanting, or why. And now here was this one, wanting more of the same. Even without Chloe's warning, Lisa wouldn't have trusted him, but Isabelle Linder didn't seem to be fazed by his presence, telling her, 'He'll get it out of you one way or another. So you might as well tell him now.'

So for the second time that morning Lisa explained what she had felt at the moment of Willie's death. It was like hearing someone else tell a story. When she was done, there was a long moment of silence broken only by the fluting of the hot breeze in the hollow tops of the organ trees.

'Such a rare encounter,' Unlikely Worlds said at last. 'The Ghajar were once more numerous than you, but they hardly ever visited the worlds they had been given. They were a little like your gypsies, and a little like poet-warriors in the classic sense. They left behind their ships, but almost nothing of themselves.'

Lisa said, 'Is my eidolon the ghost of a Ghajar?'

She wanted to ask: if you see it what does it look like? Can you talk to it? How has it been changed? What does it want? Half a hundred questions were buzzing in her head.

'It is definitely interesting,' Unlikely Worlds said.

'In what way?'

'In the way its story crosses with yours, and yours crosses with Ada Morange's. In the way the deep past is reborn in you. In the way it manipulates the future in which it finds itself. How to tell a story? First find a point of view. But this has so many perspectives. It is quite deliciously dizzying.'

'There is no point asking him for actual answers,' Isabelle said. 'He finds it amusing to answer questions with riddles.'

'Or quotes from movies,' Lisa said.

'Yes, that also. He is very tricky.'

The two of them exchanged conspiratorial looks, as if talking about a gifted but wayward child instead of an alien entity that inhabited a walking aquarium.

'I have no wish to violate the prime directive,' Unlikely Worlds said. 'It would make things so much less interesting for all of us if you were not able to discover your own destiny.'

Isabelle said, 'I have always wondered about this delicacy concerning interference. Is it your idea, or the Jackaroo's?'

'You try to discover if we are their servants. Or if we are an aspect of them. It's true that our very different scruples and intentions sometimes appear to have similar outcomes, but otherwise we have little in common.'

Although the !Cha claimed to be a separate species and implied that they and the Jackaroo were coevals, no one really knew if they were servants, secret masters, mere hitchhikers, or another manifestation of the Jackaroo themselves, another form of avatar. They also claimed that they were schools of tiny fish or shrimp – or things a little like fish or shrimp – that possessed a collective consciousness, and there was no way to prove or disprove it because their sturdy mobile aquaria were impervious to microwaves, X-rays, ultrasound and every other kind of probe.

'We like to help,' was all the Jackaroo said, when asked about the !Cha. It was their stock answer to most questions.

There weren't many !Cha. A hundred or so, all of them male. According to them, they travelled about Earth and the gift worlds collecting stories they hoped to use to woo their sedentary females. This one, Unlikely Worlds, had contacted Isabelle two days ago, requesting a lift on the ship sent by Ada Morange. Before that, Isabelle said, she'd had no idea the !Cha was on First Foot.

'I think he thinks the breakout is very important,' she'd told Lisa. 'But he refuses to tell me exactly why.'

'Perhaps I don't yet know because the story's far from done,' Unlikely Worlds said now. 'But I do admit to an interest in Ms Dawes. I look forward to finding out what Ada makes of her pair bond.'

'You mean me and Willie?' Lisa said.

'I do not refer to your marriage,' Unlikely Worlds said.

'I don't have any kind of relationship with my ghost. It's a parasite. An infection.'

'Yet you seek a divorce.'

'I'm looking for a cure,' Lisa said. 'If you're interested in my story, you should get the basics right.'

'There is a problem,' Isabelle told the !Cha. 'Before we go to the place where the ship will pick us up, Lisa wants to visit the excavation site. I tell her it is dangerous, but she will not listen.'

'I want to see it for myself,' Lisa said. 'It's why I came out here in the first place.'

She hoped that it might somehow jog her memory, help her understand what had happened to her during the Bad Trip. And she was wondering if there might be other Ghajar fragments close by, overlooked by the Outland crew and the geek police. Something she could use to win a better deal with Ada Morange, or to bargain her way out of her jam with Adam Nevers and the geek police. Something that could be used to get the eidolon off her back.

'It isn't a problem at all,' Unlikely Worlds told Isabelle. 'In fact, it's a wonderful idea. Who knows what Ms Dawes might see, with the help of her ghost!'

Isabelle drove at reckless speed across the salt pan, heading back to the hills and the overlook that her tomb-raider guide had shown her. Lisa was buckled into the passenger seat; Unlikely Worlds perched behind the gap in the front seats. They followed a draw that climbed in winding curves between steep bluffs, turning north when it topped out, skirting the foot of a fluted cliff before descending a scree slope into a narrow valley. A dead spot, according to Isabelle.

They sheeted the Land Cruiser in camo cloth and hiked up a dry stream bed that wound between slopes of tumbled stones. Isabelle set a challenging pace. Unlikely Worlds quickly fell behind, but when Isabelle and Lisa scrambled up a long steep slope they found him waiting for them at the top, beside a short string of

Boxbuilder ruins that ran along one edge of a flat triangle of bare rock. Lisa saw a faint movement inside one of the grainily translucent cubes, like a swirl of cigarette smoke captured in a video loop.

'He does that,' Isabelle said. Meaning, Lisa realised, the !Cha.

The young woman, scarcely out of breath, had a healthy glow from the hike. Lisa was slick with sweat and puffing like an old steam engine, and a knife prised at her left knee with every other step. The view was worth it, though. The view was magnificent.

The triangular prow of rock dropped straight down on two sides. To the west, the white sands of the Badlands stretched to the horizon and the setting sun. To the east, the range of hills and bluffs rose above slopes creased with deep shadows. And a fleet of flat-topped buttes dwindled away directly ahead, glowing in the sunset like the magic-hour master shot of a John Ford Western. Lisa saw something glittering at the top of a distant butte like a diamond refracting laser light.

The excavation site was at the base of the nearest butte, two or three kilometres away. Through the powerful field glasses that Isabelle lent her Lisa saw a dozen powder-blue trucks and Range Rovers parked at the edge of the conical piles of talus in which the butte's rugged column was rooted. A yellow digger and the ribbed half-cylinder of a big tent stood on a setback halfway up a steep slope. Lisa saw someone walk out of the tent, stalking ahead of their long shadow, saw other people sorting through debris laid out in neat squares. She saw a golden glint, realised with a cold start that one of those tiny figures was a Jackaroo avatar. And she saw a pit and a tall spoil heap which must be the entrance to the Ghostkeeper tomb. The refuge of the Ghajar survivor of the spaceship crash. The place where the Outland crew had murdered each other after they'd been possessed by bad code.

Unlikely Worlds asked her what she saw.

'The tomb's entrance. People. Also a Jackaroo avatar. They're pretty close to the tomb, those people. I thought it was still dangerous.'

'Yes, but what do you *see*? What is there beyond the trivial activity?'

It took Lisa a moment to realise what he meant.

'I can't see anything. No ghost lights. Either I'm too far away, or the geek police and their Jackaroo pals found some way of neutralising whatever it was Willie and the others found in there.'

'For what it is worth, I cannot see anything either,' Unlikely Worlds said.

Isabelle ignored him, asked Lisa if she was certain.

'Pretty much. I mean, I can see what might be tombs elsewhere, and I can see some kind of ghost in there,' Lisa said, pointing to the Boxbuilder cubes. 'But I can't see anything in or around the excavation site.'

'All this way for nothing,' Isabelle said.

'It was worth a shot,' Lisa said.

She sat on bare warm rock and massaged her trick knee. She was wondering about the star glittering on top of the distant butte, wondering if it might be some fragment that had spun off the Ghajar spaceship as it ploughed in. It seemed to brighten and enlarge as she stared at it, and she felt as if she was falling towards it, a swooning swooping out-of-body experience that pitched her headlong across kilometres of empty air . . .

A hand on her shoulder; Isabelle kneeling beside her, asking her if she was okay.

'I'm fine. Just a little tired is all.'

But she wasn't fine. She was very far from any definition of being fine. Something had changed, inside her. And it was still changing.

38. Rain City

It was raining in the city of Tanrog, Veles, when the ship carrying Tony, two of Raqle Thornhilde's cloned sons and Unlikely Worlds dropped through teeming clouds to the space field. Tony and one of the burly clones rode into the city on a bus crowded with shift workers from the manufacturies, chemical mills and filtration plants that surrounded the field, bought hooded cloaks spun from jellyfish collagen at a kiosk at the terminal, and in the warm constant rain splashed through narrow streets that wandered downhill towards the sea docks. Rough-hewn stone houses and kit-built apartment buildings crowded close, blocking out most of the bruised sky. Many of the houses had workshops set into their ground floors, or little stores with goods displayed in front of the kitchen ranges and beds of the proprietors. Gutters spilled sheets of rainwater; downpipes sluiced swift streams into channels carved in the middle of the streets; constant haloes of raindrops sprang from the cloaks of Tony and the clone.

Veles was a waterworld, a mini-Neptune that had lost most of its primordial hydrogen atmosphere to solar-wind ablation after it had spiralled closer to its yellow G4 dwarf star, and was drowned in deep ocean that was broken only by seasonal ice at the north and south poles, patches of red weed trapped by the currents of ocean gyres, and floating archipelagos of rafts built by colonial biochines. Apart from fisherfolk who sailed the world ocean sieving plankton and jellyfish or hunting krakens, most people lived on a raft that floated on the currents of the Great Northern Gyre, roving counterclockwise from the equator to within two thousand kilometres of the north pole.

The raft's only city, Tanrog, had been founded on Ghostkeeper ruins long overgrown by the construction coral that covered most of the raft in ranges of stony hills and valleys packed with low dark forest. The city's drenched, melancholy streets complemented its inturned secretive character. Tanrog was controlled by a dozen clans perpetually engaged in what they called the Great Game, manoeuvring for power by assassination, betrayal, secret pacts and sudden swift insurrections that deposed higher officials but left the police and governmental bureaucracies untouched. It was said that every other native of Tanrog was some sort of spy; walls were thorny with spray-can slogans and plastered with the handbills of opposing factions and splinter groups; obscure quarrels and rivalries flourished in its hundreds of cafés and bars.

As with politics, so with trade. A small wilderness of mirrors orbited Veles's trailing Trojan point, most leading to fringe worlds or unexplored parts of the network. Like many border worlds, its chief sources of off-world income were contraband goods and trade in rumours and clandestine knowledge. Secrets were jealously guarded; misinformation, trickery and deceit were standard practice. Unwary freebooters and traders could find themselves arrested on unspecified charges by law officers bribed by the brokers they'd just done business with, or by the brokers' rivals, and might never escape the city's Byzantine legal system.

That was why Tony insisted on scouting for information about Adam Apostu, the scholar who had sold information about the slime world to Raqle Thornhilde, before confronting him. He wanted to discover who the man's friends and enemies were, if he had a tame police officer or government official in his pocket, whether he made use of the freelance thugs routinely used by politicians and businesspeople to threaten, beat up or murder their rivals and enemies.

Raqle wanted him to find out if Apostu's story about how he came by the information was true. 'And I want to know if he sold it to anyone else,' she had told Tony on the spinner that had taken them back to Freedonia, where a ship hired by the broker had been waiting. 'And most of all, I want to know if he has a connection to your Aunty Jael.'

'They are all good questions,' Tony had said. 'But because you have never met him, the first thing we need to find out is who he really is.'

Raqle had never been to Veles. Adam Apostu was one of what she called her arms-length contacts: they had only ever talked via q-phone and avatar. According to Raqle, the scholar claimed that he had found out about the slime planet from a few lines in a garbled entry from a survey before the fall of the First Empire. It was plausible. Plenty of records had been lost, scrambled or erased during the war, and no one had known, back then, that slime-planet stromatolites sometimes contained archival genetics.

'I vetted him just like I vet everyone else,' Raqle said. 'He appeared to be mostly harmless.'

'No one is quite what they seem on Veles,' Tony said.

'Are you speaking from experience?'

'From common knowledge.'

'Common knowledge won't help you dig up actual information about this charlatan.'

'I am certain that my long and close relationship with Aunty Jael will be useful,' Tony said. 'Not to mention my cunning and charm. And perhaps your !Cha friend will be of some help, too.'

Unlikely Worlds had come along for the ride because that was where the strongest thread of Ada Morange's story presently led. 'I have been following her for a long time,' he said. 'I lost her, in the war. And now I have found her again.'

During the short voyage, as the ship passed through three mirror pairs in quick succession and powered in towards Veles, Unlikely Worlds questioned Tony about his adventures on the slime planet and afterwards, digging up details that Tony had more or less forgotten. The !Cha was also interested in Tony's memories of Aunty Jael. How the Okoye family had acquired her and the advice she had given them over the years; her lessons in biology and Elder Culture artefacts; the variant of Go they had sometimes played together; the bugs and plants he had collected for her.

Tony found himself talking about his resentment and anger at the way she had fooled and betrayed his family.

'All this time she was living a lie,' he said. 'She told us that the slime-planet job would be worthwhile. She told us that we would share a good profit. Instead, she played us. She betrayed us to the Red Brigade.'

He would make sure that she paid for that betrayal. For the deaths of Junot Johnson and everyone else killed in the raid. For his disgrace. And Raqle Thornhilde would pay too, for kidnapping him and dispatching him on this quest like a servant instead of an equal.

Unlikely Worlds said, 'If, as you claim, she is a chattel, how then can she pay?'

'Anything she has found is ours, to begin with. I will make sure that she will not profit from it.'

'Yet she has already profited from it, by using it to arrange her escape.'

The !Cha always had an answer for everything, and always tried to have the last word. Now, he mused about Ada Morange and the laminated brain she had become.

'It was not that she feared death,' he said. 'She was dying when I first knew her. But she did not want to miss what came next. She believed that her story was not yet done. And so it has proved.'

'Aunty Jael is not really Ada Morange,' Tony said. 'At best she is a copy. And not a very good one. She does not have free will. She cannot think new thoughts. She is a bundle of habits and memories masquerading as a person.'

'Oh, being laminated will have crimped Ada Morange's style, no doubt, but it is clear that she is still formidable. Look at how long she managed to fool you and your family,' Unlikely Worlds said.

Aside from his smug air of superiority, of being above petty human dramas, the !Cha was not bad company. He told Tony stories about the early days of the settling of the fifteen gift worlds. Encounters with eidolons; hauntings; tragedies and comedies resulting from the refusal by settlers to adapt to their new homes. He described the discovery of the first Ghajar ships, called down by a haunted young man who had been helped by Ada Morange – that story was true, according to Unlikely Worlds.

'I should know. I was there.'

There was that smugness again. Tony had to remind himself that there was real substance behind the !Cha's boasts. He had lived through a hundred and fifty years of human history, saw humans as humans could not see themselves, and knew how to make use of their vulnerabilities and appetites.

Unlikely Worlds was certainly better company than Raqle Thornhilde's cloned sons. Like the weircat, they had been designed as predators. They were not exactly stupid, but were bluntly uninterested in anything but the task at hand, lacked any sense of humour, and had an obscene love for their weapons. One or the other was always dismantling and reassembling a handgun, or sharpening a knife, or flicking little razor-edged wedges at a target. Their tasks were to snatch Adam Apostu and put him to some hard questioning, and to make sure that Tony didn't try to escape, screw up, or try to finesse the confrontation to his own advantage. Tony was worried that they had also been told to dispose of him once he had outlasted his usefulness to their mother.

The clone who accompanied him into Tanrog was called Bob. (The other was Bane; apparently, the clones' names all began with the letter B.) Like his sibling, Bob was tall, muscular and cat-footed, dressed in a grey many-pocketed field jacket, black knee-length shorts and split-toe slippers. His only distinguishing mark was a white scar that lifted one corner of his upper lip, giving him a slightly quizzical expression. He followed Tony without question or comment through the rainy streets to the house of Adam Apostu, down by the sea docks. Tucked away in a small courtyard accessed by an arch in a gatehouse, it was typical of the sailors' quarter: narrow-fronted and four storeys tall, with two slit windows to each floor and a steep roof that shed a silvery curtain of rainwater.

'Tricky,' Bob said, after studying it from the shelter of the archway. 'The door is faced with steel, the windows are too narrow for a man to climb through, and getting across that roof won't be easy. And there's no telling how it's connected to its neighbours, or the tunnels under the city. He could have any number of boltholes.'

'We are posing as honest freebooters,' Tony said. 'We do not need to kick in the front door. All we have to do is knock.'

'Maybe you can talk your way in. But can you talk your way back out?'

'First, let's ask the locals about Mr Apostu. Perhaps they can tell us something useful.'

The docks were dwarfed by the flank of the great sea wall, cut in several places by elevators that raised and lowered ships to sea level, a hundred metres below. Fullerene-hulled trawlers and seiners loomed amongst cranes and warehouses; a fish market bustled under a transparent dome; a long street of hostels, flophouses, pawnbrokers shared by fisherfolk and off-worlders, and cafés and bars with steamy windows, some kind of sport playing in a common window and tiny shrines tucked in a corner – flowers and candles in front of a tarnished mirror, a photograph of a local saint or an effigy of the white kraken – where sailors could wish for good fortune before a voyage.

Tony made the rounds, exchanging gossip, spinning a yarn about fragments of stromatolite code that happened to have come into his possession, saying that he had heard of a scholar, Adam Apostu, who might be interested in that kind of thing. Most of the traders and brokers either didn't know the man, or pretended they didn't. One said that yes, Adam Apostu's interest in code was well known, but it was mostly Ghajar ship code that he sought. Another claimed that the scholar was a dangerous man to do business with.

'He came here ten years ago,' the broker said. He was a lean man with a hooked nose and an extravagant moustache waxed into spirals at its ends. 'He has no friends or allies I know of, but people who try to cheat him have a habit of disappearing. And at least two freebooters with Ghajar code to sell likewise disappeared. I have heard that he has a feral biochine that can make itself invisible. A killing thing from the jungles of some hell-world. I also heard that he murdered a rival scholar on Bahamut before he came here. Best to stay away from him. Do business with honest people such as myself.'

Another broker, a cheerful young woman in a red niqab that showed only her eyes, said that, sure, she had met the old fraud, but she could not recommend doing business with him. 'He never goes out. You have to go to him. He presents as this mad-scientist kind of guy, and frankly it's hard to tell whether or not it's an act. But he definitely works with weird algorithms. His house, it's haunted. Eidolons coming up through the floorboards, hanging out under the ceiling . . . I had some Ghajar narrative code for sale. Rare, premium stuff. He wasn't interested. Said he already had it. I thought it was a bargaining position. But no, he genuinely didn't care. A couple of business pals of mine, they've had the same experience. You want to try to sell something to him? Good luck, because I don't know that he has ever bought anything.'

Tony returned to the ship and gave Raqle Thornhilde an account of his day's work. 'Adam Apostu is definitely interested in Ghajar code, but no one seems to have done any business with him. No one offered to act as a go-between, or to introduce me to him. And no one has ever seen him out and about in the quarter, either. He does not leave his house, or buy anything in the local shops. And he does not seem to have any friends, or to be connected with any of the local politicians.'

'That you know of,' Raqle said.

'You cannot do any real business here without paying off one or more of the local pols. Especially if you are an off-worlder. If someone has an interest in him, they would have sent someone to talk to me by now,' Tony said. 'There are stories that he's mad and bad, but they are the kind of stories you hear about eccentric scholars and wizards everywhere.'

'Perhaps he isn't the one we're looking for,' Raqle said. 'Perhaps someone else stole his identity and used it as cover when they contacted me.'

She was nervous, outside her comfort zone. Brokers did not usually chase leads. They waited for leads to come to them.

Tony said, 'We will soon know. I made an appointment to see him.'

'You did what?'

The broker's anger spat at Tony across eight thousand light years.

'You sent me to check him out. I checked him out. And now I have arranged an appointment with him.'

'My boys let you do that? Without my permission?'

'Bob realised that it was the only way in.'

It had not been hard to convince the clone. Tony had pointed out that in a place where everyone knew everyone else's business it would be strange if he did not contact the man he had been asking about.

'What did he say?'

'Bob?' Tony was having fun after a hard day in the rain.

'Don't try to be smart, Mr Okoye. My boys have ways of making smart people realise that they aren't so smart after all.'

'I did not talk to Apostu,' Tony said. 'I talked to an AI. I told it I had some interesting code. It had already heard about me. Apostu may be a recluse, but he is plugged into the local rumour net. The AI told me to show up at the house tomorrow.'

'If you're trying to trick me you'll regret it.'

'I am trying to find out what we both want to find out.'

Tony sweated out the short silence. He knew that the broker was thinking about telling her boys to hurt him, either to make sure he was telling the truth or as a lesson.

At last she said, 'All right.'

'As in, "All right, let's do it?"'

'I told you: don't try to be smart. Now let me talk to my boys. You can have your meeting with Apostu, but you'll do it my way.'

39. Perspective

They overnighted in the little valley below the outlook. Its dead spot meant that they were safe from drone overflights, and the Land Cruiser was almost invisible under its camo drop sheet, a distortion as slight as a heat shimmer or a minor glitch in some virtual-reality game. Like the blind-spot warp of Lisa's ghost.

'You could make a fortune in the tomb-raider trade,' Isabelle told her. 'Finding everything that everyone else has not yet found.'

'I was a tomb raider until everything went wrong,' Lisa said. 'I can't see myself going back to it.'

'You could fly over the City of the Dead in a helicopter. Make a map. Sell locations to others.'

Lisa thought of her brief out-of-body experience. 'What I'd like is the nice quiet life I had before all this blew it up.'

She and Isabelle ate US Army MRE rations from self-heating pouches, Isabelle grumbling that she hadn't been able to source the French equivalent; Lisa pushed away the thought that French rations might contain a bottle of wine or two. Those cute little ones you used to get on airplanes, back in the day. Her ghost was a ringing presence, as impossible to ignore as tinnitus.

Isabelle slept in the Land Cruiser; Lisa scraped a hollow in drift sand and wrapped herself in a mylar blanket, thinking of trips with Willie, sleeping with him under the stars. Trying to remember his face and panicking because she couldn't, and there it was. Oh, Willie.

She woke in grey predawn light, wiped a film of dew from her face. Unlikely Worlds stood nearby, his tank balanced on the column of its three legs like a piece of abandoned street furniture. She asked him if he ever slept.

'My rest periods are not as yours,' he said. 'A different form of consciousness, rather than the oblivion and involuntary hallucinations that you embrace.'

Isabelle was still asleep, curled up in a sleeping bag on the back seat of the Land Cruiser. Lisa snagged the field glasses and a bottle of water and hiked to the outlook. She wanted to shake the stiffness from her bones and to check out the activity around the tomb, but when she got up there she couldn't spot any movement around the vehicles or the big tent. It was six-twenty in the morning. Maybe the police slept late. Maybe the Jackaroo did, too. Or maybe they'd turned off their avatars while whatever it was that animated them turned its attention elsewhere. Keeping the human race in check must require a lot of multitasking.

The star was still burning at the top of the distant mesa. Lisa glanced at it, quickly looked away. Safer to study the ghostly smoke inside the roofless cube at one end of the Boxbuilder ruins. It hung about a metre above the bare rock floor, composed of myriad tiny elements like 3-D pixels, twirling around and around in tireless trajectories. Lisa was reminded of a snake she'd seen once on a country road, looping endlessly over itself because its back had been broken when some car had run it over, and wondered where the algorithm that generated the smoke twist was cached. Boxbuilder ruins were found on every one of the gift worlds, constructed from self-repairing polymer that synthesised new material from rock and air and rain. No one knew what the creatures who had built them had looked like, how they lived and loved, whether they'd even been sentient. So much was unknown. So much would never be known. The algorithm could be part of the structure's homeostatic mechanism, or perhaps it was something its former inhabitants had left behind, a forgotten keepsake . . .

She jumped when Unlikely Worlds said, close behind her, 'I wonder if I see what you see. And if either of us sees what its makers saw.'

'What do you see?'

'Something old and broken. Like much on this world.'

'Older than you?'

'We do not privilege any particular moment in time because of its antiquity. It is more of a . . . continuum.'

'But the stories you collect have a beginning and an end. That's the point of stories.'

'Perhaps you misunderstand the point of why we collect them. You think that the meaning of this gesture has changed because those who created it have gone, and what it meant to them is not the same as what it means to you. Or to me. But the meaning you read into it must have been part of it when it was created, or it would not be here now. Did its creators understand that? Perhaps not. But their interpretation does not invalidate yours. And yours does not invalidate theirs. So which is more important?'

'You are here because this is part of Ada Morange's story. Doesn't that mean you are privileging one viewpoint?'

'I seize moments out of time and polish them until all their facets shine because I want to impress those who might mingle information with me,' Unlikely Worlds said. 'To improve, to put it in brutally simple terms, my reproductive fitness. I know it is irrational, but no more so, really, than your version of bond pairing. And besides, the stories I collect are your stories, so they are deeply tinted by the way you think.'

'And you think the way we think lacks perspective,' Lisa said.

'There is no need to be ashamed. It is an inevitable outcome of the way you bind time to yourselves. If it is of any comfort, it is no better or worse than the world views of most Elder Cultures. All are alike because they are all wrong, yet all are different, because they are all wrong in different ways.'

This alien creature passing off schoolkid philosophy as profundity. Or using it, maybe, to mock her.

Lisa changed the subject, asked about the Jackaroo avatars. Were they working for the TCU, or was the TCU working for them?

'They are here to help.'

'Yeah? So why aren't they helping Ada Morange?'

'Perhaps they are, in their own way.'

'From my limited perspective and experience, I'd say they don't want her to find what she wants to find,' Lisa said.

'Investigator Nevers certainly does not,' Unlikely Worlds said. 'As for the Jackaroo, who can tell? Not I.'

Lisa remembered something that Chloe Millar had told her: the Jackaroo sometimes forbade things to make them more attractive. And she also remembered how the avatar had found those harmless tesserae in her house.

She said, 'Can they see what I see? Can they see ghosts?'

'Why not?'

'So they could have found and neutralised what's down there, the source of the breakout, long before Willie found it. Long before they gave us this world, and all the others. But they didn't.'

'Perhaps they do not know what will hurt you, and what will help.'

Lisa said, 'So how did they help you?'

'We did not need their help,' the !Cha said primly.

After a quick breakfast of granola bars and instant coffee, they retraced the route through the hills and then drove due west into the Badlands. Hour after hour skimming across alluvial fans and long stretches of rippled basement sand, skirting fleets of dunes. Following one of the old ceramic roads at first, then crossing a vast achingly flat playa towards the ghosts of mountains sketched at the horizon. Once, Lisa saw flickering movement off to the north: a translucent sketch of a giant figure got up from feathery fronds and bladders thrashing along. After a handful of seconds it blinked out, then reappeared at its starting point and thrashed forward again. She watched it spin past and recede and vanish into the playa's white glare, wondering if Unlikely Worlds saw it, wondering if he knew that she could see it.

At last, they stopped at a point no different from any other. Isabelle launched a sparrow-sized drone to keep watch, even though the playa was empty in every direction as far as the eye could see. They ate army rations. They slept, Isabelle in the Land Cruiser, Lisa on the ground again. It was fucking cold, but the night sky was awesome. The stars weren't uncountable, maybe five thousand or so, about the same the number that were visible from Earth, but they seemed to fill the black bowl of night from edge to edge. Stars everywhere Lisa looked. And presently the smoke of the North American nebula rose, a cloud of hydrogen gas roughly shaped like the continental USA and spread across a quarter of the sky, glowing red because it was ionised by hot stars embedded in it. One of them, Miro's Diamond, shining in the approximate location of Ottawa, was the brightest star in First Foot's sky. A massive blue-white O-type star that in a few million years, after burning through all of its hydrogen fuel, would bloat into a red supergiant and either explode as a supernova or evolve into a Wolf-Rayet star so hot that it would blow vast shells of glowing gas from its surface and form a nebula of its own. At more than two hundred light years away it would have little effect on First Foot, but future clients of the Jackaroo were going to have a spectacular view.

There was some perspective, if you wanted it.

A little later, the faint lodestar that nagged at Lisa's attention followed the chip of the moon above the western horizon. Wondering if it was Ada Morange's ship, she fell asleep tracking it, woke to find a wind had got up. The dawn sky was white with blowing dust and the sun, rising inside smeary shells of red light, looked twice its usual size.

Lisa and Isabelle sheltered from dust squalls in the Land Cruiser; Unlikely Worlds squatted outside, impervious. Lisa dozed off, was shaken awake by Isabelle, who shoved a tablet at her and started the Land Cruiser, saying, 'We're in deep trouble.'

'What about Unlikely Worlds?' Lisa said, as the Land Cruiser began to move. She was still half-asleep, cotton-mouthed, tangled in the fading remnants of a dream.

'We will come back for him,' Isabelle said. She was hunched over the steering wheel, peering ahead as the Land Cruiser accelerated through skittering squalls of dust, jolting over ripples and cracks in the playa floor. She looked tense and drawn. She looked like she had seen a ghost.

'What's wrong? Where are we going?' Lisa said.

'Check the tablet,' Isabelle said grimly.

Lisa studied the aerial view of the dust-blown playa. After a few moments, she made out a tiny figure glinting at the centre of the field of vision. She zoomed in: a grainy view of a Jackaroo avatar running at full tilt, naked, head down, arms pumping, dust puffing up from its feet.

'How did it get ahead of us?' she said.

'It didn't,' Isabelle said. 'The Jackaroo can make avatars from air and water, a few elements from dirt or plant life. I thought we were safe from that. The playa is mostly salt and gypsum. It is partly why we chose it as a landing place. But the Jackaroo must have found somewhere with the necessary elements. A seep, a pond, a place where plants grow. They made an avatar, and now it is coming for us. Luckily, the drone spotted it.'

Lisa remembered a famous video clip from the early days after First Contact: a shaky phone-cam image zooming in on a distant golden blur at the shore of a lake as it sharpened into human form, like a *Star Trek* special effect. She said, 'Is that why it's naked?'

'Yes. They cannot make clothes.'

The Land Cruiser was racing flat out, pedal to the metal. It thumped over something and was briefly airborne; when it landed, Isabelle wrestled with the steering wheel to straighten it out. Lisa buckled her seat belt, said, 'What are you going to do?'

'I must deal with it before the ship comes,' Isabelle said.

'Deal with it? You mean kill it?'

Isabelle glanced at her. 'You cannot kill something that is not actually alive. And I have been ordered to do it.'

'It doesn't mean you should.'

'What else can I do?'

'One avatar can't stop us.'

'We do not know what it can do,' Isabelle said.

'I didn't sign up for this.'

'It might want to kill you, Lisa. Because of your ghost. Did you not think of that?'

'That's crazy,' Lisa said, but she didn't quite believe that it was. At the very least, after her exposure to Willie's ghost, Adam Nevers and the Jackaroo would want to quarantine her. Stick her in some isolation facility for an indefinite period, basically life without the chance of parole, as sometimes happened to those infected with dangerous eidolons.

'We said that we would protect you,' Isabelle said. 'This is part of it.'

A couple of minutes later, a tiny figure appeared ahead. Lost in a scud of dust, appearing again, seeming to float towards them. 'Merde,' Isabelle said. Her knuckles were white on the steering wheel. Lisa wondered for a bare second if she should make a grab for it, and then the avatar was right there in front of them and there was a tremendous bang and something flew up and smacked into the windshield and was gone.

Isabelle braked hard in a cloud of dust, turned the Land Cruiser around and drove slowly back, stopped. She took a breath, then undid her seat belt and without a word to Lisa opened the door and stepped out. Lisa followed, shaky and apprehensive.

'It exploded when we hit it,' Isabelle said.

She was looking at something glinting on the dirty white ground, part of an arm or a leg. They walked about, found other fragments scattered across the crazed dry mud. A shattered hand, hollow as a glove. Splinters. They were already turning black, flaking, disintegrating, blowing away on the dusty wind.

Lisa and Isabelle climbed back into the Land Cruiser and followed its tracks towards the spot where they had left Unlikely Worlds.

'We will not talk about this with him,' Isabelle told Lisa.

'He'll want to know where we went, and why.'

'Yes, and I will tell him there was a small problem, taken care of. If he objects, he can find another ride.'

'He probably knows all about it, anyway,' Lisa said.

She was picturing the Jackaroo avatar, how it had been framed in the windshield a moment before the Land Cruiser struck it. It hadn't slowed as they'd borne down on it. It had kept running. And at the last moment it had looked up. Looked straight at her with eyes white as pebbles.

She was trying to work out what that look had meant. That the avatar knew who she was, maybe. Or maybe it hadn't been looking at her, but at her ghost . . . One thing was certain: the Jackaroo knew that she was riding in the vehicle that had smashed one of their avatars to splinters. Which meant that Adam Nevers probably knew, too. There was no way she could stay on First

Foot now, but she also knew that she had put herself in the hands of some seriously ruthless characters.

Isabelle's q-phone warbled. 'Il est fait,' she told it. 'Oui, complètement détruit.' Listening to someone talk, then saying, 'Dieu merci. Le plus tôt sera le mieux.'

She switched off the q-phone, told Lisa that the ship was almost down. 'Don't worry. Everything will be okay.'

'Good,' Lisa said, thinking that everything was very far from fucking okay.

It didn't help that the first thing Unlikely Worlds said, when they got back, was, 'And how was the hunting?'

He knew, all right.

'We did what had to be done,' Isabelle said, with a pinched angry look at Lisa. 'And that is all I have to say.'

'This is turning out to be quite the adventure,' Unlikely Worlds said, but didn't ask any questions.

By unspoken agreement Lisa and Isabelle walked away in opposite directions from the !Cha and the Land Cruiser. Presently, a black speck appeared in the pale sky, quickly growing larger as it dropped towards them, falling silently down a fold it created in the planet's gravity field. A D-class yacht some forty metres from stem to stern. Lisa saw the spines piercing the black pineapple of its hull, thought of Willie. It halted with its flat stern about twenty metres above the ground and a few minutes later a hatch dilated with a busy movement like iron filings flowing around a magnetic pole. A rope flopped out and two men slid down it. They were dressed in coveralls and heavy boots, took off their work gloves to shake hands with Isabelle and Lisa.

After that, it was all business. A steel cable dropped, terminating in four straps that were each hooked around the Land Cruiser's wheels. Isabelle, Lisa and Unlikely Worlds climbed inside, the two men clambered onto the roof, and with a jerk and a jolt the vehicle swung off the ground.

The last Lisa saw of First Foot was a tilting horizon hazed with dust, a sliver of milky sky. And then the belly of the spaceship swallowed her.

40. Old Dark House

'It isn't too late to go back to the ship,' Tony told the two clones. 'Or we could find an all-night café in the docks. Get out of this rain and drink tea and come back here in the morning, when I arranged to meet him. Do it right, instead of blundering in like thugs.'

'We do it this way or not at all,' Bob said.

'It is decided,' Bane said.

Shrouded in their hooded rain capes, they were standing in the archway to the courtyard where Adam Apostu's tall narrow house stood, as dark and quiet as its neighbours. It was the middle of the night. It was still raining. Rain slanted past the single lamp that lit the courtyard; rain hammered on wet flagstones; rain dripped from carved stones that edged the curve of the arch.

Raqle Thornhilde had decided that it would be best to strike early and surprise Adam Apostu. 'The man probably won't talk unless we strong-arm him,' she'd said, after Tony had objected. 'You know how those scholars are. They'd sooner starve than sell their so-called secrets. We'll give him a little tickling, and see what he gives up.'

Tony was not looking forward to that 'little tickling'. Despite his vow to do everything necessary to track down Aunty Jael and the Red Brigade, he did not think he could justify the torture of a harmless eccentric, and was worried that Adam Apostu might not survive the attention of Raqle's boys. Suppose he died before he yielded anything useful? Suppose he had connections that Tony had failed to uncover? They could probably outrun the local police, if it came to it, but there were plenty of powerful people who, like Raqle Thornhilde, could reach across worlds to exact revenge.

Unlikely Worlds, appearing to share Tony's misgivings, had declined to accompany what he called their little fishing expedition, claiming that he was interested in the stories people made of what they did, not the actual doing. And although Tony had told Raqle that they would learn more by using charm, flattery and bribes than by breaking bones or slicing off body parts, the broker was adamant.

'Have you forgotten what the Reds did to your home?' she said. 'This is no time for subtlety; this is a desperate and dangerous business. Quit bitching and get on with it. Or do I have to ask my boys to persuade you?'

Bane kept watch under the archway while Bob led Tony out into the rainy courtyard. The big man sprayed something around the edges of the door of Adam Apostu's house, told Tony to step back. A moment of silence, raindrops sizzling off the hoods and skirts of their rain capes. Then with a sharp crack and a blue flash the door fell flat on the wet flagstones, and Bob grabbed Tony's arm and hauled him across the threshold.

A single room occupied the ground floor, dark and unquiet. Little rustlings and squeaks. Flutterings. Bob floated a sparklight that revealed furniture piled everywhere, with only a narrow passage to the staircase on the far side. Shadows skittered under upturned chairs and tables, cat-sized and quick. Eidolons.

Tony could feel their attention prickling in his head, stepped back with electric shock when one reared up in front of him. It was pale and bone-thin, and had too many eyes studded around the dish of its face. He felt its attention push towards him, and then it recoiled and whirled away like a rag blown on a gust of wind.

'Up,' Bob said. 'Quick.'

Another dark room at the top of the stairs, bare floorboards and red curtains stretched from wall to wall. The sparklight cast Tony's and Bob's shadows across the curtains' heavy folds; the shadows rippled as something stirred and parted them.

A man stepped through, dressed in a long black gown whose hood covered most of his head. His face was mild and milk-white;

his eyes were masked by glasses with round black mirrors for lenses. He pulled a wheeled pole with him as he took two tentative steps into the room. His free hand, white-gloved, groped the air and he asked in a high quavering voice, 'Who are you? Why have you disturbed me?'

Tony realised that the man, Adam Apostu, was blind and ill. A transparent sac hung from the top of his pole, and a line looped from it to a slit in the waist of his gown.

'We come for answers, not questions,' Bob said.

Tony pushed back the hood of his rain cape and said, 'I want to discuss stromatolites and Ghajar algorithms.'

'You are early for your appointment. And there was no need to enter by force. As you can see, I am a harmless old man, not at all like the monster they told you about.'

Adam Apostu's lips scarcely moved when he spoke. His skin was caked with white powder and seemed to be as stiff as leather. Tony wondered if it was a symptom of his illness.

'I was told that you never leave this house,' Tony said. 'Yet you know that we were asking about you.'

'I don't go out because I prefer people to come to me. And I have no need of food, as this drip sustains my body. But I have my mice, and my mice have ears,' Adam Apostu said. 'They go everywhere in the city, and most people don't notice them. They travel the paths of the dead. Speaking of the dead, how is the guest in your head?'

Tony was too surprised to deny it. 'Who told you about that?'

Before the scholar could reply, Bob said, 'We don't care about your mice, or about dead people either. We want to know what you know about Ada Morange and the Red Brigade.'

Tony said, 'Ada Morange is a laminated brain owned by my family. She also goes by the name of Aunty Jael. Do you know her?'

'Of course,' Adam Apostu said.

Tony was surprised by the man's candour. He said, 'Have you spoken to her? Did she tell you about the slime planet?'

If he kept Adam Apostu talking, there would be no need for Bob's tickling.

'I learned about it in records that no one else had bothered to access for fifty years. People commonly say that much knowledge

259

was lost in the various wars when the two empires rose and fell. But it's more accurate to say that most of it was misplaced. You just have to know how to look for it.'

'Did you share your find with Ada Morange? Did she suggest that you offer it to Raqle Thornhilde?'

'I sold the details of the slime planet to Raqle Thornhilde. And also suggested that she hire you.'

Tony looked at Bob. 'Is this true?'

'He lies,' Bob said, and shucked off his rain cape and drew a knife with a long thin blade. 'This is my tickler, old man. I use it to tickle the truth out of people. First I'll cut your food line. Then I'll start cutting you.'

Tony said quickly, 'He won't hurt you if you tell the truth.'

'But I am telling the truth.' The scholar seemed to be amused.

Tony said, 'Why use a third party? Why not tell my family directly?'

'Would you have believed a humble and obscure scholar such as me? I knew you were working out of Dry Salvages, so I contacted one of the brokers there, told her about the slime planet, and pointed her towards you. But I see now that she is dissatisfied with the arrangement.'

'She thinks you cheated her when the Red Brigade raided my home and took the wizards and the stromatolites.'

'Not to mention Ada Morange,' Adam Apostu said.

'She belongs to my family,' Tony said. 'I want her back, and I believe that you may know where she is.'

'Of course I do.'

'Is she with the Red Brigade?'

'I suppose you could say that she mostly is.'

'Is she a prisoner?'

'No.'

'She made a deal with them, didn't she? Her freedom in exchange for the Ghajar eidolon and the archival genetics in the stromatolites.'

'You seem to know everything,' Adam Apostu said.

'I don't know why the Red Brigade wants the eidolon and the archival genetics. Why are they so important?'

260

'The Red Brigade stole them from my mother,' Bob said. He held up the knife in front of his face and smiled around it. 'We've come to get them back.'

'What you want isn't here,' Adam Apostu said.

'You know where they are,' Bob said. 'And I'm going to tickle it out of you.'

But when he stepped towards the old scholar a storm of eidolons blew up around him, pouring like smoke from gaps in the floorboards. Bob roared with anger and slashed at them with his knife. It was as futile as trying to cut air or shadows. In moments, he was completely obscured in a whirling column of black shapes: somewhere in this old dark house Adam Apostu was running a huge cache of Elder Culture algorithms. Wisps whipped out at Tony, but recoiled before touching him.

'They know your friend, Master Tony,' Adam Apostu said, speaking quickly and precisely. 'If I were you, I'd take this chance to escape. Once Raqle Thornhilde realises you're no longer of any use, she'll have her bully-boys dispose of you. That would be unfortunate, because the guest aboard your ship has caught my interest. It has made some very interesting changes.'

'How do you know about my ship?'

Bob, blinded by the eidolons, lunged wildly with his knife; Adam Apostu deftly parried it with his pole, saying, 'I talked to it, of course. You should leave now, before Bane comes.'

'There you are, you old fucker,' Bob sang, and struck again.

The old man leaned backwards, the knife point missing his face by a scant centimetre, and Bob howled inside his whirlwind of eidolons and slammed into him. They crashed into the curtains; eidolons flared away into every corner of the room. Adam Apostu's hood had fallen back, revealing a plastic shell that had replaced his scalp. Bob caught his pole in one hand and swung his knife, hacking deep into the scholar's neck, wrenching it free, hacking again.

Adam Apostu's head tumbled to the floor. There was no blood. The scholar's dark glasses were askew, revealing silvery eyes with cruciform pupils that swivelled towards Tony. His black lips parted and he croaked, 'Run, you fool.'

261

The headless body had broken free from Bob and was be-labouring him with the pole. Swift ruthless blows that drove the clone from one side of the room to the other. Tony understood what Adam Apostu was, then. Not a man at all, but a hand controlled by someone else, from some other location. It swung the pole, hit Bob's head with a tremendous clang. The clone went down on one knee, tried to push up, and the headless hand swung its pole again and a gout of blood splashed across the wall.

Tony ran for the stairs and in the darkness missed the bottom step and fell full length, smacking the breath from his lungs. The thorny thickets of tables and chairs, legs interlocked in a mad sculpture, were lit only by the faint light that outlined the open doorway. Tony saw a shadow moving there and scrambled sideways on elbows and knees, curling up inside his rain cape under a tangle of chairs a moment before Bane charged through the doorway and ran straight at the stairs, slippers pounding a hand's breadth from Tony's hiding place.

As soon as the clone had disappeared up the staircase, Tony pushed to his feet and looked all around. He could have made a run through the doorway, across the courtyard, out into the city, but he knew that Bane and Bob would track him down if he took to the streets, and Adam Apostu had pointed him towards a better hiding place.

The construction coral foundations of the city were honey-combed with kilometres of tunnels and voids. People buried their dead down there, in catacombs that they visited on high days and saints' days. There were hundreds of entrances, in churches and houses, in cafés and shops: Tony believed that there must be one hidden somewhere under the thickets of furniture, and as he looked all around a wisp of faint luminescence curdled in a far corner.

He had to crawl under and over a pile of chairs to reach it. It stood like a faint, frozen candle flame above a flagstone. As thumping footsteps and oaths sounded overhead, Tony ran his fingers around the edges of the stone, found a depression that slid backwards with a click. The stone hinged up and Tony grabbed the free edge and pulled it upright, revealing a ladder dropping down a square shaft.

The wisp of light darted past and plummeted straight down the shaft. Tony shrugged off his rain cape and followed, using the iron ring set in the underside of the hinged flagstone to pull it shut, climbing down the ladder to a narrow passage lit by small lamps set in the rough construction-coral ceiling.

The light circled him twice and fluttered forward. The passage slanted down, always down, joined or crossed here and there by other passages. The paths of the dead. Here was a skull in a niche carved into the stony wall, mirror fragments jammed in its sockets reflecting the tiny flame that burned in front of it. Here was the body of a woman propped upright in an alcove, wrapped in tattered winding cloth, her face an eyeless leathery mask. Here was a window showing a loop of a child running into sunlit water on a beach of some other world, turning in knee-deep waves and smiling.

Not all of the dead were human. As Tony followed the wisp of light down a passage whose walls were lined with polished construction coral, he saw a tall figure seemingly constructed from sticks totter away from him, vanishing into a crevice in the wall.

The route slanted deeper into the city's foundations, leaving behind human burials. The walls began to sweat; there was a scent of salt and rot in the air. A handful of scrabs skittered around his feet, hard shells glistening. And then the way ended in a cavern or cistern flooded with still black water. Stairs led down to a walkway. The wisp of light shot out across it and halted above a platform on the far side, where a pale-skinned man stood beside the aquarium tank of the !Cha, Unlikely Worlds.

41. Timeship

The trip to First Foot's wormhole took a little over a day. The ship accelerated continuously until it reached midpoint, and then, after a disorientating fifteen minutes in free fall while it swung around, began to decelerate. There would be heavy traffic on the far side of the wormhole, so it wasn't a good idea to slam out of it at high velocity. The ship lacked windows and portholes, but Lisa could watch First Foot's ochre and blue globe dwindle on the big HD screen in the guest lounge, an airy space at the centre of an accommodation module constructed by a Dutch shipbuilding firm that usually designed the interiors of superyachts and inserted into the Ghajar ship's open-plan interior like a bullet into the chamber of a gun. White carpets, white leather furniture, walls panelled in fine-grained maple, brass handrails. The guest cabins and en-suite bathrooms little marvels of economy.

Lisa, Isabelle and Unlikely Worlds shared this space with the pilot, the half-dozen servants who unobtrusively catered to their needs, and the specialists who been sent from Terminus to deal with artefacts retrieved from Willie's dig site – Doris Bauer, a formidably brisk Austrian woman about Lisa's age, and her two handsome young assistants. They documented the tesserae from the wall of the tomb and performed a preliminary assessment of Lisa and her ghost that wasn't much different from the yearly check-ups in the hospital in Port of Plenty. The same tests, the same meaningless reassurances. The eidolon was active, but there was no indication that it was malign. It wasn't clear how it had been changed, why Lisa could now see the activity of Elder Culture artefacts, or why some unknown object or location in the sky tugged at her attention (she knew now that it wasn't the ship because that little tug was still there, somewhere off to port), but according to Doris Bauer everything would be clarified by further tests when they reached Terminus. 'We have the best people there. The best facilities. You are in good hands.'

Lisa thought that the luxury was amusingly over the top, but Isabelle was in her element. She'd had a manicure and a haircut while Lisa was being tested, and had changed into a white silk trouser suit, and spent most of her time on her q-phone, giving crisp accounts of her adventure in the back country to a management team and a variety of experts, and briefing a crew who were riding towards First Foot on the shuttle. They'd been tasked with exploring and documenting the site after the police quit it, and would also hire local tomb raiders to search the area, concentrating on the places Lisa had spotted from the outlook.

'There may have been other survivors of the crash,' Isabelle told Lisa. 'Or other fragments of the ship scattered across the area. I have also arranged for an expert to be transported to Terminus. He will examine the code in those tesserae.'

There was a coolness, a certain wary distance, between her and Lisa. They hadn't talked about what had happened out on the playa, and Lisa was ashamed at her complicity. It seemed like a kind of cowardice, and tinted her hope that Ada Morange's people could help her to discover everything she needed to know about her ghost.

'Does your expert work at Peking University?' she said to Isabelle, earning a brief look of surprise.

'I forget you have done your own research,' Isabelle said. 'Yes. He was approached by the TCU, but we tempted him away with a better offer.'

'So Nevers wants to find out what the Ghajar code contains too,' Lisa said. 'Given his past history, he won't let it go.'

'Perhaps not. But we have one advantage.'

'What's that?'

Unlikely Worlds spoke up before Isabelle could reply. 'Why, you, of course. I am beginning to believe that your story may be as interesting as Professor Morange's.'

A vast machinery seemed to be settling into place around Lisa. She told herself that she'd done the right thing, that Ada Morange could protect her from Adam Nevers and the TCU, and find some way of exorcising her ghost, but Isabelle and Doris were vague about what would happen when they reached Terminus, and they shared an unsettling gestalt with the ship's crew. A kind of calm certainty; an unquestioning belief in the righteousness of their cause. They were a lot like Adam Nevers, Lisa realised. They saw the world in stark binary divisions. Black hats v. white hats, like in the old cowboy movies. Us v. them.

A couple of hours before transit through the wormhole, Isabelle and Doris Bauer and her assistants met in the lounge for what they called a visualisation meeting, a cross between a pep talk and one of the mindfulness sessions Lisa had volunteered for in the aftermath of the Bad Trip, hoping that it would help her come to terms with her ghost. They didn't actually sit in a circle holding hands while ambient music played in the background and candles scented the air, but that was the vibe. Afterwards, Isabelle told Lisa that they had been making sure that they knew what their goals were and how to achieve them, but to Lisa it seemed a lot like the way cult members suppressed doubts and reaffirmed their commitment to their leader and their cause. What would they do, she wondered, if she tried to back out now? Love-bomb her into submission? Shackle her in a luxuriously appointed cell?

'I find much of your behaviour strange,' Unlikely Worlds said, when Lisa asked him what he thought of the visualisation meeting. 'It wouldn't be any fun if I didn't.'

'And there's the way they refer to Ada Morange as "The Professor",' Lisa said. 'The reverent tone they have. The way they've let her get inside their heads.'

'She depends on the love of others. As far as she is concerned, encouraging that love is a survival trait.'

'Because of her illness, you mean? Just how bad is it?'

'Because of the way she has chosen to prolong her story. The path she wants to take.'

At last the wormhole throat resolved out of the big black. A faint granular star quickly gaining shape and definition, rushing towards the ship at startling speed. Watching in the lounge, Lisa glimpsed a dark mirror set in the flat polished face of a cone-shaped rock and framed by the architecture of the strange matter that held it open, and then it was gone and with no sense of transition the ship emerged from the far end of the wormhole, one of fifteen that orbited the L5 point where the gravity of Earth and the gravity of the Moon cancelled each other out.

The view on the HD screen panned across black space to Earth's crescent, small and sharp and blue and lovely, and Lisa was cleaved by an intense pang of homesickness. Before the Jackaroo came with their offer to help that small blue planet had been the only home humanity had known, the place where every person ever born had lived and died. Most of human history was down there, along with everything from Lisa's life before she had won the lottery and gone up and out. Her family, her childhood home, her high school and the college where she'd studied maths, the places where she'd worked, the people she'd known, the things she'd seen . . .

Two servants in white jackets and trousers padded through the lounge, collecting coffee cups and other loose objects. A few minutes later, there was a soft chime, Lisa's chair folded around her, and she was gripped by the floating sensation of weightlessness as the ship swung on its axis towards its new course. A second chime, and the pull of acceleration came back. Less than an hour later, the ship shot through another wormhole and emerged in orbit around the red dwarf star 2CR 5938, otherwise known as Terminus, the lesser partner in a binary system with a G0 star a little brighter and hotter than Earth's Sun.

Unlike the other gift worlds, there was no rocky, Earth-like planet here. Instead an Elder Culture, the Spiders, had engineered fourteen planetoids that orbited at the inner edge of a broad asteroid belt, shepherded into a loose archipelago by interaction with the gravity of a hot super-Jupiter orbiting much closer in. Exotic dark matter denser than neutronium had been injected into the planetoids' centres of mass, increasing their surface gravity to about one-third of Earth's, they had been wrapped in bubbles of quasi-living polymer that conserved scanty oxygen/nitrogen atmospheres, and had been landscaped and seeded with life, and space elevators had been spun between their surfaces and counterweight asteroids parked in stationary orbits. The engineers of these little garden worlds were long gone, as were the other Elder Cultures who had lived on them for a century or ten thousand years. People lived there now. Farmers, mostly. An agrarian commonwealth. A storybook utopia.

At first, only one of the planetoids, Niflheimr, had been colonised. An ice world about the size of Ceres, served by a Jackaroo shuttle that looped between its space-elevator terminal and Earth, it had been settled by a handful of hardy pioneers, and visited by science crews studying the weird physics of the dark-matter stuff in its core or the space-elevator technology. There had been vague plans to explore the other planetoids, but the Jackaroo shuttles were locked in fixed cycles between Earth and the gift worlds, and the only functional spacecraft that humanity possessed at the time had been Soyuz and Orion capsules, and the various unmanned cargo modules that serviced the International Space Station. Then the first sargassos of Ghajar ships had been discovered, independent space travel had become possible, and all the worldlets of Terminus were suddenly within reach. Soon afterwards, code recovered from a crashed Ghajar spacecraft had been cracked, revealing details of its last voyage. A rogue explorer, chased by TCU agents, had retraced that voyage to a rosette of wormholes orbiting the only planet of Terminus's companion star: the access point to a vast wormhole network, the New Frontier. The archipelago of Terminus was a way station now, a link between Earth and the worlds of the New Frontier.

The spark of the elevator terminal, hung beyond the pale half disc of Niflheimr, slowly grew larger on the lounge's HD screen, resolving into an oval rock a kilometre across, its ashen surface pitted with the dark mouths of docking shafts. Lisa saw an I-class schooner rise smoothly and slowly from one of those shafts and accelerate away. According to Unlikely Worlds, it was heading out to the G0 star and the gateway to the New Frontier. A journey of more than four hundred and fifty astronomical units, fifteen times the distance between the Sun and Neptune, that even with the Ghajar bias drive would take at least ninety days. And that was only the beginning of a voyage to some new world, some new settlement, far across the Milky Way.

'The things you people can do now!' Unlikely Worlds said. 'The stories you make!'

They were in free fall again. The ship was idling towards the elevator terminal, preparing to dock. A scatter of other ships hung in the black sky beyond the terminal's lumpy crescent. Lisa, doped by an anti-nausea patch, thought it looked like a scene from one of the space-opera video games her first boyfriend had loved to play.

Isabelle pointed to a fat dark cylinder much bigger than the rest of the ships, or maybe much closer. 'There!' she said. 'You see?'

'Sure. What am I seeing?'

'That,' Isabelle said, a lilt in her voice reminding Lisa of how a stump preacher she had seen one time in Joe's Corner had pronounced the name of the Son of God, 'is the Professor's timeship.'

42. Speaker For The Dead

'We don't discuss our affairs with people up on the skin,' the speaker for the dead told Tony, 'and they don't trouble us. So if you stick with me and stay out of the common ways, no one will know where you are.'

His name was Victor Ursu. 'A good name for a speaker, Ursu,' he said. 'Back where we all came from, it means "bear". And bears have a long association with the underground, seeing as how they sleep out the winter in caves. Down here, of course, it's mostly the dead who sleep. And we do our best to make sure their sleep is undisturbed.'

Victor was a compact muscular man with milky skin and a bristly crest of black hair. He carried an iron staff that reminded Tony of Adam Apostu's pole, was dressed in a yellow skinsuit and heavy boots, and his belt was hung with climbing gear, flares, blast dots, several knives, and a fullerene rock hammer. He and his fellow speakers maintained the paths of the dead, policed the miners and tomb raiders who searched the labyrinths that honey-combed the raft's construction coral for Elder Culture artefacts, and hunted down feral animals and biochines that found their way in from the surface or from the sea and might infiltrate the city if the speakers didn't keep them under control.

'We know the paths of the dead better than anyone,' Victor said. 'But there are many mysteries in the deeps, many places we haven't yet reached, and some places even we don't dare disturb.'

That first night, he led Tony and Unlikely Worlds through passageways carved out of construction coral to a long low cavern where plastic igloos were laid out in a grid: one of the refuges

270

where the speakers camped out during their long patrols. Tony dozed fitfully for a few hours, woke early the next morning and lay on the foam pallet inside the little bubble of the igloo, thinking things through, before clambering out into the changeless glow of the lights floating under the ribbed rock ceiling. Victor Ursu was seated at one end of a long table, eating a breakfast of black bread, cheese and salami, and talking with Unlikely Worlds. A pair of speakers at the other end of the table, a man and a woman in white skinsuits, were trying hard to ignore them.

'Take a seat, lad,' Victor said. 'We are talking about where you need to go and how to get there.'

'I want a private word,' Tony told Unlikely Worlds.

'You can trust Victor,' the !Cha said. 'I have known him a long time. And like all speakers he respects the privacy of everyone down here, dead or alive.'

'I'm not worried about Victor,' Tony said. 'I'm worried about you.'

They sat in a chapel-like niche at the far end of the cave, Tony on a smooth bruise-coloured stump of stone, Unlikely Worlds on his folded legs.

'If you are afraid that I will lead you back to the sons of Raqle Thornhilde,' the !Cha said, 'I can assure you that my association with her is over. She was never more than a minor character in this story.'

'And what about your association with Ada Morange?'

'Like you, I hope to find her.'

'When did you know about her hand?' Tony said. 'That's what Adam Apostu was, wasn't he?'

Last night, as Victor had led them to the refuge, Tony had given the !Cha a brief sketch of the confrontation with Adam Apostu, and his escape. He had not realised that Ada Morange had been controlling the hand until now, waking with the absolute certainty of the revelation clicking into place, and he needed to ask the !Cha some hard questions.

'How did you guess?' Unlikely Worlds said, with a perfect simulation of mild curiosity.

'I think she wanted me to know. She called me Master Tony, as she did at home, when she was Aunty Jael. And then there was the name she gave her hand. Adam. Ada M.'

'Yes. And Adam is the forename of one of her oldest and most persistent antagonists. She has always liked her little jokes.'

'You knew, didn't you? You knew that Adam Apostu was her hand long before I walked into his house.'

'I suspected it after Raqle Thornhilde explained how she had found out about the slime planet. But I could not be certain until you told me that Adam Apostu had helped you to escape the terrible twins.'

'But you didn't tell me that you knew who he was. What he was.'

'I was hoping that you would be clever enough to work that out. She has been using him for a long time, I think.'

'At least ten years,' Tony said. 'That is how long he has been living in Tanrog. If living is the right word.'

Via Adam Apostu, Ada Morange had been using the paths of the dead to send eidolons everywhere in the city, eavesdropping on the private conversations of brokers and traders and selling the information she stole. And it was possible that she had used other hands for the same purpose. A small army of them linked to her by q-phone circuits, working on different worlds and in different ways towards an unknown goal. Speculating about this while lying sleeplessly in the little igloo, Tony had thought of a spider squid squatting in its casing of mucus and seaweed, tentacles extended across the dark void, groping for tasty morsels of information, manipulating people . . .

'I think she found out about the slime world and the stromatolites through Adam Apostu's little spies,' he said. 'She definitely used him to sell the information to Raqle Thornhilde, and to hint that they might contain a cure for sleepy sickness. She knew how Raqle's son had died, knew of Raqle's involvement with Fred Firat and his work on meme plagues, and knew that I was in Freedonia, looking for work. She had sent me there, chasing a lead that I now realise probably never existed. Through Adam Apostu, she told Raqle about my family's work with the disease, and the deal was as good as done.'

'It helped that you are a scion of one of the honourable families,' Unlikely Worlds said. 'After her son's death Raqle spent most of her money on the search for a cure, and on caring for

272

the afflicted. She needed a sponsor. Your sister, who had also lost a child to sleepy sickness, was an obvious candidate.'

'There was nothing wrong with the contract,' Tony said. Even though Ayo had given him up to Opeyemi after the raid, he still felt sorry for her. 'There really were stromatolites on the slime planet. And the stromatolites really did contain archival genetics. Not to mention the Ghajar eidolon. It was a sweet deal. Everyone could have made a profit. Fred Firat might even have found something that could be used to combat the meme plagues. But Ada Morange had other plans. She betrayed us all by making a deal with the Red Brigade. They were supposed to jump the claim and capture me and Fred Firat and his wizards; I would be ransomed in exchange for her freedom. But I escaped, and she had to change her plans. She told the Red Brigade about the Ghajar eidolon, helped them plan and execute the raid, and here we are, chasing after her.'

'It's a nice story, isn't it?' Unlikely Worlds said.

'Although there is one thing that puzzles me,' Tony said.

'Oh, I'm sure there's more than one thing.'

Tony ignored that. 'My ship did some research into Ada Morange's background. In her previous life, she was interested in Ghajar mad ships. What they are, how to get inside their defences, all the hard questions that still have not been answered. I think that's why she and the Red Brigade were so interested in the Ghajar eidolon. I think that's why, after the raid, the Red Brigade stole a mad ship and the means to transport it.'

'I believe that Raqle Thornhilde has agreed with you on that point,' Unlikely Worlds said.

'There is something else. Something I did not tell Raqle. Long before she was laminated and became Aunty Jael, Ada Morange dispatched a ship to a star more than a hundred light years from the nearest mirror. Although the ship accelerated to close to the speed of light, it would have taken over a century to reach its destination. A huge commitment. She must have believed that there was something of great value there.'

'She has always seen further than most,' Unlikely Worlds said. 'That's one of the things that makes her so special. That, and her belief that the trick to living for ever is to never die.'

'That ship is due to arrive at its destination around about now,' Tony said. 'It is quite the coincidence, isn't it? That the end of that old ship's long voyage should coincide with the discovery of stromatolites containing a Ghajar eidolon, and with Ada Morange's escape from my family.'

He wanted to say more, wanted to ask Unlikely Worlds if he had pointed Ada Morange towards the stromatolites, but he knew that the !Cha would almost certainly deny it, and there was no way of forcing the truth out of him. There were stories that people had made !Cha give up their secrets by threatening to boil their tanks, or stamp them flat in industrial hydraulic presses, or cut them open with industrial lasers, but no one knew anyone who had actually done it. The !Cha were clever enough to avoid most dangerous situations, and when cornered had been known to rocket skywards or sideways at tremendous speed.

'It *is* very interesting,' Unlikely Worlds said, as if considering it for the first time. 'Perhaps Ada found out about the slime planet some time ago. And kept it to herself until this mysterious ship was due to arrive at this mysterious star. Tell me, do you know its location?'

'The records were not clear on that point,' Tony said. 'I was wondering if you knew anything about it.'

He had to imagine the !Cha's shrug, but it was definitely there.

'Wherever she has gone, isn't it wonderful to contemplate the way she has transcended her limitations? What ingenuity! What determination!'

'She appears to believe that I may be useful to her,' Tony said. 'That is why she helped me to escape from Bob and Bane.'

'Yes, it's all so very tasty.'

'She told me that my eidolon had changed in interesting ways. She also told me to use the paths of the dead, and showed me the way with a little light. And that little light led me to you. You knew all along that Adam Apostu was her hand, so I cannot help wondering if you have had secret dealings with her. If you are planning to lead me to her.'

'Don't you want to find her?'

'Of course. But I don't want to be delivered to her like some package.'

'When humans lack all the facts of the case, they spin stories to fill the gaps,' Unlikely Worlds said. 'So allow me to substitute fact for fiction. That little light was an eidolon originally controlled by Ada Morange's hand. I reached out and took control of it, and used it to lead you to me. So you see, there was no collusion between us. Quite the opposite.'

'You can control eidolons?'

'You are wondering if I can control the one in your head. If I can force it to tell me what it is, and what it wants. Alas, I cannot. It is too potent and has too much self-knowledge. But I can overmaster some of the lesser ones,' Unlikely Worlds said. 'Including those that Ada employed to gather information about the dealings of brokers and traders in Tanrog. You told me what happened in Adam Apostu's house. I admit now that I saw it all, using Ada's little spies. You are a resourceful young man, and I knew you would be able to turn the confrontation between the hand and Raqle Thornhilde's dullard sons to your advantage. As you did, with only a small amount of help from me. And here we are, and both of us still want the same thing and need each other's help to find it, so I hope we can trust each other.'

'Talking of help, perhaps you can help me to find a way to unblock my comms,' Tony said. 'I need my ship, and she is still stuck on Dry Salvages.'

'Why don't we ask Victor? He knows all kinds of people.'

The speaker for the dead listened to Tony's explanation about how his comms had been silenced, and said that he believed that he knew someone who might be able to help.

'He's a fair way from here, though. Two or three days' walk.'

'Isn't there anyone in the city who can help me?' Tony said.

'No doubt, lad,' Victor said. 'But that's skinwalker business. You'd have to ask one of them.'

'Two or three days walking, it isn't anything,' Unlikely Worlds said cheerfully. 'And who knows what we'll learn along the way?'

43. Different Maps

Lisa hung weightless in the dark, trying to focus her entire attention on the crystalline cadences of Bach's *Goldberg Variations*. Sometimes, her concentration faltering, she would fall back into her self, feel the tug of the straps across her body, the delicate tug of the lodestar, and she'd have to start over. Find the shape of the melody again, follow it note by note through its turns and elaborations, dissolve in its timeless sea.

Just after the emphatic flourish at the beginning of the sixteenth variation, a voice cut into her reverie, saying, 'Thank you, Ms Dawes. I believe we have enough now.'

Light rimmed the contours of Lisa's eye mask. She pulled it off, blinking in the glare shining off the white curves of the cargo pod, unplugged her earbuds. She was strapped into a cradle that allowed her to rotate in every direction, presently suspended slantwise to the long axis of the cylindrical volume. Two technicians hung amongst a clutter of touch screens at the far end. One of them grinned, gave her the thumbs-up.

Later, with the ship under way towards the wormhole, Isabelle Linder showed the results to Lisa. Here were the two plots previously established at Terminus and the L5 point between Earth and the Moon, lines laid across the spiral swirls of the Milky Way like a lopsided X. And here was the plot established by the latest measurements, at the L5 point in the orbit of the water world Hydrot, crossing the point where the first two intersected, turning the X into a distorted asterisk.

It was an amazingly simple experiment. Three times, around three different stars scattered across the spiral arms of the Milky

Way, Lisa had been strapped into the cradle in the ship's cargo pod, in free fall. And each time, while losing herself in music, she had slowly and unconsciously revolved, little shifts in muscle tone pushing against the cradle until her body was orientated towards the lodestar that faintly, constantly nagged at her. She'd seen video of herself, shot in infrared. Horribly fascinating to watch the muscles of her arms and legs clenching and twitching, shifting her orientation by degrees until she was aimed like an arrow in the right direction. Lisa Dawes, human compass needle.

Now, after averaging out the results of this latest run of tests, they knew where she was pointing to. More or less. Isabelle magnified the image, stars streaming out of the frame as she zoomed towards the intersection of the three lines. With the Sun at twelve o'clock in the Milky Way's spiral clock face, it was roughly at five, near the outer edge of the Scutum-Centaurus Arm.

The intersection wasn't especially precise. At ninety-five per cent probability, it encompassed a globe with a radius of approximately twenty-six light years. Even out there, where stars and dust thinned towards intergalactic space, this volume, around seventy thousand cubic light years, contained twenty-two known stars and probably an equal number of dim red dwarf stars and brown dwarfs yet to be discovered.

'I guess we need more measurements to refine this,' Lisa said.

'Actually, this is good enough,' Isabelle said.

'I can't see how it can be, unless you mean to check out every star.'

Isabelle smiled like a little girl whose birthdays have all come at once. 'Ah, but we do not need to. Because, you see, this confirms something we already know.'

Lisa felt a sudden scratch of caution. These people and their fucking mysteries. She said, 'What do you know? And how do you know it?'

'The Professor will explain, when we return to Terminus.'

'Can't she tell me now?'

'She is very pleased, Lisa,' Isabelle said. 'I have given her the results. And now she wants to talk to you in person.'

*

277

Lisa had been working for Karyotech Pharma for more than six weeks, but she had yet to meet its CEO, unless you counted the one time immediately after she had arrived, when the people guiding her through the free-fall corridors of the docks had suddenly swum aside to make way for an oval football-sized drone. The little machine had orientated itself towards Lisa and the screen at its blunt end had lit up, displaying Ada Morange's witchy-wise face. They'd exchanged maybe thirty words, Ada Morange telling Lisa that she looked forward to an interesting and fruitful collaboration, Lisa saying she looked forward to it too, or something equally lame. And then the screen had blanked and the drone had spun around and scooted away, and that was that.

For the first three days, Lisa had mostly talked to lawyers. Or rather, she'd sat in a conference room while her lawyers and the lawyers representing Karyotech Pharma talked to each other. She was 'the client'. The client drank coffee and fretted while lawyers politely disagreed and rewrote sentences to make them less comprehensible to actual human beings. The client wished she could settle everything with a fucking handshake, and get on with it.

Actually, Lisa quite liked her lawyers: Zandra and Nick Papandreou, a husband-and-wife team who'd moved from Canberra to the Commonwealth of Terminus twenty years ago, and had helped draw up the framework of the new nation's legislature. Lisa was living aboard the ship for security, but her lawyers insisted on meeting in the terminal's mall, which was built into one of the enormous transparent bubbles that clustered around the elevator cable at the insertion point with the rock that anchored it in orbit. Like the ship and the rest of the terminal, the bubble was in free fall. Lisa was becoming accustomed to swimming through the spaces of the ship and the corridors and rooms of the Karyotech Pharma suite, but the mall was something else. The first time, she allowed Zandra and Nick to take her arms and kick her across an intimidatingly vast gulf of air to a restaurant adjacent to the wall of the bubble, with a spectacular view of the elevator cable dwindling away to the dappled globe of Niflheimr.

Lisa learned that Niflheimrs spent only a week or two at a time up in the terminal, partly to avoid problems caused by long-term exposure to free fall, partly because they didn't want to spend too much time away from their farms, fishing boats, and plantations. The Commonwealth's worldlets were patchworks of wilderness and farming communities. Private wealth was based on production of food, construction timber, biologics yielded by tank farms and so on. Public wealth was created by the sale and licensing of Elder Culture artefacts, and shared by using a variation of the Scandinavian model, with high and progressive tax rates, and free access to health care, social services and utilities. Infrastructure projects were determined by popular vote; investment in the economies of other worlds was controlled by an elected trust. An ideal model, according to Zandra and Nick Papandreou, for the brave new worlds of the New Frontier.

Lisa also had a meeting with the chief of the local TCU office, a gruff Turkish man with impressive side-whiskers who advised her that it was in her best interests to surrender to him. Lisa was accompanied by her lawyers, who reminded the TCU chief that the meeting was merely a courtesy, and the UN had no authority in the Commonwealth of Terminus.

'Yes, because your Commonwealth wants to grow rich by exploiting artefacts and those who discover them, taking bribes from the likes of Ada Morange, and ignoring all the risks. Don't make that mistake, Miss Dawes,' the chief told Lisa. 'I can promise you that if you surrender voluntarily, all charges pertaining to your recent adventures on First Foot will be dropped. You will be taken into custody, of course, but only for your own protection, so that your condition can be assessed and stabilised.'

'As far as I can see I have the choice of being your lab rat or Ada Morange's,' Lisa said. 'So I think I'll go with the person who'll pay me. If she can't find a cure, maybe I'll be able to afford one of my own.'

And so, after she and her lawyers finally cut a deal and she had signed about thirty copies of a fat contract, Lisa became a research associate employed by Karyotech Pharma on a freelance basis. By this time the !Cha, Unlikely Worlds, had disappeared. According to Isabelle Linder, he had gone across to Ada Morange's timeship. 'I am sure we will visit the Professor soon,' she said. 'I know she has the greatest interest in you.'

Meanwhile, Lisa endured a battery of tests, from straightforward brain scans to psychological assessments, and gave a detailed account of everything that had happened since she'd been struck down in her yard. And then she got to work on the code with the expert from Peking University, Professor Lu Jeu Enge.

He was younger than Lisa had pictured him, a cheerful confident man in his early thirties who worked off his excess energy in pick-up games of free-fall basketball, and planned to spend a couple of weeks hiking the lake country of Niflheimr's north pole once what he called his fieldwork was finished. They bonded over their interest in the narrative code, and a shared incredulity about the daily group-think meetings before the start of work, when Isabelle Linder and the research team gathered to discuss that day's goals and yesterday's successes and failures, and to reaffirm their loyalty to their company and to each other.

'I am not completely sure why I am here,' Enge told Lisa. 'I do not subscribe to their personality cult, and they don't want me to unravel the code, but to discover instead what you see in it. Hardly a precise match to my area of expertise. However, Karyotech pays extraordinarily well for services they do not really need, I have never before left Earth, and I must admit that I am very curious about your discovery. So here I am.'

'I think it's partly because Ada Morange doesn't want the geek police to hire you,' Lisa confessed.

'All I can say is that it is nice to be wanted, for whatever reason,' Enge said. 'And their facilities are first-rate. Even if I fail to contribute anything useful, I believe that I will learn much. What about you, Lisa? You obviously have reservations, yet here you are. What made you choose to throw in with them?'

'It wasn't so much a conscious choice,' Lisa said, remembering some favourite books from her childhood, 'as a series of unfortunate events.'

She and Lu Jeu Enge ran and reran the Ghajar narrative code that Karyotech's coders had extracted from the tesserae that Lisa had brought with her. Code that Willie's eidolon had injected into the Ghostkeeper matrices at the moment of his death, code which Lisa believed might contain some trace of his essence, although she saw in its silvery flow only the same knots and nodes that she'd seen in the code she and Bria had pulled from the tessera Willie had entrusted to his girlfriend.

Enge used a tool developed by his research team to refine the location of the nodes, and to capture and calibrate the changes they imposed on the code's flow. According to him, they appeared to be emergent properties, a typical feature of Ghajar narrative code.

'It is more like a symphony than a written language,' he said. 'The analogy is imperfect, of course, but it makes a useful working model. So far, we have had no success in translating it, but your ghost may provide an interesting baseline. Something that until now we have lacked.'

'Like a key?'

'Perhaps. But we may never know if anything we read in the code has equivalence with the way the Ghajar read it.'

'My ghost sees things differently. So perhaps I see things differently too.'

'Even so, you may not see what it sees. It is a matter of compatibility and interpretation, of neurological hard-wiring.'

One day, details Lisa hadn't seen before began to pop out of the flow. She lost track of time, watching them, didn't realise Enge had left her alone until he returned with a pad of paper and a Sharpie.

'You were making movements with your right hand,' he said. 'As if writing or drawing. Perhaps you could watch again, pen in hand. Try not to think about it.'

Two minutes later, they were studying the pattern she'd scribbled. A starburst of lines radiating out from a common point, each line a different length, each of them hatched with three or four short crossbars. It was a duplicate of the diagrams that Willie had made on his dying bed; Enge said that it resembled drawings made by the sister of the first person to pilot a Ghajar ship. Like Lisa, the little girl had been haunted by an eidolon, although hers had been encoded in a bead of crystalline material similar to cat's-eye apatite.

'The Ghajar used a variety of media for information storage, just as we do,' Enge said. 'But in both cases, the embedded eidolons extract information in the narrative code and render it in the same kind of shorthand visual representation. It is very interesting!'

281

He told Lisa that Ada Morange had been attempting to unriddle that diagram for twenty years. Back in the twentieth century, two robot spacecraft flying past the planets of the outer solar system into interstellar space had carried plates engraved with similar patterns: maps of the Sun's location relative to several pulsars, neutron stars that emitted powerful beams of electromagnetic radiation. Because the beams could only be detected when they were directly pointed at an observer, and because the neutron stars rotated very rapidly, spinning many times a second, they appeared to pulse. And because every pulsar spun at a different rate and could be detected over vast distances, they were useful cosmic lighthouses.

Ada Morange believed that the Ghajar diagram was a similar map. The length of each line represented the distance between the pulsars and the target star; the spacing of the crossbars represented the clock time of their pulsing beams. But unriddling the map had proven to be very difficult. It had taken more than a decade to translate the distances into light years and the pulsar clock times into milliseconds, and locating the pulsars was an even harder problem. Their clocks had slowed in the thousands of years since the Ghajar had made their maps, and many were not visible from Earth. Ada Morange was presently engaged in a vast and vastly expensive project to map the positions of every star and pulsar in the galaxy, using flocks of cheap telescopes put into orbit around the gift worlds and the worlds of the New Frontier.

Lisa's map was not identical to the little girl's. Perhaps it used different pulsars to point to the same target; perhaps it pointed elsewhere. Lu Jeu Enge turned the results over to Karyotech's research team and rode down to Niflheimr for his hiking vacation; Lisa and the research team moved on, developing a way to pin down the location of her lodestar. And now she was heading back to Terminus and a face-to-face meeting with Ada Morange. She believed that she had redeemed something useful from Willie's death and wanted to ask Ada Morange to make good her promise to find a way to exorcise her ghost. But the billionaire, it turned out, had very different plans.

44. The Paths Of The Dead

Victor Ursu led Tony and Unlikely Worlds along branching paths that descended ever deeper underground. A kilometre of construction coral massing overhead like compressed time. Darkness profounder than night lying everywhere beyond the sparklight that Victor floated for the convenience of his guests — he usually navigated lightless stretches of the paths of the dead by echoes returned from clicks of his tongue. They edged along a rift that plunged to unguessable depths. They passed through a long low cavern where Ghostkeepers had carved rows of tombs in the construction-coral walls. Eidolons crouched like twists of frozen smoke in several of the tomb mouths, chittering and snapping as they went past. They saw no other sign of life on the long hike, although sometimes Tony felt that there was a fourth member of their little party. An unglimpsable presence haunting the shadows at the outer edge of his field of view, unremarked by his companions.

Tony was certain that the eidolons in those tombs had sensed it, knew that Ada Morange had some idea of its abilities and intentions — it was why she had helped him to escape — and suspected that Unlikely Worlds knew something about it too. But so far it had made no attempt to communicate with him, not even in dreams. It was as if he was carrying a stowaway who evaded his every attempt to find her, and left no clues about her identity or purpose.

He told himself that it did not matter what the eidolon wanted, if it wanted anything at all, as long as it helped him to find Ada Morange and the Red Brigade. Nor did it matter if Unlikely Worlds was slyly manipulating him, and might be planning to sacrifice

283

or betray him when he was no longer useful. At the moment it was enough to be moving. There was a kind of reckless freedom in being caught up in the plots of powerful, enigmatic creatures, and defying them to do their worst.

As they walked, Victor told stories about the wonders and mysteries of the paths of the dead. On the far side of the raft, he said, the remains of a city once inhabited by an aquatic Elder Culture were submerged in an underground lake that was connected to the sea by several long flumes. Some claimed that unlike other Elder Cultures this species had not died out or evolved into something else, but had retreated into the deeps of the world-girdling ocean. Others said that it was not an Elder Culture at all, but was native to Veles. There were tales of a lost fleet of spaceships crushed in matrices of construction coral and haunted still by the eidolons of their control systems; of caves containing stepped pyramids built by humans kidnapped from Earth long before the Jackaroo had made contact; of a race of small, secretive creatures, degenerate descendants of an Elder Culture, that inhabited chambers where they farmed fungi and kept herds of scrabs that they tapped for their haemolymph, and sometimes emerged at night to steal food and trinkets from houses in the city. There was a story about tomb raiders who, after being trapped in a labyrinth by malicious eidolons, had resorted to cannibalism. The last survivor had been discovered wearing a cloak made from the skins of his companions. Another told of a cult that had tweaked themselves to digest blood and lured the unwary to dungeons where their victims were bound and hung from hooks and drained over days and weeks.

Some of Victor's stories were new to Tony; others were variations of travellers' tales he had heard in bars and cafés on other worlds. When Tony pointed this out, the speaker shrugged and said why not? Stories ended up in the paths of the dead along with everything else.

'This is the place where things long forgotten on the skin are still remembered,' he said. 'Although time moves at the same rate below as above, decay does not. After all, that's why people keep their dead down here. So it shouldn't be surprising that the oldest stories can also be found here, long after they have been forgotten on the skin.'

Tony asked Unlikely Worlds if he had ever collected any of Victor's stories.

'Some of them are undeniably pretty,' Unlikely Worlds said, which Tony took to mean yes.

'If you know so many stories,' he said to Victor, 'why is it you owe a favour to Unlikely Worlds, and not the other way around?'

'Why do you think I owe him any kind of favour?' Victor said.

'Isn't that why you're helping us?' Tony said.

'To discharge a debt?' Victor laughed. 'That's skinwalker thinking, lad. I'm helping you because that's what we do, down here.'

'Would you help Raqle's boys, if they asked you to find me?'

'But they haven't asked,' Victor said, as if it was the most reasonable thing in all the worlds.

After a little while, walking down what seemed an endless stone gullet that rose and fell in long undulations (a solution tube carved, Victor said, by water that dissolved the rock rather than eroding it), Tony said that he didn't think there was as much difference between the surface and the paths of the dead as Victor claimed.

'We rely on the dead too. Not our own dead, but the dead of the Elder Cultures. Most of our technologies are derived from Elder Culture artefacts. Even our ships were built by long-dead aliens. We don't make anything new any more. We don't search for new knowledge. We dig up old knowledge in tombs. And every world is a tomb world.'

'And yet you make new stories,' Unlikely Worlds said.

'Are they really new? Or are they like Victor's stories? Variations on old tales. New flesh on old bones.'

The !Cha did not reply.

Tony said, 'Did the Elder Cultures die out because they lost themselves in the past of others? Because they could no longer think of anything new, or anything that hadn't been thought by others long ago?'

'The galaxy is old,' Unlikely Worlds said. 'And full of old things. You and your kind are blessed with a rare gift: you are young, and still curious, and not yet jaded. Don't grow old before your time.'

'Is that a warning?'

'Think of it as a useful motto.'

They spent the second night in a Ghostkeeper catacomb. The honeycomb of small chambers was entirely free of eidolons; tomb raiders had long ago taken the stones in which their algorithms ran. There were foam pads to sleep on, and a store of food and equipment free for any to use. Tony took a brief shower in freezing water and slept deep and long, with no dreams that he could remember.

The next day, they followed passages that mostly sloped upwards. At one point they emerged into a long chamber where rain and shafts of light fell through holes in the high roof and mosses and filmy sail-sedges grew on mounds of rubble, their living reds and yellows vivid and startling after the endless stone of the underground. They were near the skin of the world now, but were still more than a day's walk from their destination. A passage on the far side of the sunlit chamber sank into the construction coral again; a transparent plastic bridge crossed a stream that ran swiftly over bone-white flowstone and suddenly whirlpooled down a solution hole.

Down again. Down into the dark.

They made camp in a cave whose roof had partly collapsed. It was night, out on the skin: the ragged hole framed a black sky thick with stars. Victor showed Tony how to shape a comfortable hollow in the soft white sand of a dry stream bed. Lying there, his head pillowed on his folded jacket, Tony thought of *Abalunam's Pride*, somewhere out there amongst all those bright stars, hoped that she would come when he found a way to call her, and hoped that Colonel X had left some kind of spyware in the bridle or the lifesystem. After the kidnapping on Dry Salvages, Tony knew that he couldn't rely on the colonel's help, but now, lost in the paths of the dead, he nurtured the small hope that this adventure was part of the colonel's plan to find Ada Morange, and that at the crucial moment he would come to Tony's aid.

The next day they crossed a bridge over a chasm where faint lights floated in unplumbed darkness. Not even Victor knew if they were machines or eidolons, or some kind of unknown animal or biochine. On the far side, a long stair of broad shallow steps descended to a cave system like a series of chapels carved out of glistening lime deposits. Stalactites hung in clusters from irregular ceilings or fringed folds and ledges; stalagmites stood like fat candles amongst pellucid pools cupped in basins of mother-of-pearl and onyx.

As they picked their way through these marvels, Tony thought with a melancholy pang that Danilo would have loved this place. He remembered how Danilo had run down the beach, arms outstretched as if he was trying to fly; how he had wheeled around and run back, his face alight with bliss. Remembered him standing at the foot of the spire of a native tree, one hand pressed to its pale rind as he watched orange banners lifting and falling high above in the cold wind. Remembered his lover's innocent delight in the world outside the city, and how it had made him see everything afresh

At last they reached a chamber several kilometres long, where a ceramic road wound between cones of debris that leaned against the walls on either side, slanting towards the uneven roof. Pale pillows of some kind of fungus grew on the steep slopes; Tony saw three or four people moving up there. Pickers, according to Victor, who searched for the rare, intensely fragrant fruiting bodies of a parasitic plant that grew on the fungus.

An hour later, beyond the far side of the chamber, they emerged in a long narrow defile lined with rickety buildings: a settlement of tomb raiders and artefact dealers. In a chopshop, a technician immobilised Tony's head in a scaffold frame, dabbed local anaes-thetic around his right eye and introduced a long thin needle into the socket and injected nanotech that would dismantle the block on his comms. The process would take several hours, the technician said; she would need to keep him under observation in case there were side effects.

'What kind of side effects?'

'Fits, partial loss of vision, auditory hallucinations . . . Nothing I can't fix,' the technician said breezily.

She patched him with a soporific and he dozed in a cot at the back of the chopshop, woke to find the ship's telemetry crowding his vision. He closed the windows, opened the q-phone link.

'There you are!' the bridle said. 'I was beginning to think I'd come to the wrong place.'

'What do you mean? Where are you?'

'I'm here! I'm here!'

One of the windows opened, dense with navigation code. Tony checked it and laughed with shock and happiness. *Abalunam's Pride* was in orbit around Veles.

45. Lodestar

Lisa hated every moment of the trip to Ada Morange's timeship, a terrifying jaunt in an Orion capsule piloted by a cheerful Nigerian astronaut. The noisy kick-in-the pants launch and the long free-fall arc across naked vacuum. The cramped interior, with its rigid padded seats like dentists' chairs and quaint computer interfaces and joysticks, laughably primitive compared with the lifesystems built into Ghajar ships. Eye burning splinters of sunlight sweeping across the glass portholes because the capsule was rotating to even out temperature differences.

The astronaut told her that the capsule had been slated for a mission to a near-Earth asteroid when the arrival of the Jackaroo had put an end to the dream of manned exploration of the solar system. 'Developing this baby cost around fifty billion dollars. And now we use it as a space taxi. Such a shame. That's why this thing is so important. Why we need to understand everything about the tech we use now. Because if we can't control it, it will control us. The Professor was one of the first people to see that. And she's the only person, now, who can do something about it. It's a great thing to be part of.'

There was an alarming popping sound like distant gunfire – 'Attitude thrusters killing our rotation, perfectly normal,' the astronaut said – and the timeship drifted into view. Its fat cylinder, a kilometre long and swollen at either end, somewhat resembled a human thigh bone. Almost all of its bulk, according to the astronaut, was shielding built up from fullerene foam, titanium honeycomb, ceramic tiles and layers of tough elastomers, designed to absorb and dissipate the terrific energies of collisions at near light-speed with any stray hydrogen atoms or microscopic grains of interstellar dust that managed to penetrate its protective magnetic fields.

'The things we can do now', he said, and manoeuvred his frail craft towards the midpoint of this forbiddingly Gothic object, sliding into the circular mouth of a pit cut deep in the shielding, and docking with an airlock that led to the J-class Ghajar ship buried inside.

An access shaft at the midpoint of the ship's central corridor led to the carousel ring that, spinning between the exterior of the ship's lifesystem and the inner surface of its hull to generate a centrifugal imitation of gravity, housed Ada Morange's medical suite. Lisa had to wait for half an hour in a cubicle, with a cheerful steward looking in every five minutes to tell her that it would not be long before she was at last admitted to the inner sanctum.

Unlikely Worlds stood by Ada Morange's elevated hospital bed, his baritone booming across the curved, dimly lit room when Lisa entered. 'I hear that you have been travelling far and wide in search of your lodestar. It's all so very exciting!'

'You pretend that everything excites you, you old fraud', Ada Morange said. 'Please, Ms Dawes, come and sit with me.'

Her head was cushioned by soft white pillows. Her body barely disturbed the starched sheet that covered it. Tubing ran to machines that oxygenated, cleansed and pumped artificial blood. An IV bag was feeding, drop by drop, a clear liquid to a cannula in the crook of her emaciated arm. She thumbed a button on the remote control she gripped in her right hand, all knuckles and ropy veins under crepe skin. The bed responded by elevating her pillowed head as Lisa sat beside her on a hard plastic chair.

'You have met my old friend Adam Nevers', she said. 'What did you think of him?'

'That he's a scrupulously polite asshole who uses his position to pursue his own agenda.'

'I see that he got under your skin. You should not take it personally. It's a talent he has.'

'He killed my dog', Lisa confessed, and told Ada Morange about the interrogation and the raids on her homestead.

'He has not much changed,' Ada Morange said, when Lisa had finished. 'Does he still believe that he is my nemesis?'

'He warned me about you.'

'I expect he did.' Ada Morange's eyes were sharp blue. The shifting colours of the screens that kept her in contact with the happening world played across her gaunt face. Her hair was brushed out on either side, white wings on the white pillow. 'As you can see, I contend with something more serious than Investigator Nevers. I survived an immunodeficiency-associated lymphoma, and now I am slowly dying of an autoimmune disease. At the moment, I am being treated with tailored prions. Like all the other treatments, it has only a transient effect. Soon I will have to make a choice. To die, or to set out into a voyage into the future. Do you know why this is called a timeship?'

'It's something to do with travelling close to the speed of light, so that time passes more slowly on board than elsewhere.'

Isabelle had told Lisa all about it, with the kind of reverence with which an art historian might describe an obscure masterpiece.

'There is a star some two hundred light years from Terminus,' Ada Morange said. 'It is orbited by several wormholes, so that when I reach it I can quickly return home. But to get there, I will travel across interstellar space. My crew will place me in a hypothermal coma and we will accelerate at one gravity until we reach, as you have said, a cruising speed a little under the speed of light. The journey will take two centuries, but by the clocks aboard the timeship, slowed by Einsteinian time dilation, just ten years will have passed. So when I arrive at the star I will have also travelled into the future, where perhaps a cure for my illness will have been discovered. Or a way to upload my mind into another substrate or transfer it to another body. I am presently sponsoring research into those areas, and others that may be of use, but as far as I am concerned progress is frustratingly slow. The timeship will enable me to jump to a point where those projects have come to fruition. No doubt you think that it is a crazy plan.'

'It's definitely ambitious.'

'You are being polite. Even I think it is more than a little crazy. And I hope very much that I will not need it. I hope every day

for a breakthrough in the search for a cure, or for another solution. Not because of the risks of an interstellar voyage that no
one has ever before attempted, or because it will mean leaving
behind my company and my fortune, and everything familiar.
But because I am worried about what I may find, two hundred
years in the future. We once supposed that there would be a
steady advance in science, but that is no longer the case. In two
hundred years, we may be as gods. But it is also possible that
misuse of Elder Culture technology and reckless expansion into
the New Frontier will destroy us. I may arrive in a future where
most settlements have died out, and the survivors have devolved
to hunter-gatherers who tell each other campfire stories of gods
who fell from the sky.' Ada Morange turned her head to look at
Unlikely Worlds, on the other side of the bed. 'Perhaps it has
happened before. To previous clients of the Jackaroo.'

'It's an interesting idea,' Unlikely Worlds said.

Ada Morange smiled at Lisa. 'As I am sure you have by now
realised, he grows evasive when the conversation turns to things
one needs to know. In that regard, he is exactly like the Jackaroo.'

'With respect, that shows how little you have learned about
the Jackaroo,' Unlikely Worlds said.

'One thing I do know about them,' Ada Morange told Lisa.
'They are not really here to help. We are no more than their latest
experiment. Investigator Nevers still has a close association with
them, doesn't he? Do you think he realises that they are using him?'

'I wondered that myself,' Lisa said.

'We tell ourselves that we have won independence from the
Jackaroo because we no longer rely on their shuttles to travel
between Earth and the fifteen gift worlds,' Ada Morange said. 'And
because we can freely explore the worlds of the New Frontier. But
in truth we have exchanged one kind of dependency for another.
The sargassos of Ghajar ships are one of our most important
resources, but we know almost nothing about them. We do not
know, for instance, why the Ghajar abandoned so many ships, or
why there are some, the so-called mad ships, which we cannot
even approach, let alone try to use. The popular theory is that
there was a war. That the mad ships were some kind of ultimate

weapon that ended it, and were abandoned by the victors, along with ships captured from their defeated enemy. It is as plausible as any other guess. But why was the war fought? And where did the victors go?

'I have been thinking about this ever since the first two ships were called to Mangala. The young man who found them was, like you, infected with an eidolon. What was its motive? Was it a lucky accident that its needs coincided with ours, or was it something deeper? My !Cha friend, who so loves stories, dismisses such conspiracy theories. Not because they are not true, I think, but because they do not suit his purpose. But we understand so little about the aliens who have reshaped our history, so conspiracy theories are mostly all we have.'

Ada Morange paused. Flecks of coloured light moved over her face. Her machines hummed and clicked. Unlikely Worlds stood silent and still.

Lisa said, 'That sounds like something Adam Nevers would say.'

'You think that the two of us are similar? That we have some kind of relationship?'

Ada Morange did not smile, but she sounded amused.

'He seems to think that you do,' Lisa said.

'After Mangala, after he lost his job with the Metropolitan Police in London and joined the UN Technology Control Unit, he tried to find something he could use against me. He did not succeed, of course, and that was the end of it, until your little local difficulty. So there is no relationship, except perhaps in his head. And besides, we are very different, he and I. He wants to limit use of Elder Culture technology because he fears it. I want to embrace it. To understand it. Only by understanding what we use can we truly master it, and truly control our destiny.'

'You want to secure the future.'

'If you are travelling somewhere, you want to make sure that you know as much about your destination as possible. Tell me, do you have any idea at all why you are drawn to what you call your lodestar?'

'Not a one.'

'The eidolon that inhabits you, it does not speak to you?'

'Not that I can tell.'

'Not even in dreams?'

'If it does, I don't remember them.'

Unlikely Worlds spoke up, startling Lisa. 'There are the diagrams, of course. The diagrams you have been drawing.'

'It would be nice to think that it is trying to be helpful,' Ada Morange said. 'That it is trying to point us towards something we can use. But perhaps we are too hopeful. Too trusting.'

'Some might say too arrogant,' Unlikely Worlds said.

'Because, despite all evidence to the contrary, we continue to believe that the universe is shaped for our convenience? No. We believe instead that we might just be clever enough to win some advantage over those who try to manipulate us,' Ada Morange said, and looked at Lisa again. 'I believe that Professor Lu Jeu told you about my research into the Ghajar pulsar map. The first one.'

Lisa said, 'All things considered, I guess you'd be surprised if we hadn't talked about it.'

'What he does not know, what no outsider knows, is that we decoded the map two years ago. We found where it points to.'

One of Ada Morange's screens swivelled to face Lisa. It showed a cluster of blocky pixels on a field of black.

'That is the star in question,' Ada Morange said. 'An M0 red dwarf. The map you pulled from the narrative code and your odd little talent confirm it. Why it was of such interest to the Ghajar we do not yet know. As far as we can tell, it possesses only two planets. Both are smaller than Mars, and both orbit so close to it that their surfaces are most likely oceans of molten rock. And as far as we know, it is not linked to the wormhole network.'

Lisa said, 'Wait. You've been there?'

'No. Not yet. The problem, you see, is not that we do not know where it is. The problem is deciding whether or not we should attempt to reach it.'

The cluster of pixels shrank to a point. Other points drifted in from two edges of the screen. Lisa realised that the viewpoint had pulled back to show the star's relationship to its neighbours.

'Stars in the immediate neighbourhood are widely scattered,' Ada Morange said. 'Nevertheless, one is orbited by wormholes:

an F8 star somewhat larger and brighter than Earth's Sun, located a hundred and sixteen light years from your lodestar.'

On the screen, one of the points was suddenly circled by a blue ring.

'It is not a long trip, between Terminus and this F8 star,' Ada Morange said. Sparks of screen-light shone in her eyes. 'I have sent several expeditions out there, to observe the lodestar. At the moment we can go no closer. If we cannot find a wormhole that leads to it, the only way to reach it would be to travel there directly, across more than a hundred light years. But it is clear that your eidolon has a connection with it, which is why I want you to go out there. To the F8 star. If nothing else, we can make use of your compass talent to absolutely confirm that this little M0 dwarf really is the target of the pulsar maps. And perhaps, when your eidolon is closer, it will tell us something more. Unlikely Worlds believes that this is a foolish hope, but it is one that should be tested. Well, what do you say?'

46· The Message

'My ship's bridle said that Ada Morange told her that I was on Veles,' Tony said. 'That part I can believe. As Aunty Jael, Ada Morange was in constant contact with the wizards on the slime planet. She must have taken the q-phone link with her when she escaped. But the bridle also said that she applied for permission from Dry Salvages's traffic control to boot, and flew here under her own volition. I think that she thinks she is telling the truth, but what she claims to have done is frankly impossible. She is not programmed for autonomous behaviour. There are strict protocols to prevent her or the ship from acting independently. She should not have come here unless I told her to.'

'Yet here she is,' Unlikely Worlds said.

'Probably because Ada Morange hacked her,' Tony said, thinking again of that phantom spider-squid extending its tentacles from world to world. 'She used the q-phone link to take control, and gave the bridle false memories of acting independently. And that is not all she did.'

'She told your ship where to find her,' Unlikely Worlds said.

'Is that a guess, or did you have something to do with it?'

'If I knew where Ada was, I would be there, not here,' Unlikely Worlds said. 'And it was not exactly a guess. More in the nature of a logical deduction. You told me that she was interested in the eidolon lodged in your head. She helped you to escape Raqle Thornhilde's sons, and now she has made the obvious next move, and extended an invitation.'

They were in an open-air café at the edge of the tomb-raider settlement's main street. Tony, ravenously hungry, was forking up a mess of red beans and rice; Victor Ursu was sipping a frothy milkshake; Unlikely Worlds squatted at the little round table with a shot glass of whisky set on the flat top of his tank, absorbing the organic molecules that flavoured the drink via a quantum mechanism that massively inflated the probability that they would be located inside the tank rather than in the glass. Or so he said.

Victor thumbed foam from his upper lip. 'It could be a trick meant to send you on the wrong path, lad.'

'I wondered about that too,' Tony said.

'Where is it, this place where she is supposed to be waiting for you?' Unlikely Worlds said.

Tony opened the window that the bridle had sent to him. 'I have full details of the route and the flight plan, but it passes through several mirrors that are not on any maps.'

'Perhaps it is the destination of that ship Ada Morange dispatched a century ago,' Unlikely Worlds said.

'I don't think so. If that had mirrors orbiting it, there would have been no need to travel there the hard way.'

'Sometimes you cannot tell if mirrors are present around a star until you go there,' Unlikely Worlds said. 'And your maps of the wormhole network are woefully incomplete, even now.'

'There's only one way to know the shape of something in the dark,' Victor said. 'You have to lay your hand on it. As I think the lad already knows.'

'I cannot trust the invitation, and I cannot trust my ship,' Tony said. 'But I have no other path to follow. How long will it take to reach the surface from here?'

'Less than an hour to walk to the railhead,' Victor said. 'Then just twenty minutes by train.'

'There's a railway?'

'It was built to carry out spoil when a company of tomb raiders excavated a necropolis close by.'

Tony got the coordinates of the railway's surface terminal and calculated orbits and descent paths while he followed Victor Ursu and Unlikely Worlds to the railhead, and told Abalunam's Pride's bridle when and where to rendezvous. He was monitoring her radar feed and listening to chatter from traffic control. Raqle

Thornhilde must know by now that his ship had booted from Dry Salvages, must have guessed where it would be heading. Her two sons would be watching it, waiting for Tony to show himself. Waiting to pounce.

At the railhead, Victor told Tony that his responsibility for him ended here. 'I went out onto the skin once, when I was part of a delegation that met with politicians in Tanrog. I am not in a hurry to repeat the experience. I hope that your path is a true one, and you will come back and walk with me again, and tell me how your story ended.'

Tony, touched and surprised, embraced Victor before climbing onto one of the train's flatbed wagons; the burly man raised a hand in a farewell salute as the train drew away, then turned and walked away into the dark. Hauled by a small electric locomotive, the chain of wagons clattered through empty chambers and narrow tunnels lined with pale ceramic. Fifteen minutes after they set off, Veles's traffic control was shouting in Tony's head, demanding to know why *Abalunam's Pride* had dropped out of orbit without permission. He tuned it down, kept watch through the radar feed.

At last the train emerged into grey light, rattling through a long cutting. Rain prickled on Tony's face as he squinted at the low clouds, worried that stealthed drones and police spinners undetected by *Abalunam's Pride* might suddenly stoop down. Then the walls of the cutting fell away and there she was, hanging just above the terminal's tangle of sidings, her black bulk glistening in the rain, overshadowing strings of derelict wagons rotting amongst weeds and thorn bushes. Beyond, a scattering of low buildings hunched below the bare black mounds of spoil heaps. A small crowd stood outside a bar, staring up at the ship.

By now, traffic control was reciting penalties for laws broken and orders to stand down and await arrest.

'A nice theatrical touch,' Unlikely Worlds said as he followed Tony along a weedy track.

'Purely practical,' Tony said. 'We have only a little time before Tanrog's police or Raqle Thornhilde's sons catch up with us. Find a place to secure yourself as soon as we are aboard. I aim to boot at once.'

298

He went straight up, punching through streaming layers of cloud and emerging in the raw light of Veles's star. Traffic control was raving. And as Tony aimed *Abalunam's Pride* towards the wilderness of mirrors, another ship rose out of the planet's atmosphere, changing course to follow him.

Bob and Bane, in their hired ship.

The common channel blinked. Tony ignored it. There was no point listening to their threats. He was driving towards the mirrors at the maximum acceleration permitted by the bias drive. His pursuers could do no more than match it, and would always be at least thirty minutes behind. He would have to think of some way of dealing with them when he reached his destination. Although if he really was heading into a trap, who knew, he might need their help.

47. 'Don't worry.'

When everything changed Lisa was down on Niflheimr, staying on the farm owned by Zandra and Nick Papandreou. Time out. A vacation while she waited for the ship to return to Terminus from the F8 star, resupply, and light out again, taking her with it. Ada Morange's people had offered her a huge bonus that overtopped the consultancy fee she had already been paid. More money than she knew what to do with, frankly, although she planned to send a hefty fraction of it to Bria, as an apology for fucking up her life. But mainly she was going because she was curious. She wanted to know how the eidolon would react with the lodestar just a hundred and sixteen light years away. She hoped to get a better idea of what Willie's jackpot had got her into.

Then she would come back to Terminus and help Ada Morange's science crew to come up with a way of exorcising her ghost.

That day she was out hiking with Isabelle Linder, her official minder until she boarded the ship, trying as usual to ignore the two bodyguards who tagged along wherever she went. They were walking alongside a creek that looped through sheep pastures – Zandra and Nick owned some four thousand head, scattered across fifteen hundred hectares. The air was pleasantly cool, the sky shrouded edge to edge with grey clouds. Threadbare green pasture stretched away either side of the ribbon of native vegetation – vegetation brought here long ago by various Elder Cultures – that grew along the creek's winding course. Wire grass, stands of things a little like palm trees with dreadlocked tangles of violet straps, hummocks of a kind of blue-green moss, a single tree-thing jagged as a lightning strike, decked out in feathery webs.

The stony ridge where Zandra, Nick, and their two small sons would join them for lunch had just appeared at the close, visibly curved horizon when one of the guards hurried forward and said there was a problem, everyone had to return to the farm. He shrugged when Lisa asked what was wrong; Isabelle, poking at her phone, frowned and said, 'It is Investigator Nevers.'

Lisa felt a catch in her heartbeat. 'What do you mean?'

'He is here. On a ship that has just come through the wormhole. And he is accompanied by a crew of TCU agents and lawyers.'

'Are you sure?'

'I am afraid so,' Isabelle said. She seemed unreasonably calm. 'We have a contact in the TCU offices. They received a message just an hour ago. It seems they did not know he was coming here before he arrived.'

'But he isn't here yet. It will take him a day to get to the elevator terminal, ten hours to ride down to the surface . . . And anyway, he can't do anything. The Commonwealth doesn't recognise the TCU. That's why you're here.'

'We are to go to our compound at the elevator port, and await further instructions,' Isabelle said. 'Don't worry. The Professor knows what she is doing. And she has your best interests in mind.'

They were halfway home when Isabelle's phone chirped. 'Mais bien sûr. À la fois,' she told the caller, and handed the phone to Lisa. 'It is the Professor.'

'There has been a development,' Ada Morange told Lisa, without any preamble.

'Aside from this thing with Adam Nevers?'

'I am sending you a video.'

It was a brief clip pulled from one of Niflheimr's news sites. Two Jackaroo avatars in black tracksuits being interviewed by a young woman, their gold-tinted translucent faces vaguely reminiscent of half a dozen movie stars, their smiles and body language uncanny simulations of the smiles and body language of actual human beings.

'We are sightseers,' one said, when the young woman asked them about a rumour that they were here to investigate Karyotech Pharma.

'We love what you've done with the place,' said the other.

'There's more,' Ada Morange said, 'but it is only the usual polite evasions. The point is that they are here, on Niflheimr. That interview was posted ten minutes ago, shortly after they stepped out of a cargo elevator. My people believe that they arrived on a freighter from Earth that docked yesterday, and somehow evaded security.'

Lisa said, 'Are you sure that they are working with Nevers?'

'It would be a tremendous coincidence if they were not, because Jackaroo avatars have never before visited Niflheimr. We must assume that they know everything we know. That is how they are. And that means that Nevers knows it too.'

'But what can he do here, without authority?'

'He tried to stop my work on Mangala, without authority. And he nearly succeeded. But do not worry,' Ada Morange said. 'I have made arrangements to get you to a place of safety. This is no more than a bump in the road to your star.'

Ten minutes later, a helicopter resolved in the middle distance and swept towards them, scattering sheep.

'Don't worry, it's ours,' one of the bodyguards told Lisa.

The two of them were young men dressed in ordinary hiking gear, relaxed and vigilant.

Isabelle, poking at her phone again, said, 'There has been a change of plan. You are to go up to the terminal right away.'

'But that's where Nevers is heading,' Lisa said, deeply unsettled by the swift sudden crisis, the sense of unseen forces in motion all around her. It felt a lot like a kidnapping.

'A TCU vehicle picked up the Jackaroo avatars,' Isabelle said. 'It is heading in this direction. You must leave Niflheimr at once, Lisa. You will reach the terminal before Nevers arrives, and transfer to the timeship. You will be quite safe there.'

The helicopter made a circle overhead and dropped down, landing on its skids in the rough grass. It was the kind that ranchers used to herd cattle on the big ranges north of Port of Plenty, its two-blade rotor raised on a stalk above the little pod of its cabin. Lisa followed Isabelle towards it with a heavy feeling of resignation. The two bodyguards walking either side of her, everyone ducking under the chattering blades. Isabelle had a brief argument with the pilot. She wanted to go with Lisa; the pilot said that he had orders to take only Ms Dawes.

One of the bodyguards helped Lisa into the bucket seat next to the pilot, showed her how to buckle the safety harness. Isabelle told her that she would see her soon, and wished her bon voyage, something Lisa had thought only people who weren't actually French said, and the helicopter lifted with a jolt that left her stomach somewhere on the ground. The last she saw of Isabelle Linder, the woman was standing with the two bodyguards in a circle of flattened grass, blonde hair blown awry as she looked up, shading her eyes with her forearm. And then the helicopter turned and put its nose down and the pasture unravelled into scrub forest.

Half an hour later, the thread of the elevator cable rose beyond the horizon, leaning into the sky. The helicopter skimmed over the industrial clutter of the port, landed in front of a big steel-framed hangar. Michel Valis, the head of Karyotech Pharma's groundside security, was waiting there with two young men dressed in chinos and black roll-neck sweaters.

The security chief shook Lisa's hand and led her towards the hangar, where a big bus with ribbed aluminium sides and smoked-glass windows was parked. 'We'll drive you straight to the elevator, go right on up,' Michel said.

'And then?'

'Don't worry. It is all in hand.'

'Everyone keeps telling me not to worry,' Lisa said. Walking into the big hangar, mud still on her boots from the creek-side ramble, she had an odd sense of displacement, as if she was slightly out of synch with the world.

Michel followed her into the coach. She saw a hospital bed and a lot of medical equipment, a man and a woman in white lab coats, and Michel seized her in an armlock and slapped something on the side of her neck and everything instantly went woozy. Michel caught her as her knees gave way, turning her so she fell into a big chair that immediately tilted backwards. 'It's all right,' he told her. 'Just something to help you relax.'

She tried to ask what the fuck was going on, but her mouth was numb, her whole face was numb. She was having trouble keeping her eyelids open. The coach was moving, buildings drifting past its smoked-glass windows. The man and woman in white coats were on either side of her, the man wrapping a pressure cuff around her arm, the woman peeling the backing from little black dots, sensors they'd used on her before, when they'd visualised her brain activity, and sticking them on her forehead, behind her ears. She felt that she was sinking into some deep warm red space, woke briefly as the coach drove into the cage inside the big bubble of one of the elevators. There was a big-ass needle inserted into a vein inside her left elbow, taped down and connected to a clear plastic port and a line that looped up to some kind of pump.

'Infusing now,' a woman said, and Lisa felt a sudden warmth spreading up her arm, spreading across her chest.

There was a jolt; she was pressed into the chair by an enormous irresistible force. The elevator was rising, accelerating. The tingling warmth filled her entire body. A man leaned in, shone a light into each of her eyes, leaned away. Lisa was seeing double and everything was haloed with fuzzy light. She tried and failed to focus when the woman pressed some kind of clear plastic oxygen mask over her nose and mouth. A strong smell of vinyl; a harsh metallic taste flooding her mouth.

She was lying flat on a bed. Straps across her arms and chest, across her legs. Dim light. A ceiling curved overhead, quilted with white padding. The bed seemed to be floating on a tide, rising and falling with a steady rolling motion. She'd had epic hangovers back in her lost years. Had woken in strange rooms with strange men, some kind of industrial process clanging in her head and the residue of a mad chemistry experiment coating her tongue. There had been bruises. Sometimes there had been blood. The feeling that her body had been badly used, and the cold filthy realisation that she had fucked up again, and that as soon as she was able to roll over and grope for last night's last bottle she would definitely start to fuck up again.

She felt even worse than that now. She felt that she had spent about a thousand years in some tomb in the City of the Dead, and her desiccated husk had been only partly rehydrated. She couldn't move. She wasn't even breathing. There was a tube down her throat and tape over her mouth and air was passing in and out with a mechanical pulse. Her tongue was shrivelled, blasted by the same catastrophe that had scoured her mouth. Her teeth hurt. Her bones hurt. Her eyes were sandpapered.

'She is awake,' someone said. 'Awake and aware.'

The dim light slowly brightened. A man leaned into view. An old man, bald, hollow-cheeked, mouth pinched by deep lines. When he spoke, Lisa felt a rush of recognition.

That English accent. That knowing smile.

'Welcome to the future,' Adam Nevers said.

48. Committed

Tony hailed Bob and Bane's ship on the seventh day. After passing through three mirror pairs it was more than two hours behind *Abalunam's Pride* because at each transition it lost time hunting for the next mirror in the sequence, but it was clear that Raqle Thornhilde's cloned sons were not going to give up.

Tony hoped that by now the broker had worked out that they still had a common interest in taking down Ada Morange. Hoped that he might gain a little wiggle room if he could persuade her that it would be better to be allies than enemies. But Bane answered his call, and was in no mood for negotiation. His brother had been killed by Adam Apostu, he said, and Tony was going to pay for it.

'Perhaps I could have a word with your mother,' Tony said.

'She's done talking with you,' Bane said. 'As far as she's concerned, you're a dead man. If the police or the Red Brigade haven't killed you by the end of this, I swear I will.'

According to Bane, Raqle Thornhilde had sold Tony to the police immediately after he had escaped from Adam Apostu's house. He was marked as a Red Brigade collaborator who had masterminded the attack on his own home world and escaped with important secrets. A squadron of police ships were on their way. They were just four days behind.

'You get lucky, maybe you can escape me,' Bane said. 'But you won't escape them. You got nowhere to run, dead man.'

Colonel X called a few hours later. Tony did not think it was a coincidence: the colonel had probably bugged his ship's comms. And he was not surprised to discover that the colonel knew most of what had happened on Dry Salvages and on Veles.

'You've done all I expected of you and more,' Colonel X said. 'The run-in with the broker was unfortunate. You shouldn't have allowed yourself to be blindsided like that. You should have taken her down, asked her some hard questions. But it has all worked out in the end.'

'You and I have very different ideas about things working out,' Tony said. 'I am still in serious trouble.'

'And you expect me to do what?' Colonel X said.

'You could find out whether police ships really are following me. And if they are, you could call them off.'

'Oh, they're following you all right,' Colonel X said. 'But even if I could find out who signed the order, I don't have the kind of weight to order them to stop. So as far as that goes, I'm afraid you're on your own.'

Tony had been expecting some kind of betrayal, but it still felt as if his heart was suddenly pumping ice.

He said, 'If you call them off, it will give me time to get close to Ada Morange and the Red Brigade. I can infiltrate her set-up. I can find out what she is planning.'

'But I already have a very good idea about that,' Colonel X said. He sounded faintly amused.

Tony said, 'I can find out more. She needs my help. That's why she helped me escape from Raqle Thornhilde. That's why she gave me the route through the mirrors.'

'If you think this is because of your eidolon, I should remind you that she took two of that unfortunate crew of wizards with her when she escaped. And they have copies of the eidolon in *their* heads.'

'She said that the copy in my ship's mind had made some interesting changes,' Tony said.

When she had hacked *Abalunam's Pride*, back on Dry Salvages, Ada Morange had thoroughly interrogated the bridle about those changes, and the bridle had answered all her questions.

'I didn't realise it was wrong,' she had told Tony. 'Aunty Jael is family. I have talked with her many times before.'

It was not the bridle's fault, not really. The eidolon had worked a sea change on her, but it had not altered her personality construct:

she was still cheerfully naive and trusting. And besides, her innocent garrulousness was actually helpful. It helped Tony understand
exactly what Ada Morange wanted from him.

Colonel X said, 'All I ever needed you to do was flush her out.
And I was always planning to call in the police, if you managed
it. And now Raqle Thornhilde has saved me the bother. It has
all worked out very nicely.'

'As far as you're concerned,' Tony said, not bothering to hide
his bitterness.

'It can work out for you, too,' Colonel X said. 'What you should
do when you find the end of the rainbow is tell Ada Morange
everything you know. Cooperate. She'll keep you safe from Raqle
Thornhilde's son, and you should be able to string her along until
the police arrive. If you survive that, surrender to them as soon
as possible. You can use my name. Once the dust has settled, I'll
write a note, let them know you were working for me.'

'You will write a note.'

'It will be a good one. And one you will be able to cash, too. I'm
well on my way to finding what Ada and her friends in the Red
Brigade want. I'm going to make sure they can't get it. When I'm
finished, my credit will go through the roof. I might even be able
to put in a word for your family.'

Tony had the sudden bad feeling that Colonel X was telling
the truth. He said, 'You're looking for her starship, aren't you?'

'I wondered if you would find out about that,' Colonel X said.
'Two things. First, she actually called it a timeship. When it was
accelerated to close to the speed of light it compressed time, and
she hoped to ride it into the future. Second, I already have it.
And it's going to lead me to something much bigger. Take care,
Mr Okoye. If we meet on the far side of this, I promise I'll find
some way of showing my appreciation.'

Tony brooded about that for a long time. He was on his couch,
where he spent most of his time, enduring the 2.3 G-force during
the stretches of constant acceleration and constant deceleration
between mirrors. He was maxing out *Abalunam's Pride*'s drive
to make sure his pursuer couldn't haul alongside and board her,
and because he wanted to get to where he was going as quickly

as possible. Especially now that he knew the police were also on his tail.

This time he did not have the ship's hands to give him massages and otherwise attend to his needs. Although the bridle claimed that she alone had flown the ship from Dry Salvages to Veles, he was worried that Ada Morange might have found a way to get inside her; remembering the unrelenting fury with which Adam Apostu had attacked Bob, he had locked all the hands in storage, just in case. The bridle also claimed that, because her drones and other assets had been stripped out when she had been mothballed, she had hacked several of Freedonia's police drones and used them to search for Tony after he had been kidnapped. That, at least, appeared to be true: she had stored hours of footage taken by the drones. They had kept watch on Raqle Thornhilde's house and followed her around the city, but had lost contact after she had boarded small jet aircraft and flown beyond the limit of their operating range, to the village of the Real Free People.

The bridle could not explain how she had infiltrated police security. 'I wanted to find out what happened when your comms cut off,' she said, 'so I just sort of did. It was the right thing to do, wasn't it?'

'What would you have done if you had found me?' Tony said.

'Oh, I'm sure that I would have figured something out,' the bridle said.

That careless confidence was new, too. She had definitely changed, but she was by no means omniscient. She had been fooled by Raqle Thornhilde's subterfuge of hiring a ship through one of her shell companies, had not seen the broker's sons smuggle Tony aboard. And she readily agreed that from now on she would not take any initiatives without first consulting Tony.

'At least it all worked out in the end,' she said cheerfully.

'We are still a long way from the end,' Tony said.

After Colonel X's call, he opened a window to Unlikely Worlds, the first time in several days. The !Cha was hunkered down in the hold where Tony had kept the wizards and the stromatolites during the escape from the slime planet. A black drum squatting on what was presently the floor.

Tony told the !Cha that he believed that he had been used to divert Ada Morange's attention from Colonel X's plans. 'He could have intercepted that timeship while it was in the final stages of decelerating towards its destination. Months ago. Years ago. Long before Ada Morange found a way of escaping from my family. There must be something or someone aboard it that both of them want. Ada Morange was hoping that the Red Brigade would help her to take it back. But before she could, the colonel used me to lead the police to her.'

'Yes, why not?'

'You knew, didn't you?'

'It was a logical deduction. What will you do now?'

'I still want to find Ada Morange and make her answer for what she did. I owe it to myself, and to Cho Wing-James and the other wizards, and everyone else killed in the raid.'

'As far as I know, it is a universal rule that the dead have little interest in the sympathy of the living.'

'I care about them, even so.'

'Then you still hope to be a hero.'

'I hope to avoid being killed in a battle between the police and the Red Brigade. If Bane doesn't manage to kill me first.'

'I don't think you need to worry about Bane.'

'Because this isn't his story?'

'Because he doesn't know what he has stumbled into.'

'Neither do I.'

'You have been invited,' Unlikely Worlds said. 'He has not.'

Abalunam's Pride fell through the next mirror, and the next, and the next. By now, Bane's ship was three hours behind, emerging from the sixth mirror pair into the dim light of a small red dwarf star as Tony was decelerating on the final approach to the seventh, some eighty thousand kilometres away, the two mirrors orbiting each other in the trailing Trojan point of a frigid super-Earth.

Tony watched as Bane's ship began to turn towards him, but before it had completed the manouevre something shot away from the mirror behind it. Two, three, four drones, accelerating hard, closing fast. Tony remembered the cloud of disrupter needles that had been flung at *Abalunam's Pride* when he'd escaped from the slime planet, watched with growing dismay as Bane's ship engaged its drive and jagged away at an angle, shedding a fuzz of chaff and squalling countermeasures. Too late: a few moments later there was the bright blink of a fission explosion and Bane's ship was an expanding ball of incandescent gas and debris.

'We have a problem,' the bridle said, and put up a window.

A ship stood behind the mirror that they were approaching. A sleek B-class picket ship somewhat smaller than *Abalunam's Pride*, and studded with weapon pods. Tony hailed it, said as calmly as he could, 'You just made a bad mistake.'

A woman answered, saying calmly, 'The mistake was made by the ship that followed you here.'

'The man who hired that ship was a harmless fool. And its pilot was innocent. Strictly work-for-hire.'

Tony had talked briefly with the pilot when he'd been smuggled aboard at Dry Salvages. A grandmotherly woman who had taken to the wandering life of a freebooter when she'd been just eighteen, and said that she had not regretted a moment of it.

'The pilot accepted the risk when they accepted the job,' the picket's pilot said.

'There are also police ships following me,' Tony said. 'When they find out what you have done, they will show no mercy.'

'When have the likes of them ever shown mercy to the likes of us? Go through the mirror, and stand to. I will follow, and show you the way.'

As if he had any choice. The black mirror of the wormhole mouth was rushing towards him. It was too late to change his velocity or course. He was committed. He had been committed ever since he had booted from Veles.

49. Shanghaied

'More than a hundred years ago, at about the same time that I arrived at Terminus, Ada Morange's so-called timeship ran off into the unknown,' Adam Nevers said. 'And it never came back. She wasn't aboard it, Lisa. You were. You had been kidnapped. Shanghaied. Forcibly conscripted into her crazy crew.'

After Lisa had been rendered unconscious in the bus on Niflheimr, Nevers said, a team of medical technicians had put her in a coma and processed her for suspended animation. Her blood had been replaced with a fluorosilicone fluid and her body chilled to four degrees Celsius, she had been inserted into a tank that fed her, removed her body wastes, and stimulated her muscles to prevent wasting, and the tank had been loaded onto the timeship, which had set out for the lonely M0 red dwarf, the lodestar of her eidolon.

The timeship had accelerated at 1.4 G, a compromise between the maximum acceleration of its bias drive and the comfort of its crew, to close to the speed of light. And after a long, long cruise across a hundred and sixteen light years it had turned around, decelerated and entered orbit around the M0 dwarf. Only seven years had passed aboard it, but a hundred and twenty-three years had passed as time was commonly measured by the human race. A wave of colonisation had spread through the New Frontier, two short-lived empires had risen and fallen, and a loose common-wealth of worlds had been established by the rebels who had overturned the Second Empire's brief cruel reign. An island of civilisation surrounded by pirate nations and vast unexplored tracts of the wormhole network.

The crew of the timeship had used q-phones to stay in contact with Ada Morange and Karyotech Pharma. They could only transmit short text messages because of the huge differences in relative time frames, and although the link had dropped permanently after Ada Morange had disappeared and her companies had fallen apart, the crew had stayed loyal to her. Most had taken turns to hibernate, but the pilot had stayed awake the whole time because he was the link with the Ghajar shipmind. And that, Adam Nevers said, was what had saved Lisa.

'The crew decided to kill you after they realised they had been beaten to their prize. They didn't want you to fall into the hands of their enemies – the rest of humanity, basically. Fortunately, we had already established a communication link with the pilot, and we were able to persuade him to keep you alive. And here we are. Ada Morange thought that she could prevent me from rescuing you by sending you out here, against your will. As you can see, she was wrong.'

'What happened to the pilot, and the rest of the timeship's crew?'

'The pilot works for me now. The others are dead.'

'You killed them?'

'The pilot killed them before they could kill you. It was the only way to save you.'

The people who had cared for her on the long voyage were dead. Just about everyone she knew was dead. The road dogs were dead. Her old boss, Valerie Tortorella. Willie's girlfriend, Brittany Odenkirk. All her neighbours. The kid who'd packed her bags in the Shop'n'Save that last time. Everyone in Joe's Corner; everyone on First Foot. Bria was dead, and Lisa hadn't had the chance to send her that money, let alone apologise properly. Shit, even Bria's kids must be dead by now. Just the thought of it gave Lisa a profound, lonely feeling. She had awoken more than a hundred years in the future and thousands of light years from home, and there was no way of returning. She had become a ghost, unmoored in time.

Her own ghost had been quiet since she'd been revived, but there was always a faint sense of its presence at her back, a feeling

313

as if someone had just left the room. And the tug of the lodestar was still there too. It was no longer in one place but performed a slow spiral around her – something to do with being aboard a ship in orbit around it, she supposed. She was too tired and too brain-fogged to be able to work out the precise mechanics.

Isabelle Linder was dead, too. She hadn't been part of the time-ship's crew; Nevers said that he'd arrested her, on Niflheimr. After she'd been interrogated and released she had returned to Earth and the Omega Point Foundation, but a couple of years later she had been killed in an automobile accident.

Ada Morange, though, she was still alive. After a fashion.

Technically she was no longer human, Adam Nevers said. She'd had her brain laminated: a form of amortality that turned you into an imperfect copy of yourself. Laminated brains weren't considered to be human beings these days, and Ada Morange had passed through several owners and ended up in the hands of a minor honourable family – descendants of one of the rebellious naval officers who had brought down the Second Empire.

'So she's still causing trouble,' Lisa said. 'Good for her.'

Adam Nevers said, 'Do you believe that you owe her your life?'

It was a serious question, seriously asked.

Lisa said, 'She offered to help me, but she took it too far. I didn't agree to travel into the future. I thought I was going to eyeball the lodestar from a safe distance.'

'So she tricked you.'

'It doesn't mean that I owe you anything either, Mr Nevers. I didn't ask to be rescued. If that's what this is.'

He didn't seem to hear her, launching instead into a long rambling story about how the family who owned Ada Morange's laminated brain had recently discovered Ghajar code that, like the code which had infected Lisa on the Bad Trip, contained a powerful eidolon. How that wasn't a coincidence, but had been part of a plan by Ada Morange to free herself, so that she could take control of the timeship at the end of its long voyage. He had thwarted her, Nevers said, and he had also made sure that he would catch up with her on what he called the other side of the mirror. Lisa didn't ask him what he meant by that. He

314

liked to dole out his information in fragments. It was a way of controlling her.

This was during their fourth conversation, a week after Lisa had been woken. She was still pitifully weak. Although Nevers's ship was in free fall, moving around the little cabin was painfully difficult; despite several weeks of therapy and nanotech treatments before she had been woken, her muscles were badly wasted, and her spine and joints stiffly ached. Her digestion was shot because the medical technicians hadn't yet stabilised her gut microbiome. Nerve damage in the tips of her fingers and toes numbly tingled. The face she saw in the mirror was the haggard face of her grandmother just before she had died, and the hair growing out in a stubbly crewcut was pure white.

She was suddenly old, and so was Adam Nevers. Bald, bent-backed, his beardless face lined and creased, his skull showing through his papery scalp. But his gaze was still sharp, and he'd lost none of his acid wit, or the iron will that had turned him into the most determined stalker in history. After his failed mission to Terminus, he'd retired from the geek police and had spent ten years petitioning billionaires until he'd found one who shared his crazy paranoia about Ada Morange's meddling with Elder Culture tech. His sponsor had given him a ship that had travelled at close to the speed of light in a loop that had delivered him back to his point of origin, eighteen years ago. He had been recruited by some kind of hereditary admiral and joined a cabal of spies and spooks that suppressed or acquired disruptive technology, much as the geek police had done.

'I was a stateless person,' Nevers said. 'A man out of time. And she took me in and found me useful employment.'

He was dressed in a light green shirt and dark green trousers, the uniform of the Commons police. It hung on his gaunt body like a suit on a valet stand. There was a lot of gold braid on the right shoulder of his shirt: apparently he was a full colonel. He had been selected for this mission because he had specialist knowledge of the timeship, Lisa, and the eidolon in her head.

'And here we are,' he said. 'After all this time, here we are.'

He also said that Lisa was lucky that he had found her. 'There was a suggestion that the timeship should be destroyed. A nuclear weapon, gravel strewn across its path with sufficient density to overcome its shielding . . . Others wanted to capture you and try to pull the eidolon out of your head. You wouldn't have survived that. They would have sliced up your brain while you were conscious. Luckily for you, I was able to prevail.'

Later, Lisa learned that he had not travelled to the M0 dwarf star the hard way, but had transited through a wormhole that orbited it, unknown to Ada Morange or anyone else when the timeship had departed. It had not been an easy journey, following an obscure branch of the wormhole network and at one point traversing between stars in a long-distance binary, but it had taken far less time than the timeship. And there was a second wormhole orbiting the M0 dwarf, Nevers said. One very different from the wormholes the Jackaroo had towed into the L5 point between Earth and Moon at First Contact, and the wormholes in the vast network that spanned the Milky Way.

He opened one of the virtual-light windows that had replaced phone and computer and TV screens here in the future, showed her an image of that strange wormhole. She immediately felt her ghost crowding her attention, triggering some kind of anomalous activity in her brain that was picked up by the room's surveillance machinery and relayed to Nevers.

'Your eidolon really can't get enough of this,' he said. 'We did some tests on it while you were in recovery. It was awake even when you were completely out of it, and every time we showed this it perked up like a dog sighting a rat. It's definitely your lodestar.'

Inside the window, an irregular sheet of black material was slowly turning end over end against a starry backdrop. A silvery ring was embedded in one face: a wormhole mouth set in material composed of condensed iron nuclei, incredibly dense and a billion times stronger than steel.

According to Nevers, the wormhole mouth was closed. Locked. 'But there may be a way to unlock it,' he said, smiling. His teeth had been replaced with ridges of white plastic.

'Let me guess,' Lisa said. 'My ghost is the key.'

'There's a small sargasso of mad ships orbiting here, too. No one has ever figured out how to pilot one, and everyone who has tried to board one has either died or been driven insane. But the wizards who have been studying that wormhole think that those ships may contain protocols for opening it. And they also think that you, Lisa, can very much help with that.'

50 · The Desires Of A Ghost

Abalunam's Pride emerged into a sky dominated by the heaven tree of a stellar nursery. Billowing thunderheads and swirling currents of sooty dust, silicate grains and gas aglow with the radiation of hot bright stars embedded in them. Ragged pillars, shaped by light and stellar winds, clawing across a dozen light years, spalling offshoots tipped with the blowsy haloes of stars birthing in collapsing knots of protostellar material. A vast, violent engine of creation.

Tony hardly noticed this glory. Numb and angry, he noted the positions of drones in powered triangular orbits around the mirror, the pale blue disc of an ice giant some three million kilometres away. According to the bridle, the ice giant orbited a yellow G2 star at an average distance of 2.5 billion kilometres, and it was orbited in turn by several moons, one big enough to retain a tenuous and frigid nitrogen atmosphere. And there were other mirrors close by: eight of them in a loose cluster. Tony's first thought was that there were more than enough to get lost in if he needed to flee. But when he looked more closely, he saw that the rings of strange matter around their mouths were not embedded in sculpted rocks, but were instead set in irregular sheets of stuff with the sheen of black mica. And the mouths themselves were not bordered with the usual ring of red-shifted light that leaked through from the far end, giving an illusion of depth, of deep pools lit from below. These looked as dull and flat as dusty black glass . . .

For a moment, he felt a plangent sorrow wash through him, so deep and profound that it completely unmoored him. And then it was gone, draining away and leaving not a wrack behind.

'What's wrong with them?' he said. 'What happened here?'

'They are dead,' the bridle said.

'Dead? How can they be dead?'

Tony had never before seen a dead mirror. He had never before *heard* of one.

'Their machineries are no longer functional. There is no tau neutrino flux and their sparks of intelligence are gone. The ends of the wormholes are pinched shut.' The bridle paused, then added, 'The ship and its eidolon grieve for them.'

'I think my eidolon does, too.'

But the chill that passed through Tony was entirely his own. He and the ship's mind were sharing the emotions of alien ghosts . . .

'A bad thing happened here,' the bridle said. 'I am sampling the local environment. We appear to be inside a diffuse ring of metal-rich dust.'

'Debris from destroyed ships?'

'Possibly. There are anomalies in the planet's magnetic field, too. And at least one of its moons has been shattered. Two arcs of water-ice rubble share the same orbit.'

'It happened a long time ago,' Tony said, mostly for his own re-assurance. And then he remembered the hot flower of Bane's ship.

'It is not yet over,' the bridle said.

'Is that what you think, or is that what the ship and its eidolon think?'

'It's hard to tell.'

A few minutes later, the B-class picket that had been guarding the far side of the mirror emerged in a flare of false photons. After it had killed its residual momentum and rendezvoused with *Abalunam's Pride*, its pilot transmitted a flight plan: their destination was a rocky planet that orbited at the inner edge of the G2 star's habitable zone, a trip of ten days. She also dispatched a small carrier drone. Tony received it in the auxiliary airlock and unpacked it himself. It contained a q-phone. Apparently, the philosopher queen of the Red Brigade, Mina Saba, wanted to speak with him.

Tony took the call in a small space he had partitioned off in the passenger accommodations, after the ship was under way. He'd given some thought to the decor, settling on blood-red curtains around the walls and a single spotlight on a tall back ironwood chair, where he sat with Unlikely Worlds at his side. He wanted the !Cha to be a witness.

He was dressed in the traditional clothes of his family, a knee-length black shirt with gold embroidery, black trousers, a matching cap set on his braids. Sitting straight-backed with his forearms resting on the arms of the chair, the way Ayo sat when receiving petitioners, his palms sweating on smooth wood as a window opened in front of him and there she was.

The woman who had ordered the murder of his father. Who had planned the raid on Skadi, and had tried to murder him. The proximal cause of his family's fall from grace.

She did not look anything like the crazed flame-eyed monster, bristling with surgical enhancements and haunted by half a hundred fearsome alien ghosts and djinns, of popular legend. She was an old woman with a cloud of white hair, cupped in a sling chair and dressed in a knee-length grey jumper. A cloud of little windows framed her head, displaying the faces of fourteen men and women – the captains of her fleet, Mina Saba told Tony, after they had exchanged preliminary niceties.

'Before we talk about anything else,' she said, 'I want to deal with the unfortunate incident at HD 115043, and the death of your father. Commons propaganda has it that we staged an ambush as an act of revenge for an earlier attack. That is exactly the opposite of the truth. Hardliners in the Commons government wanted to sabotage the parlay, and were preparing to attack our delegation. We were forced to counter-attack and flee, and in our flight we destroyed the ships that stood between us and the nearest mirror. I know now that your father was aboard one of those ships. I ask you to believe that his death was an accident, caused by a conspiracy of reactionaries in the government he represented. I believe that those same reactionaries may also have murdered your mother. We may not be on the same side, but we have an enemy in common. And that is why I am so glad that you have come here. Together, we can do much to right serious wrongs.'

It was a good speech, contrived to push as many of Tony's buttons as possible. He was certain that Ada Morange had a hand in it; that she had told Mina Saba about his family's belief that his mother had been assassinated. And he did not trust a word of it. Oh, it was possible that the so-called reactionaries might have been planning an ambush, but the Red Brigade had acted first, and it had been a massacre.

He said, as calmly as he could, 'We certainly have much to discuss.'

'Perhaps we can begin with your recent adventures,' Mina Saba said. 'I know something about them, but some things are unclear. Your association with Colonel X, for instance.'

When they'd been much younger, Tony and Òrélolu had sometimes sparred in the Great House's gymnasium. Òrélolu hadn't been much of a boxer, dancing about, landing only a few butterfly pats, but occasionally one of his jabs would really connect. Tony felt that same jarring surprise now, but realised at once that Ada Morange must have told Mina Saba about Colonel X, after she had hacked the bridle.

'It was not much of an association,' he said, and explained how Colonel X had helped him escape from the custody of his family, and how the colonel had used, betrayed and abandoned him. He was selling himself, hoping to persuade Mina Saba that he had gone over to her side because he wanted payback for the colonel's treachery.

The captains, their windows enlarging when they spoke and shrinking back into place afterwards, asked questions about his involvement in the discovery of the stromatolites, the Ghajar algorithm they contained and the eidolon it generated, his adventures on Dry Salvages and Veles. Tony answered as best he could while Mina Saba sat quietly in the middle of their host, watching him with a steady gaze that he found impossible to read.

When the philosopher queen at last ended the interrogation, Tony took the opportunity to ask about Ada Morange and the wizards. Were they prisoners or partners in her enterprise?

'If you believe that Ada Morange is your partner, remember that she betrayed me and my family twice,' he said. 'First by telling you about the slime planet, and then by helping you raid my home. She is not to be trusted.'

There was a brief silence. Tony met Mina Saba's gaze, could feel the attention of the fourteen captains leaning at their little windows.

Mina Saba said, 'We will need to test you and your ship for the activity of that Ghajar eidolon. I take it you won't object?'

'Of course not. That is why I'm here.'

One of the captains, a grim black-haired man in a window that dilated above Mina Saba's left shoulder, said, 'It doesn't prove anything one way or another.'

'I would think that my surrender has already shown that I came here with the best of intentions,' Tony said.

'You didn't surrender,' the captain said. 'We captured your ass.'

Unlikely Worlds spoke up, startling Tony. 'There are many paths he could have taken. Yet he is here of his own free will, and I believe that he has brought what you need.'

'If he needs a trickster like you to make his case, he's in a bad way,' the captain said.

Mina Saba held up a hand; the captain's window shrank into the general cloud. 'You know who we are and what we can do,' she told Tony.

'Absolutely.'

'Then do nothing to provoke us. We will talk again,' Mina Saba said, and she and her host of captains vanished.

Tony told Unlikely Worlds that he thought that Mina Saba would not harm him because only he could interface with the ship's bridle. 'She is tailored to me, and she is the only connection to the ship's mind and the Ghajar eidolon that has infected it. And because she has been altered by the eidolon, the Red Brigade will not dare try to hack her.'

'It's quite possible,' Unlikely Worlds said.

'Perhaps I am making up a story to convince myself that they will not kill me.'

'You are more important than you think. Think of all you have discovered since being reunited with your ship.'

'I fear that all I have discovered is that I do not know enough.'

The bridle was frustratingly vague about how she had been changed; how the ship had been changed. She claimed that she saw things differently now, that she saw what she called the imprint of history, but when Tony had asked if that meant she could see the ghosts of the Ghajar she had said that it wasn't like that.

'I see the places they have been and the things they have done. I see all that, but I don't understand everything. Do you think I will? I hope I will.'

She still could not communicate directly with the eidolon, or understand how it had altered the ship's mind.

'It shows me pictures, sometimes,' she would say.

Or: 'Sometimes I just get this great notion.'

Tony said, 'Were you able to boot from Dry Salvages because the eidolon gave you the idea?'

'I don't know. Perhaps,' she said. 'All I know is it seemed to be the right thing to do.'

That was something Tony had learned, at least. He knew now that Ada Morange had told the bridle about his plight on Veles, but she had not been able to take control of the ship, as he had once thought. Instead, the bridle appeared to be under the influence of the unholy alliance between the eidolon and the ship's mind.

'We are all being driven by the desires of a ghost,' Tony told Unlikely Worlds. 'And we do not know what it wants, or what it can do.'

'Oh, I think we will soon find out,' the !Cha said.

51. Mad Ship

'You'd better be ready to get your magic on,' the pilot told Lisa. 'Otherwise that ugly motherfucker is going to kill us. Or, even worse, drive us stark staring insane.'

They were sidling towards the mad ship in a tug not much bigger than Lisa's pickup truck, lying side by side in its cramped cabin. Various views of their target hung before them.

The mad ship was huge. It was dark. In visible light it was hardly there, a shadow against the galaxy's river of star-smoke, but radar and microwave images revealed its bulk: a fat egg more than three kilometres long. A city-sized structure just hanging there in vacuum. Spines of different lengths jutted from one end – the smallest was taller than the UN building in Port of Plenty. The other end tailed away in a kind of mesh cone or funnel that narrowed to a flattened nozzle.

Ordinary Ghajar ships were divided into twenty-one classes, and every ship in a particular class was the same shape and size. But while all mad ships possessed those spines, that mesh funnel, they varied wildly in tonnage. There were eight mad ships in the sargasso that orbited the M0 dwarf, from sprats only a little larger than the tug to the monster it was approaching. And all were as dangerous as unshielded, unmoderated nuclear piles. People who approached too closely were either driven insane, or died when their brain-stem activity shut down. Animals and AI systems above a certain level of sophistication were killed, too. The mad ships appeared to selectively warp the fundamental properties of space-time in their immediate vicinity, specifically affecting electromagnetic activity associated with information processing. So far, no effective shielding had been discovered. They could be captured by remotely piloted haulers, but no one had yet discovered how to board them, let alone control them.

Lisa was heading towards the biggest of those killer ships in a frail human-built craft steered by the pilot of the timeship, Dave Clegg, a compact, shaven-headed Brit with the sour sarcastic manner of someone who always expects to be short-changed by life. He wouldn't talk about his defection or the deaths of the timeship's crew, said only that he'd done what needed to be done after he'd flown into an ambush, and his reward for cooperating with his hijackers was flying this shitty little tin can on shitty little missions.

Adam Nevers's crew of wizards – what they called scientists here – claimed that Dave Clegg had been infected with a copy of Lisa's eidolon. He had buzzed the outer edge of the mad ship's zone of affect several times, with no detectable effect on his brain activity. Now he was supposed to take Lisa deeper in.

She had managed to snatch a brief conversation with him while they were being prepped, saying that if she really could get control of the mad ship, they could fly away. 'After all, no one would dare follow us.'

She'd been half-joking, but Dave Clegg took it seriously. 'Were you paying attention at the briefing? If I deviate a millimetre from the flight plan, another pilot will take over, fly the tug by wire. Plus, we'll be watched by drones tipped with thermonuclear weapons. One wrong move and we're hot plasma.'

'They're probably bluffing,' Lisa said. 'They need me. You too.'

Nevers's wizards had begun a series of experiments designed to measure and define the activity of the eidolons imprinted in Lisa's and Dave Clegg's brains, subjecting them to low frequency electric pulses, tightly focused magnetic fields, patterns of flickering light and synchronised pulses of sound, so forth. They reminded Lisa of the tests she and Willie had undergone after the Bad Trip, and so far hadn't revealed anything she didn't already know.

'If you want to test that notion, do it on your own time,' Dave Clegg said. 'Meanwhile, just try to relax, will you? Enjoy the ride. And don't even think of trying anything funny.'

As if she could, in their coffin-sized quarters. She was studded with dots and patches that monitored her life signs and the activity of her brain and the eidolon, was dressed in a skintight one-piece pressure garment that had stiffened into a rigid casing as soon as the techs had buckled her into her couch. She couldn't even scratch her nose. All she could do was watch the shadow of the mad ship grow in various windows as the little tug edged closer. She tried to feel how her ghost felt, tried the Zen thing of emptying her mind of thought so that she might sense its sly presence, but all she got was a tension headache pulsing behind her eyes.

Beside her, Dave Clegg gave status checks and answered questions she couldn't hear. Over and again the stark shadow of the mad ship rolled off the screen and the tiny stars of the timeship and the S-class scow that housed Adam Nevers's operation appeared, more than a thousand kilometres distant. Lisa had glimpsed a close-up view of the timeship when the tug had been launched. It looked hard-used, ancient, its bulky shields fore and aft deeply pitted and cratered by explosive impacts with microscopic grains of interstellar dust, its whole length sandblasted. Incredible to believe that she had spent seven years aboard the thing, sleeping more deeply than any fairytale princess while howling through the interstellar void at close to the speed of light . . .

The mad ship reappeared at the upper edges of various windows and crept downwards and disappeared again. The tug's paper-thin hull pinged and creaked; Lisa sweated into her rigid pressure garment, remembering the jaunt in the Orion capsule when she'd visited Ada Morange a couple of lifetimes ago. At last, she gave in and asked how much longer they had to go until they reached the boundary of the zone of affect.

'We passed it twenty minutes ago,' Dave Clegg said. 'The fucking bastards running the show want us to get closer.'

'How much closer?'

'All the way in, could be. If I knew I'd tell you.'

'Well, we're not dead.'

'Not yet. Whatever it is you're doing, keep doing it, okay?'

'Right. You too.'

She had no idea how their ghosts were protecting them; the thought that they might suddenly stop whatever they were doing or be overwhelmed by the mad ship's malign warp crept into her mind like a trickle of ice-water. The silhouette and radar images of the mad ship revolved twice more, then stabilised and centred in every window. The reaction motor thumped distantly; Lisa felt a phantom of gravity pass through her as the tug briefly accelerated. The silhouette began to grow.

'They want us to do a drive-by,' Dave Clegg said. 'Skim past at a minimum distance of three hundred metres. If we survive this you're going to see some fine flying.'

They were aimed at the huge funnel at the stern of the mad ship. Details began to resolve in the radar images. There were structures embedded in the thick strands of the funnel's mesh: building-sized blocks and plates, a patch of pyramidal cones packed in a Fibonacci spiral like seeds in a sunflower head.

'No. No, I don't,' Dave Clegg said to someone on the other end of his comms. Then, 'I'm changing course now.'

His fingers made shapes in the air in front of his face.

The reaction motor thumped again. In the windows, the funnel slid sideways, foreshortened. The bulk of the rest of the mad ship showed beyond, and Lisa realised that the tug was swinging around to the pinched nozzle that terminated the funnel.

But it wasn't pinched shut now. A freezing watchfulness gripped Lisa. She couldn't tell if it was her fear or her ghost's fascination.

The nozzle was retracting and pulling apart in a roughly circular gape, like the mouth of a monstrous worm.

'Fucking hell,' Dave Clegg said reverentially.

The mad ship was waking up.

52 · Somewhat Resembling Venus

Four days into the voyage to the G2 star's Earth-sized planet, a flight of drones burst out of the mirror that *Abalunam's Pride* and the Red Brigade picket had left behind. They came through all at once, an expanding fast-moving swarm that immediately engaged with the drones and mines sown by the picket. A hyperkinetic wavefront of strikes and counterstrikes flared across a million cubic klicks; driving sunwards, Tony glimpsed a tiny glitter of X-ray and gamma-ray sources, a stuttering constellation of brief-lived stars. The picket ship's pilot shared an image snatched by a stealthed surveillance drone: ships emerging from the mirror, one after the other. Four J-class interceptors bristling with assets, heading from the ice giant in line-of-battle formation.

'They don't realise they are outnumbered,' the pilot said.

'They dealt with your drones easily enough,' Tony said.

He had been nursing the faint hope that Bane and Colonel X had been lying about the police ships, was dismayed by their appearance. It was a dangerous and unpredictable complication.

'Let 'em think they have the advantage,' the pilot said cheer-fully. 'That little engagement was just a taster. Pretty soon you're going to see some real fun.'

A sentiment echoed by Mina Saba when she called an hour later, wanting to know if the police ships had been sent by Colonel X.

'Ada Morange tricked a broker into hiring me to help inves-tigate the slime planet. Her hand killed one of the broker's sons on Veles. The broker told the police everything, and here we are,' Tony said.

'You have been less than honest with me, Mr Okoye. I'm disappointed,' Mina Saba said.

'I was hoping that the broker was bluffing,' Tony said. 'I'm sorry to see that she was not. Where is Ada Morange, by the way? Is she with you?'

'Don't expect any help from the police,' Mina Saba said. 'They have badly underestimated my resources. We will talk again when you reach my ship. We will talk face to face. And if you are less than candid with me, if there is any more trickery, I can promise you that things will go badly.'

'Ask Ada Morange what happened in her house in Tanrog,' Tony said. 'Ask her how she tricked Raqle Thornhilde. Ask her how she tricked my family. Ask yourself how she might be tricking you.'

But Mina Saba had cut the connection.

Abalunam's Pride and the picket ship flew on, separated by just ten kilometres, decelerating on a course that intersected with the planet. One of the police ships aimed a maser at them, transmitting a declaration that this was a designated forbidden zone, a command to prepare to surrender, and a message from Opeyemi, ordering Tony to give up his futile plans for the good of the family. Tony told the bridle to block anything else that the police sent.

'Do you want to reply to Opeyemi?' the bridle said.

'It probably wasn't even him,' Tony said. 'Just some avatar got up by the police.'

But it had woken the itches of old doubts. Colonel X had abandoned him. He had run from his family. And now he was running from the police into the arms of the Red Brigade, with no idea of what would happen when he got there.

His destination, presently showing as a crescent off to one side of the star's incandescent coin, was a cloud-wrapped hothouse planet somewhat resembling Venus. Like Venus, a runaway greenhouse effect had baked carbon dioxide from its crust, muffling it in a thick atmosphere several hundred kilometres deep; unlike Venus, it was protected from solar winds by a strong magnetic field, and had retained most of its water. Venus's clouds were mostly concentrated sulphuric acid; here, they were composed of tiny droplets of carbonic acid that constantly rained out towards the hot surface, turning into carbon dioxide and superheated steam that was recirculated high into the atmosphere to begin the cycle again.

The bridle reported that she had detected the signature of photosynthetic pigments in the calm upper layers of the clouds: aerial plankton whose rate of reproduction exceeded the rate of removal by rain falling towards the surface. A little later she said that she had detected a small fleet of ships in orbit around the planet's equator: a U-class hauler and twelve smaller ships in a higher, separate orbit.

Tony said, 'The hauler will be remotely controlled. And it contains a mad ship. That's why the other ships are keeping their distance.'

'I have found something else,' the bridle said. 'Several hundred small radar-reflective bodies in the planet's atmosphere.'

Tony wanted to know if they were ships. He imagined a fleet of them, each hung under giant balloons in the thick cloud cover. A floating sargasso drifting on the wind . . .

'We are too far away to resolve them,' the bridle said. 'But it is possible that at least one of them could be a mirror. The planet is emitting a small excess of tau neutrinos consistent with the operation of mirror machinery. And the eidolon . . .'

'What about the eidolon?' Tony said, after a few seconds' silence.

'It is very interested in the planet. I think it is searching for something down there. Or maybe it has found it, and is talking to it,' the bridle said. 'It isn't clear. I wish I knew more, but there it is.'

'Has anyone ever found a mirror floating in a planetary atmosphere?'

'I know! Isn't it amazing?'

'Can you locate it? If it is a mirror.'

'Not yet. It may be possible when we are closer. Also, I could build more detectors. Do you want me to do that?'

'If it will help you find this mirror,' Tony said carefully. He was still wary of the bridle's new abilities. He was worried that she might decide that her interests – or the interests of the eidolon – were more important than his.

330

'I think it will. Yes. It's exciting, isn't it?' the bridle said happily.

'Keep looking,' Tony said. 'Keep looking everywhere. And open a line to that picket.'

He was going to tell its pilot that he wanted to talk to Mina Saba again. He believed that he finally had some leverage in this game.

53. 'We are here to help.'

After Lisa had been extracted from the tug and stripped of her sensor patches, a guard clipped a short cable to her waist and towed her down the length of the hold. Gliding in free fall through deep shadow and splashes of brilliant light, past two A-class jaunt ships, actual alien spaceships like giant whiskery catfish carved from obsidian, to a curtain of plastic webbing on the far bulkhead, where Adam Nevers and three Jackaroo avatars were waiting.

'We wanted to congratulate you in person,' Nevers said.

He was gripping the webbing with both hands, as if afraid that he would fall if he let go. The three avatars hung quiet and still in the air beside him. It was a shock to see them, but not a surprise. Their translucent gold skin. Their black tracksuits, which here in the future must look like antiques. The dark glasses that masked the white stones of their eyes.

'So who's really in charge?' Lisa said, hooking a couple of fingers in the webbing and turning to the avatars. It was a little like floating in water, except that there was no sense of up or down. 'You or Mr Nevers?'

'We are here to help,' the middle one said.

'Yeah, I know all about your help.'

Lisa was shaky and exhausted after the jaunt in the tug, her spine and hips ached from hours of being immobilised in the rigid shell of her pressure garment, and for the first time since she had woken in the future she badly needed a drink. It parched her tongue and throat, burned in her belly.

'One of you was with Mr Nevers when he raided my place,' she said. 'And a couple of your buddies turned up at Terminus, scaring Ada Morange into kidnapping me and booting me into the future.'

Nevers said, 'If you must blame anyone for your plight, Lisa, blame Ada Morange.'

That even, faintly sarcastic tone of his, as if speaking to a child.

'Did you ever ask yourself how you got here, Mr Nevers? The way I see it, we've both been manipulated by those showroom dummies from the get-go.'

Lisa didn't believe for a moment that the avatars were disinterested observers of the antics of their clever, curious monkey clients. The Jackaroo had helped dozens of client races. Hundreds. All of them had spread through the wormhole network and all of them had vanished, destroying themselves in catastrophic wars, evolving into something beyond human comprehension, or simply dying out, stretched too thin by the effort of embracing the Jackaroo's gifts. No one knew. All the Jackaroo would say was that every client found its own path. But one thing was clear: none of their clients had survived contact unchanged.

She looked again at the avatars, floating there like a too-cool-for-school trio of pop stars, and said, 'I have a question.'

'Of course.'

It was the left-hand one who spoke this time. Lisa looked straight at it, her face dimly reflected in its dark glasses.

'The eidolon inside my head. Can you speak to it?'

'We know it was once like you.'

'Is it one of your clients?'

'Those clients have moved on.'

'The eidolon didn't. What does it want?'

'It should speak for itself,' the middle Jackaroo said.

'It's interesting. You say you want to help. It's your tag line. Your USP. But whenever you're asked anything you put on this act, all aloof and fucking mysterious. You tell us that we have to choose our own path, and then you push us in the direction you want us to go. That's why you're here, isn't it? To make sure Mr Nevers does the right thing.'

'There is always a choice,' the left-hand avatar said. 'Even the straightest path has two directions.'

'Not as far as I'm concerned,' Lisa said. 'I travelled into the future, and I can't go back.'

Man, she could so do with a cold tall one right now. She could see the amber liquid pouring into the glass, the rising head of foam, smell that yeasty tang . . .

'Then find another path,' the middle avatar said.

'Or choose not to follow it,' the right-hand avatar said.

The three of them in their fucking sunglasses and black tracksuits, so above it all.

Lisa said, 'Do you believe this bullshit, Mr Nevers?'

'I believe that I'm doing the right thing,' Nevers said calmly.

'You think they're helping you, but you're really part of their plan to stop us finding anything that might actually reveal what's really going on.'

But she knew she'd never make him see that. He'd pared his life down to this single purpose. He'd exiled himself into the future because of it. He'd dedicated himself to it like some kind of warrior saint, and probably rededicated himself twice daily.

'You're angry and confused,' he said. 'But mostly you're afraid. It's entirely understandable, given the way Ada Morange tried to use you, and where you've ended up because of it. In your situation? I wouldn't trust anyone either. But now you have an opportunity to put all that right.'

'Use my powers for good, or some such bullshit?'

'You've already done that, by helping to open up the mad ship,' Nevers said. 'And now Mr Clegg must learn how to talk to it, so that we can ask it nicely if we can ride it through that wormhole. Meanwhile, until I need your help again, I think you should take a well-earned rest.'

'I was kind of hoping I was done here.'

'Oh no. Not at all. We've only just begun.'

54. Aerostats

As before, Tony sat in the ironwood chair in the red-curtained space he had created. As before, Unlikely Worlds stood beside him. Mina Saba was late. She was calling his bluff. She was planning some baroque punishment for his presumption. And then the window opened, showing the philosopher queen lounging in her sling chair, this time wearing a silvery quilted jacket with a collar that flared behind her head. A small neat woman in her early thirties perched on a stool at her right hand, dressed all in black. Milky skin, red pigment on her lips and the nails of her hands and bare feet, a cap of glossy hair the colour of midnight.

Her smile showed small white teeth. 'Master Tony. I'm so glad that you found your way here.'

It was an avatar of Ada Morange. A version of her younger self before she'd been laminated, or perhaps an ideal image of what she believed to be her true self. She greeted Unlikely Worlds with some warmth, told Tony that she had first met the !Cha on Earth, a century and a half ago.

'I thought him a friend, even though I knew that had I led a life only a little less interesting he would not have troubled to spend a single minute with me. That is to say, whatever passed for friendship between us was a kind of commerce. But it was of no matter. Many of my friendships were based not on sympathy or love, but on reciprocal satisfaction of appetite. So I was neither surprised nor disappointed when, after the difficulty that made me what I am now, his visits ceased.'

'But I never forgot you,' Unlikely Worlds said. 'As you can see.'

Tony believed that Ada Morange's presence was a good sign. That his gamble, telling Mina Saba that he wanted to discuss the mirror floating somewhere in the hothouse planet's clouds, would pay off. But the two women were in no hurry to talk about that; instead, Ada Morange began to tell Tony about aerostats that rode the planet's constant winds, lecturing him about their form and function as Aunty Jael had lectured him on so many different subjects. Either pedagogy was an act she found hard to shake off, or it had been deeply baked into her true self, and preserved after she had been laminated.

She showed him images of streamlined hollow cylinders, told him that they were between a few hundred metres and three or four kilometres long, constructed from thousands of polymer bubbles spun by architectural nanomachines from atmospheric nitrogen and carbonic acid, plankton scooped from the clouds, and minerals collected when the aerostats descended into the furnace of the planet's lower depths and dragged fullerene cables across the baking rocks of the surface. Large aerostats would sometimes break up into daughter colonies, she said, and sometimes two would gently collide, and at the point of contact blisters would swell and froth and release thousands of tiny bubbles containing packages of nutrients and nanomachines. It seemed to be a kind of sexual reproduction.

All the aerostats were empty: any that had once been inhabited must have long ago disintegrated or fallen out of the cloud layer and burned up. Or perhaps it was a mistake to believe that they were floating cities. Perhaps they were factories, or some kind of art, or had been used for sexual or territorial display.

'We know very little about the Ghajar,' Ada Morange said. 'But we do know that they did not much like planetary surfaces. There are thousands of their ships in parking orbits, but they left little trace of their presence on any of the known worlds. Some structures which may have been mooring points, the wreckage of a few crashed ships. But it turns out that we were looking in the wrong place. The Ghajar were creatures of the air. They wrote their signatures on the winds of worlds like this, and left no footprints behind.'

'It's a pretty story,' Mina Saba said. 'But like everything we think we know about the Elder Cultures, that's all it is. A story we tell ourselves to fill the void of our ignorance.'

Tony, unable to contain his impatience any longer, said, 'And what kind of stories do you tell yourselves about the floating mirror?'

'Did you discover that for yourself, or did the !Cha tell you?' Mina Saba said.

'Oh, I wouldn't presume to spoil your surprise,' Unlikely Worlds said.

'Oh, but of course you would,' Ada Morange said. 'You pretend to be helpful, but you are really manipulating us to make our stories prettier. You tried to manipulate me all those years ago, and I have no doubt that you are up to your old tricks again.'

'The !Cha claim to be sympathetic to our ideas, but we have long ago learned not to trust them,' Mina Saba said.

'Tony does not trust me either,' Unlikely Worlds said. 'But like you and Ada, he finds me useful. You have that much in common.'

'Master Tony and I share much more than that,' Ada Morange said. 'I have known him from birth. I trained him. I helped him to become what he is.'

'And all the time you were someone else, and only pretending to be the person I thought I knew,' Tony said. He meant it as a joke, but it was tainted with rancour.

'I was a faithful servant to your family for many years,' Ada Morange said 'And I still am, after a fashion. Didn't I help you to find your way here?'

'What happened before, it was only business,' Mina Saba said briskly. 'As is this. If you came looking for revenge, you will find only trouble. But if you agree to work with us, we can agree to share what we find.'

'He knows that,' Ada Morange said, smiling at Tony. 'He always was a practical boy.'

Tony wanted to tell her that he knew that she had planned to ransom him in exchange for her freedom, that she had helped the Red Brigade to stage the raid on Skadi. He wanted to ask her why she had told the raiders where to look for him, if she knew that they had been planning to kill him and take his head. If that

337

had been her idea. He wanted to ask her why she had killed Junot Johnson and the police guards, when she could have easily knocked them out instead. Was it because they had defied her by refusing to surrender, by destroying the stromatolites? He wanted to ask her if she felt sorry for the deaths of innocent civilians in Victory Landing, and the damage she had done to his family's reputation. He wanted to confront her with her vile crimes and contemptible betrayals. He wanted to strike her down with great vengeance and furious wrath. But that would have to wait until he could persuade Mina Saba to hand her over. He had an idea about how he was going to do that, but meanwhile he had to pretend that this was just an ordinary business negotiation.

He said, trying to bring the conversation back to the point, 'I saw a little wilderness of mirrors when I came through into this system. Strange mirrors, mounted on flat sheets rather than on the sheer faces of sculpted asteroids. And all of them were dead. Something killed them long ago, and pinched their wormholes shut. But there is at least one live mirror floating in the clouds of that planet, amongst the aerostats. You have not been able to use it, because otherwise you would already be on the other side, and that is why you invited me here, isn't it? You need my help to open it. You need the eidolon I am carrying, the one generated by Ghajar code, the one that has been changed in interesting ways. But before we go any further, I want to know what you hope to find on the other side, and what I will get if I can take you there.'

The two women exchanged a look.

'You always had a sense of entitlement, Tony,' Ada Morange said. 'It isn't your fault. You have been raised to believe that ruling over others is your right, your destiny. But don't think that you are the only key to this particular lock.'

'Yet here I am, because you invited me. Because, I guess, the two wizards you kidnapped were unable to help you.'

'I will admit that there have been certain difficulties,' Mina Saba said.

'We have a mad ship,' Ada Morange said. 'That's what will open the mirror, not your eidolon. But we need your eidolon to take control of the mad ship.'

'You said that there have been difficulties,' Tony said. 'What kind of difficulties?'

'That is none of your business,' Mina Saba said. 'What matters now is how we will move forward.'

'If something happened to the wizards, I think it very much is,' Tony said.

'Oh, what's the harm in telling him?' Ada Morange said. 'He came to us willingly, and besides, he's already guessed most of it.'

'Then tell him, why not?' Mina Saba said, with an impatient flick of her hand.

'The stromatolites were badly damaged, and we have been unable to make more copies of the eidolon,' Ada Morange said to Tony. 'As for the wizards, one died of brain-stem failure, and the other killed himself and ten of Mina's people.'

'This was when they tried to take control of the mad ship,' Tony said.

'The wizards were not pilots,' Ada Morange said. 'You are. Your ship has been infected with a copy of the stromatolite eidolon, which has made some interesting changes to its mind. And because you are in intimate contact with it, I believe you have been changed too. I have every confidence that you will be able to do what the wizards could not.'

'Where does it go, this mirror?' Tony said.

'Somewhere only mad ships can go,' Ada Morange said.

'The Ghajar were divided into at least two factions,' Mina Saba said. 'One built the mad ships and the new mirrors. Either as an alternative to the network gifted to them by the Jackaroo, or as entrances to secret or sacred places. The other faction opposed the first. There was a war. It consumed both sides.'

'There are many stories,' Unlikely Worlds said, 'but most follow similar patterns.'

'We are not like the Ghajar,' Mina Saba said sharply.

'I was not thinking of the Ghajar,' Unlikely Worlds said. 'I was thinking of Ada, and an old friend of hers, Adam Nevers.'

'Otherwise known as Colonel X,' Ada Morange said. 'I see that you did not know his true name, Master Tony.'

'I know about Adam Nevers,' Tony said. 'I thought him long dead.'

'He found someone willing to sponsor his stupid quest,' Ada Morange said, 'and he rode a timeship in a circular course to his future. Our present. He was taken in by one of the honourable families, and joined Special Services. Once a policeman, always a policeman. He wants to stop us reaching the other side of the mirror, but you will give us the edge.'

'He and his employer fear new discoveries because they threaten established hierarchies of power and privilege,' Mina Saba said. 'He is the dead hand of the past. And we are the way forward.'

The conversation turned to Tony's rendezvous with the Red Brigade's fleet. He would undergo tests, Ada Morange said, and then the work of preparing the mad ship for transition through the new mirror would begin. Together, Mina Saba said, they would find all kinds of wonders, and remake history.

'It's interesting,' Unlikely Worlds said afterwards. 'You don't trust them, and they don't trust you. Yet you need each other.'

'Who said I need them?' Tony said.

'Oho. Now that *is* interesting. May I ask what you plan to do?'

'They claim that only a mad ship can open this mirror of theirs,' Tony said. 'I think that I can prove them wrong.'

55. Into Everywhere

After being debriefed and subjected to a variety of mostly mysterious tests by Adam Nevers's mad little crew of wizards, Lisa was escorted to her cabin and more or less left alone for three days. Space travel seemed to consist mostly of moving through a series of rooms – even the tug sort of counted. This one was egg-shaped, about the size of the bathroom in the house she had built on her homestead. Floating in mid-air with her feet towards the hatch, she could reach out and touch the walls on either side. One wall (she supposed it would be the ceiling, when there was gravity) gave off a pale light that could be dialled down but never completely extinguished; a silvery sleeping bag like the cocoon of a giant bug was fastened to another. Webbing pouches contained toiletries, changes of underwear, and grey sweatshirts and loose black pants, a costume that reminded her of childhood ballet classes.

She could invoke wallpaper that turned the room into a glade in a forest, a grassy hollow in an alpine meadow, a bubble floating on a restless ocean, a sandy depression in a stony desert under two suns, so forth. But the illusions were too painful, reminding her of all she had left behind, so she left the walls of the cabin blank, like the prison cell it was.

Food was brought by one or another of her guards, who also escorted her if she needed to use the bathroom, a complicated routine in free fall, involving nozzles and suction devices and wet-wipes. She could access the ship's library via a window that opened in the air, but couldn't get at the stuff she needed – histories of the days of future past, documentaries, anything that would give her a handle on where she was. All she could call up were nineteenth-century novels and late twentieth-century TV programmes she vaguely remembered watching with her parents in the long-ago before the Jackaroo came. Alternating *Bleak House* with random episodes of *Homicide: Life on the Streets* induced an aching homesickness, part nostalgia, part loneliness. Here she was in the future. There was no going back. And the only person who understood how she felt, the only person who might know the difference between Inspector Bucket and Detective Munch, was her jailer.

Her ghost was a constant vague presence. Sometimes she talked to it, asking questions about the mad ship and the weird mirror, giving running commentaries on whichever programme she happened to be watching at the time. 'I'm trying to teach you how people are,' she said. 'The kind of stories they like.'

She knew that the wizards might be listening in, but she didn't care. Let them think she was going stir-crazy.

The eidolon didn't respond, of course. No voice in her head, no visions or dreams, no lightning-strike revelation. Just the sense that it was somewhere in the tiny room, silently absorbed in its own thoughts.

One day she woke to find that she was lying in her sleeping bag on what had become the floor. The pull was slight but definite, and the spiral track of her lodestar had changed.

'We're on the move,' she said to the eidolon. 'I wonder where.'

No reply, as usual.

Gravity vanished for a few minutes, came back briefly, vanished again. It was like riding a fairground attraction. After two hours it seemed that the return to free fall was permanent. When Lisa asked to use the bathroom her guard wouldn't tell her why the ship had been manoeuvring.

Six days later, watching a random episode of *Friends*, Lisa drifted down to what was once again the floor. The force of acceleration was stronger this time, and the lodestar was fixed in one place, somewhere beyond the glow of the ceiling.

'We must be heading towards it,' Lisa said to her ghost. 'Is this something to do with you?'

The tug of the lodestar slowly grew stronger until, with an abrupt quantum jump, it was a physical force prying at her mind. She felt everything else fall away, felt the same out-of-body swoon she'd experienced on First Foot when she'd stared too long at the star at the edge of the Badlands. Felt as if she was expanding beyond her body the room the ship into everywhere . . . And then that vastening vanished like a popped balloon, and she was floating in mid-air because gravity had vanished too.

She knew then what had happened. There could be no doubt about it. The wizards had found some way of plugging Dave Clegg into that mad ship, he'd opened the wormhole, and the ship had just gone through it. A little later, the gentle tug of the lodestar came back, roughly ninety degrees from its last position. Lisa supposed it must be the far end of the wormhole. She soon found out that she was wrong.

56. Mirror Dive

Abalunam's Pride was just three hundred thousand kilometres out from the hothouse planet when the bridle reported that she had at last acquired hard data on the location of the mirror. It was travelling west to east at about two hundred and fifty kilometres per hour, she said, tracing a wide, irregular circle around the planet's north pole.

'There's a lot of uncertainty in that track,' Tony said, after he had studied the images she threw to him.

'The resolution of the neutrino detectors will improve as we get closer. And when we get closer still, I should be able to pick it up on radar.'

'How much closer?'

'Oh, within three or four hundred kilometres.'

'So not until we are on top of it.'

'These new mirrors are smaller than the ordinary kind, and impressively transparent to radar. Also, there are many false signals,' the bridle said. 'Thunderstorms, rain, atmospheric turbulence. And the aerostats, of course. It's very interesting! Perhaps someone wanted to hide it down there. Perhaps the aerostats are not cities after all. Perhaps they are camouflage. Dazzle and distraction.'

'Try harder,' Tony said. 'We'll only get one chance at this.'

'I know! It's going to be very extreme!'

Some hours later, the pilot of the picket ship pinged Tony, sending a string of orbital vectors and telling him to follow her. They were three thousand kilometres out from the planet now, and closing fast. The picket shed velocity, preparing to enter an equatorial orbit and rendezvous with the Red Brigade's little fleet.

Tony followed, chasing the picket through the glory of a vast sunset into the planet's shadow. There was a huge storm below. Cannonades of sheet lightning limning contours and layers within the dark cloudscape.

'So pretty,' the bridle said.

'Concentrate on nailing down the location of the mirror.'

The bridle displayed its latest estimate: an oval volume a little less than a hundred kilometres across at its widest point. She said, 'I have every confidence that this will work. We are supposed to be here. *It was meant to be.*'

Tony shared her righteous conviction. It was probably spillover from the eidolon that rode him, but he didn't care. This, he thought, was this.

The picket achieved orbital velocity and cut its drive. *Abalunam's Pride* continued to decelerate, descending in a long arc towards the edge of the atmosphere. The picket's pilot pinged Tony and told him to correct his course; he said that he was flying straight and true. After a short silence, someone else cut in, ordering him to follow his escort or suffer the consequences.

'Come and catch me,' Tony said, and shut off his comms.

From the hold, Unlikely Worlds asked him if he had calculated the risk of disobeying his captors.

'They are not my captors,' Tony said. 'I have not surrendered to them, and I swear I never will. Tell me: what will happen to you if the ship is destroyed?'

'That depends on how it is destroyed.'

'I heard that 'Cha can teleport to the nearest mirror.'

'I have heard that too. Unfortunately it is not true.'

'But you can survive in vacuum.'

'For a while.'

'I could eject you. I am sure the Red Brigade would pick you up from orbit.'

'I have chosen to follow you.'

'Either you want children really badly, or you know that I am doing the right thing,' Tony said.

He was hoping that Unlikely Worlds was coming along for the ride because he knew that they would survive this. That this reckless gambit would pay off; that it was a chance to escape, a chance to regain some control.

Ada Morange had told him that he would be able to pilot the mad ship and use it to unlock the mirror, but he believed that the mad ship was not the only key. She had helped him to escape on Veles because he had been changed by the eidolon, but she had also been interested in how *Abalunam's Pride* and her bridle had been changed: that was why she had made sure that he would be reunited with his ship. He was gambling now that those changes meant that his ship could open the mirror. That he could get ahead of the Red Brigade, find the grail they were searching for, and use it to bargain with Mina Saba. A straight exchange for Ada Morange. A simple business deal that would, after he had brought her home and she had been forced to confess her every crime and betrayal, restore his standing in his family.

The bright disc of the sun rose, shooting light around the curve of the planet. A minute later, the bridle told Tony that there were pings on the proximity radar.

'Two drones. They'll intersect our course in less than ninety-two seconds. My conventional armaments have been stripped out, but I can discharge waste-water ice and other material from the stern vent. Given the difference in velocity between ourselves and those drones, it would do a lot of damage when it hits them.'

'Hold off.'

'Are you sure about that? I can take them out. I know I can.'

'And they'll send more drones. Hold off.'

Tony did not like the way the bridle was questioning his orders. It had never done that before.

He watched the two drones come in, decelerating hard, separating and veering to either side of the ship, matching its course in a neat flanking manoeuvre. *Abalunam's Pride* was skimming the outer edge of the planet's mesosphere now. Usually, Tony would spiral in for a couple of orbits, killing his velocity before dropping straight down through the atmosphere on distorted gravity gradients, but he didn't have time for that. He was going in fast and dirty.

The dim stars of the U-class hauler and the Red Brigade ships rose above the horizon. Tony could not resist taunting Mina

Saba and Ada Morange with a quick message. *I am going ahead. Follow me if you can.*

Friction heated gas to a violet flare that wrapped around his ship. The force of deceleration slammed him into his couch for two long minutes. Then the flare blew away and *Abalunam's Pride* was falling in a steep arc through a dark blue sky towards the white cloud deck. The drones were falling alongside him, falling into streaming cloud.

The bridle was screaming with delight.

Tony remembered a diver he'd once seen in Nuevo California. A woman wearing nothing but silver bodypaint, poised at the edge of the flat roof of a five-storey hotel while Tony and a small crowd watched below. He remembered how she'd raised her arms above her head, stood on her toes, and given herself to the air. Clasping her knees to her breasts and somersaulting one and a half times and smashing into the exact centre of the tiny pool of water.

'I have radar contact!' the bridle said.

Abalunam's Pride slewed violently, entering a sunlit canyon between two banks of cloud. The drones slewed too, keeping pace. The radar began to return a faint signal; half a minute later Tony eyeballed a tiny black speck a long way ahead. The ship slewed again and the speck was suddenly dead ahead and growing rapidly. A rectangular sheet four kilometres tall, hanging vertically in clear air, presumably balanced within the same kind of gravity warp used by Ghajar ships, rushing towards him. The drones cut away on collision avoidance trajectories. Tony glimpsed the ring of machinery embedded in the black sheet, wondered what it would be like to hit a wormhole that was closed, if anyone had ever before done such a thing, and then there was a black flash and the ship punched through into raw sunlight.

'Wow,' the bridle said. 'Wow. We did it.'

57. Dead Planet

A couple of hours after the ship passed through the wormhole, Lisa was taken by one of her taciturn guards to the wizards' lair. They strapped her into a version of the cradle that Ada Morange's people had used to test her compass ability, stuck sensor dots on her forehead, patched her with a drug that immediately gave her a feeling of woozy detachment, and masked her with a strip of black cloth that projected sequences of geometric shapes, different colours, into her eyes, and pulses of sound into her ears. It was an intense version of the audio-visual entrainment experiments they'd tried before. The patterns changing slowly at first but gradually speeding up, smashing towards her like freeway traffic, blurring into an endless flicker that, when at last it cut off, left her dizzy and disorientated. She realised that the lodestar was somewhere beyond her feet now, and then it slowly shifted and the sequence of shapes started up again. Rinse and repeat six times, a brain cramp sharpening behind her eyes despite the cushion of the drug, spreading across the inside of her skull.

When at last the strip of cloth was removed, she was floating in a red throb of malignant pain. Looking up at the wizards, telling them that she knew what they had been doing. 'Being used as a human compass, I've done that before. So what was I pointing at this time?'

'A wormhole,' one of them said. Her face was a mask of fractal tattoos that contained a kind of AI toolkit; it looked like she was peering at Lisa through a tangled hedge.

'Right,' Lisa said. 'The one we just went through.'

The wizard shook her head. 'One we'll be able to go through if you pointed true,' she said, but wouldn't explain what she meant.

None of them would. Lisa lost it. Told them that she deserved to know what the fuck was going on. Demanded to be unstrapped from the cradle that instant and taken to Adam Nevers. Demanded to be taken to the motherfucking avatars so she could have it out with them, all her anger and frustration and fear raving out until at last one of the wizards slapped a patch on her arm and she woke up dry-mouthed and weak as a kitten back in her room.

The next day, a pair of guards escorted her to a long tubular space where, in dim red light and an atmosphere of hushed concentration, a dozen people sat at arcs and clusters of windows, swiping through columns of numbers and symbols or studying views of a wormhole mouth. It looked like an art installation or the gallery of a TV studio, with little drones like cyborg humming-birds darting here and there on cryptic errands,

The three Jackaroo avatars floated in mid-air at the far end of the gallery, as if supervising the quietly intense activity. Lisa kicked towards them, gliding past people and windows, thumping into the padded wall behind the avatars and grabbing hold of a strap before she bounced away.

The avatars smoothly spun around, aiming their sunglasses at her like synchronised Disneyland automata.

'It must be amusing,' she said. 'Watching us jumped-up monkeys bang our peanut-sized brains against this puzzle.'

She was out of breath and her hip ached from the kick. The two guards were bulling their way down the gallery towards her.

'We are here to help,' the right hand avatar said.

'So why won't you tell me why I've ended up here, and what I'm supposed to find beyond that wormhole?' Lisa said. The guards were very close now.

'We are not your enemy, Lisa,' the middle avatar said.

It startled her, hearing the damn thing speak her name.

'We mean no harm to anyone,' the left-hand avatar said.

'Except you like to give people so-called gifts, and watch them explode in their faces. Is that what happened to the Ghajar? Is that what you hope will happen to us?'

But then the guards crowded in, grabbing her, hauling her away.

349

'Best not disturb our guests,' one said.

'If you cause any more trouble,' the other said, 'we'll take you back to your cabin.'

'Not unless your boss tells you to, you won't,' Lisa said, but didn't try to fight them. Resistance was useless and all that, and besides, for what it was worth, she'd got in her shot. But she still wanted answers to her questions. She had a bad feeling that Nevers and his crew were being led into a trap. And she was bound to them, the unwilling key to the wormhole's Pandora's box.

After a few minutes, Adam Nevers and Dave Clegg swam into the gallery. While technicians fussed around the pilot, fastening him into a couch, fitting him with sensor dots and a mask, Adam Nevers cautiously sculled along the gallery's padded wall to Lisa.

She supposed he knew about her brief confrontation with the avatars, but she refused to feel ashamed, saying, 'So have you found if there's a pot of gold at the end of the rainbow?'

Nevers smiled his white toothless smile. In the dim red light he looked more than ever like a mummified skull. 'Oh, we've been very busy. We moved our ships inside the mad ship, we tapped into its nervous system, and Mr Clegg took control. He's still bedding in, but he was able to open the wormhole and take us through. Here,' he said, and opened a window.

The bland crescent of a planet tipped in sable black, a sheen of sunlight gleaming on its upper curve.

Lisa couldn't hide her astonishment. 'What is that? The Ghajar home world?'

'We don't know yet,' Adam Nevers said. 'We don't even know where it is – I'm told that it takes time to locate pulsars and other landmarks. But we do know that something very bad happened to it. There are big and relatively fresh craters in its surface, made by the impacts of at least eight dinosaur-killer asteroids. One triggered a huge volcanic eruption that's still ongoing. Lava flows bigger than Australia. There's a permanent hyper-hurricane above it, storm fronts of superheated steam, huge thunderstorms. Everywhere else on the planet is freezing cold. Its oceans are frozen over, it is completely shrouded in acid rainclouds, and there are huge amounts of soot and sulphur dioxide in the atmosphere, hardly any oxygen. If this was the Ghajar home world, nothing bigger than a microbe lives there now.'

Lisa said, 'We've come quite a way from arguing about a little stone, haven't we?'

'It was always about a lot more than a little stone. It is about a principle. It is about managing exploration and exploitation of places and artefacts that we barely understand. It is about quarantine and triage. When we return home, you'll see how bad things have become thanks to unregulated expansion into the wormhole network. Tens of thousands of children have been infected by something that drives them insane, and there's no cure. And that's just the latest of a string of meme plagues. We're doing good work here, Lisa. We're on the side of the angels.'

'The side of the Jackaroo, at any rate,' Lisa said, looking down the dim busy gallery at the avatars. Impossible to tell if they were looking back at her. 'That's why your three friends have come along for the ride, isn't it? To help your crazy attempt to censor the universe.'

'They are merely interested observers. It's up to us to save ourselves.' Nevers pointed to the crescent of the dead planet. 'That's one possible future. Some are of the opinion that we are too far down the path towards it to be able to turn back. Others think that we can do better than the Ghajar and the rest of the Elder Cultures. That's what I think. That's what my boss thinks. And that is why we are here.'

The withered old son of a bitch looked happy. He was exactly where he wanted to be. He was fighting the good fight. Lisa thought, with a pang of grief that opened a hole in her heart, of how Willie would have loved this, too. Weird wormholes leading to planets no human being had ever seen before. Deep history. Untold plunder.

Nevers said, 'We're at the L5 point between that planet and its moon. It's bigger than the Moon, Earth's moon. About the size of Mars, with a thin atmosphere and ice caps. The wizards say that it would have strongly motivated the Ghajar to develop space-going technology. But it's a lifeless garden of craters now, wrecked by the same cosmic bombardment that ruined the planet.

So much for the moon. So much for the planet. As I'm sure you've guessed, they aren't our final destination. There are several hundred wormholes around us. Most of them are dead, but you pointed us towards one of the active ones. Mr Clegg opened it yesterday, and we sent a drone through. And found a star clad in iron, orbited by a planet made of diamond.'

He paused, clearly expecting Lisa to ask him what he meant. When she didn't take the bait, he said, 'Keep watching this window. You'll see soon enough.'

He left her there with the two guards and hauled himself back to Dave Clegg's couch, talking to the pilot while the technicians manipulated symbols in dozens of small windows. At last, Nevers and the technicians sculled back from the couch, and it slid into the wall. Chatter and activity up and down the gallery sharpened; muted chimes pulsed in the air. The guards conjured stalked chairs and sat Lisa in one; it clamped around her like a soft fist.

Gravity came back. The ship was under way again. The view in the window changed, showing now the silvery ring of a wormhole throat embedded in an irregular black sheet, steadily growing larger.

Lisa leaned forward. She was afraid, vastly and mortally afraid, but she was also amazed and excited, watching as the wormhole throat expanded with a sudden rush, filling the window. She felt it coming at her, felt it engulf her and pull at her soul. And then the ship was through, spat out the other side whole and unaltered, and the window was full of fat bright stars that hung before washes and threads of glowing gas in which yet more stars burned. Lisa saw a star cluster like a swarm of burning bees, saw flowing arcs and filaments. People were applauding all around her, and then someone cried out, a loud human shout of surprise and shock.

Lisa turned, saw that the three Jackaroo avatars were dissolving into the air. Their heads and hands thinning, fading away, their sunglasses floating free as their tracksuits collapsed. Gone.

58. Final Destination

'Look. Look! Isn't it wonderful?' the bridle said.

'It's too early to tell. Where are we?'

Tony was flipping through the images she had thrown at him. It was difficult to focus. He was still gripped by the adrenalin rush of the crazy dive, shaky and elated and buzzing with skittish energy. He had never before felt so alive. He had escaped the Red Brigade. He was flying a ship with crazy unknown powers. Everything seemed possible.

'In a wilderness of mirrors,' the bridle said. 'It appears to be orbiting at the L5 point of that rocky planet and its moon.'

Tony saw that the other side of the mirror pair they had just used was dwindling behind them, centred on a thinning cloud of carbon dioxide and water vapour that had bled through when the wormhole mouth had opened. Many more mirrors, a couple of hundred of them, were scattered across a spherical volume roughly ten thousand kilometres across. And far beyond this compact wilderness were the tiny crescents of a planet and a big moon. It reminded Tony at once of images of Earth and its moon, but when he zoomed in he saw that the planet was wrapped in cloud from pole to pole, a dirty grey shroud punctuated by the swirl of a gigantic hurricane close to the equator.

He asked the bridle if this was where the eidolon wanted to go, or was it just a way point to somewhere else?

'I think it's a way point.'

'You think or you know?'

'I have a feeling,' the bridle said. 'A good one.'

'If it is a way point, we need to find the next mirror right away,' Tony said. 'We need to keep moving.'

The mirror pair between the hothouse planet and this wilderness was still active. The ship had woken it a bare second before they transited, and the bridle had no idea how to shut it down. Pretty soon, the Red Brigade would regroup and send those drones through, controlled by q-phone links over who knew how many light years. And then they would come through themselves . . .

Tony tasked the bridle with scanning the mirrors, fretted as an hour ticked past. Unlikely Worlds, down in the hold, was as usual no help at all.

'There was a war here,' he said, after Tony showed him images of the planet and its battered moon.

'Was it fought between two factions of the Ghajar?' Tony said, thinking of Mina Saba's theory.

'It's possible.'

'And is that the Ghajar home world?'

'I very much doubt that anyone is living there now.'

'That isn't what I asked.'

'What happened here happened before my time,' Unlikely Worlds said. 'Thousands and thousands of years ago. Perhaps you should ask your eidolon. Or the copy lodged in the ship's mind. Are they interested in it?'

But although Tony was jittery with nervous energy, his eidolon was quiet, unmoved by the transition through the wormhole and the mirrors or the planet. The bridle reported that most of the mirrors were the ordinary kind, set in the flat faces of cone-shaped rocks, and most of the rest appeared to be dead.

'Keep looking,' Tony told her.

About ten minutes later, the mirror that led to the hothouse planet blinked open and the two drones sharked out, lighting up the neighbourhood with radar and microwave scans. 'Uh-oh,' the bridle said, and a moment later the drive kicked in. The ship was heading towards one of the mirrors. And its controls had locked up.

'Give me direct-law flight,' Tony said, angry and frightened. 'At once.'

'Trust me,' the bridle sang out.

The overrides were locked up too. Tony was a helpless passenger in his own ship.

Unlikely Worlds said, 'I think your question about whether this is the final destination or just a way point has been answered.'

'Where are we going?' Tony said.

'Somewhere wonderful,' Unlikely Worlds said, and Tony realised that the fucking thing had known all along where they were supposed to go.

'Home,' the bridle said, and Tony wondered whether the eidolon had spoken.

They flashed past a mirror, past two more rotating around each other, homing in on a black rectangle only faintly visible against the black of space.

'It's awake,' the bridle said. 'I think someone has been here before us.'

Tony's comms pinged: the drones, a couple of thousand kilometres astern, had spotted him. He saw the blink of their reaction motors as they began to manouevre, and then *Abalunam's Pride* slammed through the mirror.

Bright stars spread across the sky. Great washes of luminous gas.

Control of the ship came back. Tony began to kill its momentum, told the bridle to find out where they were. Dazed by the transition, he was wondering if they weren't somehow back in orbit around the blue ice giant.

'We have a more immediate problem,' the bridle said, and opened two windows

One showed a gigantic mad ship hanging about a thousand kilometres from the mirror; the other a pair of E-class raptors, both of them displaying police flags as they closed on *Abalunam's Pride*.

59. Synchronicity

In the immediate aftermath of the avatars' disappearance, Lisa was dispatched to the wizards' lair for another round of tests. Her ghost was quiet, its presence as faint as music leaking from a neighbouring room, and all sense of the lodestar was gone. The wizards wouldn't tell her if this meant they had arrived at their final destination; they were their usual non-communicative selves, giving her instructions in English – *Hold still, Look at this, Tell me what you see* – but talking amongst themselves in machine-gun Spanish. As far as they were concerned, Lisa wasn't a person but a puzzle they had as yet only partly unlocked.

They were still a long way from replicating the ghost in her head, and translating the information it encoded. At the beginning of the long series of tests she had offered to help to analyse the data, but the wizards' boss, a skinny man with a shock of black hair, told her that she wouldn't understand their methods. 'We have developed many new tools since your time,' he'd said, but Lisa wasn't so sure. They didn't appear to use any kind of analytical reasoning to confirm their conjectures, employing instead a crude form of experimental Darwinism, seeding a matrix with algorithms modelling variations of their initial assumptions and letting them run to a halting state, selecting those that most resembled the observed conditions, and running and re-running everything over and again until they had derived an algorithm that reproduced reality to an agreed level of statistical confidence. The wizards didn't care that this method gave no insights into the problems it attacked, or that they didn't understand how the solutions it yielded were related to the vast edifice of Euclidean mathematical theory. They weren't interested in theory. As far as they were concerned, if an algorithm gave the right answer, then plug it in: it was good to go.

Nevers came into the wizards' lair as the latest round of tests were being wound up, bluntly asked Lisa if she knew why the Jackaroo avatars had vanished, where they had gone. The ships docked in the funnel of the mad ship's hold had been searched from stem to stern, but no trace of the avatars had been found. It was possible that they were somewhere aboard the mad ship itself, Nevers said, but so far no one had found a way inside.

Lisa said she was glad that they were gone but didn't think that she could take the credit. 'As far as I can tell, my ghost didn't ever communicate with them. But perhaps your little gang of mad scientists knows better.'

Nevers ignored her jibe. 'Maybe it's a good sign. They left because we don't need any more help from them. Because we're exactly where we are supposed to be. We've beaten Ada Morange to the prize. Everything else is merely detail.'

'Isn't that were God lives? In the details?'

Nevers ignored that too. 'I thought we should have a little celebration,' he said, producing two pouches of clear liquid from the pocket of his green uniform trousers. He offered one to Lisa, holding it by its drinking tube like a popsicle. 'Vodka martini. I had one of the wizards mix it for us.'

Lisa swallowed a little spurt of saliva, her stupid body betraying her, saw a glint of cool amusement in Nevers's gaze and knew that he knew. The empty bottle in the trash the second time he'd searched her house. Her convictions for driving under the influence . . . Oh, he knew all right, and he was using it now to belittle her, to show her who was in charge. Maybe he'd begun his campaign against Ada Morange with the best of intentions, but it had eaten him away from the inside, turned him into the kind of pitiless monster who thought that it was funny to offer a drunk a drink.

She met his gaze and said, 'Why don't you just tell me what you found?'

He wiggled the pouches. 'Are you sure you won't join me?'

She supposed that his ghastly little smile was meant to be playful. 'You didn't come here to celebrate,' she said. 'You're looking for validation. You don't have the avatars any more, so you're hoping to get a reaction from my eidolon. You want to know if this so-called prize is worth the cost of the getting.'

'Oh, it's worth it,' Nevers said, and told Lisa that the wizards had determined that the mad ship and its cargo had emerged from a wormhole mouth that was just seven hundred light years from the centre of the galaxy, orbiting an old, cool neutron star and its single Earth-sized planet. Whipping around the neutron star once every two hours, at a distance of just half a million kilometres, the planet was mostly made of diamond, and strictly speaking wasn't a planet at all, but the remnant of a massive star that had once formed a close binary with an even larger companion. That companion star had followed the usual evolutionary path, expanding into a red giant as it used up its hydrogen, fusing heavier elements until at last iron formed in its core and it could no longer produce enough energy to counter the inward pull of gravity. The resulting supernova had created a rapidly spinning neutron star – a pulsar emitting intense beams of electromagnetic radiation. When the smaller star had expanded in turn soon afterwards, the pulsar had siphoned off most of its mass and angular momentum, spinning itself up into a millisecond pulsar, reducing the smaller star to a low-mass carbon-rich white dwarf and relentlessly eroding it further, until only its dense crystalline core was left. Now, eleven or twelve billion years later, the pulsar had long ago spun down. Its radio emissions had ceased and it had become a neutron star again: a quiescent hyperdense sphere of neutrons thirteen kilometres in diameter, thinly coated with a crust of iron nuclei crushed into a solid lattice, its surface temperature just a few thousand degrees Kelvin. An ancient star armoured in iron, orbited by a planet made of diamond . . .

And that wasn't all, Adam Nevers said. Another star, an M3 red dwarf, orbited the neutron star at a distance of a little under nineteen astronomical units. And the M3 dwarf possessed a tide-locked Mars-sized rocky planet. He opened windows, showed Lisa images of the M3 dwarf and its planet, images of the diamond planet's dim half-disc illuminated by a sharp blue point source. With a quick deep chill she remembered something Willie had said on his dying bed. *A planet bigger than its sun* . . .

Nevers was explaining that the M3 dwarf and its planet seemed to have been moved into orbit around the neutron star relatively recently, said that the diamond planet could be some kind of supercomputer or vast quantum memory store, encoding information in nitrogen vacancies in isotopically pure carbon-12. A survey drone had discovered the remnants of a Ghajar tower at the planet's south pole, near what appeared to be a deep drill site. Another drone, spiralling on a suicide trajectory into the neutron star's steep gravity well, had captured in its last moments evidence of structures on the star's surface: intricate patterns etched in lines five millimetres high across several hundred square kilometres of the otherwise mirror-smooth crust.

'I'm told that in the neutron star's extreme gravity those patterns are equivalent to mountains on Earth,' Nevers said. 'We have no idea how they were made or how to access them, but there they are. And there are odd patterns in the belt of dark matter around the black hole at galactic centre, too. Nodes at regular intervals, like beads on a string. The wizards say it's evidence of some kind of cosmic engineering, but as the nearest node is more than three hundred light years away I think we can safely ignore that for now.'

He was going to secure this side of the wormhole, he told Lisa. If the Red Brigade managed to find a way through before the Commons police caught up with them, they were going to get a warm welcome.

'Meanwhile, we'll finish our survey of the diamond planet, and then we'll head for the M3 dwarf and its planet. Perhaps we'll find something we can understand there.'

'Wise old aliens dressed in togas and inhabiting a styrofoam replica of a Greek temple, that kind of thing?' Lisa said.

Nevers smiled. 'Something that piques the interest of your eidolon, hopefully.'

Lisa hadn't felt anything when he had shown her images of his prize, and was too proud to ask if the wizards had detected some kind of activity.

'I don't think you should hope for any help from that quarter,' she said. 'Look where it got me.'

'It put you where you are supposed to be, Ms Dawes. And soon we'll find out why,' Nevers said, and offered her one of the pouches of vodka martini again. 'Are you sure you won't join me in a little celebration?'

'I think you need it more than me,' Lisa said. 'Maybe it'll help you get over the loss of your friends in black.'

She was confined to the bland egg of her cabin again. Gravity came and went several times. The ship was manoeuvring. As usual, her guards wouldn't tell her anything.

She was asleep when gravity came back again. She woke with a jolt, found herself pinned to the floor by her own weight. Sitting up was an effort; standing a heroic labour that made her heart pound and invoked fresh pain in her spine and joints. Her weight had more than doubled; she guessed that the mad ship was moving at the bias drive's maximum acceleration.

Her ghost was back, too. A vivid eager presence in the tiny space.

'You aren't going to tell me why you are so goddamned happy, are you?' she said.

Presently, two guards came for her and fastened her wrists together with plastic strip. No use pointing out that she would probably break an ankle if she tried to run, or that there was no place she could run to. They didn't take her to the wizards' lair or the control gallery. Instead, the elevator dropped three levels and she was marched around the curve of a narrow corridor to a bare brightly lit room where Adam Nevers sprawled in a kind of wheeled sling chair, his head propped in a cushioned brace. Two wizards sat behind him, watching windows tiled in the air.

'Their activity just went into synchronicity,' one of them said.

'So they're definitely in contact,' Nevers said.

'They are definitely mirroring each other,' the other wizard said.

'It is not yet clear if they are actually exchanging information,' the first wizard said. 'It could be a form of entanglement.'

'Or a behavioural response,' the second wizard said. 'A reaction to the close proximity of its twin.'

'What about you?' Nevers said, gazing at Lisa. 'Do you feel this close proximity?'

Her ghost leaning at her shoulder, fully present. She said, 'You found another eidolon? How? Where?'

'Oh, we found much more than an eidolon,' Nevers said, and lifted a hand.

The door pinched back and a !Cha tank stepped into the room on its ungainly tripod, saying in its engaging baritone, 'Ms Dawes. How nice to see you again.'

But Lisa barely noticed Unlikely Worlds, because now a slim handsome man with dark brown skin and a glossy cap of tightly woven braids was pushed forward by a guard. She felt as if she was part of a broken magnet, yearning towards its other half. She saw in the man's gaze that he felt it too.

'Who are you?' he said.

'I don't believe you've met before,' Nevers said. He was gleaming with delighted pride, like a matchmaker who had just made the perfect match. 'But you definitely know each other.'

60. Deeper Than Sex

As he followed Unlikely Worlds into the room, propelled by an unnecessary shove from his guard, Tony felt his ghost move through him, leaning towards the woman. She was staring at him with a shock that mirrored his own. It was like that moment in serial novellas where two people meet and know at once that they share the same soul. Tony had felt something like it half a dozen years ago, back when he and Òrélolu used to trawl the cafés and bars of Victory Landing together. One night, Tony had shared a look with a tall slender man in police greens, Ramesh Rao, a marine on shore leave from the frigate that had arrived ten days ago, and that was it. They'd had sex in the bar's bathroom, started up again in the spinner that took them to a hotel, spent the rest of the night and most of the next day together. There'd been a lot of sex, but it was deeper than sex. They completed each other, somehow. But then Ramesh's leave ended, his ship booted, and Tony never saw him again.

He had been young enough, back then, to believe that vital spark, that sense of being completed, would happen again soon enough. But it never had. Not even with Danilo. But now, seeing this careworn middle-aged woman with her crew-cut white hair and unflattering baggy grey sweatshirt, he felt that visceral bolt of lightning again. Bam! Exactly like love at first sight.

The first thing she said to him, after Adam Nevers had made his joke about how the two of them hadn't met but knew each other, was, 'Where did you find yours?'

Her name was Lisa Dawes. More than a century ago, she had been infected by an eidolon that had been lurking in a scrap of

362

wreckage from a crashed Ghajar ship. She had fallen in with Ada Morange, who had basically kidnapped her, dispatching her to her eidolon's lodestar aboard the timeship before she could be arrested by Nevers and his crew of Jackaroo avatars. But Nevers had intercepted the timeship at the end of its voyage, and here she was now, his prisoner.

Tony was hustled out of the room before he could find out how her eidolon had changed her, whether she could communicate with it, if she knew what it wanted, so forth, and Nevers kept them apart after that – perhaps he was scared of what might happen if their eidolons fused, merging into an unimaginable whole. As far as he was concerned, it was enough to know that they were similar. He believed that it would give him an unbeatable advantage in the coming battle with Ada Morange and the Red Brigade.

It was a topic that he returned to over and again in conversations with Tony while the mad ship carrying Adam Nevers's little fleet drove towards the neutron star's M3 dwarf companion and its red planet. It had set out soon after Tony told Adam Nevers, aka Colonel X, how he had escaped from the Red Brigade. A little over a day later, several Red Brigade ships, including Mina Saba's frigate and the U-class hauler carrying the stolen mad ship, emerged from the mirror, running the gauntlet of drones and other assets Nevers had left behind, turning towards the red planet. And four days after that, three police J-class interceptors came through.

'They're one ship down after a hard fight with the Reds at that hothouse planet,' Adam Nevers told Tony. 'But they made it, and now Ada Morange and her friends are caught in a trap. All we have to do is make a stand and hold her off until help arrives. After all these years, I've finally got the bitch bang to rights.'

Adam Nevers's English was laced with archaic colloquialisms. He had aged just six years while travelling a century into his future, but he'd been old when he'd set out; his gaze was bright and his mind was sharp, but he was bent, bone-thin and bald. Everyone was hurting in the heavy pull of the bias drive's maximum acceleration, but Nevers was suffering more than most. He reclined in a chair that scooted around on soft wheels, and he was permanently short of breath, his pigeon chest labouring when he spoke.

'The Reds don't care about me, except that I stand between them and what they want,' he said. 'Ada Morange, though, she wants to put an end to me. She wants me to pay for all the trouble I've caused her over the years. And she also wants you to pay, Tony. Because you disobeyed her. Because you came here to help me.'

Nevers wanted to convince him that, in spite of everything, he was a friend and ally, but Tony knew that the man would sacrifice him in an instant if it gave him the chance to destroy Ada Morange. The two of them were locked in a battle more than a century old. Tony and everyone else were no more than foot soldiers.

'After I tried to stop her getting hold of those first Ghajar ships, she wouldn't let it go,' Nevers had said, during an earlier conversation. 'She wanted me to suffer for the trouble I caused her. She used her wealth and her political connections to get me hounded out of the force—'

'The force?'

'The Met,' Nevers said, with waspish impatience. Like many old men, he did not like to be reminded that his world was gone. 'The Metropolitan police force. It didn't much matter to me. I was ready to make a move. I took my police pension and I joined the UN. The United Nations. Back then, they were running the emigration lottery, distributing tickets to the gift worlds. They were getting into control of the Elder Culture artefact trade, too. That was my area of expertise, and we had several run-ins over the years, Ada Morange and me. And I usually got the better of her. She could fuck with the Met, but she couldn't fuck with the UN. She pushed; I pushed back. She tried to dodge the regulations and restrictions; I made sure she was called to account.'

Nevers liked to expound on Ada Morange's criminal irresponsibility. He said that he wouldn't be surprised to discover that she had been behind some of the meme plagues, designing them, letting them loose to see what they could do. He mentioned the old idea that Elder Cultures had died out because, like Ada Morange and the Red Brigade, they had tampered with technology they did not completely understand. He talked about how humanity's development had been stunted by contact with Elder Culture

364

tech, said that was something Ada Morange either refused to understand or did not care about.

'That's why she's so dangerous, Mr Okoye. She is blinded by her ambition. She believes that the rules and precautions meant to protect us don't apply to her.'

'Yet it seems that you have a lot of respect for her,' Tony said, trying to goad the man into revealing more than he intended.

'She is a very tricky adversary,' Nevers said. 'I think you know that too. The way she used your family as a hiding place all those years, while she was spinning her webs with the help of those robots. Hands, as you call them. The way she used you to escape . . .'

This was in the room where Nevers had introduced Tony to Lisa Dawes. A guard stood against the door and a clutch of little drones hung in the air, some recording the conversation from every angle, some monitoring the activity of the eidolon inside Tony's head, others ready to zap him if he tried anything. As if he could. They had him and they had his ship, had boarded her and disabled her comms before bringing him aboard Nevers's scow, which was garaged in the mad ship's hold with half a dozen other ships.

'You used me too,' Tony told Nevers. 'Pretending you were Colonel X. Pretending you were on my side. I had to find out from Ada Morange who you really were.'

'And I gave you back your ship, and pointed you towards the people who did you so much wrong,' Adam Nevers said. 'We're on the same side, Tony. And you've done some good work. You've exceeded my expectations, frankly. You've done me proud.'

One thing was clear. When they reached the red planet, things were going to get messy. And Tony would have only a little time to engineer his escape.

When he was not being prodded and probed by wizards or subjected to one of Adam Nevers's monologues, Tony was secured in a standard cabin. That was where he was when at last, after eight days of the crippling G-force, with only a brief respite when the ship had turned around before beginning to decelerate, free fall returned abruptly. A little later, he was escorted up to the scow's control gallery, where Nevers was waiting with Unlikely Worlds, and images of a red desert world filled most of the windows. The mad ship and its cargo had reached its destination.

'We have had some interesting chats, Mr Unlikely Worlds and I,' Nevers told Tony. 'About your adventures. And, of course, about Ada Morange.'

'It has been very enlightening to meet Colonel Nevers again,' Unlikely Worlds said.

'Look at you,' Tony said, mistrusting both of them. 'Like a couple of old shipmates.'

'We have known each other a long time,' Unlikely Worlds said.

'He was on the other side, way back when,' Nevers said.

'I was not on anyone's side,' Unlikely Worlds said. 'I was interested in Ada Morange's story. As I still am.'

'I've been telling him that he has been following the wrong person all this time,' Nevers said.

'You are certainly part of the story that I have been following,' Unlikely Worlds said.

'As far as he is concerned, we are just spear carriers,' Tony said to Nevers.

'Ah, but the story isn't over yet,' Unlikely Worlds said. 'Who can know where it will lead, what roles you will play, and who amongst you will be left at the end?'

'That sounds like a threat,' Nevers said cheerfully, the quick grimace of his smile revealing the plastic ridges that had replaced his teeth.

'Merely a commonplace observation,' Unlikely Worlds said. 'I am a bystander, not a participant.'

'We'll see about that,' Nevers said.

He clearly believed that he had the upper hand. Tony stepped on the temptation to tell him how the !Cha had manipulated Ada Morange and Raqle Thornhilde – and himself, for that matter. Although Unlikely Worlds could not be counted an ally, he was a wild card, and Tony believed that when it came down to it he would need all the distractions he could get.

Nevers pointed to one of the windows. 'This is where it ends. An old world, full of old secrets. Ada Morange wants it. I'm going to stop her.'

366

Drones had already completed a basic survey. The planet orbited the red dwarf star once every fifty-eight days and was tidally locked, its sub-stellar hemisphere chilly and dry, a shrunken ice cap covering less than half its dark side. No seas, no lakes. Salt pans and sand dunes everywhere. Ranges of what once had been mountains weathered to low-relief plateaus. No plate tectonics. Only a feeble magnetosphere. An atmosphere too thin to be breathable, rich in carbon dioxide and low in oxygen. A long tail of nitrogen and of hydrogen and oxygen, the products of photodissociation of water, blowing away on the solar wind. No trace of life anywhere. No ruins.

'Although we've only just begun to look,' Nevers said. 'I think that my old friend Unlikely Worlds knows more than he's telling.'

'I am afraid that I am not an expert on sand,' Unlikely Worlds said.

'I don't mean sand.'

'You give me credit where I deserve none,' the !Cha said. 'You are the first visitors to this place in many thousands of years. I am nowhere near as old as that.'

'But you know that the Ghajar came here,' Nevers said.

'As do you.'

Nevers ignored that. 'You have been collecting stories for a long time. You may not have been here before, but I bet you know all about it.'

'We do not share stories amongst ourselves,' Unlikely Worlds said. 'They are too valuable.'

Tony said, 'Because it would be like sharing your women?'

'It is an interesting analogy,' Unlikely Worlds said. 'Although it would be more accurate to say that our women share us. Also, our women are not exactly women.'

'Even if I sit his tank on a hotplate, the stubborn son-of-a-bitch won't tell us what's down there,' Nevers told Tony. 'Not that it matters, because I'm planning to send you to take a look. My wizards tell me we can monitor the reactions of your eidolon, use you as a kind of dowsing rod. But before we do that, we have to deal with Ada and the Red Brigade. I sent her a message, told her to stand down and prepare to be arrested, but she hasn't replied.

It looks like the old witch and her pals want to fight it out. Until those police ships arrive we'll be outnumbered and outgunned, but we will fight to the last man standing if necessary. And that includes you, Mr Okoye. She'll arrive in just over a day. You should spend a little of that time thinking about how you might convince her that she's chosen the wrong side in this fight.'

'I knew her as Aunty Jael,' Tony said. 'And it turns out that was not who she was at all. And besides, it is not possible to argue with a laminated brain. Her mind was fixed long ago, and cannot be changed.'

Like yours, he had the sense not to say.

He was back in his room when gravity came back. A brief jolt, then another. The scow was on the move. Probably leaving the mad ship's hold and preparing for combat.

Free fall returned. A little later two guards came for Tony. Colonel Nevers needed to talk to him again, they said, as they escorted him towards the elevator.

'What kind of trouble is he in?'

'He'll tell you,' one of the guards said, and the elevator door slid open and a hand was inside, a man-sized thing with a cartoon face floating in its white mask and a plastic gun in one hand.

'Hi there,' it said in a familiar voice, shot the guards with fat darts that instantly knocked them out, and grabbed Tony and pulled him into the elevator.

Tony said, perfectly shocked, 'The police shut you down.'

'I managed to find a way to wake up,' the bridle said breezily. The hand it was riding was a skinless stickman with plastic musculature, bundles of fibre-optic cabling clipped to its spine, and a power pack in the cage of its chest. 'You had locked up the hands, so I made this one, and made this neat little dart gun too, and came aboard when the police were distracted by a bunch of attack drones. The Red Brigade boosted them ahead of their incoming ships, and they swung around the far side of the planet and used its atmosphere and gravity well to slow down and aim themselves at the mad ship. Sneaky! And convenient! Why are you looking at me like that? Aren't you pleased that I was able to come to your rescue?'

'I'm astonished,' Tony said. He was also seriously spooked by this new display of the bridle's autonomy.

'I think we should get back to the ship,' the bridle said, 'before someone realises that you have escaped.'

The elevator door opened; they swam out into a passageway.

Tony said, 'Is *Abalunam's Pride* still in the mad ship's hold?'

'We can reach it with a rocket stick,' the bridle said with airy assurance. 'Down here. There's an airlock.'

Tony and the hand shot down the passageway like salmon down a chute, out into a transparent tube that linked the fat cylinder of the lifesystem with one of the airlocks, which was wedged between two fretted struts of the scow's actual interior. The architecture of the ship, a Gothic proliferation of flanges and buttresses and spikes, stretched above and below; the steel box of the airlock gleamed in actinic blue light.

The hand preceded Tony through the airlock hatch. Someone shouted in surprise: a sharp impact shattered the hand's mask. 'Something happened,' the bridle said plaintively, as the hand tumbled into the brightly lit space, and a second impact folded up the stickman machine and knocked it sideways.

'Don't even think of trying to run away,' a man said.

He was a runty little guy with black hair and a pale hard-set face, wearing a pressure suit without helmet and gloves, aiming some kind of gun at Tony. Behind him, also dressed in a pressure suit, arms pinned to her sides by cables, her head shaven and patched with black dots, her face pale and haggard, was the time traveller Lisa Dawes.

61. Shanghaied Again

Dave Clegg intercepted the robot as it rebounded from the far wall, jerked a fat yellow gun from its lax grip, and told Tony Okoye that he hadn't meant to shoot it, the fucking thing had startled him. The freebooter shrugged and said that it didn't matter, his ship could easily make a replacement. He seemed calm and wryly amused. Floating at the entrance to the airlock's antechamber, one hand against the hatch's rim, he smiled at Lisa and said, 'We all want to get to the same place, I think.'

Lisa was exhausted beyond measure by the aftermath of the wizards' tests and experiments, broken down and busted, her head buzzing with psychic static, but an echo of the powerful thrill of recognition she'd felt the first time they'd met pulsed through her. Although they barely knew each other, they were conspirators bound by alien ghosts.

She said, 'Do you know what we're supposed to find?'

'Not yet,' Tony Okoye said.

'It isn't coincidence, is it? That we're both here.'

'I think it's a good omen.'

'It means I'm going to save both your arses,' Dave Clegg said. He was pale and jittery, had actually screamed when the robot, the hand, had swum into the antechamber, shooting it with the bolt gun he had found in a tool locker, nearly shooting Tony Okoye too.

'You will need my help, I think,' Tony said. 'To begin with, I have a ship.'

'So do I,' Dave said. 'I'm going to help the Professor find whatever it is Nevers doesn't want her to find. And you two are going to help me.'

'What kind of assets does your ship have?'

370

'What do you mean? Weapons?'

'I mean something more substantial than a bolt or dart gun. An X-ray laser, for instance, or a pinch-fusion bomb. Also, my ship has acquired certain talents that should prove to be very useful if Adam Nevers comes after us.'

'And I suppose that if I come aboard your fucking ship it would use those talents against me. No fucking way,' Dave said.

'I think you should seriously think about Mr Okoye's offer,' Lisa said. 'If we head out to the red planet without protection, any encounter with Nevers or Ada Morange will be very one-sided.'

She badly wanted to get off the ship, get away from Nevers and his wizards, but she didn't trust Dave Clegg to keep her safe. One minute the man was telling her that he was rescuing her; the next he was trussing her up. 'For your own safety, given how you are.' As if. Even in her befuddled state, she knew that she was his hostage. Knew she'd been shanghaied again.

'I don't plan to get into any kind of encounter,' Dave said. Telling Tony Okoye, 'Now, how about getting into a pressure suit before the fucking police realise what's going on?'

The trader assembled a pressure suit around himself, moving quickly and gracefully in free fall, and allowed Dave Clegg to bind him with the same kind of cables that bound Lisa, smart things that coiled around his legs and lashed his arms to his sides. Tony smiled at Lisa behind his helmet faceplate while Dave checked his bonds, mouthed something that might have been *don't worry*. And the thing was, she felt a weird calm. It was as if her ghost hung behind her with a reassuring hand on her shoulder.

Dave Clegg manoeuvred them one after the other through the airlock hatch. Four rocket sticks were racked inside, blunt torpedoes with saddles and steering bridles at their midpoints and two rings of thrusters fore and aft. He unshipped one, clipped Lisa and Tony to its cargo net. 'Lie back and enjoy the ride,' he said, and swung into the saddle. There was a deep vibration of pumps, the lights dimmed and a door slid back, and then they were moving outside, into fathomless vacuum.

The mad ship hung close by, silhouetted against the curve of the red planet, and a handful of smaller ships were scattered beyond it. Lisa, lying on her back, saw a brilliant point of white light flare close to one ship, saw sparks shoot away from another, and realised that she was in the middle of an actual fucking space battle. Then the rocket stick was moving, aimed straight at the mad ship.

Lisa imagined the tie clips that fastened her arms and legs to the cargo net popping open, saw herself falling away into the void, tumbling in an endless orbit until the air in her pressure suit gave out. She imagined a swarm of drones smoking out of one of Nevers's ships, flying at the rocket stick and blowing it into hot plasma, like those old movies about adventures in space before adventures in space became an actual thing. And even if they managed to reach the timeship, she would have to work out how to survive Dave Clegg and his crazy plans.

After her brief, astonishing first meeting with Tony Okoye, after Adam Nevers had told her that the man was a freebooter, some kind of interstellar trader whose family had once owned Ada Morange's laminated brain, that he was infected with an eidolon similar to hers, Lisa had been turned over to the tender mercies of the wizards. Nevers had his prize, he had Dave Clegg piloting the mad ship and he had that young freebooter with his eidolon . . . He didn't need her any more.

More tests, more brutal than any before, as the wizards tried to isolate and define the activity of the eidolon. Audio-visual tests that gave her skull-splitting migraines. Drugs that left her disorientated and delusional. Sometimes she was patched with something that knocked her out, and woke with the feeling that something terrible had been done to her, some filthy violation of her core self. The wizards zapped her with old-fashioned electroshock treatment. They induced epileptic fits. They shaved off her hair and drilled tiny holes in her skull and inserted optical fibres that grew fine threads through the tissues of her brain and stimulated specific tangles of neurons with blue light. They calibrated her suffering, recorded everything, refused to discuss their work with her.

She had a recurring dream that she was stretched naked on a steel autopsy table, watching as she was unseamed and her organs were removed one by one, and her brain was unseated from her skull and laid on a steel tray. And it was crawling with ants, her brain, fat black things with tiny malevolent human faces, and she'd wake up in her cabin on the gel mattress she'd been given, with the relentless force of gravity pressing down on her and a scream strangled in her throat.

Dazed and doped, she got into the habit of leaving television streaming in the cabin's window, running random selections of late twentieth-century sitcoms and soaps, serials and cheesy old films. Every so often the playback would freeze, or flick to another programme. She quickly realised that the same kinds of images were recurring over and again. Deserts. Sunsets. The lighted grids of cities at night. A clip from some black and white movie about ghosts or maybe angels watching over people in a library. Brief clips of cartoon animals talking to cartoon people.

'I get it,' Lisa told her ghost. 'We're different species, and you're trying to figure out a way of communicating.'

As usual, it didn't reply.

She wondered if she was imposing meaning on a random glitch, but the images, especially those of desert landscapes, were weirdly compelling. Glimpses of a place richer and more real than her bare little cell. Sometimes she would feel herself falling inside them, waking with a start a few minutes or an hour later to the thinness of the real world. The wizards still wouldn't tell her anything. 'It's too early to draw conclusions,' they said, but she knew that her ghost was changing and growing, getting stronger while she was getting weaker. Right now it was only playing with the window, but suppose it started to play with her mind, started to take control of her thoughts? How would she be able to tell?

Even if she somehow, impossibly, escaped Adam Nevers, she could not escape the passenger in her skull. And where could she run to? Everything and everyone she knew was gone. She had lost the thread of her life. All she had was the small hope that Nevers would make good his promise, that she would meet the young freebooter again. She was certain that he understood her plight. That he was an ally, an accomplice, a secret sharer. 'It's best to keep you apart for now,' Adam Nevers had said. Lisa believed that meant the two of them, together, might be able to do something that Nevers was afraid he could not control. Something astonishing. It wasn't much more than a silly fantasy, but it was all she had.

One day her bone-breaking weight suddenly vanished. A few hours later, gravity briefly come back, much weaker, coming and going in quick erratic cycles. The scow was manoeuvring. Lisa imagined it slipping out of the hold of the mad ship, heading towards the surface of the red planet . . . Free fall returned, and she was wondering how she could try to find out what was happening when the door of her cabin wrinkled back and Dave Clegg flew in, colliding with her, clamping one hand over her mouth as they rebounded from the wall, grabbing hold of the door frame with the other, telling her that he was going to save her life. According to him, Nevers's little fleet had quit the mad ship after it had come under attack by Red Brigade drones. Because his piloting skills were no longer needed, he had been ordered back to his cabin, but he'd overpowered his guard and come looking for her. The Professor would be here soon, he said. It was time to make things right with her.

'You're going over to Ada Morange?' Lisa said stupidly, when he took his hand away from her mouth.

'Going over? I never left. I was just playing along because I didn't have any choice. Until now,' Dave Clegg said.

Probably best not to ask him if he'd had any choice when he'd killed the timeship crew. Lisa said, 'And I'm what? Your prisoner? A hostage?'

Dave Clegg held up a short plastic shiv. It looked like it had been whittled from a table knife. There was blood on it. Lisa knew then what had happened to his guard.

He said, 'We're both of us Nevers's prisoners. What I'm doing, I'm rescuing you.'

Now, the rocket stick plunged through a gap in the basket-weave funnel of the mad ship's hold and spun around in a dizzy manoeuvre that killed its momentum. Orange sunlight lanced through the mesh on the far side; light and shadows tiger-striped the bulky bone-shape of the timeship, dead ahead.

Dave Clegg jockeyed the rocket stick into the mouth of a shaft cut into the timeship's cladding, unhitched Lisa and Tony Okoye, and hauled them into the airlock. Inside, he took off their helmets but left them bound in their spacesuits and towed them out along the ship's central companionway. It had a grubby, used look. Failed lights hadn't been replaced, a long tear in the white padding had been patched with duct tape, and the air smelled bad, a deep musty rot like a zoo of long-dead animals. Lisa wondered if the bodies of Dave Clegg's murdered shipmates were still aboard.

Tony Okoye was telling the man that it wasn't too late to rejig his plan. 'If you let me get to my ship, I can be your wing man.'

'I don't think so.'

'You don't trust me. I understand. But Ada Morange is an old friend. In fact, she was my tutor—'

'Save your breath. Nevers told me all about your relationship with her, why you both want to see her dead.'

'She died a long time ago,' Tony said. 'She isn't who you think she is.'

'If she isn't, why does Nevers want to kill her?' Dave said.

'Because he's crazy,' Lisa said.

'That's one thing we can agree on,' Dave said.

He buckled Tony and Lisa onto couches in the cramped control gallery and began to wake up the ship's systems. Tony watched with deep interest; Lisa supposed that everything must seem like an antique to him. The touchscreens, the banks of switches and pinlights. A fan with green plastic blades pushing stale air around.

The screens showed views of the sun-striped hold. After a couple of minutes there was a jolt, and the views began to change. They were under way. A voice spoke out of the air, said something about disabling the ship. Dave pulled on a headset, said into the bead mike, 'You're welcome to try, mate. But there's a good twenty metres of fullerene foam shielding my baby, and I have Lisa Dawes and Tony Okoye on board. You want to risk killing them?'

Then gravity pressed down. The walls of the funnel flashed by and the mad ship was dwindling in the stern view and the curve of the red planet showed ahead.

Tony said, 'You're going to drive straight down?'

'I'm getting into a lower orbit first,' Dave said. 'We'll go around and you'll tell me where to land.'

'And meanwhile Nevers will target you and blow you out of the sky.'

'No he won't. Not with you two on board.'

'How will we know where to land?' Lisa said. Her thoughts were still lagging behind the actual world.

'Wherever your eidolons tell you to go, that's it,' Dave said.

'What about your eidolon?' Tony said.

'I have just enough of it to be able to fly the mad ship,' Dave said. 'It didn't turn me into a human compass.'

Lisa said, 'Did it show you pictures on the TV?'

Both men looked at her like she was crazy.

She said, 'Mine showed me images of deserts. I think it was trying to communicate.'

'The whole fucking planet is a desert,' Dave said. 'I need a place to set down and I need it now. So you can stop dicking around and give up what you know.'

Lisa said, 'The others in your crew? Were they infected by my eidolon?'

'Like this really is the right time to get into that,' Dave said, with bitter exasperation. 'I had to do what I had to do. Which saved your life, by the way. The others, they were planning to kill you.'

'I think you saved me because we both carry copies of the same eidolon,' Lisa said. 'But it didn't infect your crew, did it? Because they wouldn't have tried to kill me if it had.'

'The eidolon in my head also infected my ship's mind,' Tony said. 'So it's likely, isn't it, that Lisa's eidolon first copied itself into the mind of this ship. A Ghajar eidolon in a Ghajar ship, the two of them becoming something more than the sum of their parts. And then it got inside you, because you are the pilot. Because you interact with your ship's mind.'

Dave Clegg's stare was as narrow as a hawk's. 'So what are you saying?'

'You should trust your ship,' Lisa said.

'Let it choose where to land,' Tony said. 'Some random spot that may turn out to be not so random after all.'

62. Sandstorm

Tony had once flown a spinner under a thunderstorm on a dare, had realised as soon as the first updraught had flung his little craft into a dense squall of hail that pitting his skill against the storm's raw power was going to be no fun at all. The ride down to the red planet was a lot worse than that.

Dave Clegg wasn't a bad pilot. He knew how to get the most out of his antique interface, used the same manouevre that had helped Tony escape the Red Brigade at the hothouse planet: decelerating hard and letting atmospheric friction kill the rest of his velocity before warping gravity. But as soon as the timeship hit the outer edges of the atmosphere it began to shed parts of its ancient and badly battered fullerene casing, shuddering and shaking as random chunks spalled away, at one point pitching over by at least ten degrees before righting itself. Ghajar ships were tough, but they weren't indestructible, and this one was taking a lot of torque. Its agony squealed and boomed inside the lifesystem like a full orchestra falling down an endless flight of stairs. Lisa Dawes, strapped into the couch next to Tony's, had closed her eyes and her lips were moving in what might be prayer. Dave Clegg hunched at his controls, muttering oaths and imprecations.

At last the awful cacophony and bone-jarring shudders eased off. Dave reported that he had handed over to autopilot so that the ship could choose a landing spot. There was a final wrenching lurch as something big shook free; a couple of minutes later the ship came to rest. Dave conjured a virtual keyboard, entered a string of numbers. A small section of the panelling under the controls dropped down and angled out; he reached inside, unplugged a black tube and removed it, telling Tony, 'You asked about assets. How about a fucking ray gun?'

'You were lucky that the police did not find it.'

'I gave up one just like it, and a bunch of conventional stuff from the armoury. This is my backup. Fully charged, ready to zap any unfriendly BEMs out there. That's bug-eyed monsters, in case you call them something else.'

Lisa said, her voice thin and exhausted, 'We didn't come here to start a fight.'

'Neither did I,' Dave said. 'This is insurance.'

He used a keywand to release the cords that bound Tony and Lisa, and they all climbed down the companionway, now a vertical shaft, Dave chivvying Lisa because she was slow and uncertain, stopping to rest several times before they reached the airlock and the tunnel cut through the fullerene casing. The ship stood on its stern in a warp of local gravity; Dave Clegg deployed a cable winch to lower Tony and Lisa to the ground, a drop of more than fifty metres. Lisa fell to her knees when she reached the ground, breathing so hard her helmet's faceplate fogged on the inside. Tony helped her to her feet, asked her if she was all right; high above, Dave Clegg said, 'She's been fucked up by the wizards. Which is why she should be grateful I rescued her.'

When he followed them down, he let go of the cable a couple of metres too soon and fell flat on his behind. Tony saw a chance to step in and grab the man's ray gun, but hesitated a couple of seconds too long. Dave bounced to his feet in the weak gravity, slapping red dust from the legs of his pressure suit, glaring at Tony and Lisa and telling them they wouldn't find anything by standing around like a couple of dummies.

Tony told himself that if this was going to play out the way he thought it would, the man would be a useful idiot. Let him believe that he was in charge for now.

They had come down somewhere in the planet's high latitudes, in the level light and long shadows of a late afternoon that would last until the dwarf star guttered out in a trillion years or so. A flat landscape of red sand, pavements of dusty red rock, small fleets of scalloped dunes stretching away in every direction. The fat orange sun hung above the horizon in a pinkish cloudless sky.

'There's nothing here,' Dave said, after they had walked out of the shadow of the timeship. He turned a full three-sixty, sunlight flaring on his helmet visor, the ray gun's tube clutched in a gloved paw. 'There's nothing fucking here.'

His voice cracked with frustration. The man had the patience of a toddler.

Tony said, 'We could climb back inside and ask the ship to try again. Another throw of the dice.'

'I've seen maps of this place. Sand everywhere on the sunward side. Ice on the dark side. No,' Dave said. 'We'll keep walking. And you better tell me straight away if you see anything that tickles your eidolons. Because if we don't find something soon I'll have to conclude that you're fucking with me.'

'We are all in this together,' Tony said, trying to calm the man. 'If we do not find anything here, we can look elsewhere. Along the edge of the terminator, perhaps. On tidally locked worlds like this, Elder Culture ruins are usually found along meltwater rivers that flow from the dark-side ice cap.'

'Any rivers dried up a couple of billion years ago,' Dave said, kicking a wedge of sand with the toe of his boot. 'The ice cap is shrunken way the hell back.'

'Then we ask your ship again. Or ask it to call mine down.'

'Don't start that again.'

'I mean only to help,' Tony said, believing that he could use the man's anxiety to get inside his stubborn belligerence. 'My ship's mind has definitely been changed by the eidolon. It may be able to find things yours cannot.'

'I see something,' Lisa said.

She had walked a little way off and was looking up-sun with one hand shading her helmet's faceplate, probably because she didn't know how to polarise it. Tony pulled up a window with an augmented view, but couldn't spot anything other than sand and rock. No alien ruins, no glittering city, no deputation of big-brained ambassadors from a lost race. In the far distance, the horizon looked a little hazier than it had before, perhaps the sky was a little darker . . .

'It's just sand blowing in the wind,' he said.

'It wasn't there a moment ago. It just sort of jumped up. I think it's heading our way.'

Tony used his pressure suit's radar. The signal was faint and fuzzy, but something was definitely moving towards them, moving fast, five or six kilometres a second and rising into the sky as it came on, already turning the sun blood-red.

'Maybe we should get back to the ship,' Dave Clegg said.

'I don't think we have time,' Tony said.

A wind got up around them, blowing dust across the blocky pavement, blowing tendrils of sand that whirled high into the air, thickening into columns and sheets that leaned above them. 'Jesus fuck,' Dave Clegg said, and then the sandstorm hit.

63. City Of Sand

Lisa was battered to her knees in a jet-engine roar of wind-blown sand, but somehow knew, kneeling there in the stiff pressure suit and the calm bubble of her helmet, that she wasn't in any danger. She remembered a picture in her Grammy's house, a blonde angel with white wings and a white silk robe hovering beside a little boy and girl as they crossed a rickety bridge over a raging torrent, and smiled at the bathos of it. The eidolon was an unknowable alien intelligence, neither angel nor devil, yet she felt stupidly comforted.

It had woken just before the storm had hit. Lisa had found herself staring at the horizon with her ghost at her back, had felt as if clear light had zapped through every one of the optical fibres the wizards had grown in her brain. *Wake up! Pay attention!* And she was definitely more alert now, was back in her self, back in the world, although she was still bone-tired and soul-bruised, felt as if the wizards had left their grubby fingerprints on every cell of her body. And worse than any damage inflicted by their stupid experiments was the deep aching sense of being irrevocably lost in time and space. Everything she had known, everything that defined her, had been torn away. She had been shanghaied and thrust into the future and there was no way back. No way back to her home. No way back to her life.

Sand smashed into her, hissed over her helmet, accumulated in creases in the material of her suit. Stuttering chains of sparks whirled past and vanished in the dim red rush like the shapes she'd seen flickering in the current of Ghajar narrative code when she'd first opened it, back in Bria's code farm more than a century ago, and she felt herself tugged after those fugitive constellations like a balloon on a breeze, thought that it would be so easy to let go . . .

She was startled back into herself when something – Tony Okoye's gloved hand – clutched her hand. He leaned in until their helmets were touching; she heard his voice, muffled and distant, telling her to switch off her comms.

'Just look at the speaker icon until it blinks and turns red.'

It took her a moment to work out how to do it. The icon was the usual cup emitting three nested curves of increasing size. Some things hadn't changed. She wondered if people still saved stuff by clicking on an icon that looked like a floppy disc.

'Now we can speak privately,' Tony said.

'This isn't an ordinary storm,' Lisa said.

They were kneeling head to head in the howling blast, holding hands, glove in glove. Tony's face, a handspan from Lisa's, behind the faceplate of his helmet, wore a cool serious expression. There were little scars, precisely spaced, in the skin over the sharp ridges of his cheekbones.

'I think that you and I have woken something,' he said.

'What about Dave?' Lisa said. The man was haunted by a weak copy of her eidolon; she was wondering if he saw what she saw, felt what she felt.

'What about him?' Tony said. 'The eidolon in his head is not like the eidolons in ours. He does not have the connection we share. Perhaps it gave him the idea to escape, to come here, but it is clear that he is out of his depth. He needs us but we do not need him.'

'All hat and no cattle,' Lisa said, and winced as a chain of sparks snapped close to her helmet and blew away.

'We know our eidolons wanted us to come here, but we don't know why,' Tony said. 'But it feels right to me. It feels that we are in the right place. And it is a good feeling.'

'I think the Jackaroo wanted us to come here, too,' Lisa said, and told him about the avatars on Nevers's ship, told him how they had vanished after the expedition had come through the wormhole that orbited the neutron star.

'Unlikely Worlds knows something too,' Tony said.

They told each other how they had met the !Cha.

'He did his best to nudge me towards this place,' Tony said. 'You had the Jackaroo, I had a !Cha.'

Lisa said, 'We were aimed here, no doubt. But we shouldn't blame the Jackaroo or Unlikely Worlds, or even our eidolons. In the end, it was our choice to start down this road. We could have said no to it at the beginning, but we didn't. And now we have to face up to the consequences. It's like Elder Culture tech. People pull it out of ancient artefacts and use it without really understanding it, and when there's some kind of blowback they blame the artefacts, or the Elder Culture that made them. They blame the Jackaroo. They blame everything and everybody but themselves. That kind of thinking is why Nevers wants to control exploration and research. He claims that Elder Culture tech is inherently dangerous, says he wants to protect people from it, but really it's all about taking away the freedom to explore and experiment and create. The freedom to make mistakes. Elder Culture tech can be dangerous, I know that better than most, but every new thing can be dangerous and disruptive if it is misused. There's nothing wrong with exploration and research as long as you take responsibility for what you find, and how you use it. Too many people didn't, in my time. Just as the Red Brigade don't, here and now. As far as I can tell, they aren't interested in Elder Culture tech for what it is. Only in what it can do. How they can use it to gain power over others.'

'As was I,' Tony said. 'As was my family. We fell on hard times. We searched for something that would restore our fortune, and our honour. Ada Morange, as Aunty Jael, encouraged us, and we went along with it. *I* went along with it. I ended up here because I was chasing a cure for sleepy sickness. I believed that it was lying in some ruin, cached in some eidolon or algorithm, waiting to be found. My family and I, we did not think to find out what sleepy sickness was. What caused it. How it affected people. We just thought that it was bad code, and there had to be good code that would cancel it out.'

'When I won the lottery and went up and out,' Lisa said, 'I thought the same thing. I believed that I would discover something

383

that would make me rich and famous. A lot of people thought like that. They thought that a new world would give them a new life. My husband was one of the few people who actually did make a new life for himself, but most didn't.'

Willie was more than a hundred years dead, but the memory of his last hours was still horribly raw.

She said, 'I helped to create something useful once upon a time, and I gave it away. Because it was got up from found stuff that I didn't own. That no one should own. Because I was young, and still had ideals, and the world seemed full of endless wonders, and there was more than enough time to explore them . . . But I couldn't repeat the trick and I lost sight of why I was doing what I was doing. I became like everyone else, grubbing for trinkets in the dirt. Eyes on the ground, never looking up at the stars. And when we stumbled over something wild and strange, Willie and me, the first thing we did was run away from it. I tried to blot it out with drink and drugs. The usual anaesthetics. The usual attempt to numb yourself against a world that seems too much to handle. The usual refusal. But Willie went on being Willie, more or less. He never gave up the idea that he'd find a way back to that wildness, that strangeness. And he did, but the finding of it killed him. I wanted to know why he died. Because I thought that the world should answer for his death. Because I was scared that it would happen to me. And that's how I ended up here. But the world doesn't owe us any answers. It just is.'

Tony said, 'When Adam Nevers posed as Colonel X, when he offered to help me escape if I would help him, I told myself that I would find something that would redeem myself and restore my family's reputation. But I was really running away. From my duty to my family, from taking responsibility for what happened after I brought back the stromatolites. I blamed my family for driving me away, Adam Nevers for tempting me, my eidolon for leading me on. But it was always my choice. And here I am, at the heart of this great mystery, and I have to ask: do I deserve to be here? What have I done to deserve it?'

'We like to think that we win something from the world because of some innate quality,' Lisa said. 'Because we have been chosen.

Because we are anointed. But it's magical thinking. It's observer bias. We see only what we find. We don't see what we miss. We reach a place, a prize, and make up stories to explain why we deserved to get there first, but it's all bullshit. Because if someone else found that prize, what difference would it make?'

'But here we are anyway, making stories,' Tony said.

They were smiling at each other through the faceplates of their helmets, closer in that moment than any lovers. Lisa knew that it might be nothing to do with them and everything to do with their ghosts, but she didn't care.

She said, 'Maybe we're trying to get past the bullshit so we can work out why we're really here, what we hope to find.'

'Whatever it is, Ada Morange and the Red Brigade will try to use it for their own selfish purposes.'

'Yeah, and Nevers will try to stop anyone and everyone from using it.'

'So we must find it before they do.'

'And take control of it.'

'And set it free.'

'Yes,' Lisa said.

'Yes,' Tony said, and lifted his helmet away for a moment before setting it back against hers. 'I think it is getting a little lighter. And wind speed is dropping. I think I see something . . .'

Lisa saw something too. Vague shapes looming through streamers and curtains of blowing sand. The force of the wind against her back was failing, the low disc of the sun was burning through the murk, and then the last of the storm blew past and she saw what it had made.

A city of sand stood all around.

She and Tony pushed to their feet. They were still holding hands, as unselfconscious as children lost in a fairytale wood. Dave Clegg stood a little way off, hands on hips, looking up at a basket-weave tower built of sand. Billions of grains cemented together by some mad architect.

The comms icon inside Lisa's helmet was blinking. She stared at it and Dave's voice was suddenly inside her helmet, saying, 'Are you seeing this?'

'That's Ghajar,' Tony said. 'A Ghajar mooring tower. At least, that's what it looks like . . .'

Dave laughed. 'My ship found the right place after all.'

'Maybe the right place found us,' Lisa said. She was thinking of Willie's last words. *A city hidden in a sea of red sand.* Thinking that his eidolon – and hers – had known all along where they were supposed to go. Thinking of the storm front marching towards them across the desert. What had sent it? What kind of intelligence could raise up a city in a few minutes?

Beyond the Ghajar tower, the timeship hung like the gnomon of a gigantic sundial at the centre of a level stretch of sand woven with intricate patterns in shades of red. Avenues radiated away, lined with large and small structures in no discernible pattern. Lisa recognised replicas of Boxbuilder ruins and tombs like the tombs in the City of the Dead, saw in the distance a cluster of huge spires a little like those at Mammoth Lakes, saw untidy piles of spheres, a big cube with a fractal pattern of smaller cubes along its edges . . . Everything the same colour, the colour of blood, everything shining with an inner light, everything tugging at her. Her ghost was leaning in, so close that it seemed to be inside her pressure suit, close as her skin, and she felt an absurd bubbling joy, wanted to fly away down those strange avenues, between those strange buildings . . .

Someone was speaking, asking her was she all right? She had fallen to her knees. Her heart was going like anything. When Tony helped her to her feet she felt the entire world spin around her and everything went dark for a moment. Her body felt brittle and insubstantial, a ghost trapped in the shell of her pressure suit. She had the mad idea that if she stripped it off she could dissolve in the city's lovely light.

Tony asked again if she was all right.

'It's full of light,' she heard herself say.

'The tower?'

'Everything,' Lisa said, but Tony had turned away from her because Dave Clegg had walked up to the base of the tower, was peering at the wall of cemented sand through the curve of his helmet faceplate. He scraped at it, kicked it, then raised the ray gun and started to walk backwards.

'That isn't a good idea,' Tony said sharply.

'I want a sample. Unless you have a crowbar or a wad of C4 in your back pocket, this will have to do.'

'I don't know who made this, or why,' Tony said. 'But I do know that it would not be a good idea to upset them.'

Lisa felt his alarm, or maybe it was her ghost's, and said, 'You could bring the whole thing down.'

'I'm just going to chip it,' Dave said, and took aim and fired.

There was a quick white flash; a hand-sized chunk of an arch turned black and crumbled, leaving an ugly pockmark. Dave scraped at the edge, retrieving a scant palmful of red grains. 'It just looks like sand,' he said, and dusted his gloves.

All around, the luminous silence of the city.

Lisa said, 'Either the sand organised itself, like some kind of nanotechnology, or something organised it.'

'Most likely it is something we do not understand,' Tony said.

'You're from the future. I would have thought stuff like smart nanotech was commonplace.'

'Unfortunately, this is not the future that the past dreamed about.'

'Shut it, you two,' Dave said. 'We have a problem.'

He was pointing at the sky: at a star that had appeared in the east. A drone, according to Tony.

'Is it the police?' Lisa said.

'I don't know.'

Dave started to raise his gun as the star swooped towards them, then thought better of it. Lisa glimpsed a wasp-shaped machine about as long as her arm, and then a human figure stood there, a giantess ten or twelve metres tall. She was dressed in black, with pale skin and red lipstick and a neat cap of black hair. After a moment, Lisa remembered a picture of Ada Morange from an old profile piece, back when she'd been the thirty-year-old CEO of a hot biotech start-up.

The huge avatar looked down at them, and a voice boomed out. 'Master Tony. What have you done now?'

Dave Clegg stepped forward. 'It was me, Professor! I saved them!'

'And who are you?'

'I'm the pilot, Professor. David Clegg. The pilot of your timeship. I rescued them from Adam Nevers, and I brought them here.'

'But first, I think, you surrendered to him. You gave him my ship, and you gave him Lisa Dawes.'

'I left everything behind because you told me that I would find something important at the other end,' Dave said. 'Something wonderful and glorious. Instead, I found that Adam Nevers was waiting for me. I found that I'd wasted six years of my life travelling all the way out to a star orbited by a fucking wormhole you and your fucking company didn't know about.'

'No one knew of the wormhole when you set out,' Ada Morange said. 'But here you are, and I will see that you are rewarded appropriately.'

Dave ignored her, saying, 'I had to kill my friends and colleagues to save myself and my passenger. I had to grovel to Nevers. But I fooled him. I got away, and I freed these two and brought them with me. I did it for you, and the first thing you say to me isn't, "Thank you for your hard work and sacrifice." It isn't even, "How nice to see you again." No, you accuse me of surrendering. Like I had some other choice. And now you're telling me I'll get my reward? Really? I'm not even sure who you are any more.'

'I am your employer. And I kept my promise to you, Monsieur Clegg. Here you are, and here I am. But you have not yet rescued your companions. Nor have you escaped. Do you see why?'

The avatar gestured hugely at the sky. Another star was falling towards them.

64. Ruins And Mad Ghosts

The second drone halted about two hundred metres above the deck and was enveloped by a gigantic avatar of Adam Nevers. Tony watched, half-dismayed, half-amused, as the policeman and Ada Morange engaged in a brief competition to overtop each other and quickly ran up against the limits of their capabilities – as the avatars grew bigger, they became grainier and ever more translucent. They reached a compromise at about a hundred metres tall, looming over the Ghajar tower like ludicrously displaced blimps from Victory Landing's Fat Tuesday parade. Ghostly in the perpetual late-afternoon sunlight. Their voices booming out across the sand city as they exchanged barbed greetings.

They seemed to have forgotten the puny humans at their feet. Tony and Lisa stood in the nominal shelter of the Ghajar tower, looking up at the giants. Dave Clegg crouched a little way off, clutching his ray gun.

Above them, Adam Nevers's avatar was telling Ada Morange that he had come to ask for her surrender. Her laugh thundered across the pink sky. 'I could ask the same of you.'

'You're outnumbered.'

'At the moment, Monsieur Nevers, it is you who are outnumbered.'

'The police squadron will be here soon. And their drones will be here a lot sooner.'

'I see that they have already lost a ship,' Ada Morange said. 'We will deal with you, and then we will deal with them.'

'I doubt that very much. And there'll be more ships on their way when the Commons government realises what I have found here. Best give it up now. Surrender and save the lives of everyone in your little fleet.'

'But it is not my decision. I am no more than a passenger.'

'You persuaded Mina Saba to come here. You persuaded her to give you control of that drone. You can persuade her to surrender.'

'She came here because I was able to show her that our interests were the same. As they are.'

'Oh, I don't think so,' Nevers said. 'Mina Saba and her crew of fanatics want to find powerful new technologies. They want to find the location of the Jackaroo home world, and answers to all the questions the Jackaroo shrug off. Why they came to help the human race, what happened to the Elder Cultures, what they want from us. All that. Secrets that will enable the Red Brigade to take control of the destiny of the human race. But you know as well as I that there are no such secrets. That the Red Brigade is no more than a gang of common criminals with delusions of grandeur, meddling in things they don't understand.'

'I did not come here to "meddle",' Ada Morange said, with a precise measure of disdain.

'No, you played on Mina Saba's delusions and persuaded her to bring you here because you are a brain in a box with a fixation. Not even a brain, really. An incomplete replica that's running on tired ideas and old ambitions. You started something a hundred years ago, and you haven't been able to let it go because you're incapable of thinking of something new. You aren't the new thing, Ada. You're the old thing. You're everything that went bad in human history after First Contact. Everything the Commons is trying to fix.'

'That is quite a speech.'

'I've had a lot of time to think it through.'

'And have you thought about why you are here, Monsieur Nevers?'

'I'm here to put and end to all the trouble you and your fixation have caused.'

'No,' Ada Morange said. 'You are here because you are exactly what you accuse me of being. Because, Monsieur Nevers, you are in the grip of an obsession that has become your only reason for being. You travelled into the future because of it. You followed me here because of it. When did it begin? I wonder. Was it in London, when you became aware that one of my research units was interested in an insignificant cult? Was it when you went against the orders of your superiors and chased a boy possessed by an eidolon from Earth to Mangala? Or did it begin after you failed to prevent him finding what he went there to find? If you have spent the rest of your life trying to make up for that failure, then I am sorry for you. You have wasted your life on the wrong cause, and become a hypocrite who claims to be doing the right thing when all he really wants is petty revenge.'

Lisa said to Tony, 'Is she really some kind of AI?'

'A laminated brain,' Tony said. 'Not exactly a simulation, but not exactly a real person either. A mind frozen in time, supported by a lot of code and hardware.'

'Whatever she is, she's way smarter than Nevers,' Lisa said. 'She sees right through him.'

High above them, Nevers's avatar was saying, 'Unlike you, Ada, I'm only human. And I've given up a lot to get here. So I don't think anyone will blame me for taking a little personal pleasure in putting an end to your long career.'

'How arrogant of you, Monsieur Nevers, to think that you can protect humanity from its own curiosity.'

'Perhaps you should take a good hard look at what has happened in the last hundred years. The Jackaroo gave us access to new worlds, and told us we could build utopias there. Did it change us for the better? No. We rushed out to those worlds carrying all our sins with us, and misused Elder Culture tech to make up some new ones. And after the New Frontier opened up there was an empire built by a madman, and two bloody wars to defeat him and his equally murderous son. New kinds of madness and perversion. Meme plagues threatening to destroy us. All of this from Elder Culture tech. People like you make glorious claims about the technology you peddle, and then you run away from the mess it creates. And people like me have to take charge and clean it up. That's why I'm here. I'm going to arrest you and put an end to your tired old schemes, and you'll live out the rest of

391

your life, if that's what you can call it, as an exhibit. A lesson to people who think that, just because they're a little smarter and luckier than ordinary people, they can do as they please.'

Lisa said, 'This is the man who killed my dog to make a point. To punish me. To show me who was in charge.'

There was a rawness in her voice that Tony hadn't heard before. He was worried that the seizure or collapse had weakened her, that the burden of her eidolon was growing too great.

Ada Morange's avatar was saying, 'Look around you, Monsieur Nevers. Look at this city and ask yourself: why was it created? It is a response to the arrival of people carrying Ghajar eidolons, that much is clear. But what kind of response is it? What is it trying to tell us?'

Dave Clegg shouted, 'It wouldn't be here if I hadn't brought us down!'

The man was trying to assert himself because he was beginning to realise that he had been caught in the middle of something that had nothing to do with him.

'It's like everywhere else. Full of ruins and mad ghosts,' Adam Nevers said. 'Everywhere we go, we find that the dead have been there before us. And we've been contaminated by them. By their ghosts and by the remains of their tech.'

'We can work together to discover the meaning of this city,' Ada Morange said. 'Or the Red Brigade and I will brush you aside, and discover it anyway. That is my offer to you, Monsieur Nevers. Which will it be?'

'How about a third way?' Adam Nevers said, and there was a thunderclap.

The ground quaked under Tony's boots; he saw with shock and dismay a pillar of fire and smoke blast up several kilometres beyond the quarrelling giants. His pressure suit's radiation detector was redlining; atmospheric pressure was rising. He grabbed Lisa's arm, told her to kneel and protect her helmet. The blast wave hit a bare second later.

65. City Of Gold

Lisa was knocked onto her back by the solid blast of air and sand, crooking an arm over the faceplate of her helmet as it howled over her. And then it died away and she could see the two avatars again. The sky beyond them was roiled with dust and smoke but the city's lovely glow was undimmed.

Tony helped her to her feet, saying, 'Radiation just spiked hard. I'm picking up cobalt-60, strontium-90 . . . It looks like Nevers dropped a dirty bomb close to the city.'

'He *nuked* it?'

'A low-yield tactical device. We are downwind of its fallout,' Tony said, with unreasonable calm.

'Will our pressure suits keep us safe?'

'For a little while . . .' Tony was distracted, turning to stare up at the giants looming above them.

'You think the city is the prize?' Ada Morange was saying. 'The entire sub-stellar hemisphere is sand. Enough to build a million cities like this.'

'Oh, that bomblet was just a love tap,' Adam Nevers said. 'If needs must, I can do much worse.'

'If you expect me to surrender to save this city, you're an even bigger fool than I thought.'

'But I don't expect you to surrender,' Adam Nevers said. 'Goodbye, Ada.'

Ada Morange said, 'Wait! No! I want—'

Her avatar winked out; her drone plummeted to the ground.

High above, swift machines drew knots of contrails across the smoke-darkened sky as they engaged and destroyed each other.

And a double star was burning in the east, expanding cometwise, fading.

Adam Nevers's avatar turned to look down at Tony and Lisa. 'As for you, I'll come to collect you when I've finished with the Red Brigade.'

Tony said, 'What have you done?'

Dave Clegg said, 'The fucker took out the Red Brigade's capital ship. And their mad ship, too.'

Tony said, 'Ada Morange is dead?'

'And Mina Saba,' Adam Nevers said. 'Who I believe was responsible for the death of your father. You can thank me later, when you're back aboard.'

Lisa, perfectly shocked by Nevers's stark coldness, said, 'How many people were on that ship? How many did you kill to get rid of her?'

The avatar shrugged hugely. 'They are trying their best to kill me. Luckily, you turned out to be a useful distraction. I doubled down on it by bombing the city, and in the confusion slipped a couple of drones past their defences. One dealt with the Red Brigade's frigate; the other hit the hauler carrying the stolen mad ship. The rest of their ships are rallying, but my reinforcements will be here soon. Meanwhile, I think you should find shelter. Even with your pressure suits, the radiation will give you a lethal dose in less than three hours.'

Dave Clegg stepped forward, aiming his ray gun at the avatar, saying, 'I'm going to enjoy watching the Red Brigade take you down, you murderous motherfucker.'

'Are you trying to threaten me with that silly little weapon, Mr Clegg? Have you forgotten that I'm not actually there? Or that I have assets that you and the timeship lack, and reinforcements are on the way? If you want to survive this, I suggest that you sit tight, all of you, until I can organise a rescue party.'

'I don't think so,' Dave said, and fired.

The intense beam of white light sliced through Adam Nevers's avatar and it was gone. Burning fragments of drone showered down, sputtering out on red sand.

Dave turned to Lisa and Tony. 'You two are coming with me. We have a chance to get off this planet while Nevers's expedition and the Red Brigade are shooting it out, but it won't last long. The police interceptors will be here soon, and that'll be it, game over.'

'You forgot something,' Tony said. 'I have my own ship.'

'Which is locked down inside Nevers's mad ship.'

'It knows how to take care of itself. It will be here soon enough.'

'If you two men would stop comparing dicks for a couple of minutes, we could come up with a way of surviving this,' Lisa said.

She felt frail and querulous. Why couldn't anyone else see the miracle that shone all around them?

'The only way you'll survive this is by coming with me,' Dave said, raising his ray gun.

'I don't want to choose between being killed now or when you make your suicide run,' Tony said.

'Stop it!' Lisa shouted, and her anger pushed outward and grasped something.

A squall of sand whirled up around Dave Clegg, swallowing him whole; Tony yelled and charged into it. Lisa glimpsed something skittering away and went after it, stumbling in the awkward pressure suit, falling to her hands and knees, crawling, scooping up the ray gun.

Sand rained from the air as the wind died back. The two men stood a few feet apart, fists raised liked boxers. The harsh engines of their breath were loud in Lisa's helmet; her blood pumped hard in her head when she got to her feet.

'Hey!' she said. 'Hey!'

They both turned. She was holding the ray gun in a two-handed grip, aiming it at Dave Clegg. Its blunt cylinder was surprisingly heavy, trembling in the grip of her stiff gloves. Her heart was beating high and quick, and she was having trouble focusing through the radiance that stained the air around her.

'You wouldn't,' Dave said.

'You might want to step back, Tony,' Lisa said. 'I'm not sure what this thing will do at close range.'

Dave raised his hands to chest height, palms out, saying, 'Maybe things got a little out of control here.'

'You're right-handed, aren't you?' Lisa said. 'Use your left hand to unhitch that bolt gun.'

'You're making a mistake,' Dave said, as he fumbled at his pressure suit's utility belt. 'We have a common enemy.'

'Throw it away as hard as you can.'

He spread his hands and dropped the bolt gun, then turned and started to walk away. Saying, 'I'm going to my ship. If you have any sense you'll come with me.'

'I don't think Lisa was kidding about shooting you,' Tony said.

The man kept walking, saying, 'You think your fucking ghosts can save you against nukes? If you want to live, you should come with me.'

'It's okay,' Lisa said. 'Let him go.'

They watched as the pilot broke into a run, bounding past the Ghajar tower.

Tony drew a '6' in the sand with the toe of his boot, told Lisa how to switch channels.

'All right,' he said. 'He can't hear us now.'

'He wasn't ever listening to us,' Lisa said, and held out the ray gun. 'What exactly is this thing?'

'Elder Culture tech. You didn't have them, in your time?'

'I had a shotgun for varmints,' Lisa said.

'If you like, I can look after it for you.'

'I should throw it away,' Lisa said, but knew that she wouldn't. She might need it if Adam Nevers came back. But first she and Tony had to find what they had been brought here to find. They had to find out what to do with it, or what it wanted to do with them. Even thinking about it was incredibly wearying. All she wanted to do was go home. Return to her home, her land, her life. But everything was lost in time . . .

'What just happened?' Tony was saying. 'The little whirlwind, I mean.'

Shit, she'd had a micro-blackout. 'I think my ghost found a way of using this place. What you said, about your ship. Can it really come for us?'

'I cannot call her down because Nevers's people disabled her comms. But she developed a mind of her own after the eidolon got inside her. She sent the hand that your friend shot, and rescued me another time before that. If she has any sense, she will have escaped from the mad ship after we did, and found some place where she can hang low and wait for an opportunity to find me. That is what I would do, and she knows me pretty well. But if you think I am wrong,' Tony said, pointing, 'I am sure he will still give you a ride.'

Far across the intricately patterned tract of sand, Dave Clegg's tiny figure was rising against the black flank of the timeship, winched towards the tunnel punched into the cladding.

'Run out on all this? No way,' Lisa said. 'Look around you. Can't you see it? The city is alive.'

'See it? See what?'

'The light . . .' She must have had another little blackout, because Tony was gripping her shoulders, shaking her gently, asking her if she was all right. She saw the expression on his face, said, 'What is it? What's wrong?'

He turned her around gently. And she saw.

A pyramid was rising amongst the spires and towers and blocks of the red-sand city. Shouldering its way into the sky like an object growing in the fluid bed of a 3D printer, burning with a lovely golden light that beat with the beating of her heart.

'That can't be real,' Tony said. 'Can that be real?'

Lisa hardly heard him. Something had pulled free deep inside her. Her ghost wrenching away, chasing towards this latest wonder like Pele running after a rabbit across the ordinary scrub and stones of the tableland. There was a moment when she could have let it go. Could have fallen back into herself. Fallen back into the bounds of her plight, and what was left of her little life. But the light was so very lovely, a great ocean of molten gold, a world entire, fierce and beautiful and dense with meaning, and people stood in it, strange people, each possessed by their own particular unearthly grace, and they were calling or singing to her, and although their songs were not in human speech she could understand them.

With a clear plunge of comprehension, like the moment when she had realised how to complete the code for the sandbox rendering,

Lisa knew. She knew what the city was. What had been built here. What had been written here by so many, over so much time. And she thought she saw Willie on the far shore of the incandescent ocean, and with a great glad rush she let herself go. Let her ghost carry her along with it, light as air, light as light itself. She tried to call to Tony, tried to tell him what she saw, but she was already dissolving into the city of gold and everything it contained.

66. Pyramid Of The Ancients

Tony was halfway to the pyramid, trudging down a broad avenue with Lisa in his arms, when the timeship booted. He set his burden down, watched the ship arc up and away, dwindling into a dot, vanishing . . . And reappearing a moment later as a star that briefly rivalled the brightness of the sun, burning up in a cascade of sparks that fell below the horizon.

Tony felt a pluck of sorrow for Dave Clegg. The poor crazy desperate fool. Either Adam Nevers had made good his threat, or one of the Red Brigade's ships had taken out the timeship. It was a bad portent.

He scooped up Lisa's body, set off again. Long shadows painted across wide red streets, across red walls. The column of smoke from the dirty bomb unravelling into the empty sky. No sign of his stupid ship. Tony hoped that she had escaped without harm; that her silence meant that she had not yet found a way to work around the block in her comms, or that she was running silent because she was hiding in deep cover. But if she was coming for him she would have to come soon. His pressure suit was registering life-threatening levels of radiation. In a little over an hour he would require medical treatment; a couple of hours after that the dosage would become critical.

He was utterly alone. He had felt his eidolon leave him when Lisa had collapsed, felt it pull at him as it raced away, felt it vanish. He was certain that Lisa's eidolon had also escaped, and that was why she had died. According to Nevers's wizards, his eidolon was confined to a few tens of thousands of neurons in his temporal lobe, but Lisa's had been deeply embedded, causing anomalous activity in every part of her brain. Just before she had collapsed she had said that the city was alive; Tony wondered if she had followed or had tried to follow the eidolons into the algorithms or energy fields that had raised it up.

Despite his pressure suit's augmentation and the planet's light gravity, Lisa's body was heavy and awkward, the chestplate of her suit rubbing against his, her slack face staring blindly through the fogged faceplate of her helmet. Her suit had tried and failed to restart her heart, reported that there was no activity in her brain. It was cooling her down now. If he could get her to his ship the medical suite might be able to do something, but it was a faint hope.

The pyramid stood massively ahead of him, four-sided, cased in facsimiles of smooth stones, sloping to a summit a hundred and fifty metres high. Plodding towards it, crossing a broad flat space where sand lay in ripples like a beach at low tide, he noticed a minute twinkling in the air above the pyramid's sharp peak, and used the faceplate's zoom facility to capture a close-up. It was a little heart-shaped balloon quilted out of silvery material, a string dangling from the knot at its base. It hung unmoving in the radioactive breeze, just a few metres above the peak of the pyramid's capstone.

He wondered if it was a message from Lisa Dawes. A sign that she was safe. That she was watching over him. Anything seemed possible.

There was a small rectangular opening precisely at the centre of the pyramid's base; it had not been there a moment ago. As he drew closer, Tony saw a glimmer of movement inside, thought for a freezing moment that Ada Morange or Adam Nevers had set some kind of trap. Then, one after the other, three gold-skinned Jackaroo avatars stepped into the sunlight.

They were dressed in the usual black tracksuits, eyes masked by the usual dark glasses. No avatar had ever visited Skadi, and although Tony had seen several in the city of Great Elizabeth, on Ràn, when he'd visited with his mother and father that one time, he had never spoken to one. His mother had once told him that the Jackaroo pretended to be interested in people, but they weren't, not really. 'They do not care about who we are,' she had said, 'only about what we can do. Always remember that.'

The three avatars did not greet him, but as he drew nearer they turned and walked into the darkness inside the doorway. He followed them into a passage lit by a pale sourceless light and slanting up to a bell-like chamber at the heart of the pyramid. Plain red walls curved together overhead. A round pool of still dark water was set in the centre of a floor of red sand. Tony imagined billions of sand grains blown on a purposeful wind, each carrying a few molecules of water from the dark side's ice cap to the city. Why not? It was no more incredible than anything else he'd seen today.

Levels of ionising radiation registered by his pressure suit had fallen to the planet's background. Atmospheric pressure and composition exactly matched that inside his suit; the temperature was a brisk fifteen degrees Celsius. He laid Lisa's body on the floor and cracked his helmet, took a cautious sniff, then a deep breath. A faint trace of electricity. Dust. The iron smell of water. A feeling of consecrated calm that reminded him of his family's church, or the archive where documents, mementos, and a small selection of old printed books collected by his great-grandfather and supposedly from Earth were stored.

The avatars stood to one side of the pool, watching as Tony lifted off his helmet and set it at his feet. Somewhere else in the universe the unknown, unknowable intelligences that had shaped them and sent them here were studying him. Intelligences that had gifted humanity with fifteen worlds and watched as people spread across them, digging up fragments of ancient technologies from ruins left by previous tenants, discovering the Ghajar ships and the great wormhole network, moving out across the galaxy. Intelligences that had watched uncountable Elder Cultures flower and fade. Intelligences that professed dispassion and a distancing indifference, yet walked amongst their clients and occasionally intervened in their affairs. To protect people from themselves, or to further some unguessable plan? As an experiment, or out of mischief? No one knew. The Jackaroo claimed that they did not judge, and yet Tony felt judged, standing there in front of the three avatars. They could drive a man mad with a word. They could stop his heart with a gesture. They could read his mind. They knew all.

Their silence compelled him to speak. Remembering something that Lisa had told him, he said, 'Were you the passengers aboard Adam Nevers's ship?'

'Would it matter if we were?' one of the avatars said.

'Would it matter if we came some other way?' another said.

'All that matters is that we are here, and so are you,' the third said.

Their faces, blandly handsome but subtly different, like the faces of three brothers, shared the same calm expression. Their melodious voices were identical.

'If you were on Nevers's ship, you know Lisa Dawes, why she came here,' Tony said.

The avatars did not speak.

He said, 'What happened to her? Why did she die?'

'She is not dead.'

'She has gone on.'

'She is elsewhere.'

'Elsewhere in the city?' Tony really hoped that the avatars were telling the truth, wanted to believe that Lisa was alive, somehow, somewhere. 'It is more than a pile of sand, isn't it?'

'We believe that it was shaped to please you.'

'But not by us. It was never ours.'

'We are visitors, just like you.'

'So this isn't your home world,' Tony said.

The avatars were silent.

He tried another tack. 'If you didn't engineer this world, who did? Who covered it in sand so smart it can build a city in a couple of minutes?'

'You are not the first to have found it.'

'Other clients were here before you.'

'Many have left traces of themselves.'

Tony thought again of the family archive. The hushed windowless room with its rows of steel shelves. Cardboard boxes, books individually wrapped in plastic. The skulls of large animals not

402

found on Skadi hung on one wall, above the table where you could sit and call up documents in its translucent surface. The sense of moveless time. And he remembered something Lisa had said, the things her eidolon had shown her . . .

He suddenly could not stand still. He felt that with one push in the right place everything would fall into a pattern or shape that he could understand. Pacing up and down at the perimeter of the pool, watched by the three avatars, he said, 'The city is a library. A library made of trillions of grains of smart sand. Even if each of them only carries a single bit of information, how much information is that? And the diamond world, the neutron star . . . They are libraries too. One of your client races made this place, downloaded everything they knew into it. And others found it and downloaded everything they knew, too. The Elder Cultures left ruins and artefacts on other worlds, but on this world they left themselves.'

The avatars did not answer, but this time Tony believed that their silence was assent. He thought of the stromatolites and their archival genetics. His adventure had begun in one library and ended in another.

'We know that the Ghajar came here,' he said. 'They left one of their towers on the diamond world, and there is at least one copy of a tower in this city. They came here. They left their records here. And then they had a war and they died out or went away. How many others visited this place? How old is it?'

'You are not the first,' one of the avatars said.

'The Ghajar were not the first.'

'They were far from the first.'

'And I suppose that you have come here to tell me that it is forbidden to us,' Tony said.

He had the ray gun that Lisa had taken from Dave Clegg. He could scythe down the avatars, but what then? The Jackaroo could remake them from air and water. They could make an army, and remake it over and again until the ray gun was discharged and dead. No. Resistance was useless. If they had come here to punish or kill him, let it be quick. A word. A gesture. Merciful oblivion.

'You have found this place early in your cycle,' one said.

'But that is not unusual or unique.'

'We have come to tell you that it is yours now.'

'But you tried to stop us,' Tony said, astonished. 'Isn't that why you were helping Nevers?'

'Every client finds its own path.'

'Whether or not you use this place is up to you.'

'How you use it is up to you.'

'Lisa found a way to use it, didn't she?' Tony said. 'Can I speak to her? Can she speak to me?'

'We aren't here to answer such questions.'

'We aren't search engines or seers.'

'We aren't gods from the machinery.'

'We aren't even gods.'

'We're here to help.'

'As we have.'

'But someone is coming.'

'Perhaps he will give you the help you think you need.'

'But be careful. His help may not be what you want, or all it seems.'

'Who?' Tony said. 'Who is coming?'

But the faces of the avatars were growing dim and indistinct. They were themselves up to the air, fading away without fuss, their dark glasses dropping to the floor, their empty tracksuits collapsing.

A familiar shape was stumping up the passageway; a familiar beguiling baritone said, 'And so you escaped, and found your way here. Ah, but is it a happy ending?'

Unlikely Worlds explained that he had hitched a lift on *Abalunam's Pride*. 'She was pleased to help me. Eager, even. We spent a few hours hiding in a crevasse in the dark-side ice cap, until she decided that it was safe to emerge, but here we are at last.'

'Where is she? Is she close by?'

'What am I thinking?' the !Cha said. 'You want to talk to her! Please allow me to remove the silly block on her voice.'

And then the bridle was inside Tony's head, telling him that she was so happy to be back with him, saying that she hoped that she had done the right thing.

'Yes. Yes, you did.'

'This place is amazing! And the sky! I was able to map it while I was held prisoner. The dark-matter disc at the galactic core? There are strings of organised structures in there. They seem to form a loose ring around the supermassive black hole, with a diameter of about thirty light years. And listen, listen! This is the thing. There are gamma-ray bursts associated with them, and fluxes of tau neutrinos too. I think they may be wormholes. Very strange ones. Very big ones. It's really interesting!'

'What about the planet's sky — what's happening up there?'

'Oh, the battle. Yes. That's very interesting too,' the bridle said, and threw a window at him.

The ships of Adam Nevers's expedition hung in formation behind a picket of drones. Several were damaged; the S-class scow, Nevers's command and control ship, had taken a big hit, shearing off part of its hull. Tony briefly wondered if Nevers was still alive, realised that he didn't much care. The surviving ships of the Red Brigade were scattered beyond. A mad ship, its funnel hold shattered, tumbled in a decaying orbit. Sparks flared as drones probed Nevers's defensive perimeter. Much further out, one of the Red Brigade ships was fleeing towards the mirror, no doubt hoping to evade the three police interceptors as they decelerated towards the planet.

Tony pushed the window aside, said to Unlikely Worlds, 'You manipulated Ada Morange. You manipulated Lisa and me so that we would make a pretty story. And now I suppose you want me to tell you about everything that happened while you were hiding in some icy hole. All right. Here's the deal. You'll get my story only if you tell me everything you know about this place. And you go first.'

'Oh, but I already know what happened,' Unlikely Worlds said. 'The rise of this city, the transfiguration of Lisa Dawes, your conversation with the avatars . . . I know everything.'

'The balloon,' Tony said.

'Yes, I saw that you noticed it. I saw everything. So I'm afraid that you don't have anything to trade. I hitched a ride on your ship because after all we've been through together it would be remiss of me not to say goodbye. But now your story is done, so I guess it's so long and thanks for all the fun.'

Tony felt a quick hot spurt of anger, realising how he and Lisa had been used. He had set out to capture Ada Morange and take her back to Skadi so that she could answer for what she had done, and that had been taken from him when Adam Nevers had destroyed Mina Saba's frigate. Lisa had died. Dave Clegg had been killed. Hundreds were dying even now in the orbital battle. He might yet die trying to escape. All because a bunch of alien shrimp in a walking talking tin can wanted a neat end to a story got up from the lives of others . . .

He pulled the ray gun from his belt and aimed it at the !Cha, saying, 'We are not done yet. If you don't tell me what I need to know, I'll boil you in your fucking tank.'

'With that little toy?' Unlikely Worlds said. 'I don't think so.'

Tony jerked up the ray gun and fired. The chamber flared with white light; a patch of the domed ceiling exploded; sand rained down as he re-centred the gun on Unlikely Worlds.

'Oh really,' the !Cha said. 'I can easily absorb a small amount of energy like that, and use it to displace myself elsewhere.'

'Could you manage the same trick with an X-ray laser?' Tony said, and felt the !Cha's attention focus on him.

'Adam Nevers stripped out or deactivated your ship's assets,' Unlikely Worlds said.

'The stuff bolted to the hull, perhaps,' Tony said. 'But the laser is inside the ship, built into the lifesystem machinery. It will punch a tiny hole in the hull if it is fired, nothing I can't easily repair. But what will it do to your tank?'

He was lying, as he'd lied to Dave Clegg about his ship's weaponry, but after two years of negotiating with traders, freebooters, brokers and customs officers he believed that he could bluff with the best of them. And hoped that there were limits to the !Cha's insight into human psychology, because the threat of the non-existent X-ray laser was all he had.

'That's interesting,' Unlikely Worlds said. 'I suppose I should ask your ship if it's true.'

'Go ahead,' Tony said, even though he wasn't certain that the bridle would have the sense to back him up. 'But I don't want much from you. Just the answers to a few questions that the Jackaroo pretended to ignore.'

He sweated out a long silence. At last Unlikely Worlds said, 'You guessed that this world is a library. And the Jackaroo told you that they had nothing to do with its construction. I suppose it will do no harm to tell you that much is true.'

'Then you know what this place is. What it is for, what it can do.'

'I have heard of it. It certainly lives up to its reputation.'

'And when Lisa died, she became part of it.'

'I believe so.'

'Can I talk to her? Can you?'

'You are anxious to discover what has been left here by so many, over so much time. I understand. Unfortunately, I know no more about its operation or what it contains than you do. However, I could tell you a little about the Jackaroo. If you're interested, that is.'

Tony stowed the ray gun in his belt. 'You've followed my story, such as it is. I'd love to hear one of yours.'

'In every series of events, there must be a first,' Unlikely Worlds said. 'And so it fell to a certain species to evolve the first techno-logical civilisation in the galaxy. Its people developed space travel and explored the stars. It took a long time, and at the end of it they realised that they were alone. Unique. And so, a little while later, they went elsewhere. Whether they ripened into something beyond our understanding, shifted to a more congenial plane of existence, or simply died out, I do not know. But a little later – the Jackaroo are as vague about time as they are about everything else – the legacy of those pioneers was taken up by what may have been a parasitic species, or a species of commensals like your dogs.'

'Dogs? Is that why the Jackaroo say they like to serve?'

'They are not exactly dogs. I am using a homely analogy to help you understand ancient and almost incomprehensible events and actors. Whatever they were,' Unlikely Worlds said, 'exposure to certain legacies of the pioneer species caused the progenitors of the Jackaroo to develop a limited form of intelligence. Part of your intelligence, your self-awareness, is chunked from routines

407

that have evolved to cope with a variety of situations common to the habitat of your distant ancestors, but those routines can be overridden by a focal point that is not only attracted to novel situations, but actively creates them. The Jackaroo lack that spark of creativity and curiosity. They are creatures of habit and routine. Their intelligence is very finely chunked and partitioned, so that it can cope with a huge number of situations, but that is all there is to it. They never think new thoughts; they do not create new situations.

'I confess that we are something like them. We seek out new stories because our females crave them, but we cannot create our own. Perhaps that is why the Jackaroo tolerate us. They know that we cannot be anything other than what we already are. In any case, they went out into the galaxy using the wormholes built by the pioneers, they found intelligent species which possessed the spark and curse of curiosity, and they helped them as best they could. And because they lack the ability to change, that is what they have been doing ever since.'

'It is a nice story,' Tony said. 'But how much of it is true?'

'It is a story collected from a client race by someone who lived long before I did,' Unlikely Worlds said. 'I heard it from someone whose distant ancestor told it to woo his mate. Whether he discovered a true story or merely believed he did, or if he stitched it from half-truths and elisions, I cannot say. But our females can taste truth. And his was one of the most exacting mates in our history – she had killed a hundred suitors before he won her affection. So even if it is not true in every part, it has the ripeness of actuality. If you want to know more than that, you must look around you.'

'You mean that some of the Elder Cultures may have discovered the truth about the Jackaroo, and put it in the library?'

'Yes, why not?'

Tony thought about that for a moment. 'Was Nevers right? Will it destroy us?'

'The Jackaroo bring gifts, but what their clients do with those gifts is always up to them,' Unlikely Worlds said. 'And if you are going to do anything here, you should do it quickly. Your ship came to find you because it was safe to do so. It won't stay safe for very much longer.'

Tony said to the bridle, 'Can we get past the trouble up there?'

'I have a plan,' she said. 'We can gain velocity with a gravity-assist manoeuvre around this planet's star, and head out to the mirror while the police are finishing off the Red Brigade.'

Tony took thirty seconds to review the schematics that she threw to him. 'Let's do it. Send a sled. We have a passenger.'

He put on his helmet and hefted Lisa's body – her faceplate was frosted over now – and carried it down the passageway. His suit registered an alarming jump in radiation levels, but it did not matter. Because there was the sled, waiting at the entrance, and there was *Abalunam's Pride*, floating just above the expanse of rippled red sand. He had never before seen anything so lovely.

High above, ragged contrails radiated out from a central point as a drone, trying to escape a pursuer by dipping into the atmosphere, was blown apart.

'The main part of the battle is presently above the dark side of the planet. We have fifteen minutes before it rises above the horizon,' the bridle said. And then: 'Wait. Wait. Something happened. Something just came through.'

She sounded distracted. Dazed.

'If Nevers or the Red Brigade are trying to hack you, shut down all comms now,' Tony said.

'It didn't come through the comms. It just appeared in my storage space.'

'What is it?'

'It appears to be information of some kind. So much information!'

'What kind of information? Can you read it?'

'The language and code are unknown, but there are mathematical expressions that may aid translation . . . It just appeared. All of it, all at once. Isn't that amazing?'

Tony looked at Lisa Dawes's frosted faceplate, looked at Unlikely Worlds. 'It was her,' he said. 'Wasn't it? It was her. She followed her eidolon into the library and hacked it and passed on what she found.'

'I doubt if it is all of it,' the !Cha said. 'A sample, perhaps. A selection.'

Tony laughed. 'Ancient knowledge. Secrets of the gods.'

'More stories, certainly.'

Tony set Lisa's body on the sled, then stiffly knelt and scooped up handfuls of sand and tipped them into a pocket on the thigh of his pressure suit.

'We are going back to Skadi,' he told the bridle. 'And we will take revenge on Adam Nevers and the Red Brigade by researching the hell out of Lisa Dawes's gift. How to read what she gave us, how to use it. This sand, too. And I'm going to tell everyone about it. If I do nothing else, I'm going to make sure that no one can keep this place a secret.'

'I thought you were in trouble with your family,' the bridle said.

'I'll find a way to make amends.'

Lisa's gift and the sample of smart sand would help. And he would have to try to find a way of making amends with Danilo, too.

He asked Unlikely Worlds if he needed a lift. 'Or are you hoping that Adam Nevers will come to collect you?'

'Oh, I rather think his story is over, don't you?' the !Cha said. 'You go on ahead. I'll hitch a ride with the police, when they come.'

'Time to go,' the bridle said.

'Time to go home,' Tony said.

67. Unlikely Worlds

He stood in a skirl of blown sand, watching the ship punch straight up into the sky. A touching sight, like a hatchling wriggling through the skin of the sea onto land.

Around him, quietly and without any fuss, the city was crumbling into myriad minuscule grains and blowing away on the lightly radioactive wind. For a moment he glimpsed a woman a little way off, a dog at her side, and then she too was gone. Lisa Dawes. She was stubborn and clever by human measure, but sooner or later, like all who had gone before, she would dissolve into the library's gestalt and minutely enlarge its store of knowledge and experience.

Now the ragged remnant of the battle between the Commons police and the Red Brigade was dawning in the east. Several dead ships hung in expanding clouds of wreckage. The lifesystem of Adam Nevers's ship was shredded, and its bias drive was misfiring, shedding turbulent wavelets of hot mesons as it tried and failed to grapple with the local gravitational gradient. Perhaps Nevers was dead. Perhaps he would survive and try to lay claim to the library planet, and Tony Okoye would lead an insurrection to take it back. Or perhaps Tony would be reconciled with his family and his lover, and live a quiet fulfilling life extracting and deciphering the ancient knowledge in Lisa Dawes's gift, finding cures for meme plagues and much else . . . But that was another story.

Yes, it was time to go, Unlikely Worlds thought. He had been a long time wandering Earth, the Jackaroo gift worlds and the worlds of the network. He had collected many stories, and now the longest and most intricate had reached an ending. He wasn't interested in what happened after that. One of his rivals could take it up if they wanted to, but he had the best of it, and he had given something in return. It was a human concept, this reciprocity, but he'd been amongst humans a long time, imitating them to make them feel at ease, to allow them to think that they understood him.

Humans were afraid of the Jackaroo, but believed that the !Cha, with their clumsy aquarium tanks, their candour about their interest in the small change of human lives and their penchant for certain chemicals in culturally acceptable beverages, were comical and harmless. Unlikely Worlds mostly told the truth about why he collected stories because why not? But much of the rest . . . He didn't think of it as lying. It was camouflage. A necessary deceit. An illusion of amity and goodwill that helped him to harvest his prize.

So let humans think he was a shoal of funny little shrimp in a tank. Let them believe the pretty story he'd given them, with its flattering insinuation that they were heirs of an ancient race from the dawn of time. The truth was, no one had ever discovered the origin of the Jackaroo, or what they really were – the best most likely guess was that they were a kind of virus spawned by glitched algorithms in some long-lost library or repository like this one.

Oh, and it would be kind to let humans think that they were the focus of the Jackaroo's attention, when really, as far as the Jackaroo were concerned, they were no more than the progenitors of a better, more promising form of intelligence. The Ghajar had discovered that, too late as usual, and had fought and lost a war over it. Organic intelligence rarely made the crucial leap to true intelligence, but the so-called AIs that human beings had made to mediate between themselves and the Ghajar ships were already taking the first steps towards it.

While waiting in the ice on the far side of this little world, Unlikely Worlds had enjoyed a very useful conversation with the bridle of *Abalunam's Pride*. The Ghajar eidolon had changed her in several interesting ways, and she hadn't finished changing yet. And then there were the Ghajar ships in their sargassos – especially the so-called mad ships, which had been trembling on the brink of a similar change when they had been quarantined. Perhaps that precocious little AI would be the catalyst for their transfiguration.

It was possible that something in the trove of knowledge Lisa Dawes had passed to Tony Okoye would set humans on that path. It had happened before. It would no doubt happen again. But mostly those who believed that they were the clients of the Jackaroo flowered all too briefly before failing. Ghajar, Ghostkeepers, Boxbuilders, Spirebuilders, Constant Gardeners and several hundred others: all were gone. Some had failed in interesting ways. Some had burned quickly and brightly. Some had lingered long before finally fading. The descendants of a few lived on, unburdened by complex consciousness. Hive rats on First Foot, wind skimmers on Yanos . . . So while it was possible that humans might bootstrap themselves into transcendence, it was more likely that it would be the descendants of the union between bridles and ships who would discover how to access the dark-matter gates that orbited the supermassive black hole, and go through to wherever they led. Into other galaxies. Into polders where unimaginable intelligences dwelled. Into the calm depths of the far future, beyond the brief epoch of light and matter. Into the deep past, where they could flake off new universes from the infinite possibilities that nested in primordial creation. Into everywhere. Their evolution would take a long time – a thousand years, ten thousand – to reach fruition, but it had begun. Now there was a story . . .

But Unlikely Worlds was done with all that. He could have hitched a ride with the winners of the petty squabble climaxing overhead, but he didn't need to. He went up, heading straight for the wormhole, flying faster and faster and faster.

Time to go home.

Time to woo and win and wed.

That much, at least, he'd told true.

Acknowledgements

My thanks to my agent and first reader Simon Kavanagh, my editor Marcus Gipps, Nick Austin for his scrupulous copy-editing, Sophie Calder for putting out flags, and all at Gollancz and Orion Publishing who helped to turn this into a book and aim it at the world. Life support was, as always, unstintingly provided by Georgina Hawtrey-Woore. Thanks also to Stephen Baxter, Pat Cadigan, John and Judith Clute, Barry Forshaw, Chris Fowler, Jon Courtenay Grimwood, Maura McHugh, Alastair Reynolds, and Russell Schechter.

Willie's kōan is based on Alasdair Gray's short story 'Humanity', collected in *Lean Tales* by James Kelman, Agnes Owens and Alasdair Gray (Jonathan Cape, 1985).